Divorced, Desperate and Deceived

Divorced, Desperate and Deceived

Christie Craig

LOVE SPELL NEW YORK CITY

LOVE SPELL®

December 2009

Published by

Dorchester Publishing Co., Inc.
200 Madison Avenue
New York, NY 10016

Copyright © 2009 by Christie Craig

ISBN-13: 978-1-61523-684-8

To my dad, Pete Hunt, plumber extraordinaire, and to Ginger Curtis, proud mama, whose approach to life taught me that if you can laugh at it, you can live with it. The message resonates in all of my books. And to Faye Hughes, who is as crazy as I am, and as supportive as an underwire bra.

ACKNOWLEDGMENTS

To my guardian angels, who swear they aren't angels, but I love them, clipped wings, bent halos and all: Jody Payne, Teri Thackston, and Suzan Harden. You girls rock! To my hubby and son who understand that deadlines mean scrambled eggs and frozen dinners for supper. To all the readers who take the time to e-mail me and say I made them laugh. Never stop laughing, guys. To my editor, Chris Keeslar, and my agent, Kim Lionetti, who took a chance on a quirky writer with quirkier stories and made her dreams come true.

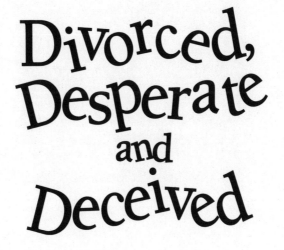

Divorced,
Desperate
and
Deceived

Chapter One

Kathy Callahan needed a man, but Hell would be renting ice skates and serving bubblegum-flavored snow cones before she chose one of the three specimens presently being offered to her.

She looked at Sue and Lacy, at their expressions of sheer anticipation, then back at the pictures. All three were photos of buddies of her friends' husbands, men Kathy had met at one or more of Lacy's get-togethers. And all three men were cops.

Kathy placed her index finger on picture number one. "No." Picture number two. "No." Picture number three. "No."

Lacy waved her hand across the photographs. "*Pleeease.* What lame excuses do you have to reject these men?"

Kathy pointed to Danny's picture. "Too nice." She pointed to Cary's. "Too egotistical." She pointed to Turner. "Too much of a player."

There was truth to each statement. The fact that there was a deeper reason for her rejections didn't matter; Kathy never showed all her cards. Which probably explained why she always felt a bit like an outsider, even with her two best friends.

"You're just chickening out," Sue accused. "Bawk, bawk, bawk." She flapped her arms like a demented chicken.

"I'm not chickening out. I just haven't found the right . . . rooster yet." Well, actually she had, but it seemed like she'd put all her eggs in the wrong basket. For close to three years, she'd had her eye on Stan Bradley, plumber extraordinaire.

How many times had she turned him down? Now that she was finally emotionally ready to crack a few eggs, he seemed to have lost interest in breakfast in bed.

"But you've wasted a week of your month without Tommy," Lacy pointed out.

The point—not necessarily the one Lacy wanted to make—went straight to Kathy's heart. She forgot all about men and thought about her little man. A week. A whole week that she hadn't seen her seven-year-old son's freckle-faced smile, or felt those little boy arms wrap around her neck as he said, "Love you more than dirt, Mom." And to her son, dirt rocked.

As the memory whispered over her heart, the pain of missing him yanked the oxygen right out of her lungs. Everything else was irrelevant. "I should have never let him go," she muttered.

"Your ex?" Sue asked.

"No!" Kathy said, and damn if she didn't feel like crying. "Tommy." She stiffened her backbone. How many times had she sworn she wouldn't turn into one of those moms whose whole world revolved around her child? But to stop that from happening, she needed to get her own life. She knew that.

Maternal understanding filled both her friends' expressions.

"He's with his dad. He's *fine*," Lacy said.

Sue reached over and touched Kathy's hand. "She's right."

"It will be a great education for him," Lacy continued. "How many seven-year-olds get a chance to visit Europe?"

"Yeah, he'll get to see all those naked statues." Sue grinned. When Kathy didn't respond, she added, "His dad will take care of him."

Kathy wanted to argue that her ex was about as trustworthy as a cockroach, with bad hygiene and a prison record to boot—not that she wanted to insult roaches, or the average everyday criminal who needed a bath. Still, she had to admit that while Tom had failed miserably as a husband, so far the man hadn't let down their son. Like it or not—and for the record, she didn't like it one iota—she had to give him that.

She sighed. "I know. It's just . . . a whole month is too long."

"A month you swore you were going to use to get your life back on track," Lacy reminded her. "You've refused to join a dating service, refused our offer to go barhopping with you, and now you're saying no to all our suggestions."

"Cruising bars with two pregnant women?" Kathy said, eyeing the rounded bellies of her friends. And while she should have been proud of her flat abdomen and size-five jeans, it wasn't pride shooting through her earlier when she placed her hand on Sue's tummy to feel the baby kick. "I'm sure the men would be all over us. Besides, I'm *going* to do it. I'm going to find a man to date if it kills me. Though, for the record, it just might."

"Did he bring *her* with him when he picked up Tommy?" Sue asked.

Kathy wished she could pretend she didn't understand the question. Wished she'd never told them that Tom had married the TOW, "The Other Woman." But during the last Jack Daniel's night—at which, quite unfairly, neither Sue nor Lacy could imbibe—Kathy had accidentally spilled her guts. Or at least she'd spilled a bit of them. The big secrets were still in the bag. And they could stay bagged. It would take more than a couple shots of Jack for her to hang out her dirty laundry. Even to her two closest friends.

The pause hung heavy in the air, and Kathy realized they were waiting for a response. "The TOW was in the car but didn't get out."

"I'll bet she's twenty-one, has fake boobs and more tattoos than her IQ quotient," Sue suggested.

Her friends had no idea how much Kathy wished that was so.

The clatter of heavy machinery shot across Lacy's patio, interrupting the soft sounds of a spring day. Lacy looked over her shoulder. "The lot next door sold, and they're starting— Hot damn!" Her head whipped back around. "Guess whose truck is next door?"

"Whose?" Kathy and Sue both shifted to see.

Lacy giggled. "Mr. Lost-My-Screwdriver the Plumber."

"You mean Mr. I-Wanna-Clean-Out-Kathy's-Pipes?" Sue added.

Kathy's gaze shot from the truck parked at the curb to the nearby group of men. A fluttery feeling hit her stomach. Not the fluttery feeling that required Beano.

"This is a sign," Sue said.

Even across the distance, Kathy could pick Stan out. He stood taller than the others, and no doubt had the sexiest smile. He was probably the only one who smelled like freshly cut grass with a hint of mint. From the first time she'd laid eyes (and nose) on Mr. Bradley, he'd taken over all her fantasies.

Normally Kathy selected her leading men from movies. They were Matthew McConaughey types, and a tad more white-collar. Who knew she'd go weak-kneed over a tall, dark and fine-looking man wielding a pipe wrench? But no matter how hard she worked at bringing in a new star, Stan pushed his way into her bedroom fantasies, shoved Matthew off the mattress and crawled in beside her.

"Why don't you go say hello?" Sue wiggled in her chair like a kid who had to pee.

"He's not alone," Kathy replied, feeling her pulse race.

"So?" Lacy said. "If he gives you the cold shoulder like he did on the phone, turn your charm on his buddies. That'll teach him." Lacy looked again. "One or two of them might even be worth smiling at."

"It *would* teach him, wouldn't it?"

Kathy remembered the hollow feeling she'd gotten last week when she'd called and he told her he didn't have time to come check her leaky faucet. He'd always made time before. He'd even found a way to make things like changing toilet rings into a three-day job, without charging for his time, of course. She'd known what he was doing, finding a reason to hang around. The man knew how to flirt. She'd enjoyed every moment of it, too, even if at the end of each day she'd refused all his advances. He had no idea how much he and he alone had repaired her mangled self-esteem. How his heated glances had added a bounce to her step and fueled her fantasies. . . .

The question was: Had Stan just gotten tired of getting nowhere, or had he found some other lady with more exciting plumbing? Someone who didn't look away when he leaned in a little close, someone who claimed to have time for memorable nights. Maybe he was roostering it up somewhere else. Kathy took a deep breath. Maybe it was time for her to stop questioning and go find out.

Damn right it is. "I need lipstick." She sniffed her right underarm. "And a squirt of perfume."

"And how about a lower-cut blouse?" Lacy jiggled her breasts, which were a cup size larger now that she was pregnant. "One that lets the girls breathe a little."

Kathy glanced down at her *Don't mess with Texas* T-shirt. True, she hadn't dressed today with seduction in mind. "The girls do like breathing," she admitted.

Her friends shot up from the table and herded her off to get dolled up. Outsider or not, she loved her two divorced-and-remarried best friends. And they were right. It was high time she started having a little fun.

"Look, Stan, I just want—"

"I gave you my bid," said Luke Hunter, aka Stan Bradley,

shooting the contractor a disgruntled look. "I'm not lowering it." He focused his gaze and his bad mood on James Johnson, the asshole plumber here to underbid him. Something about Johnson and his men reminded Luke of lowlife scum. One might say it took one to know one, and that wouldn't be too far off. Luke had played the part and brushed shoulders with enough; some of their bad habits were bound to have rubbed off.

He considered just leaving, making the decision easy for the contractor. In truth, he didn't want the job, didn't know if he'd be around to see it through. Stan Bradley the plumber was about to fall off the face of the earth. And about damn time, too. Luke wanted his life back. Never mind that his life sucked. What was supposed to be only a nine-month stay in this tiny Texas town had stretched into almost three years. But something about letting Johnson think he'd walked because he couldn't handle the heat of a little competition was about as appealing as a case of third-degree jock itch.

"You've seen my work," he told the contractor, whose company worked in about six of the minuscule towns clustered in the area.

"That's why he's gonna go with me," Johnson quipped.

Luke ignored that. "You either know I'm worth it, or—"

"Come to papa!" one of Johnson's men said, interrupting Luke.

Johnson spoke up, "This one's mine. I got dibs."

"You had dibs on the last one," another man complained.

Luke looked over at his competitors, trying to figure out what they were talking about, but before his gaze found the lowlifes, his gaze found . . . heaven. His gaze found Kathy Callahan. Her long, red hair bounced off her shoulders, her jeans fit her even longer legs like a glove, and that scooped-neck green tank top hugged her breasts. Her saucy steps had everything beneath the tank top moving in a way that . . . moved a man. No doubt about it, the sight of her scored a direct hit. A hit, so to speak, below the belt.

"Shit," he muttered. In the three years he'd been stowed away here, there was only one thing he was going to miss when he finally left. And that something was walking right toward him.

Her gaze was on him. Her smile brightened, and then she seemed to notice he wasn't smiling back. Just like that, her attention shifted to the group of men to Luke's right, the group of lowlifes who, odds were, had already mentally stripped her naked. Sure, he'd done the same a thousand times, but the thought of other men doing it chapped his ass.

He took a step—a possessive step—forward. He had no claim on her. Zero. Zilch. In a week or less, he'd be long gone from her world. But damn it to Hell and back, as long as he was here, he wasn't about to let any trash near Kathy Callahan.

"Hi." Luke forced a friendlier look onto his face and moved between them. "You need something?"

His tone must have missed the friendly range, because her smile faded. "I need a plumber."

"Well, then this is your lucky day!" Johnson moved in so close that his shoulder brushed Kathy's.

Luke shot the jerk a warning glance, which was ignored.

"Name's James." The jerk held out his hand, which Kathy took, but Johnson held on a second longer than was warranted. "And it would be my pleasure to work on your pipes."

Johnson's men snickered, and Kathy flinched. Luke moved forward, his blood pressure soaring. "Back off," he growled. "She's here to see me."

Kathy's gaze, one eyebrow arched in challenge, shot to him. "I am?"

Johnson chuckled. "Sounds as if the woman's got a mind of her own, Bradley."

Luke frowned, hoping like hell she got the message that now wasn't the time to play games.

"You think you could swing by?" Kathy asked. She addressed Luke, and from the way she scooted a bit closer, he saw she understood.

"Now, don't go making any hasty decisions," Johnson spoke up. "Why don't you let us both make a bid and see who comes in cheaper? I can guarantee your sweet ass that I'll beat this man's bid, 'pants' down. And I got better equipment to do the job with, too." He winked.

Kathy frowned and took another step closer to Luke.

Johnson wasn't ready to call it quits. He moved forward and wrapped his arm around her shoulders. "Now, sweetheart—"

Luke didn't hear what Johnson was going to tell her. Neither did Kathy, because Luke yanked the man up by his shirt and physically repulsed him several feet. "I said, back off!" He looked at Kathy. "Now get out of here before—"

His words were cut short as Johnson's fist slammed into his cheek, and the next thing he knew it was him against Johnson and all three of Johnson's men. The contractor just stood there, yelling. Good thing Luke knew how to fight.

Luke had just knocked Johnson to the ground with a hard right to the nose when he heard Kathy scream. He swung around to make sure no one was messing with her. They weren't. She stood there, dancing from one foot to the other, screaming like a female—and looking good doing it. Her breasts bounced with the up-and-down motion, and . . . and that's when he caught his second punch to the face.

Women, Luke thought, ignoring the pain. Spinning, he lunged to give someone a taste of his own medicine. A taste that held almost four years of frustration. And with so much pent-up fury to spend, this was one fight he was destined to win.

Luke slammed the front door to his rented house and went to the freezer in hopes of finding anything to help ease the swelling of his face. His mug was supposed to appear before a judge and twelve jurors next week, and being black and blue wasn't part of the plan.

"Shit," he muttered, and touched his swelling eye. Then, in spite of the fact that he hurt like Hell on roller skates, he laughed. Damn, if he didn't almost feel like himself again! It had been a long time since he'd let himself do what he did best. Well, *second* best. But he hadn't done number one in a damn long time either.

Remembering what he would be up against when he went back to his real life, he stopped laughing and yanked open the freezer. Not a damn thing in there. Not even an ice tray. He wasn't exactly surprised. He wasn't even sure why he looked, considering it was his freezer and for anything to be in there would mean he'd have to have to put it there. His mind jumped back in time to when he might have opened his freezer and found all sorts of frozen vegetables, Weight Watchers meals, and 90% ground round made up into ready-to-grill patties. Things his wife, Sandy, would have put in there.

Slamming the door so hard that it banged against the wall, he yanked off his shirt and tossed it to the floor. He unsnapped his jeans and got two steps toward the shower. Then his doorbell rang.

It was probably Claire, his elderly landlady, wanting him to change another lightbulb. He liked the woman, appreciated the food she regularly dropped off. Many days he'd come back to find a homemade meal waiting on the stove top. But tonight he was so *not* in the mood to listen to her go on about her irritable bowel syndrome.

Taking a deep breath, preparing to send her off to tend her bulbs and bowels alone, Luke yanked open the door. But it wasn't his blue-haired neighbor. Not even close.

Could his day possibly get any worse?

Chapter Two

He didn't look happy to see her. Quite the opposite, actually. Kathy had sort of expected that. The fight was . . . well, kind of her fault. But with luck she could turn his mood around. Couldn't she?

"Hi." Her voice rang too chipper. She tried to wipe the cheerful expression from her face, but unsure as she was of what approach to take, it was hard to change her facial features to anything appropriate. "So this is your place, huh?"

He didn't answer. She couldn't exactly say he was glaring at her, but then again, because one of his eyes was almost swollen shut, she couldn't be sure. Her gaze slid from his puffy eye to his puffy lip. He still had blood on his forehead, and she flinched.

Shifting her gaze past his lips, she found his chest, his oh-so-gorgeous naked chest. As she remembered not to gawk at that, her gaze whispered through the trail of dark hair tiptoeing down into his unsnapped jeans. Elastic from his Calvin Klein's peeked out from his unfastened Levi's, and those darn flutters started up again in her stomach.

"This really isn't a good time," he said, and his voice rumbled deep in his chest.

Kathy snapped her gaze back up to his face, to see his frown. She offered him her hundred-watt smile. And, hey, she didn't offer that to everyone! "I brought . . . butter beans. Plus a very big apology."

"Butter beans?" The brow over his good eye arched.

"Well, they're lima beans, but I guess they're still butter beans." She reached inside her purse and held out a cold-to-the-touch bag. "You know, frozen. To help reduce the swelling and pain."

He stood there staring, so she went ahead and pressed the bag to his puffed-up eye. Then, because her position was kind of awkward, she moved a little closer. Closer to his naked chest. Her next breath came scented with freshly cut grass and mint.

He didn't pull back, and while half his face was covered by a pack of baby lima beans, he continued to stare at her through his good eye.

"I've always heard peas are better, but Lacy didn't have any peas," Kathy continued. "Or steak. I know some people use a steak. But it was either broccoli or limas. I don't care much for broccoli, so . . ." Oh, Lordy, she was beginning to sound like Sue, chattering just to fill the silence. She continued to hold the beans to his face and took a deep breath. "Are you okay?"

"Do I look okay?" His voice sounded tight—not quite angry but definitely annoyed. And since she was the only one close, his annoyance had to be aimed at her. Not that she could blame him, Kathy reminded herself.

"No, you look like hell." She shrugged. "Then again, you look better than the four jerks you left flat on their backs in that empty field." She moved the veggie pack for just a second to get a good look at his eye. "Ouch."

"I'm fine." He reached up and took the limas, pressed them to his face and stepped back enough so she had to drop her hand, but not far enough for her to slip inside his house. "Look," he said. "I'll take the beans." His gaze lowered, and Kathy was almost certain he was staring at her breasts. "But you should probably go."

"I'd rather not." Just the thought of him looking at her breasts had her heart racing, and darn if she didn't feel her nipples tightening. For a very awkward second, she considered crossing her arms over her chest. But hadn't she dressed for him to notice? "I mean, the least I can do is make sure you're okay. You know, clean you up a little. You still have blood . . . here." She reached up and touched his brow.

He swiped his finger across his forehead. "I can take care of it."

"I know, but it will make me feel a lot better if you'd let me do it."

Joey Hinkle watched the florist van park in front of the house down the street and hoped like hell it would leave just as quickly. When it didn't, he reached into the backseat, snagged his briefcase and pulled out the binoculars. He'd brought them to bird-watch, not to spy—not that he'd ever admit it. In the circles in which he ran, bird-watching pretty much labeled you queer. Joey wasn't queer, he just liked birds.

Adjusting the focus, he spotted the redhead on the porch. She'd driven the florist van, but she didn't have any flowers in her hands.

He cut his gaze toward Donald, the bulldog-faced man sitting next to him. "It's a woman. Maybe you should call Corky and Pablo and tell them to wait awhile."

"They're on their way."

"I know, but why do this now?"

"Why not do it?" was Donald's reply.

Joey stared at the man and felt his revulsion grow. By God, sometimes he didn't like these people. "Why can't we wait until she leaves?"

Donald looked at him and laughed. "What's wrong, kid? You soft just because it's a woman?"

At almost forty, Joey didn't see himself as a kid, but most

of Lorenzo's other help had at least ten years on him. "No. I'm just saying that—"

"Well, stop saying it. It's not our fault some bitch drops by for a visit, probably wanting a little dick. The boss wants this done. What the boss wants, he gets. Or haven't you worked for him long enough to figure that out?"

Joey dropped his binoculars into his lap. Yeah, unfortunately, he'd already learned that lesson. He'd had to bury the evidence in a patch of woods outside of town. The memory still made him queasy.

Kathy stood on Stan's porch, waiting for him to answer. He still didn't look happy to see her. "Please, can I come in?" she asked.

The bag of lima beans held to his face, he backed up, which she took as an invitation. Advancing two steps inside, she looked around at the combo living and kitchen area. His home was small, probably built in the late sixties, and looked . . . clean. Eclectic, garage-sale style, but bland, generic. Not at all what she'd expected. For some reason she'd imagined it as a tad more masculine, a tad more like a bachelor pad. Okay, and she had expected it would be messy.

She made another quick inspection. Nothing was out of place except his button-down shirt tossed on the floor. The sofa was a dark tan. Centered before the couch was a glass-topped coffee table that needed refinishing. In the corner was a La-Z-Boy recliner that had seen better days facing a twenty-six-inch television set. The kitchen held an old oak table surrounded by four chairs. The kitchen floor was linoleum, and the yellow and brown faded design screamed it was from the eighties. The carpet in the living room was beige and newer than the rest of the furnishings. All the walls were painted white—bright white—and not a picture or a piece of artwork decorated any of them. Kathy got a feeling the place was rented and had come furnished and that Stan hadn't added or changed a thing since he moved in.

Her gaze shifted back to him, shirtless with his jeans unsnapped. He was without a doubt the best-looking furnishing in the room, and she had a sense he didn't belong.

"How did you know where I live?" he asked, breaking his silence.

"You gave me the address to mail your check, remember?"

"Oh."

The fact that she'd memorized it and had even driven by once—okay, six or seven times, okay, a dozen, but no more than that—didn't need to be said. She wasn't really a stalker. Just infatuated and unavailable. Unavailable until she decided to become available.

For just a second, she wondered about her timing. Was it a coincidence that she'd decided to open herself up to dating—or, as she'd told Sue, "join the fornicating masses"—less than a month after her ex went and tied the knot with the woman who'd broken up their marriage? Surely she hadn't been secretly hoping he'd come to his senses and return to her, had she? No! She wasn't that pathetic. Obviously, she'd just needed some time to rebound. And now she was ready.

Watch out, world. Watch out, Stan Bradley.

The thought sent a wave of something like fear running down her spine. Honestly, she didn't know what she wanted from Stan. Well, she knew *some* of what she wanted. She wanted some company, someone to chase away the empty feeling that always hit after she went to bed. She wanted to laugh with someone—a *male* someone. To share pillow talk, long lingering glances and desserts. But most of all, she wanted the loneliness to go away. Ever since Lacy and Sue remarried, her hangout time with her friends had been shortened. Not that she blamed them.

Okay, maybe she did blame them just a bit, but she tried really hard not to let it show.

Her gaze went back to Stan, who was still staring at her. Darn, even beat up and holding a pack of frozen beans to his face, he looked good. Too good. And right then she was forced to admit the other thing she wanted from Stan Bradley: sex.

Yup, sex would be great. Not that she could expect it to be like her fantasies. He couldn't be that good. Could he?

Feeling her cheeks heat, she moved into the kitchen and dropped her purse on the table. "Why don't you sit down here and I'll grab a washcloth." She looked around. "Where would you have a—?"

"Bathroom, second door to the right." He waved toward the hall. "In the closet beside the hamper."

The bathroom wasn't quite as neat as the living room and kitchen. Good thing, too, because the man had been at her home, and Neat just wasn't her middle name. Her middle name and Neat didn't even share an initial.

She spotted a pair of dirty socks on the floor, and strewn over the bathroom counter was some deodorant, after-shave and a razor. Unable to resist, she pulled the top off the aftershave and gave it a sniff. "Mmm . . ." It smelled clean and masculine. It smelled like him.

"Find it?" he called.

Feeling chastised for snooping, Kathy swung around to the closet and locked her eyes on the washcloths so she didn't have to lie. "Yup, got it!" Then she looked around for a medicine cabinet, which she opened to see if Stan had any alcohol or antibiotic cream.

The only things lining the cabinet were aspirin and condoms. An open box of condoms. A frown pulled at her lips, and she muttered to her reflection in the mirror, "Looks as if Mr. Bradley hasn't been wasting his time waiting for me to come around."

"Did you say something?" Stan called.

"Talking to myself," she answered. "You got any alcohol or peroxide?"

"Look under the sink. There might be some alcohol there."

She found it—and another pack of condoms. Okay, one pack was acceptable, but two meant . . . What did it mean? Was he involved with someone? If he was, she was so not gonna go there. Fantasies or no fantasies, lonely or not, the last thing she wanted was to become the TOW. Which meant that before she let things get hot and heavy, she had to find out whether he was committed to someone else.

She grabbed the alcohol, and that's when she noticed another box tucked in the back of the cabinet. This box didn't hold condoms, but a hundred pack of 9mm bullets. And beside that was a gun.

Okay, it wasn't as if she'd never seen a gun before. She had. Heck, she'd learned to shoot before she learned how to whistle. She lived in Texas, for God's sake! Everyone and their pet guinea pigs had guns. Her own Smith & Wesson, from her rebellious days, was tucked away in a closest at her mom's, because no way would she have a gun with Tommy in the house. But the craziest questions fluttered through her: Did she really know Stan Bradley? Did she know him well enough to entertain the possibility of . . . of what she was considering? Did she even know him well enough to be alone with him in his home?

She almost laughed. Duh! The man had been alone with her in her own house a couple dozen times. If he were some sort of psycho pervert, he'd have already played that card.

Right?

Luke dropped into a chair. The frozen beans held to his face slowed the throbbing, and he hoped it minimized the swelling and bruising as well. He heard Kathy walking down the hall and looked up. The soft sway of her hips, the gentle way she moved—it all started a new throbbing.

For a moment she looked as if she was having second thoughts about being here. She had no idea how right she was. If she knew what was good for her, she'd snatch her purse and get out while the getting was good. Hell, if he were a better man, Luke would have done her a favor and told her as much.

He was not a better man. At least, he didn't think he was.

Not that any red-blooded man could blame him. Damn, she looked good in that green tank top and tight jeans. Add the fact that she wore her hair loose instead of up in one of those tight knots she usually favored, and that those auburn strands danced around her shoulders, playing peek-a-boo with that scooped neckline, and, well . . . suggesting she leave seemed downright stupid.

Luke's gaze shifted upward, all the way to her hazel eyes, and his breath caught. Kathy Callahan had traded in her usual teasing glint for a deep, seriously sultry look—a look promising that if he played his cards right, he could peel off those jeans and that shirt. How many times had he removed her clothes in his mind? The thought of doing it in actuality made the throbbing of his body painful. What he wouldn't have given to have seen that look from her over the past three years! *But not now,* the voice of reason whispered in his head. Now was too late. Wasn't it?

She edged closer, moved between his legs. He was eye level with her breasts, and the sweet swell of cleavage had him dropping the frozen lima beans to get a better look. The veggies landed in his lap, a nice, chilling way to cover up the evidence of his thoughts. Except, the heat between his legs would cook those beans before too long. And when he looked up again and saw the tightening of her nipples under the green tank top, damn, he really wanted it not to be too late.

She reached behind him to set the bottle of rubbing alcohol on the table. Her stretch brought soft feminine flesh within inches of his mouth. He entertained the idea of pressing his lips to that naked cleavage, but she pulled back and the tiniest bit of willpower had him rethinking the urge.

He opened his mouth to tell her to go. He really needed to tell her to go before he forgot that come next week he'd be dead to her. Gone. It would be too late. But she reached out and touched him: a gentle finger to his chin, lifting his face. He hadn't been touched like that in a long time, and it made his chest ache.

"Does it hurt?" She smoothed the tips of her fingers over his jaw, and he imagined her touching other places similarly.

"Like hell." But he wasn't talking about his face. He'd gone hard the moment he first laid eyes on her.

"I'm so sorry." She pressed the damp cloth she carried to his swollen lip.

He reached up and held a finger to her mouth. Her lips were so soft, it made his body throb harder. He imagined they would taste sweet, like peaches or raspberries. "Don't," he whispered.

She jerked back, as if afraid she'd hurt him. "Don't what?"

"Don't apologize. This wasn't your fault."

She started again with the washcloth, her touch so gentle that he remembered seeing her doctoring her son's knee after he'd fallen off his bike. Luke remembered that day so clearly because it had contained an epiphany: He could never, ever forgive his ex-wife. But now wasn't the time to go down that dark alley.

"If I hadn't gone out there to talk to you, none of this would have happened," she remarked.

He couldn't argue with that, but: "They were jerks. Needed to be taught a lesson."

"Maybe," she agreed. "But you didn't have to be the one to teach them."

If it got me this close to you, it was worth it, he didn't say.

Her gaze locked with his. "You're a good guy, Stan Bradley."

He wasn't sure if she said those words to him or herself, but Luke answered. "Don't put me on pedestal, Kathy. It will be hell falling off." He'd made his share of mistakes. And right now, letting her stay was likely among them.

She moved her washcloth to the corner of his eye. "Can I ask you a question?"

He stared up at her through his lashes. "Is it personal?"

"Yes." A smile whispered across her lips.

Her tone sounded so coy that he smiled. Pain reminded him of his swollen lip, but he ignored it and focused on the look in her eyes. "Good," he said. And just like that, they were back at the comfortable niche their relationship fit into: teasing, flirting. He loved that place, and, damn, he would have loved to take it a few steps further.

"Actually," she clarified, "I have several questions."

"Shoot," he said.

She leaned back and considered him. "The perfect segue into one of my questions." She folded three fingers back and made a pretend gun, then took a deep breath. "But I'll start with this one: Why did you tell me I'd have to find someone else to fix my leaky pipe?"

He stared at her hand. Shit, Luke realized. His gun was under the bathroom sink. "I thought it was the faucet," he replied, remembering their telephone conversation, remembering how hard it was to suggest finding someone else. That he was the wrong guy. Something he should be saying right now but couldn't.

"Faucet, pipe—doesn't matter," she said. "Why didn't you want . . . my business? Or is it my company you didn't want? I guess what I'm asking is . . . if you're not . . . interested anymore? And if there's a reason that you stopped being interested."

She reached again toward the table, bringing her soft

cleavage a breath away from his face. When she pulled back, she had the bottle of alcohol in her hands. She unscrewed the top and doused the cloth. A stinging medicinal smell filled his nose, while his eyes saw only her breasts.

"Maybe I just got tired of being told no." The words slipped out before he could stop them.

He forced himself to look at her face. She nipped at her bottom lip with her straight white teeth and said, "This might sting." Then, after shifting to set the bottle back on the table, she touched the cloth to the side of his brow. It did sting.

When he flinched, she leaned in and blew softly on the hurt. The feel of her warm breath brought a dozen or so erotic images to his mind: her mouth in other places doing wonderful things to his body, while he returned the pleasure. He'd never been selfish when it came to sex.

"Maybe you shouldn't have given up so soon." Her words were merely a whisper, but the invitation rang loud and clear. And it wasn't an invitation he could refuse.

He reached up, curled his hand behind her neck and brought her face to his. But before he let himself take it further he asked, "So if I kissed you right now, you wouldn't go Texan on me and freak out?"

"Haven't I told you? I'm originally from Alabama."

She didn't pull away, so he kissed her, tasted her for the first time. Just a little taste, he told himself, something to take with him. To remember her. But the moment his mouth touched hers, he knew he'd screwed up Royally with a capital R. Because a little taste of Kathy wasn't going to be enough.

He slipped his tongue between her lips, knocked the lima beans from his lap and pulled her soft behind into place. The sweet weight of her backside pressed against his hard-on, and he forgot all the reasons he shouldn't do this. He just let himself enjoy what he'd wanted for too damn long.

Chapter Three

Stan tasted *so* good. Like dark chocolate with a touch of mint. Even better than he smelled.

Kathy didn't hesitate when he pulled her onto his lap. Didn't hesitate to open her mouth to allow his tongue inside. Didn't hesitate to move her tongue against his. All her senses seemed heightened.

Taste.

Smell.

Touch.

Especially touch, both on the receiving and the giving ends. She brushed her hand across his stomach and shifted on his lap, and the hardness between his legs told her she wasn't alone in that wonderful place called passion. A place she had missed. A place she had longed to visit for a very long time.

The ache between her thighs intensified and before she realized it, she pressed herself harder against him. The wanton movement almost brought her out of the moment. Wanton wasn't her normal mode of operation. She started to move away, but he pulled her even closer, held her extra tight and then released only to pull her close again. The gentle back and forth fueled the fire burning inside her—the heat burning hottest between her thighs. Maybe she could get used to wanton.

She threaded her fingers through his dark hair, then moved down to touch his bare chest again. She felt the tiny nubs of his nipples, flicked them lightly with her nails, stroked the hardness of his muscled chest and smoothed her palm over the tightness of his abs. Oh, goodness, she had forgotten how good it was to touch and to be touched in return!

His lips moved from her mouth to her neck, suckling, nipping and lowering until his mouth was on the tops of her breasts. Her nipples tightened, and she leaned her head back, allowing him room to do his magic.

His hand slid around her back, slipped under her tank top, and he expertly released the hook of her bra with a gentle twist of his fingers. Her breasts fell forward with the bra's release, and his face moved lower into the swells of flesh. The hand against her back moved to her waist, slipped between their bodies and underneath the loose bra to cup her right breast. He caught her taut nipple between his fingers and teased it into an even tighter bud. The touch, not too rough, not too gentle, brought a moan from her lips and had her shifting her hips to assuage the ache between her legs.

She felt the bra being slipped from her shoulders and then the satin material sliding across her abdomen. He gently pulled it from under her shirt and let it fall to the floor. Somewhere deep in the cortex of her brain she heard the slightest warning that she was supposed to ask him something before she let things go this far, but that warning wasn't nearly loud enough to stop her and was nowhere near as loud as what came next.

A pounding against the front door startled them both. The banging shattered the oh-so-perfect moment, and all the wonderful things he was doing to her breast came to a sudden halt. Stan shot a look at the door and yanked his hand free. Then came the sound of keys being jangled.

"Shit," he muttered, and in less than a second he picked her up and set her down on her own feet as if she weighed little more than feathers. Her knees were still jelly, and he needed to stop using her key whenever she wanted. Taking a gulp of oxygen into his lungs, Luke vowed not to take his mood out on the old woman.

She stared at him. "I was just going to leave some of my famous turkey meatloaf on the counter."

Claire was short, barely reaching the middle of his chest, and seventy if she was a day. He generally liked his landlady, who happened to be a damn good cook and lonely enough to want to feed strays like himself. But right now, turkey meatloaf was the last thing on his mind. Not with the feel of Kathy's breast still in his hand.

When the old woman took another step, Luke met her by the door and took the plate. "Thank you so much. I . . . was sleeping. Not feeling well. Wouldn't want you to catch anything, so . . ." He coughed into his hand. "Maybe you should just—"

"What happened to your eye?"

Shit. "A tree. I ran into a tree. Damn—er, dang tree." Claire didn't tolerate bad language, and he could only guess finding a braless woman in his home wouldn't sit well with her either. He put the plate on the coffee table and motioned to the door.

She eyed him. "Those men. They came back again, didn't they?"

It took a moment for her words to register. "What men?"

"Those men who came here this afternoon looking for you. Big guys. Not very friendly looking."

Luke tried to figure out if James Johnson could have somehow made it here before him. But no, he'd left all those men flat on their backs when he'd taken off, and he'd come straight home. Then her words "big guys" hit a nerve. Surely they weren't—

"Yankees," Claire finished with a sniff of displeasure.

Yankees. The hair on the back of Luke's neck stood up. "Did they leave their names?"

caught her around her waist. Then, pulling back, h
hand over his face. "It's Claire." He pushed Kath
the hall. "Look, could you step into the bathroom
rid of her."

Just like that, the truth ran over Kathy with all th
of an eighteen-wheeler carrying lead bars. "I'm the
she gasped, and put a hand over her mouth to keep
of anguish from escaping.

He stared. "What?"

"I didn't want to be a TOW! Never, *ever* wanted
TOW!"

His gaze shot to her feet. "A toe? What's wrong wi

The doorknob rattled again, and she grabbed her
tore down the hall into the bathroom. She slammed
inside, not so much for effect as from bone-deep ang
ger at herself. Anger at him.

I'm a TOW.

She dropped her bra to hug herself, to offer just
comfort. It didn't work. Then, because she thought sh
voices, she put her ear against the door.

The damn thing was solid, and much more sour
than she would have liked. Closing her eyes, she took
breath and tried to decide whether she should storm ou
her glory and let his other woman know just what ki
man Stan Bradley really was, or stay put and save hers
embarrassment. Decisions, decisions. And this one wa
doozy. She hated making them in the spur of the mom

Kathy had no sooner slammed the door to the bath
when Luke's front door opened and Claire stepped ins

"Oh," she said. "I knocked. You didn't answer. I
know you were home."

And my truck and Kathy's damn florist van weren't a
He almost spat the words out, but bit them back. Tru
liked the homemade meals Claire provided, but the w

"Nope, and I asked them for one, too. Didn't much care for them. They did that to your face, didn't they?"

"No. Uh . . ." His mind reeled. He needed to call Calvin Hodges and check in. Putting a hand to Claire's back, he nudged her toward the door. "Thank you for the meatloaf."

Unfortunately, she took one step, then stopped. "I can't eat much of it myself. Irritable bowel syndrome and all." She took a step out the door, then looked back. "You're a good man, Stan. You pay the rent on time, and you never complain about screwing in a lightbulb for an old lady. But I don't want hoodlums hanging out here."

"I understand," he promised. He watched until she got down the steps, then shut the door and ran for his cell phone.

Calvin's line rang once . . . twice . . .

"Come on, Calvin—answer, damn it!" Luke's head told him he was overreacting, but his gut told him different. He'd known Lorenzo's men would track him to the ends of the earth to prevent him from testifying. Unfortunately, they'd only had to manage Piper, Texas. And they weren't here to buy him a beer. He breathed in a deep gulp of air. "Answer, damn it!"

Only, Calvin didn't pick up. And Calvin always answered his freaking phone.

Luke paced, trying to decide what to do. "Think!" He couldn't stay here. If the men who'd come were Lorenzo's, he was a sitting duck. He knew damn well he could take out one or two, but Lorenzo would have sent a whole crew of his best men, each with bigger guns than Luke. Lorenzo wanted him dead that bad. And while Luke wanted the asshole Lorenzo behind bars just as much, well, dying didn't appeal to Luke anymore. He supposed there had been a time . . .

He redialed, praying this time Calvin would answer, that Calvin would tell him everything was fine. That he would feel silly for working himself up over nothing. But as the line rang once, he spotted Kathy's purse. "Damn." He'd forgotten all about her. He hung up and shot for the bathroom door.

"Kathy?" He drew in a breath and forced calm into his voice that he didn't feel. He knocked on the door. "You can come—"

The door swung open. She pointed a finger at him. "Why? Why do men do this?"

He studied her, confused. "Do what?"

"Cheat. I never would have let you . . . let you touch me if I'd known you were seeing someone else."

He shook his head. "Seeing . . . ?" She thought Claire was his girlfriend? "That wasn't . . ." But it didn't matter what she thought. He needed to get her out of here and as far away from him as possible. Now. "You should go. I'm sure Tommy is worried about you."

"Damn right I should go. I should have never come here in the first place!" She stormed past him and snagged her purse. "And I'm taking my lima beans with me!" Stooping, she snagged the bag of veggies and stuffed it into her purse. She took one step and then touched her chest. "Oh. My bra. You wouldn't want me to leave it, now would you? Claire might see it!" She took off for the hall, sweeping past in a wave of cold fury.

And that's when his phone rang. *Calvin?* He answered as the bathroom door slammed. "Hello?"

"Stan?" Luke recognized Claire's voice. She sounded worried. She was worried a lot about health issues, but something told him this wasn't bowel related. "I think they're back. Those men . . . I just saw a car pull into your driveway. They're just sitting there. I think it's the same car as earlier.

"Fuck," he muttered.

"Stan! You know I don't approve of such language."

"Lock your doors, Claire. And call 911."

"But—"

"Just do it, Claire."

He snapped his phone closed, stormed over to the bathroom, burst inside and ignored the "Do you mind?" snarl from a half-naked Kathy, who was standing with her shirt off and her bra half on. He dove under the cabinet for his gun. Turning around, he took her by the arm.

"Listen to me, and listen good. You need to get out of here. The back door is through the laundry room." He pulled her out of the bathroom and shoved her toward it. A noise echoed out front—a car door? He looked down the hall, then back to Kathy. "Run. Don't come back. Hide in the woods until you see the police."

"Police?" Her eyes were wide, and she stared at the gun he held. He knew he owed her an explanation, but damn it, he didn't have time.

"Stay away from the house, Kathy. Go. They're bad men." He gave her a shove. "Damn it, go!"

He started down the hall, his gun aimed, not really giving a damn if he took a bullet. His mind was on Tommy, Kathy's seven-year-old son. A boy needed his mother, Goddamn it. Kathy had to make it out of here alive. Unlike him, she had a whole hell of a lot to live for.

But what if . . . ? His heart thundered in his chest. What if one of the men had gone around back? He almost swung around to check. Then he remembered Claire's words: *They're sitting in their car.* He prayed she was telling the truth. He would gladly die ten times over if Kathy got away safely.

He'd barely cleared the hall when bullets exploded through his front door.

Chapter Four

Shit! Was that gunfire? Kathy's heart started to pound, and she felt her chest tighten. No. It couldn't have been gunfire. That didn't make any sense. Except for Stan carrying his own pistol. So—

Run. Don't come back. Hide in the woods until you see the police. Kathy hated taking orders, especially from men, but right now getting the hell out of the house sounded like a good idea. And she would, just as soon as she got dressed.

She'd been so wrong, she thought, yanking her bra into place and slipping on her top; Stan Bradley wasn't her rooster. He was a cheating no-good louse like all the rest of the male population. Why had she thought he was different? Oh, and he was also a psycho freak! Or at least he hung out with psycho freaks, because illogical or not, that sounded a hell of a lot like bullets popping off in the other room. The sound echoed childhood memories, which she shoved back.

She ran through the laundry room and turned the knob. It was locked. With shaking hands, she turned the catch and yanked at the door. Still locked. *Double shit!*

Another turn lock was above the doorknob. She gave it a violent twist and tried the door again, but it didn't budge. Maybe she'd locked one and unlocked the other, but she didn't want to wait around to keep trying combinations. Heart pounding, she went in search of a window.

She had no more than stepped out of the laundry room when all hell broke loose again in the living room. She heard booming voices and more gunfire. There was no mistaking it this time. People were shooting in Stan's living room. She dove into the bathroom and shut the door.

Dashing to the window, she slung her purse over her shoulder and put every bit of elbow grease she had into opening the window. The damn thing didn't budge. She ran her hand on top to see if it had a turn lock. Nothing. Was it painted shut or just too damn old to work? Not that the reason mattered. She had to get the hell out of Dodge.

More popping sounds echoed through the house. Each threatened to take her back to when she was eight.

Taking short, about-to-pass-out breaths, she considered hiding. But the shower curtain was clear. What kind of weirdo bought a clear shower curtain?

She yanked open the closet, but with shelves lining the back, she wouldn't fit. The hamper? Too small. Under the sink with the condoms? She yanked open the doors. Too small. And there was nowhere else. Nowhere to hide.

More voices. More gunshots. Was Stan, her leading fantasy man, shot? Not that it mattered, because she was not going to be using him again. Bring on Matthew! Stan Bradley was a cheater! But the idea of him being harmed, shot, killed, slammed against her brain and had her hyperventilating. And suddenly she realized she was screaming, which might lead the psycho freaks in the living room to her, so she slapped a hand over her mouth.

Desperate, she grabbed the heavy ceramic top off the back of the toilet. Climbing on the bathroom counter, she moved against the side wall so that if someone came in, they wouldn't see her when they first entered. Then, holding her breath and the toilet tank lid over her head, she listened.

Thump. Thump. Thump. Was that her heart thudding in her ears or footsteps?

The door squeaked open. The tip of a gun appeared. Then, moving an inch through the door came a hand attached to it, a hairy hand with a finger on the trigger, which meant he planned on firing. Firing at her. Attached to that hand was a hairy arm. The kind of hair that needed a good waxing. Not Stan.

Not that it mattered. Fantasy man or not, if Stan came at her with his gun drawn, she'd use the toilet lid on him, too. She knew what guns did to people. A bloody image from the past flashed in her head and she immediately chased it away. What the hell had Stan Bradley gotten her into!

She waited until the man moved in just enough for her to see his head of thick dark hair, and then she let him have it. *Crunch!* The sound of thick ceramic hitting his skull wasn't pretty, and the man—definitely not Stan—fell face-first to the bathroom floor. His gun dropped and skated across the linoleum, bounced off the base of the toilet and spun around and around and around.

A loud crash echoed in the other room. Footsteps thundered down the hall. Panic made everything feel surreal, and the next few seconds passed as if the sand had gotten caught in the hourglass. Time flowed in slow motion; even the clanks and clatters in the next room sounded drawn out.

A man's tennis shoe appeared at the threshold of the bathroom. Still on the counter, Kathy held the heavy toilet tank lid ready. Breath caught, she waited. Finally, the tip of a gun appeared at the edge of the door molding. Then a hand. A not-so-hairy hand this time. She swung the toilet tank lid.

She swung too soon and missed the man's head. Her grip on her weapon loosened. The tank lid went flying across the bathroom, dented the door to the closet, then shattered on the floor beside the big hairy man, who hadn't moved since his nose met the floor.

Not moving? That wasn't good. And then she saw the red pooling around the man's head. Red. Bright red blood. Lots of bright red blood against the aged yellow linoleum. Which was definitely not good.

The nasty sound of the tank lid hitting his head replayed in her ears. *Bam. Crunch.* A crunch like bone. Her stomach turned. She couldn't look away from the blood. Had she killed him? With a toilet tank lid? Black spots started popping in her vision like fireworks. Memories started spinning through her befuddled brain. The next thing she knew, someone—the second someone with a gun, the one she'd missed with the toilet lid, the one she'd completely forgotten about—was yanking her off the counter.

She kicked. She screamed. Then she recognized Stan.

Didn't matter. He had a gun. *Fight,* her panicked instincts shrieked.

He tossed her over his back, caveman style, and shot off down the hall in a dead run. She bounced on his shoulder, each jolt making her stomach slap against her lungs and sending her bladder dancing around her pelvis. Her purse, still hung over her shoulder, slipped down her arm. Bending her elbow, she caught it before it dropped. Stan took a sharp turn into another room.

"Put me down!" she shrieked. Her heart raced. She started squirming, but his arm tightened around the back of her thighs. Feeling trapped, she sank her teeth into his back and bit.

"Stop!" He slapped her butt so hard it stung. He turned the locks in the back door, then twisted the top one again and swung it open. Bolting outside, he dropped her on her feet. Her knees folded, presently having the consistency of toothpaste, and she fell to the porch.

"We've got to get out of here," he grunted. He cut his eyes to the back door as if he'd heard something, grabbed her by the arm and yanked her up on her feet. "Now!"

The moment he released her, her gaze shot to his gun. She took a swing at him, which he ducked.

"Kathy, stop it! I'm trying to help."

She couldn't stop. Her heart wouldn't stop pounding, and

her instincts still screamed *fight*. His words replayed in her head: *I'm trying to help.* But she didn't believe him, did she? *No.* She took another swing.

He ducked again. And then he leaned down, grabbed her around her legs and threw her over his back again. Before she could catch her breath, he had taken off in another dead run.

Back to having her stomach bouncing on his shoulder, she pounded her fist on his butt. "Put me down!" And the next thing she knew, he did what she said. But he could have done it nicer. She was unceremoniously tossed to the ground. The hard thud bruised her backside, and she fought to catch her breath.

He tore her purse off her arm, and the lima beans flew out and hit the ground. Stan Bradley was a cheater, he hung out with murdering thugs, *and* he was a purse thief? Could she pick 'em or what?

He yanked her keys out of her purse and pulled her to her feet. "Get in," he told her, and motioned toward her van.

"No!"

He forced her into the passenger side. Add auto thief and kidnapper to his sins! Then, crawling over her—all six foot plus of hard muscle, probably weighing in at over two hundred pounds—he settled in the driver's seat, jabbed her key into the ignition, started the van and sped off.

Before he got out of the drive, she heard a loud pop. The windshield crackled and something pinged around the back of the van. That something was probably—

"Shit!" She recognized that sound: bullets hitting a vehicle. A buried memory resurfaced. She was eight and so damn scared.

"Get down!" Stan yelled. Before she could react, he caught her by the arm and threw her to the floorboards. The van, swaying back and forth, spun off his driveway and onto the road.

Pulling herself up and away from the past, Kathy glared at him. "Stop this van right now and get out!" she shrilled.

His gaze cut into her. "I know you're scared and—" His attention shot to the rearview mirror. "Damn it, I knew there had to be more."

Kathy's focus shot to the side mirror. A black sedan sped behind them. The words printed on the mirror stood out, Objects might be closer than they appear. She hoped like hell that was wrong, because the car practically kissed her van's bumper. And the guy leaning out of the passenger window had a gun.

"Get back down!" Stan growled.

Get down, Sweet Pea, get down. Her dad's voice vibrated through her mind, but she refused to go there.

She dropped to the floorboards and not a second too soon. Her van—her beloved White Elephant—took another bullet. *Ping. Ping. Ping.* The bullets hitting the road around them sounded deadly. "I'm not happy," she yelled at the man driving.

"Me either." He didn't look at her. His focus moved between the road and the rearview mirror.

A big jolt brought Kathy's head up against the dashboard. The van swerved, rocked on its left tires, and for a second she felt certain they were about to tip over. "Why are they after you?" she snapped.

"Long story." Thuds and pings, which Kathy pretty much figured were more bullets, echoed outside the van. Then another one hit the vehicle.

"Can you give me the short version?" she hissed. "I'd really like to know why I'm about to die."

He didn't answer.

Why I'm about to die. That last word vibrated in her head. *Die.*

He jerked the steering wheel to the right, then to the left; the van bounced back and forth.

Die. She really was going to die. An image of Tommy filled her mind. Tears stung her eyes. She thought of all the things she'd miss in her son's life. His smiles. The bedtime stories. His first date. His graduation. Oh God, his sweet hugs and his little boy smell. And if she died, her ex and his TOW would raise her son. Tommy would be telling that old biddy that he loved her more than dirt.

"Oh, hell no!" she cried. And, curled into a ball on the floorboards, she buried her face between her knees and prayed. Prayed for a miracle. Reminded Whoever Might Be Listening that she'd given living an honest life a good shot. Reminded Whoever Might Be Listening that she'd taken some hard knocks, first with her father, then with her mom's illness and then with her husband and his TOW, and that she'd forgone any serious whining beforehand but this was too much. She absolutely, without exception, refused to die.

She heard a big crash. It didn't involve her or the White Elephant. It came from behind them. She looked up at Stan Bradley, who seemed completely comfortable driving without a shirt, his jeans still unsnapped, as if . . . as if someone hadn't stormed into his house and sprayed it with bullets. He stared in the rearview mirror, and a slow smile pulled at his lips, and he dropped into his lap the gun he'd had locked in his right hand.

His gaze shot to her. "I don't think they'll be following us now."

Okay, she was seriously going to have to pray more. "Thank you. Thank you. Thank you." She dropped her face back onto her knees.

"You're welcome," Stan said.

Her gaze shot back to him. "Oh, *pleeeeaase!* I wasn't talking to you! Why in holy hell would I thank you? You got me into that mess!" She swiped the tears from her cheeks and pulled herself up into the passenger seat.

She didn't look at him, but she could feel his gaze on her.

He touched her arm. She slapped his hand . . . and slapped it again as he pulled it away. "Do not. Do *not* touch me, you . . . you . . . I don't even know what you are, but whatever it is, I don't like it! I don't like you!"

"I'm sorry—"

"Sorry? You say 'I'm sorry' when you step on someone's toe." Her voice rose, but she didn't care. "'I'm sorry' doesn't cover . . . bullets and . . . and someone trying to kill me." A few more unwanted tears filled her eyes.

Stan glanced into the rearview mirror and then toward her. "Okay, what kind of an apology covers bullets?"

How could he be so calm? *What kind of an apology covers bullets?* She wouldn't know, because she hadn't gotten an apology when she was eight. She hadn't even gotten one when she went looking for one at eighteen. Not that this made Stan's apology mean anything—especially when his mouth twisted and, she wasn't absolutely sure, but it looked as if he wanted to laugh at her.

"Is this your idea of how to show a girl a good time?" she spluttered. "Because if it is, I got news for you, buster. I'm *so* not your kind of girl."

The brow over his swollen eye arched. "We seemed to be doing pretty well before . . . before everything happened."

"You mean before your girlfriend showed up?" she snapped, and latched both her hands to the dashboard. "The girlfriend I didn't know about."

His blue eyes cut to her briefly. "You totally misunderstood—"

"Misunderstood? I was the TOW!"

He made a face. "What's a—?"

"Did I misunderstand all those popping sounds, too? Was that a squirt gun that . . . that Neanderthal brought into your bathroom? Or how about the one in your lap right now? Does a sign with the word BANG pop out of that semiautomatic when you pull the trigger?" She looked at her van's windows. "Is that a bullet hole, or am I misunderstanding that too?" She let out a big huff of air.

The sight of the hairy man on the floor of Stan's bathroom with blood pooling around his head filled her mind. She felt her insides start to tremble. Was he dead? Had she really killed a man with a toilet tank lid? And what about the men in the car who'd been shooting at them and had wrecked? Oh, gawd! Was she more like her father than she cared to admit? Her sinuses stung with unshed tears.

She fought against the memory and tried to focus on what was important. Right at this moment, what seemed important was getting herself as far removed from this situation as possible—which meant getting a dozen or so miles away from Stan Bradley, then going straight to the police. Yeah, she'd go to the police. That'd prove it. Prove she wasn't like dear ol' dad.

That's when she remembered her new fandangled cell phone. Damn, she could have *already* called the police.

She reached down, but her purse wasn't there. Bits and pieces of its contents littered the floorboards, but not her cell phone, which must have been thrown to the back. She started to go for it, but then her gaze shot to the man driving the van—the man who had a gun.

Fear settled like a bad burrito in her gut. "Seriously, I want you to pull over and get out of my van."

He frowned, let out a gush of air, passed his hand over his face, then met her gaze. But he didn't say a word.

"Pull over right now! I don't know what's going on here, but I want you far, far away from me." She put some punch in her voice. Or at least she tried.

"I really wish I could do that."

"You *can* do that."

She didn't like the nervous little tickle she got in her belly. It wasn't a he's-a-hunk tickle; this was a the-shit's-about-to-hit-the-fan kind of tickle. This was the first sign she always got before life plopped something terrible into her lap, and she didn't need anything else in her lap. She hadn't shoveled the crap from her lap that had appeared at Stan's place ten minutes ago. Oh, heck, who was she kidding? She hadn't dealt with the crap her husband laid on her four years ago. She hadn't dealt with the crap she'd gotten herself into on her little trip back to Alabama to make things right, either. In fact, if you asked the court-mandated therapist she'd visited when she'd gotten caught shoplifting at the ripe old age of twelve, the good doc would say she hadn't dealt with the crap her dear old dad had laid on her in the first eight years of her life. If there was one thing Kathy Callahan was good at, it was *not* dealing with crap. But her lap was too full to take any more. No more crap room.

"Look. There's a nice spot to pull over, right there." She leaned close and wrapped her hand around the steering wheel. "Just turn here and—"

He put his hand on her wrist and tightened his hold on the wheel. "I can't do that, Kathy. I can't let you go now."

She kept her eyes fixed on his face, on his swollen eye, so he wouldn't know what she intended to do next. Truth was, she wasn't sure when it had become the plan. Not that it was a good plan, but it was the only plan she had. And she was going for it.

She released the steering wheel and, lickety-split, her hand shot straight for his crotch. It wasn't the prize behind the zipper she was going for—not that she hadn't once entertained the idea—but the prize that lay in his lap. Unfortunately, with her eyes still on his face, she found the behind-the-zipper object first.

Before Stan Bradley could do more than widen his eyes— yup, even his swollen eye widened—she rebounded and wrapped her fingers around the gun. Then, breath held, she pulled back, drew the gun to her chest, wrapped her right hand over her left, kept her trigger finger to the side of the gun, just the way she'd been taught to do for safety, and pointed the weapon at his gorgeous naked chest.

"I said, pull over and get out of my van!"

Chapter Five

Joey crawled his 300-pound ass out of the car, spitting out the white powder from the air bag. He was madder than hell and feeling like . . . like he'd just been in a car crash. Which he had.

Fighting back adrenaline, he focused enough to make sure he didn't have any serious injuries. His neck ached, but mostly his head, and he remembered hitting the driver-side door when the car flipped. If he hadn't been wearing his seatbelt, no telling what would have happened.

Leaning down a bit, he looked back into the wrecked car at Donald. The man's nose and head were bleeding, and he looked half out of it; but he wasn't dead. Not yet, anyway. But both Joey's and Donald's ass would be grass if they didn't catch Luke Hunter fast. The boss didn't like people who couldn't get the job done. And Joey and Donald had sure as hell screwed up. Of course, they hadn't been alone. Boss would also have to whack Pablo and Corky. Joey could only hope that digging four graves might prove too much for their boss.

Corky and Pablo were supposed to take care of the problem. Joey didn't take care of these types of problems; he didn't have the stomach for it. And Pablo and Corky had been the ones to let Hunter and his woman friend escape his house in the first place. But would Lorenzo blame Pablo and Corky? Who knew?

Sometimes the boss chose one guy to make an example of, just to keep everyone else on their toes. Joey still remembered Freddy, Lorenzo's last example, still remembered having to pull his cold, dead body from the trunk and then burying it in a patch of woods. Joey hadn't really liked the man, but he hadn't disliked him enough to see him dead. For a week, Joey had puked every time he thought about Freddy and the hole in the back of his head.

Damn, he didn't want to be the boss's next example. He didn't want to be the reason someone else puked their guts out. Not that most of Lorenzo's hired help would care enough to lose their lunch. Killing was what most of them did.

Not for the first time, Joey regretted accepting Lorenzo's job offer. But with Joey's size and his lack of education, he didn't have a lot of employment opportunities. Being a bouncer had paid his rent, put food on his table and given him dough enough to occasionally take a woman out to dinner. From bouncing jobs he'd gotten a few gigs working as a bodyguard—and that was what he'd signed on to do for Lorenzo. Only, Lorenzo paid a hell of a lot more than anyone else. Sure, Joey knew Lorenzo was dirty, but he'd fooled himself into believing he could work for him without getting involved. And for what? The money. Why the fuck had he thought the money would make a difference? It didn't.

Joey kicked a tire so hard that he heard the bone in his big toe crack; then he let out another string of curses, words his crackwhore of a mother would have taken a toilet brush to his mouth for saying. His mom had sold her body for ten dollars a pop and then used most of the money to pay for her drug habit, saving her dimes and nickels to buy peanut butter and bread so her two sons wouldn't starve. Sometimes, when the money was all used up, she'd sent them to the store to steal the peanut butter. Stealing and whoring were okay, but let him or his brother use a four-letter word, and they'd have toilet breath for weeks. To this day Joey didn't eat peanut butter, and every time he really let loose with bad language he got a bad taste in his mouth.

Jeezus! Why was he thinking of his dead mom and peanut butter? It had to be the accident, getting his brain knocked sideways. He reached up to the goose-egg-size lump on his head. He hadn't given his mom this much thought in years. Some things were just best forgotten.

A string of curses came from the car. With his toe throbbing, Joey limped around the other side and opened the passenger door.

"I bet you wish you'd worn your seat belt like I told you now."

Donald spat. Blood oozed down the man's face and dripped onto his black suit coat. "Why the fuck are some people so hard to kill?"

Donald was talking about Luke Hunter and the redhead, of course. That's when Joey realized why he'd been thinking about his mom. It was that woman, the one with Hunter. His mom had had red hair, too.

"What the hell happened?" Donald snapped. "How did we wreck?"

"I don't know."

Joey let the question run around his addled brain. He remembered Donald shooting at the van and thinking that, if they caught up, he'd either have to help Donald kill the pair or at least witness it. The next thing Joey knew the car had gone into a swerve and started flipping.

Not that he believed he'd done on it purpose. Surely he hadn't done it on purpose. He wasn't that stupid, was he? He sure as hell wouldn't put his own life on the line to help save some woman he didn't know. Not even a redhead who made him think about his mom. Nah, he wasn't that good of a person. If he was, he'd have told Freddy about the orders to take him out. The thought sent a gush of acid into Joey's gut.

He looked at the cut over Donald's brow. "You're gonna need stitches."

"Why? I'm going to get a bullet in the brain if we don't find that asshole."

Joey looked closer. "Bet I've told you a hundred times to wear your seat belt. Maybe now you'll listen."

"Fuck you," Donald said, and pulled out his cell phone. He dialed and waited, then: "We're on Route 5, a couple miles down the road. Get the car here now! Joey fucked up and wrecked the car." His eyes shot to Joey. "Hunter's getting away. I don't care if Corky's hurt. If he can't make it, shoot him. Just get here now before they get farther away. And make sure you wipe down the place for prints and leave the package before you go. But hurry, damn it!"

Luke studied the weapon in Kathy's hands, and then his gaze shot back to her eyes. "Put the gun down," he said calmly.

"I said pull over!"

Her hands trembled, and he could tell she was in shock or the verge of it. He looked back at the rearview mirror to make sure no one was following. "We really should keep driving in case—"

"I know how to use this," she snapped, and gave the gun in her hands a little shake.

He let out a frustrated gulp. "I can see that." He cast another glance at how she held the gun. Someone had taught her well. "I'd be more worried if you didn't."

"I said—"

Keeping one eye on the road, he held out his hand. "Give me the gun."

"I really do know how to use it!" she said again.

"We've already established that," he said. "But we both know you're not going to shoot me."

"Are you really positive of that?" Her expression hardened.

Was he? "You *won't* do it." He looked her way again, watched her finger move toward the trigger. He really hoped he was right. Then again, he remembered how she'd taken down that armed gorilla in his bathroom. Most of Lorenzo's men weighed in at 250 or more. *Hire them big and dumb* seemed to be the man's motto. Nevertheless, Kathy had managed to fight the goon off. Damn impressive.

So she wasn't a wimp, but he still didn't think she'd shoot him. "I'm not the bad guy here, Kathy."

"Really? Is that why those people were shooting at you? Good plumbers don't get shot at!" Her voice trembled. "Wait, don't tell me. You failed to unclog someone's toilet and they came after you."

He almost laughed, but then he saw her eyes glisten with unshed tears.

"Good people don't have hairy men with guns trying to kill them," she continued. She blinked several times, and her hands shook as if she was about to lose it.

Luke glanced again at the rearview mirror, assuring himself that no one was following the van. Then, against his better judgment, he pulled off the main highway onto a side road.

"Now, get out!" Kathy snapped as soon as he cut the engine.

He looked at her and tried to decide how much of the truth he could tell her. As little as possible, his training dictated. But weren't these unusual circumstances?

"Have you ever heard of the Witness Protection Program?"

Her mouth dropped open, and he remembered kissing that mouth—and damn if he didn't want to do it again.

She closed her eyes for a second. "You're not a plumber?"

"Not really." After the last four years of his life, he wasn't really sure what he was anymore. From the special task force, he'd gone undercover. From undercover, he'd gone into the WitSec program.

He watched her eyes grow round, and then her whole body shook. The fact that she was processing information told him she wasn't in full-blown shock, but that didn't mean she couldn't yet go there. "I'm supposed to testify next week—"

"Your name's not Stan Bradley?"

"No. It's not." He wondered if telling the truth was the right choice. Face it, he'd gotten better at lying.

"Right." Sarcasm dripped from her words. "Get out."

His gaze shot back to his gun, which was still aimed at him. "Kathy, think just a minute. Why would I lie to you?"

"That falls in the 'don't know, don't care' category. What's important is why I would believe you."

"You should believe me because I'm not lying," he replied.

It looked as if his calm words helped. Her finger moved away from the trigger.

"I'm telling the truth," he repeated. Relief loosened the knot in his gut—or it did until her finger went back to the trigger. He heard her taking short gulps of air, which was another sign of panic. "Kathy, you need to breathe. Long deep breaths. It will help you."

She must have heard, because she took a deeper gulp of oxygen. "You're telling the truth about lying to me. So if I believe you, what I'm believing is that you're a liar. So if you're telling the truth, I really shouldn't believe you, because I know you're capable of lying."

He got dizzy trying to follow her logic. "I have no idea what you just said," he admitted. "It doesn't make sense."

"It does to me," she snapped.

"I'm not the bad guy."

"Really?" She stared at him. "Okay, prove it."

"How?" he asked.

"Call the police," she answered. "My purse is in the backseat, and my cell phone is in it."

He glanced back and saw her purse. He could pretend to reach for it and snag the gun, but that could get him killed. Probably it was best to reason with her. But to reason with her, he needed to explain why calling the police was a bad idea.

He cleared his throat. "I can't do that."

"Why?"

He could probably come up with some half-truth. Half-truths had become a constant in his life these past few years. But without really understanding why, he decided to stay honest. "Because until I talk to my contact, I don't know who I can trust."

She shook her head, and her hair danced around her shoulders. In spite of the situation, he remembered how it had felt to run his fingers through that hair, and he ached to touch her again.

Her hands trembled, and her finger moved away from the trigger. "I'm not much on police, either," she said. "But everything about this screams to call them."

"The people I'm testifying against have ties to the police departments in more than thirty states," he related.

"So you're not going to call?"

Had she not heard? "I already told you, I have a contact I need to get in touch with, and as soon as I talk to him I'll figure out how to get us out of this."

"Get out of my van!"

Kathy's finger was back on the trigger, but everything he knew about her said she wouldn't shoot. He held out his hands, palms up, hoping to soothe her. Whether she believed him or not, he wished walking away was an option, but it wasn't. Not now. Not when her name and her florist's were printed in bright pink letters on the side of her van. Lorenzo's men would stop at nothing to find him, and thanks to her being at his place today, Kathy Callahan was now a means to get to him. They wouldn't care what they had to do to get her to talk. It wouldn't even matter if she didn't have anything to tell them.

Fury backed with determination had him stiffening his spine. He'd gotten her into this, albeit indirectly; he was getting her out of it. No way in hell was he going to let her get hurt because of him. But figuring out how to convince her of that was another problem.

"Okay, let's say I get out. What are you planning on doing?" He ran a hand over his face and flinched when his palm passed over his bruised eye and jaw. "Don't you understand that you can't go home?"

"Why?" she asked.

He tried to remain calm. She needed calm. But a car turned down the road and his calm took a backseat to the adrenaline shooting through his veins. He froze. His gaze shot to the side mirror . . . and his gut unknotted when he saw an old man behind the wheel of a beige Saturn.

He held his breath and waited for the car to pass. Luckily, they'd taken only three or four bullets, most to the bumper, as their pursuers attempted to shoot out the tires. He didn't think the damage would call too much attention, but then again . . . His shoulders relaxed as the old man drove past.

"Why?" she asked again, her voice firmer this time.

"Because they'll come after you now. These aren't people who will care if—"

"I'm not involved in this. Whatever you've gotten yourself into, I'm not involved," she said.

He thought he heard another car, and his gaze shot to the side mirror again. Nothing. Not this time. But Lorenzo's men, the ones he'd left at his place, could be right on their tail. They wouldn't give up. It wasn't just out of loyalty, either. Lorenzo's men would die trying to complete a job because they knew they would die if they failed.

He kept glancing from Kathy to the rearview mirror. "They won't care if you're involved or not."

"They don't know who I am."

Was she blind? "Your damn name and address are painted on the van!" And that's when it hit him: It wasn't just her he had to worry about. "Fuck! Where's Tommy?" How could he have forgotten Tommy? He turned the engine on and floored the gas pedal. "Where's Tommy?" he yelled.

She sat there, eyes wide, gun still aimed at his bare chest.

"Goddamn it, Kathy! Tell me he's not at your place!"

"Why?" she asked.

"Because we've got to get him before they do! Where is he?" He slammed his hand against the steering wheel and made the turn back onto the highway, back the way they'd come, straight back toward Lorenzo's men. Men with serious motivation to see them dead. But his mind created an image of a little freckle-faced kid kneeling beside him, watching him fix a leaky pipe, and for Luke facing the men didn't seem so much to ask.

He met Kathy's eyes. "Where *is* he?"

"France." Her reply was barely more than a whisper.

"France?" The word danced around his panicked brain.

"With his dad," she added. "On vacation."

Luke took his foot off the gas and fought the alarm pulsing through his veins. The kid wasn't at home. Lorenzo's goons weren't at this minute doing something horrible to the boy. Realizing he needed to put some miles between him and Lorenzo's hit squad, he moved the van into the center lane, took only one second to exhale the fear from his lungs, and started to turn the van around.

Then again, maybe they would expect him to make a run for it. Lorenzo would have men watching for this van on all the major roads of the county. He needed to do just opposite.

Looking at Kathy, his gun still clutched in her hands, he

did what he should have done in the beginning. He simply reached over and took it.

She didn't fight. As a matter of fact, she hardly reacted. Which told him just how submerged in panic she really was. Facing what she had back at his place couldn't have been easy. He wished he had the time to pull over and hold her, to console her. Not that consoling her would be all he'd want to do. As inappropriate as it was, the memory of her on his lap, of his hand holding the sweet weight of her breast in his palms crowded into his mind.

Realizing where those inappropriate thoughts were taking him—a place where his jeans would feel way too tight—he pushed them away. "Listen to me," he said, shoving the gun under the seat and away from her reach. "I totally get that you're scared." He looked to the road, then back at her. "However, you've got to believe me. I'm the good guy. The men we left back there are the bad guys. I'm going to do everything I can to make sure you get out of this without one gorgeous red hair on your head harmed. But you've got to trust me right now. Can you do that?"

Could she? The question Stan—or whatever his name was—had asked bounced around Kathy's addled brain for the next few minutes. Trust had never been her strong point. Add having to defend herself with a toilet tank lid and having men shooting at her, and the idea of trusting this man seemed ludicrous. Oh, and that wasn't even considering he'd had her hide in the bathroom because his girlfriend had shown up while they were dry humping in a kitchen chair!

Then she remembered the look of sheer panic on his beat-up face when he'd asked about Tommy. She recalled he'd turned the van around, headed straight back toward the men—men who'd been shooting at him—when he thought Tommy was at her place. She couldn't deny that

Not-Stan, whoever this man was, cared about her son. He had placed her son's well-being before his own.

And of course there was the scene at Lacy's. Her gaze shifted to his black eye. The swelling had gone down some, but the bruising had gotten worse, going from bluish to purple. He'd been defending her when the fight broke out. But did that make him trustworthy? Maybe? A little? But not hardly enough.

She shook her head, trying to clear the fuzzy, lightheaded sensation buzzing through her. "My two girlfriends are married to cops. If I call them—"

"No." His jaw clenched. "You're not listening to me, Kathy. These people have cops in their pockets. Until I talk to—"

"I don't trust cops either, but Jason and Chase aren't like that."

He inhaled. "I'm not saying they're dirty. What I'm saying is that as soon as they report in, if someone in their department *is* dirty, they will have access to everything you tell them."

"Then I'll tell them to be careful who they—"

"And if they don't listen?" he snapped.

"I trust them," she insisted.

His jaw clenched again. "I don't."

Her mind reeled. "Fine. Then you do your thing, but let me do mine." She went for her phone.

He caught her hand and held it. "Aren't both your friends pregnant?"

Kathy blinked. "What does that have to do—?"

"I'm telling you that these people don't care who they hurt. If you get your friends involved, you could bring these people down on them. Do you really want to take that chance?"

His words flew from her ears to her brain to her heart. The thought of either Lacy or Sue being hurt made the trembling in her stomach return full force.

"Look . . ." He hesitated, as if trying to find the right

words. His hold on her hand softened, and that took her back to them in his kitchen, in that chair. She stared at his naked chest and remembered running her hand over his flesh. No! Why was she thinking about that now?

"I know I'm asking a lot," he said. He ran his thumb over the back of her hand. "Give me some time to get in touch with the right people. I'll have this taken care of."

Kathy sighed. This was crazy. Was she really going to trust him? Did she have any other choice? It seemed she didn't.

For the following half hour, she kept her eyes closed. Not that she slept. It was as if she had Dr Pepper in her veins, buzzing through her body, fizzing through her brain, accompanied by a number of flashing images and sound effects that played and replayed for her entertainment. She tried to find the button to stop it, but her mind wouldn't shut off. She could see the man lying facedown on the faded yellow linoleum floor, blood pooling around his head. She could hear the toilet lid crunching into his skull, hear the bullets pinging against the van. Her breath caught in her throat, and her heart pounded against her chest.

Then, just like that, her mental clock turned back twenty-one years and she could hear the popping sounds hitting her father's old truck. She could hear the last words her father ever said to her: *"It's gonna be okay, Sweet Pea."*

A knot formed in her throat, and she swallowed it down. Her daddy had lied. It hadn't been okay.

Sometimes, when she got wrapped up in memories, she'd feel the pinch of self-pity and it seemed nothing had been okay since that day. Then she'd think about her son. If all she ever did in this life was create him and a few good bouquets of flowers, she'd have to call her life successful. He was without a doubt the best thing she'd ever done. Maybe it was just melancholy or the aftershock of thinking she was going to die, but right now she missed that little boy so much that breathing hurt. And just as soon as she was away from all this mess, she was calling Tom and insisting he bring her son home. Screw Paris. Screw the education her son would get from traveling, the hell with trying to make a life for herself outside of being a mom. Look where her little adventure today had landed her! Nope, she didn't need anything in her life but Tommy.

"You okay?"

Not-Stan's voice pulled her from the hazy place between sleep and panic. Not-Stan? What was his real name, even? Was she an idiot to trust him? Should she attempt to jump out of the moving van? Should she . . . ? She opened her eyes, and the vision of him without a shirt had her brain misfiring with all sorts of messages and questions.

"I'm great," she said, her tone so thick with sarcasm that she could barely get the words out. She spotted her phone in his lap. She recalled him talking to someone, but for the life of her she couldn't remember anything that had been said.

"Did you talk to the person you needed to talk to?" she asked.

"He's not answering. I left a message." A flash of concern pinched his brow, right before he refocused on the road.

"Why do you suppose that is?"

"I don't know."

"Can't you call someone else?"

"It doesn't work that way."

Bam! The image of the hairy man, blood pooling around his head, flashed again in her mind's eye. "Do you think I killed him?" she asked.

"Killed who?"

"The man on your bathroom floor."

Not-Stan turned his head and stared right at her. "No."

"How can you be so sure?" She wrung her hands in her lap. In spite of being cold, her palms were slick with sweat.

"Because he was the one shooting at us as I pulled away."

"Are you sure?" She wiped her hand on her jeans.

"Positive. You heard the bullets, remember?"

"But wasn't there someone else with him?"

"Yeah, but I hit my guy harder than you hit yours. He couldn't get up so quickly." He smiled. "Of course, your guy was bigger, so I guess you should get points for that."

Somehow she sensed his attempt at humor was to make her feel better. Too bad it failed. "You're one hundred percent sure?"

His smile faded, and only concern etched his face. "Seriously, I saw him in the side mirror as I pulled away."

She nodded and wrapped her arms around herself as a chill snaked through her body. It wasn't cold in the van, but that didn't stop her from feeling an unnatural iciness all the way to her bones. Goose bumps crawled on her skin and a drop of sweat slipped between her breasts. Of course, she knew what was happening; this wasn't her first walk in this park. These were all the effects of shock. She remembered the same symptoms from when she was eight: the cold, the flashing images, the sweating.

At least she'd mostly stopped trembling. If it was like the last time, it might take a while before the images stopped. Of course, maybe this go-round wasn't as bad as the last. No one had died. Or had they?

She looked out the window again at the mirror and remembered the sound of the car crashing behind them. "What about the guys in the wreck? Do you think . . . ?"

"I don't know," he answered. "But we didn't cause that wreck. They just lost control of the car." His gaze focused on her again. "It wasn't our fault. Stop worrying."

She nodded; but even though she knew he was right, it didn't change a dang thing. Just running over a possum ruined her spirits for a week. Being responsible for another person's death might possibly ruin her life—though that hadn't stopped her from smashing the guy's head in. She supposed she could blame it on panic or maybe self-preservation.

Perhaps if a possum was after her, gun blazing, she could run it over.

She saw a road sign pass in a blur. "Where are we?"

"A couple miles off Cypress Springs."

"Shouldn't we be farther than that? I mean . . . I thought we were leaving town."

"They'll expect us to leave. I'm hoping they leave looking for us."

"So . . . where are we going?"

"First, I've to get some clothes."

Her gaze shifted to his chest again. "Clothes would be good. Maybe then I could think straight." *Did I say that out loud?*

He didn't look at her, but he smiled. "I guess I wouldn't think well if you had your shirt off."

She ignored the flirtatious remark and asked one of the questions that had been zipping around her confused mind: "What's your real name?"

She forced her gaze to stay on his face. In spite of the shock buzzing through her body, the man still looked good. Instantly she recalled how it felt to have his hands on her breasts, to feel the hardness of him pressing between her legs. Her nipples tightened against her bra and the muscles of her thighs tensed. Was she actually getting turned on? Oh, gawd, she was! Embarrassment chased around the unwanted hormones stimulating her body and fogging her brain. How could she be feeling this when she'd just been shot at, when she'd been forced to use part of a toilet to defend herself?

Maybe she was feeling this *because* of what she'd been through. Hadn't she read once that adrenaline actually heightened arousal hormones? The embarrassment filling her mind eased. The arousal, not so much. Her gaze wandered down his torso again.

Not that what she was feeling meant diddly-squat. She

had zero intention of acting upon the attraction. She'd learned her lesson.

His dark blue eyes met hers. One banged-up eyelid hung a little lower than the other.

"What's your name?" she repeated.

"Luke Hunter." Holding the wheel with one hand, he smiled and reached out his hand. "Nice to meet you, Kathy Callahan."

When she didn't shake, he placed his hand back on the steering wheel. Her gaze followed that hand to his arm, to his muscled bicep, ending at his naked chest. She recalled touching him in that chair.

Catching her breath and stopping her thoughts from returning to what had happened in his kitchen, she closed her eyes. His words replayed in her head: *Nice to meet you.* She opened her eyes just as the image of the bloody guy on the floor flashed in her head. "Nice? I had to crunch in someone's skull with a toilet tank lid."

"And you did a hell of a job."

He was smiling. Staring at his profile, she could see his bottom lip was still a little swollen. She blinked, and the image of the man on the floor flashed across her mind again.

"Nice isn't exactly how I'd describe it." She hugged herself again to ward off another chill.

He glanced over, and a look of concern appeared on his face. "The day started out nice," he offered, and there was heat in his voice. Heat that helped chase away the unnatural cold eating at her bones. For just a second, she wondered if that was why he was talking to her, to get her mind off the other stuff. And that maybe it was a good plan.

"Yeah, well, that was before I knew you had a girlfriend."

He laughed. "I don't have a girlfriend."

"Oh, so Claire's just a friend, right?"

"Claire's my landlady."

"Who just so happens to have a key to your place and feels comfortable using it? Don't deny it. I heard the key turning the lock."

"I wasn't going to deny it. But that doesn't mean she's my girlfriend."

"Just your bang toy, huh?"

"Bang toy?" He spat out the words as if they hurt him to say. His swollen eye widened again.

"That explains why you keep so many condoms on hand—for her visits."

"Condoms, for . . . Claire?" He shook his head. "My head's not wanting to wrap around that one!"

"In your medicine cabinet and below your sink." She let the accusation hang heavy in the air and fought the goose bumps crawling up her arms.

"Oh, those."

Was that guilt flashing in his eyes? Some of the anger she'd felt when she'd been ordered to the bathroom with her bra came back. She latched on to it, because at least that emotion she could deal with.

"Yeah, those. The ones you use when Claire stops by and lets herself in with her key. Of course, she's not your girl-friend, she's just your wham-bam-thank-you-ma'am toy."

"Okay, you're going to have to stop saying that, because the images are giving me stomach cramps." He let out a laugh. "If you got a peek at Claire, you'd be feeling silly right now."

"Why's that?"

"She's . . . old."

Insecurities swept over Kathy like a hurricane on oiled wheels. She actually welcomed that, because, like the anger, she understood them. "Like that matters."

"Oh, it matters," he said.

"Haven't you ever heard of cougars?"

"Claire lost her cougar status about twenty years ago. She's old enough to be my mom. Or my grandma."

So was the woman who'd managed to steal Kathy's husband—the same woman who was now Tom's wife and was prancing around France with Kathy's son. She could still remember Tommy asking her, *Why does Daddy's girlfriend look like Grandma?*

"Age doesn't have anything to do with it," Kathy said.

Her husband hadn't left her for a younger, prettier model. He'd left her for a woman almost twice Kathy's age. Maybe if the woman had been rich, Kathy would have felt better, but nope. She was old, wrinkled and poor—and yet somehow Tom had preferred her to Kathy. Had she sucked that bad as a wife that Grandma Moses could tempt him away from their marriage and his own son?

"Believe me, it has something to do with it," he said.

Neither of them spoke for a few minutes. Kathy tried to concentrate on Tom and the bucket-load of insecurities his leaving caused—anything not to think about the men and the guns. But bam, just like that she could hear the sound of the bullets hitting the van. She reached up and pressed her hands over her ears. Deep down, she knew it wouldn't help, but logic wasn't getting through right now.

"You okay?" Luke's voice seemed distant.

"No," she answered honestly, and didn't move her hands. "I keep . . . I keep hearing the bullets."

"That's normal," he said. "Try not to think about it."

She stared at the dashboard and did what he said: tried to not to think about it. She felt the back of his hand move over her shoulder and up to the side of her face.

"Breathe," he said. "That's good."

She blinked away the beginning of tears, and after a few more deep breaths dropped her hands from her ears.

"If I remember correctly, there's a place a few miles from here," he said.

"A place for what?" she asked, trying to concentrate.

"To get some clothes. I . . ."

He continued talking, but she stopped listening. When she realized he'd stopped, and was staring at her, she fixed her gaze on the side window. The landscape passed in a blue haze. The bluebonnets were out. *Yes, think about the blue-bonnets, think about anything but . . .* He was talking again and she forced herself to listen.

". . . Then we've got to lose the van."

"Lose my van?" That had her thinking a little clearer. "I don't—"

"Not *lose* it. Park it and get another ride."

"And how do you plan to do that?"

"I'll figure it out," he said.

"Oh, gawd, you're not planning to steal—"

Her cell phone rang in his lap, playing "Sweet Home Alabama." She reached for it, but he snatched it up. Once again she found herself with her hand in his crotch. The message fired from her brain was to jerk her hand away, but her brain must have been firing duds. She just sat there, half out of her seat, leaning over the cup holder, her hand stuck between his legs.

He cleared his throat. Or was that a chuckle? Either way, he gave her hand a slow perusal. A smile threatening, he turned the phone over to read the Caller ID.

Kathy sat up, removing her hand from the bulge growing in his jeans. Glancing back at him, she noted the humor dancing in his expression had vanished. "The call's coming from your house. Who could be at your house?"

"I . . . No one is at my house."

"No one?"

The seriousness of his tone had her heart racing again, and the fuzzy feeling of panic tap-danced in the way of her focus.

"Then it has to be them," Luke said.

Chapter Six

Joey parked the rental car Corky and Pablo had been driving in front of the trailer. They'd left the two banged-up guys, who looked even worse than he and Donald, at a rental dealership to get another car.

The trailer had all kinds of homey-looking flowers growing along the front, and Joey felt relief that the van wasn't parked there. But then he spotted a green Honda to the side, and he hoped that Kathy Callahan—if that was really her name—hadn't come home. Just a few phone calls to Lorenzo's local contacts had given them the florist owner's name and address. Lorenzo had more people in his pocket than a stray dog had fleas.

Pulling the keys out of the ignition, Joey noted the second, smaller trailer off to the side. There was a florist sign posted out front. He reached for the door handle—and nearly jumped out of his seat when a bird came crashing into the windshield.

"Motherfucker!" Joey spouted. At the same time, Donald yelled. Joey wiped his mouth, literally tasting the toilet brush. A bright blue bird, definitely a male blue jay, flapped its wings and haphazardly flew away. Joey smiled, thrilled at seeing the bird until he remembered a wives' tale one of his old girlfriends had told him.

"You know what they say," he asked Donald, "about birds trying to get into a house? They say it's a premonition that someone is going die."

Donald reached for the car door and looked over at him.

"This isn't a damn house. And what are you waiting on? Let's do this one first." He pointed at the trailer with the flower beds—the one that looked like a home. "I'll go around back. You take the front. If you find her, don't kill her yet. We need to talk to her."

Yet? Dread filled Joey's belly, and he started to remind Donald that his job description was bodyguard, not grim reaper, but Donald's mood didn't invite such a comment. Then it hit him: Maybe that saying about birds wasn't just an old wives' tale. Someone might indeed end up dead—if not right now, then later. Lorenzo had been less than thrilled with how this mission had gone, and there had been threats made that if it didn't get done right, there would be hell to pay.

Joey didn't doubt it. There would be hell to pay either way. If he wound up helping kill this woman, that would be hell. If she got away, Lorenzo would probably give him a ticket to Hell, just like he had Freddy. Joey just wasn't sure which he preferred. He supposed he'd better figure it out fast.

He walked up to the front porch, his damn toe throbbing like a son of a bitch. Instead of kicking in the door, he reached for the doorknob. It wasn't locked. Fighting the urge to knock, Joey stepped inside.

A blonde standing by the kitchen table holding a phone in her hand swung around to face him. He had the over-whelming need to apologize and step out. But he couldn't.

Her blue eyes widened in puzzlement. "Who . . . are you?" she asked.

His gaze shot from the shock on her face to her belly—a belly swollen with child. "Damn!" he muttered.

He spotted Donald through a window moving toward the back door. His mind created an image of what Donald would do to the pregnant lady. The bird hitting the windshield flashed in his mind; then he remembered Freddy and how he'd known the man might get offed and hadn't done anything to stop it. It was decision time. Joey guessed he had about two seconds to decide which side of the fence he was on: the killing side, or the possibly-being-killed side for not killing.

He met the blonde's eyes and reached for his gun.

Luke watched Kathy snatch her hand off his zipper, and if the situation weren't so damn serious, he would have laughed. He met her wide-eyed gaze again, a sure sign of shock.

"Kathy, I need you to take some deep breaths and think. Who could be at your house?"

"I don't know. Maybe it's either Sue or Lacy."

"Do they have keys to your place?" When she reached for the phone, he held it out of reach and repeated, "Do they have keys to your place?"

"Yes," she snapped.

Shit. Anyone in Kathy's house was in danger.

"Do they use those keys? Do they let themselves into your place?"

"No. But they're the only ones who have a key."

He let go of his fear that one of Kathy's friends was mixed up in this. Chances were the caller was one of Lorenzo's men. Had they had time to get to Kathy's and find her cell number? He mentally tallied up the time and realized that, hell yeah, they might have. If they had someone working with the authorities, a phone call would have gotten them all the intel they needed.

"Give it to me." She motioned to her phone. "I'll call and find out."

"No," he said in a calm voice. "The phone can be traced." He switched his focus back to the road.

He heard her say something. Her words bounced around his head, but instead of listening, his mind chewed on the consequences of Lorenzo's people tracing the phone.

She tried again to snag it.

"Stop, Kathy." He shut the phone off and pressed a little harder on the gas.

"It's my phone," she said, as if he didn't know. She folded her arms over her chest and glared at him. Her hazel eyes shot fire, her mouth pinched, and the haughty way she tilted her head spoke volumes about her mood.

"I know it's your phone, but considering they already have the number, they could have also gotten a trace on it."

Her expression hardened even more. "You used it a few minutes ago."

"And maybe I shouldn't have." He glanced back at the phone and then focused on her. "If they've got your number, chances are they got a trace on it. They could have someone on their way right now to find us." The thought had him speeding up the van. Maybe he should even reconsider an attempt to get them out of town. But, again, he knew that's what they would expect him to do.

His mind raced. He'd purposely driven the back roads— less traffic, less chance of being spotted—but if Lorenzo's men knew their location, it would also be easier for them to be taken out with no witnesses.

"Please!" Kathy rolled her eyes. "A trace on my phone? That's . . . that's ridiculous."

She seemed to be thinking clearer, even if she was wrong. Good, he needed her clearheaded. "It's not ridiculous."

"I want my phone."

"Sorry," he said.

He watched her fall back in her seat and glare out the window. Let her get mad, he told himself, you need to concentrate on getting her out of this mess. Damn, she doesn't deserve this.

For the last few years she'd been the one joy in his life here. When he'd accepted the job to go undercover in Lorenzo's operation, he'd said yes because at the time he thought there wasn't anything to live for. In less than two years his dad had died, his sister and her kids were in a fatal car crash that he could have prevented if he'd gone with them as they'd asked. Top that off with learning his wife had aborted his child and, when he confronted her, filed for divorce . . . well, he'd lost everyone he loved. His life sucked. Going undercover had seemed like a way to escape.

Looking back, in the beginning he hadn't been too concerned if he lived or died. When he'd gotten out alive with proof that could put an end to the operation, Lorenzo's men were taking out witnesses left and right. The top dogs working the case decided to place him in protective custody. But there was no way in hell that Luke was going to be babysat for months on end. So there was only one other option: temporarily placing him in WitSec. Most people hated walking away from their lives. Luke hadn't flinched. He hadn't thought he had a life to go back to. It wasn't as if he'd be missed. The few friends he'd had, he'd walked away from while trying to deal with his grief. He hadn't come to Texas expecting anything that would make him see his life or circumstances any differently. But Kathy, with her wholesome, picture-perfect love for her little boy, her sassy wit and sexy body, had given Luke something to believe in, something to look forward to, even if she hadn't known it.

"It's my phone," she muttered again under her breath.

"I know you're pissed, but you're going to have to trust me."

She didn't look at him.

He'd never really seen her angry before. Oh, she'd put up barriers to keep him from getting close. And while he hadn't understood her reasons, and that annoyed the hell out of him, it hadn't stopped him from coming back. He'd found reasons to see her. Just being in the same room had him looking at life differently. He liked that.

The fact that he wasn't the only one to enjoy their time

together made things even sweeter. He knew damn well she'd invented plumbing problems just to have him drop by. Not that he complained. Hell, he'd taken to ordering flowers for all his clients as a thank-you for their business. A plumber who sent flowers! He'd never heard of such, but ordering them was a reason to stop by Kathy's place once a week. Those stop-bys were never short, either. He'd always ended up spending hours there talking and laughing.

As for those condoms she'd accused him of having for Claire . . . Shit. He inwardly cringed. The first pack had been bought on an off chance that Kathy would change her mind about his offer of dinner and a memorable night. He'd become the proud owner of the second pack when she'd called him one Friday afternoon with another faux plumbing problem, and he hadn't had any on him. So now he had two packs of condoms. And not a damn one of them used.

"Taking something that belongs to someone else is rude," she snapped.

He studied the phone again. He really needed to call Calvin, but he'd have to find a different method.

"You know what?" she seethed. "I don't have to put up with this." She held out her hand. "Give me my phone or else!"

He shot her a quick glance. Or else what?

Joey darted forward and managed to get his hand around the blonde's mouth before she screamed. She started squirming, but he held her against him and dragged her to the back of the trailer and into a bedroom. Once he had her away from the windows, he yelled out the bedroom door, "No one's here, Donald! Why don't you try the other trailer?" He hoped Donald heard. Hoped even harder Donald believed.

With his hand still locked over the struggling woman's mouth, Joey opened the closet door. Before he released her, he spoke low in her ear. "You can't scream. If you scream, he'll kill you. Just stay in here and hide. Wait awhile before you come out. You understand me?"

"Open the fucking door!" Donald's shout shattered the little peace Joey had.

The blonde's gaze shot to the bedroom door. Then her eyes, still round as half dollars, slapped back to Joey.

"I'm trying to help you," he whispered. "You and your baby don't need to get mixed up in this."

Tears fell from her frightened eyes and leaked onto his hand. She released her hold on his arm, and her hands moved protectively to wrap around her belly.

"That's right. Think of your baby. Just hide and it'll be okay." He knew she was worried sick about her unborn child. And she should be.

"I'm not going to hurt you."

The sound of the back door being kicked in caused the woman to flinch. Joey's heart thudded. "Promise me you won't scream!" he whispered. "Because I really don't want to see you get hurt. You got that?"

She nodded and sniffled.

Donald's angry voice boomed through the trailer. "Where the fuck are you?"

Joey moved his fingers from around the woman's mouth, felt terrible when he saw his handprint on her pale cheeks. "Get in there now," he whispered. She looked ready to bolt.

"Joey!" Donald's voice boomed closer.

"Hide." Joey gave her a nudge.

The woman hesitated for one second. But when the sound of footsteps in the hall echoed, she bounded into the closet, pulling the door shut behind her. Joey wasn't sure, but he could swear he heard a thank-you before he took off.

Donald stood in the hall, his back to Joey. "Hey," Joey said, and Donald swung around, gun drawn. "Whoa! It's me! Just checking the bedrooms. No one's here. Why don't we check the other trailer?"

"You sure no one's here? There's a car parked outside."

"Check for yourself," Joey said, afraid he'd give himself away if he said anything different.

For some reason, his grasp on his gun tightened. Then the realization hit with a thud in Joey's chest: If Donald walked into that bedroom, Joey would shoot him. He'd kill the asshole before he let an innocent woman and her baby get hurt. Was it because the woman was pregnant? Or was it because she didn't have anything to do with all this? Not that the reason mattered. He just knew she shouldn't have to die. The same way Freddy shouldn't have died—wouldn't have died if Joey had only spoken up. And if Donald found her, he'd kill her as thoughtlessly as stepping on a roach.

The tension in Joey's broad shoulders eased when Donald started down the hall. Joey followed, but not without noticing the pictures lining the walls. In the frames was the redhead. Beside her stood a young redheaded boy, smiling ear to ear. The kid looked happy, loved—like a kid should look. Kathy Callahan was a mother.

Joey's gaze shot around the trailer. It looked lived-in but clean and sported all sorts of feminine touches. He passed the bathroom and saw the toilet adorned with those fuzzy covers on both the seat and tank lid. Joey had never lived in a house with a covered toilet seat. Not that he thought he'd like it. The damn thing would get splattered with piss the first time he took a good leak. But for some reason, a covered toilet seat lid seemed homey.

His focus shifted from the john to a bright green basket by the tub. The thing was filled with kids' toys: plastic cars and army men, even a water gun. Joey wondered what it would have been like to have had a mother who kept toys beside the bathtub. To have grown up with someone who cared about him more than she cared about her next high. His own mom hadn't cared if they ever took a bath.

He remembered the picture of the happy boy, and Joey's

toe started throbbing again. His gut twisted and . . . damn! Just like that, Joey knew that he couldn't stand by and watch scum like Lorenzo's men kill the boy's mother. But could he stop them without getting killed himself? When Blondie in the closet went to the cops with her story, Lorenzo would hear about it. He'd hear about it and tell Donald to do to Joey what had been done to Freddy.

Joey continued down the hall but stopped when Donald saw the portable phone on the floor. "You *sure* no one is here?" Donald asked.

"Blast you!" Kathy seethed, reaching again, not really caring if she sounded rational or not. She wanted her phone, damn it!

"Sorry!" he said again, holding the phone away. "We can't use this anymore."

"It's my phone! I paid a killing for it! And I would like for you to hand it over . . . *now!*"

He ignored her? How dare he ignore her! She counted to three, not sure what she would do then, but it made her feel as if she was doing something.

He examined the phone more closely. "Does it have a GPS?"

A GPS? Why was that important? Why was any of this important? They had killers after them, so why was getting her phone so important to Kathy right now? Maybe it was the principle of the thing. Maybe shock was making her loco. She didn't know. Didn't care. She just wanted her phone.

"Does it have a GPS?" he repeated.

"Yes. Now give . . ." Her words faded. She stared in disbelief as the obstinate, bullheaded man tossed her phone out the window. Her phone! He'd just tossed the one toy she'd allowed herself in the past five years out the window. "Are you bat-shit crazy, or does it just look that way?"

"It just looks that way," he answered.

She continued to stare. "I really should have shot you when I had the chance." She slammed back against her seat and let out a frustrated yelp. Damn him!

"When you calm down and are able to listen, I'll explain."

"I'm listening," she said, and noticed he was driving about eighty-five miles per hour. Speeding.

He cut his gaze back to her. "But you're not calm."

"After the day I've had, that might not happen again in this lifetime." She dropped her face into her hands and moaned.

"You hearing the bullets again?" he asked.

"No!" She pulled her hands away. "What I'm hearing is me kicking your ass!"

He grinned, and that made her even madder. She crossed her arms over her chest and glared at him.

"What you're feeling is normal. It's shock, but I need—"

"This isn't normal," she said.

"Normal for what just happened. But I need for you to focus. To be reasonable."

She continued to stare at him. He kept his eyes on the road. Was she being unreasonable? Her mind nipped at the question and somewhere logic intervened and said, *Maybe.* Maybe she was being a tad unreasonable. "You seriously think these people would have put a trace on my phone?" she asked. "That those guys are already at my place?"

"Yes, on both counts." He glanced at her.

She shook her head. "I thought only cops or FBI could do things like that."

"Well, you thought wrong. But then again, they've got plenty of powerful people in their corner. It could be a cop pulling the strings." He paused and his mouth tightened. "Even an FBI agent."

"My God, who *are* these people after you?" she finally asked.

"They're a crime organization that smuggles everything from guns to drugs into our country. But unlike common criminals, these guys are smart. They've spent years building their organization from the ground up. They've got politicians and law officers in their corner. They know how to break the law and get away with it."

"You make them sound like the mob," she said.

"You could call them that," he replied.

"And how did you get involved?"

He looked at her as if debating whether to tell her the truth. Why would he be keeping something from her? Besides her being unreasonable. "Oh, gawd, please don't tell me you used to work for those goons?"

"No. Well, yes. But—"

"You're a drug dealer?"

"No."

"Gun smuggler?"

"Do I come off like a gun smuggler?"

"I've never met a gun smuggler, so I wouldn't know."

He frowned. "I worked for their accountant."

Wonderful. Her *ex* was an accountant. She tried to visualize Luke sitting at a desk all day crunching numbers. It didn't fit. Although she had to admit he hadn't quite fit into the plumber category either. He'd never had the beer belly or the jeans that hung too low in the back, showing his profession's famous crack. She knew because she'd checked that out many times. *Many* times.

"So you're really an accountant and not a plumber."

"Sort of."

"Just what does 'sort of' mean?"

"It means it's complicated."

She watched him run a palm over his face in frustration. "Didn't you say you were under the witness protection program, and that you were supposed to testify?"

"Right."

"So did the authorities catch you doing something illegal with these people's taxes and offer you a deal to testify?"

"Not exactly."

When he didn't offer a further explanation, she glared at him. "You ask me to trust you, but you're not telling me why all this is happening."

"I did tell you why it's happening. I'm supposed to testify, and they want to make sure I don't." He took a sharp turn and the van bounced. "You should buckle up."

"Why are you driving so fast?"

His right eyebrow arched. "Why do you think I'm driving so fast?"

"Are they back?" Her gaze shot to the side mirror.

"Not yet. But if they got a trace on the phone they'll know our vicinity. And I'd rather not be here when they arrive."

She buckled her seat belt. The sound of the buckle clicking brought on the sound of the gunshots, and with that came the image of the bloody man on the bathroom floor. She flinched and tried to refocus on the conversation.

"You're still keeping things from me," she said. "And yet you want me to trust you. That falls in the 'really bad manners' category. Don't you think?"

"No. I think it falls into the 'this isn't something I can talk about' category."

"I don't like that category." She clenched her fist. "You can't expect me to just go along with everything you say and not understand why I'm doing it." She crossed her arms over her chest. Another wave of cold shot up her spine. She fought the chill and focused on seeing the passing scenery—not the bloody images flashing in her head.

Chapter Seven

Jason Dodd, Detective for the Houston Police Department, had finished giving his "Say No to Drugs" speech at one of Piper's junior high schools and was heading home early. He picked up his cell and called his wife, Sue, to see if she wanted him to pick up Chinese for dinner. With his wife being pregnant, he never knew from one day to the next what she would or wouldn't eat. Not that he cared. Hell, she was the one who carried around his kid in her belly—a fact that had him both sweating bullets and feeling giddy. Accommodating her likes and dislikes was the least he could do.

When she didn't answer the home number, he dialed her cell phone. It went straight to voice mail. Probably a run-down battery. She was famous for forgetting stuff like that when she was writing a new book.

He was leaving a message when his line beeped. He checked the name on his Caller ID: Kathy Callahan. One of Sue's good friends. That meant it was probably Sue. Kathy wasn't . . . Well, except for a nod and a casual conversation about the weather, the woman kept her distance. He would call her a cold fish, but Sue wouldn't like that.

"Hey, babe," he said.

"I . . ." Sniffle. Hiccup.

His heart flew into his throat. His wife was crying.

Luke looked over at Kathy, who was hugging herself as if cold, and he switched on the van's heater. It had to be over eighty degrees in the van. He knew her cold stemmed from her nerves, but sometimes heat helped.

"You okay?" he asked.

She moved closer to the door as if determined to ignore him.

Not that he blamed her. She'd asked for the truth. She deserved the truth, didn't she? But if there was one thing he'd gotten good at these past few years, it was keeping secrets. Then again, in a few weeks he'd be out from under all this, free from the secrets and back to . . . what? He still hadn't decided if he was returning to work for the FBI. He didn't know what he wanted. Surprisingly, these past few years working with his hands hadn't been nearly as bad as he'd envisioned. And damn if the money hadn't been pretty good, too.

He imagined his dad saying, *"See. I told you so, son."* Luke had chosen plumbing as his WitSec profession because it was what he knew. He'd put himself through school with it. Plumbing was what his dad had done.

Luke had spent a lot of time thinking about his dad the last few years, wishing the old man was still around to see him carrying on the line of work. His dad had wanted that. *"You can take over my business when I retire,"* he'd said. But Luke wanted no part of it. While he hated the fact, he'd looked down on his old man because of the manual labor— shit work, as he'd so often referred to it. It simply wasn't cool to spend your life unstopping other people's johns. He'd thought he wanted excitement: chasing bad guys, dodging bullets. After today, snaking a drain didn't look so mundane. It sounded pretty damn good.

From the corner of his vision, he saw Kathy tremble again. Would hearing the truth help? Then again, what would it hurt?

"I was working in Lorenzo's accountant's office," he said, and watched her turn to look at him. "But I was really working undercover. I work for the FBI on a special task force of the DEA."

Her expression grew pinched. "You're a cop?"

He heard accusation in her tone.

"I'm a federal agent."

"Same thing." She shivered, as if another wave of cold hit her.

"Not really." He paused and then cranked up the heater. "I was undercover for almost a year before I finally found something that could take Lorenzo down. I had a lineup of people willing to testify, but one by one they . . . became unavailable."

"They backed out?" she asked.

More like backed off a cliff or the face of the earth. One had been unfortunate enough to run into an ice pick. "Something like that."

She took several deep breaths, as if trying to fight panic. He'd been there a few times himself. His first shooting as an agent hadn't been easy. Then there was the night he stood in the emergency room and was told his sister and her entire family were gone.

He glanced at Kathy and found her staring, as if waiting for him to finish. "It became clear that someone on the inside was involved. The agency didn't know who to trust. I was the only witness they had left. They wanted to dig deeper and try to find out where the leak was coming from. It was supposed to be for nine months, but things kept getting postponed."

She closed her eyes. "You couldn't have just been a criminal, huh?"

He remembered her saying something about not trusting the police. "You don't like cops?"

She opened her eyes. "Let's just say they don't fall into my 'favorite-people' category."

"Why?"

She blinked several times, almost as if fighting tears. "Because I've found most of them to be self-serving, macho-minded, ignorant sons of bitches who think a badge makes them better than everyone else."

"Ouch!" He cut his gaze to the rearview mirror and relaxed when there wasn't a car behind them. "Kind of harsh, isn't it?"

"Yeah. Maybe." She leaned back in the seat. "Normally I keep my opinion to myself, but today I've lost some of my normal tact." She swallowed, and her bottom lip quivered until she caught it with her teeth. He watched her shiver again as she whispered, "Sorry, nothing personal."

"But didn't you say that your friends' husbands are cops? Lacy Kelly and that blonde who's a writer?"

"Yeah. What can I say? I guess my friends have no taste." It sounded as if she was trying to tease, trying to hide some real emotion. He looked over and saw a drop of sweat running down her brow. She leaned her head back. Her eyes closed and then jerked back open.

"More bullets?" he asked.

"Something like that," she muttered, and leaned against the door.

It was best to keep her talking, to get her thinking about something besides the bullets. "So . . . you don't like your friends' husbands?"

"I didn't say that."

"No, you didn't. You even said that you trusted them earlier. But then you insulted all cops." He purposely put some accusation in his tone, knowing a fire in her belly might help.

She looked over at him. "The truth is that they seem to be decent guys. But frankly, I think they're the exception to the rule." Her teeth chattered.

"Whose rule? Your rule? Like the 'categories' you judge law officers by? The category that says we're all alike?" He put even more edge in his tone.

"I . . . didn't say that." She sat up a little straighter, and her mouth tightened.

That's right. Get mad at me, it will make you feel better. "So what you're really saying is that I'm not a decent guy because I'm a federal agent."

"I didn't say that either."

"You implied it," he said.

"I didn't imply it."

"Yes, you did."

"No, I didn't, because what kind of guy you are falls into the 'I don't know and don't care' . . . er, category." She stopped hugging herself. The shift in emotions was working.

He shrugged. "You've got a lot of categories."

"You . . . you're impossible! You threw my phone out the window. How did I miss this side of you?"

He almost laughed but held it back. "I told you, I suspected they might be tracking it. But you wouldn't listen."

"Couldn't you have just cut it off?"

"If it had GPS, it could be tracked even without being turned on," he said. "I couldn't chance that. You're just going to have to get over it."

"Get over it? Are you always so pigheaded?"

"Pigheaded? Is that a slam against me being in law enforcement?"

Her hazel eyes squinted. She pulled her hair to one side and twisted it into a rope. "Take it any way you want," she said.

She stared out the window as if shutting him out. Out wasn't good. Out would take her back to the bullets.

"Are you always so difficult?" he asked. "Of course you are. You're a redhead. Hot tempered, difficult and—"

"Stop!" Her mouth fell open. "I can't believe you'd judge people by stereotypes. You're infuriating! I can't believe I didn't see this side of you."

"But most cops are self-serving, macho-minded, ignorant

sons of bitches, who think a badge makes them better than everyone else, huh?"

She sat for several seconds as if letting his words fall into place. "You worked really hard to make that point, didn't you?" she asked, sounding more rational than before.

He grinned—he couldn't help it. "I like making points. Plus, you're fun to mess with." And she was.

"Well, shucks! I'm glad I'm entertaining you," she replied.

"Me too," he said, and the idea of what might have happened earlier at his place when Lorenzo's goons had showed up had his gut clenching.

"I was being sarcastic."

"I know. But at least you're not shaking anymore."

She studied him, her mouth a tight bow. "So you purposely set out to annoy me so I'd forget about . . . about everything."

"Did it work?" His gaze slipped to the side mirror.

She paused, then inhaled. "Yes."

He turned down the heater. "If I did it purposely, would it make me come off less like a self-serving, macho-minded, ignorant son of a bitch who carries a badge?"

She bit down on her lip. He didn't think she was going to answer. But then she did. "Maybe a little."

He laughed. "Then that's what I was doing."

Again, he realized how much he liked her. She had been the one bright spot in his life these last few years. Then he let himself entertain ideas for when he got his life and name back. When he decided what he really wanted to do with the rest of his life, maybe he could knock on her door and see if they had a real chance at starting something.

The sound of a car engine entered Luke's awareness. His gaze shot to the side mirror. A black Ford truck pulled into the left lane and moved up beside him—in the lane for opposite traffic. Luke grabbed his gun.

But then he spotted the driver. It was just a teenager eager to pass, ready to get somewhere faster than he needed. But the accompanying shot of adrenaline made Luke realize that he shouldn't be thinking about the future until he knew for sure he could get himself and Kathy through the day. He really needed to get to a phone. He needed to talk to Calvin and get some reinforcements. And before he could do any of that without calling attention to himself, he needed to find a shirt.

Glancing over at Kathy, he saw that she seemed to have gotten past her shock . . . for now. While it brought him some relief, he knew damn well that this was the smallest of feats he had to accomplish. Getting her out of this alive, away from Lorenzo's reach, was going to be the hardest.

Another car pulled off a side street and fell into place behind him. His gut tight, he waited to see if the driver was one of Lorenzo's men.

Chapter Eight

Somehow Joey convinced Donald he'd knocked the phone off the receiver himself, so now they stood in the second trailer, which was set up as a florist shop. Thankfully, an unmanned florist shop. Joey stood in the middle of a room that smelled like different kinds of flowers and studied his partner, wishing he could convince the man to leave. But if he acted too eager, Donald might suspect something.

Trying to not put his weight on his toe, Joey leaned to one side and watched the older man pace the room. His head had started bleeding again, and Joey noticed he'd swayed on his feet several times. Add the fact that the man had puked earlier, and Joey figured Donald probably had a concussion or something.

Joey touched the lump on his own head. Hell, maybe he had a concussion, too. That would explain why he'd risked his life to save the blonde. But he didn't regret it. Hurting a pregnant woman was just plain wrong.

"Motherfucker!" Donald yelled, and turned over a table that held a vase of fresh yellow flowers. Glass shattered, and the water from the vase splattered the wood floor and Joey's pant legs. Tearing up the place didn't make sense, but as long it wasn't the blonde in the other trailer being torn, Joey couldn't care less. He cast a glance out the window and prayed the woman wouldn't pull a stupid stunt and try to run until she made sure their car was gone.

Donald's phone rang. Joey turned from the window and listened. "Got it," Donald said. "I'm on it!" He hung up and started out the door. "We got them. Come on."

"I'm five minutes away, baby," Jason said into the phone as he whipped around a curve so sharp he smelled rubber. He held the phone to his ear with one hand and drove with the other. Somehow he'd managed to get his gun out, and it waited in his lap. If they laid one finger on his wife, he was going to kill them. "Talk to me, Sue."

He heard her sniffle. "He had a gun. He said the other guy would kill me."

"Four minutes," he said, and pushed his foot on the gas pedal as hard as he could. "Are you sure you're not hurt?" Rage bubbled up inside him.

"I don't think so." She sniffled. "I was just so scared."

Which meant his child was scared. At the last doctor visit, the doc had said everything Sue felt, the baby felt.

"How many do you think there were?"

"Two. All I saw were two."

That was good. Because he could take on two. He could take two with his bare hands if he had to.

"Are they still in the florist shop?" he asked, acid pumping through his stomach. "Is their car still there?" He didn't have time to consider who they were or why they were at Kathy's. All that mattered was getting to Sue and keeping her safe. He considered hanging up and calling for backup, but he knew the Hoke's Bluff police response time would be at least ten minutes. Their response was even worse than Piper's and Houston's. And hanging up on Sue didn't feel right.

She inhaled shakily. "Car's still there. Maybe I should try to get to my car and leave?"

He envisioned her getting shot while running. His grip on the wheel tightened. "No! Just stay right there. If you see them coming, drop the phone and go hide. I'll be there in three minutes, baby. Three minutes."

Then he heard her yelp. The sound of the phone being dropped echoed in his ears and panic shot to his heart.

"We've got them?" Joey asked.

Donald nodded.

Joey's thoughts shot to the image of the little boy with his mother, and his stomach muscles tightened. He didn't think Corky and Pablo could have gotten a rental and caught up with Hunter and the redhead that fast. "Who has them?"

"No." Donald scowled and swiped at the blood seeping down his brow. "We got a location. Let's go before they get away."

As they made their way back to the car, Joey kept one eye on the first trailer. He could have sworn he saw the curtain flutter, and he hoped like hell Donald didn't see.

Crawling into the driver's seat, he bumped his foot on the gas pedal and let out another curse that would have had his mom grabbing the toilet brush. A minute later he was back on the highway. A Mustang came blazing past them in the oncoming lane, driving like a bat out of hell. Joey jerked the car closer to the curb.

"How did we get the lead on them?" he asked Donald.

"Cell phone," the other man answered. His eyes were closed, as if he was almost asleep.

"Who gave us that?"

Donald jerked upright, shook his head. "Does it matter?"

It might. "I guess not. Just wondering if we have anyone here to help us get the job done."

"We don't need anyone." Donald leaned his head back again and closed his eyes.

"Who is this Hunter guy, anyway?" Joey had worked for Lorenzo for about eight months—eight months too long. And he'd only heard rumors about this Hunter character. Rumors said his testimony could bring down Lorenzo's operation. Joey figured the guy was either an idiot or had a death wish. Everyone knew Lorenzo wouldn't let someone take him down.

"He's someone your boss wants to feed to the worms," Donald growled. "That's all that matters. Boss wants it? We do it. Damn, my head hurts like a fucker."

"Is it true that he's a cop?"

"Why all the questions?" Donald muttered. "Just shut the hell up." He dropped his head into his palm.

Joey didn't doubt Donald's head hurt; the man's scalp was gaping open at his hairline, and who knew what was going on inside. "There's some aspirin in my bag in the back," he offered, not sure why he cared. Hadn't he told the man to wear a seat belt? Even now, after the wreck, Donald didn't buckle up.

The guy jerked his hand from his face. "Aspirin? You fucking offer me an aspirin? You realize that if I don't catch Hunter, my ass is as good as dead?"

"I thought Pablo and Corky were supposed to do this." It was something Joey was depending on.

"But I was running it. It was my job!" Donald's face turned red. "I wouldn't be in this fix if you hadn't wrecked the fucking car." He pulled out his gun and pointed it at Joey's face. "I should shoot your ass."

Joey looked at the barrel and said, "Not unless you want to have another wreck. And since you still aren't wearing a seat belt, I'd suggest you put the gun away."

When the van pulled off the road and drove across a graveled patch of grass, Kathy sat up. "This is where you're going clothes shopping?" she asked, realizing that after her fight with Luke she almost felt normal. Almost.

"It's not the mall, but it'll do in a pinch," he said. For the last few minutes he'd grown quiet, as if worried. And, okay, she'd admit it, they had a lot to worry about; but his lapse into silence concerned her.

She stared at the parked eighteen wheeler, its trailer set up as a Goodwill donation site that he'd parked behind. She'd dropped a few bags off at Goodwill centers like this. Only thing was, they didn't sell merchandise here.

She crossed her arms over her chest and glared at him. "Oh, this is priceless. You're going to steal from Goodwill?"

"Borrow," he said. But while his tone was playful, there wasn't a hint of humor in his expression.

She remembered something he'd said about parking her van and getting a new car. "Borrow? Like you plan to 'borrow' a new car?"

He didn't deny it. Holy mother of pearls, he was actually planning on stealing a car! Cop or not, that was against the law. And . . . and she was with him. Which meant she would be an accessory to car theft. That was a real crime. A go-to-prison crime.

He reached for the door and glanced at her over his shoulder. "You'd best come with me."

"With you? Oh, hell no! I refuse to be a part of this. I refuse to become a criminal. Nope." She shook her head. She'd had a small taste of jail life, and it just didn't suit her. "Do I look like the type of woman who would do well in prison? I saw what it did to Martha Stewart. I'm not going there."

He let out a puff of air. Well, he could just be annoyed. He could stay annoyed. He could live in his own little annoyed world until it snowed in Hell for all she cared. Because, frankly, he was annoying the hell out of her, too. And yes, part of it was because he wasn't wearing a shirt, but that was beside the point. The point he needed to consider was that Kathy Callahan wasn't a thief. Not like her daddy. Nope.

"I'm a federal officer. You're not going to be charged for this."

"And I'm just supposed to believe you? Take your word for it?"

"What? You don't believe me?" He looked surprised.

"I . . . believe you're a cop."

"Federal agent," he corrected.

"Same thing," she snapped. "My problem is that I'm just not sure I won't have to pay the consequences." Face it, anyone with a black mark on her record didn't do well on a second go-round. That was part of the reason Kathy went out of her way to avoid even getting a parking ticket.

"Look," she said. "They might give you a get-out-of-jail-free card, but I'm not a certified badge-carrying *cop*." And, yes, she said *cop* again just to annoy him.

"We're wasting time arguing about this." He closed his eyes and muttered something under his breath about women.

"What did you say?" she asked.

He opened his eyes. "You won't go to jail, Kathy. Okay?" He ran another hand over his face. Then he looked back at the side mirror, a scowl firmly etched into his bruised features. She held her breath as he reached for the gun. His eyes never left the mirror. Then, she heard a car whiz past on the other side of eighteen wheeler.

She let go of a heartfelt sigh and took a moment to remember what she'd been about to say. "I've got a kid. I can't go to jail."

"Fine," he grumbled, and his annoyance was clear. He tucked the gun in the back of his jeans and just sat there staring out the window. Then he jerked his arms up. "So you'd rather just drive around in a van with your freaking name printed in pink, in huge goddamn letters, that sure as hell is going to be remembered by anyone who sees it. You'd rather let a couple of known murderers find us and let them finish us off, huh?" He hit the steering wheel with a hand. "Tell me, did you bring your toilet tank lid with you? Because frankly I'm not sure I can take them on by myself. And I don't have time to sit here and argue with you. I've got to get a shirt. Get us a different ride. Then find a phone and get us some help."

His words bounced around in her head, and he dropped back on the seat and closed his eyes.

"I'm sorry," he said after a moment. "I shouldn't have exploded like that." He passed a hand over his face. "I just need you to do what I say."

But Kathy Callahan didn't just do what people said. She always used logic and weighed her options before making a decision. Some people would say she was too commonsensical, Sue and Lacy among them. But Kathy had learned from experience that letting your emotions rule could get you in trouble. It had been emotions that got her that little black mark with the law in Alabama. And her decision to marry Tom . . . again driven by emotions. So logically, with her emotion set aside, she looked at her options: she could help him and possibly face being arrested for a second time, or not help him and possibly face being killed.

She reached for her door handle and looked at him over her shoulder. "What size shirt are we looking for?"

Joey starred into the barrel of Donald's Glock. "I offer you an aspirin and you threaten to kill me. Now, why does that feel wrong?"

Donald let go of the safety, letting Joey know he meant business. It wasn't the first time Joey had stared into a gun barrel, but he'd decided a long time ago he didn't like it. And he'd expressed his dislike by sending that idiot to the hospital. He pressed his foot harder on the gas. His toe throbbed but he ignored it. "You shoot me, I swear the last thing I'll do is flip this car over. I'll bet you won't make it this time."

Donald blinked. His gaze shot to the speedometer.

"Put the fucking gun away," Joey said.

Donald's hand wavered. Joey knew the man had no problem killing him. While Joey hadn't witnessed the act, he'd heard it was Donald who'd put the bullet in Freddy's head. However, Donald wasn't totally stupid. And shooting Joey while he was doing eighty and behind the wheel would be damn stupid.

"You best watch your back, kid." Donald's weapon lowered, and he reached up and pressed two fingers to his brow. "I swear to God if Lorenzo ever wants you dead—and he might when he hears it's your fault Hunter got away—I'll volunteer for the job."

"I'll remember that."

Joey considered pulling his own gun and making sure Donald didn't get a chance, but unlike Donald, Joey had never offed anyone. It had been one of the questions Lorenzo asked him during the interview. Joey hadn't lied either. "*No, sir. Killing isn't my thing. But I've broken my share of noses, put a few guys in the hospital when I worked the nightclub. One bozo stayed in the hospital for over a week when I caught him beating one of our waitresses.*" He wasn't proud of what he'd done, but he'd never minded a good fight, never backed down. However, the idea of killing someone didn't appeal to him either.

Or it hadn't before. When he'd thought Donald might find the pregnant blonde hiding in the closet, Joey hadn't questioned whether he'd be able to put a bullet in Donald. He would have done it. Odd, how he felt he could kill for a stranger but when his own sorry ass was threatened, he wasn't sure. Was that because his life didn't seem worth killing for?

Donald's cell phone rang. Joey's shoulders tightened. Had the blonde already reported the incident to the police? Had someone working for Lorenzo already gotten word? Holding the wheel with one hand, he tucked his other into his shirt and curled his fingers around the grip of his pistol. Maybe his life was worth killing for, after all.

Chapter Nine

Kathy watched Luke jump up into the back of the un-manned Goodwill trailer. He reached down and pulled her up. The feel of his hand in hers sent a jolt up her arm ending right at her heart, the kind of jolt that bordered on pain but felt good at the same time. As soon as her feet got planted, she pulled her hand away. He studied her, and she wondered if he'd felt the jolt as well.

She took a deep breath, and the heat in the tin box hit her first, but the heat wasn't near as bad as what came next. "Oh my!" Immediately she slapped her hand over her nose. "What's that smell?"

"Don't know. Let's just find me something to wear." Luke grabbed an enormous garbage bag and started rummaging through the clothes inside.

Kathy looked around at the stacks of bags and boxes of clothes. Wanting to get out as soon as possible, she found a bag and started sifting through it with one hand. She still had her nose pinched when she found a box of clothes that included several men's suits.

"Hey, these might work," she said, her voice funny with her nostrils pinched.

Luke looked up, and that's when she heard it: a whimper or a cry. Luke heard it, too, because he jerked upright, tucked her behind him and aimed his gun at a stack of dark green garbage bags. If the smell was any indication, they honestly contained garbage.

The noise sounded again. Kathy stood frozen, her hand pressed against Luke's warm back, listening. Luke's shoulders relaxed; his gun lowered. Motioning for her to stay, he took a few steps and pushed bags aside. The whimpering began full force. That's when Kathy saw the carrier.

"Poor cat!" she said.

Luke knelt down. "It's not a cat."

Kathy moved closer. She dropped her hand from her nose, but the hideous smell had her breathing through her mouth. She squatted beside Luke and saw the tan puppy surrounded by his own excrement. The poor thing couldn't have been more than a few months old. With its mashed-in face and bug eyes, it looked part pug and part . . . something else equally ugly. But cute ugly.

Can I have a dog? Can I please? Tommy's constant pleas rang in her ears. She'd made up her mind that when he got home they'd go puppy shopping. Hey, her ex offered her son Europe, so she had to do something to one up him.

She moved a little closer and saw that the puppy looked hot and thirsty. "Poor thing!" She reached to open the cage.

"Don't," Luke said.

She cut her gaze at him. "Why?"

He shook his head. "We can't bring that dog with us."

"We can't leave it here. It'll die. Look at it. It might be half dead now. We don't know how long it's been here like this. No water. No food." She opened the cage and the puppy inched forward. "Come here, baby. It's okay. I won't hurt you, I promise."

She lifted the puppy and held it up and out, as far from her nose as possible. The little guy stuck out his long pink tongue and tried to reach her face. "Oh, look at you," she said in a voice she reserved for babies.

"Put that thing back," Luke insisted. "It's covered in shit." He opened the cage door and motioned. "Now."

She shot him a cold glare. "It won't be covered in shit if you'll help me find something to wipe him off with."

"Kathy, we have hit men after us. We can't take this dog!"

"You would leave a puppy here to die? You could do that?"

His gaze went to the puppy and she could swear she saw an ounce of compassion in his eyes, and then he looked away. She heard him spout a few four-letter words before he faced her again. All compassion had left his expression. "To save our lives, yes. I would let that puppy die."

"Then you just go on without me. Because I will not leave this poor animal here to starve or die a slow miserable death." She bit down on her lip, knowing she was halfway back to being unreasonable, but . . . "Please. Besides, our lives aren't exactly in jeopardy at this moment."

"She's fine. The baby's fine," the doctor repeated.

The tension gripping Detective Jason Dodd's chest since he'd gotten the panicked call from his pregnant wife lightened. "You sure?"

"Positive." The doctor sent him a comforting smile.

Sue had kept reassuring him on the drive to the hospital

that she was fine, but seeing his pregnant wife in tears had lit a fire in his belly. And not the good kind either. All he could think about was getting away from Kathy's trailer where someone had threatened to kill Sue, taking her to the hospital to get every little inch of her checked out.

"Can we see the baby on one of those sonograms things again? Just to make sure."

The doctor frowned. "The baby's heartbeat is fine."

"Jason!"

Jason swung around and saw his partner and friend Detective Chase Kelly hurrying down the hall. "What the hell happened?" his friend asked. "Is Sue okay?"

Taking a deep breath and fighting the lump that suddenly lodged in his throat, he remembered leaving a half-assed message on Chase's cell phone. "She's fine," he managed to say.

"The baby?" Chase's face paled.

Jason knew his friend could relate, because Chase and his wife were on the baby path as well. Their babies were only a couple of weeks apart. And they had already talked about how great it was that their kids would grow up together, play in the mud together and become friends. "The baby's fine, too."

The empathy left his friend's face. "What the heck happened? You scared the shit out of me!"

"Sorry. I wasn't thinking straight when I called." Jason took a deep breath. "I don't know what's going on. But Sue went over to Kathy's. Supposedly there was some kind of altercation out by your house between that plumber who has a hard-on for Kathy and some other guys. Kathy left your place to—"

"I know about that," Chase said. "Lacy called and told me. She said Kathy was going to try to find Stan—the plumber."

"Well, Sue went to check on Kathy, but she wasn't home. Sue's cell phone was out of battery so she went inside Kathy's to use her phone to try to reach Kathy's cell. While she was there someone broke in. . . ." Jason chest tightened, and he trailed off.

"Shit!" Chase said. "Did you call this in?"

"Not yet. When Sue phoned, I was only a few minutes away. I knew I could get to her faster than a dispatch. . . ." He hesitated.

"So, what happened?" Chase asked.

"Sue said there were two guys. One of them forced her into a closet and told her not to scream because"—Jason's voice shook—"he said the other guy would kill her."

Chase's eyes widened. "Christ! But she's okay? Not hurt?"

"She's fine. Swears all the guy did was grab her and stop her from screaming. The doctor assures me she's fine."

"Were they robbing Kathy?"

"I . . ." He tried to remember what condition Kathy's place had been in. "It didn't appear that way. But I didn't . . . I didn't spend time looking around. The fuckers had left. I grabbed Sue and rushed her here."

"Okay . . . I'll report it and go check out Kathy's."

Jason looked toward the curtain concealing his wife and motioned Chase to step away. He lowered his voice. "Sue's been trying to call Kathy every five minutes. She's not answering."

Chase's eyes widened. "You don't think this was random? Shit! You think the fight by my house has something to do with it?"

"I don't know, but I'd feel a hell of a lot better if we knew where Kathy was."

Chase took out his phone. "Why don't I call the plumber and see what he knows?" He dialed directory assistance and got Bradley's number, then said, "Let's hope Kathy's there and they're . . . busy. That girl has gotta get laid sooner or later." He half smiled.

Jason glanced back at the curtain between him and his

wife, torn between hearing what Chase found out and returning to check on her.

"Is this Stan Bradley?" Chase asked, and Jason saw his partner's brows pinch together as if confused.

"Danny? What the hell? Is that you?" Chase asked.

"Danny who?" Jason asked. The only Danny he and Chase knew was his cop buddy who'd just gone to work for the Hoke's Bluff PD.

"It's me. Chase. Chase *Kelly*, the guy you played poker with last Friday. What the hell is going on?" Chase paused. "You're kidding!"

"What?" Jason asked.

"Damn!" Chase said.

"What's going on?" Jason repeated.

Chase held up his hand. "Is anyone hurt? No bodies?" His gaze cut toward Jason, and he ran a hand through his hair: a sure sign that the news wasn't good. "Yeah," he said into the phone. "I was looking for Kathy Callahan. There's a chance she was with Stan. I'll be right there and explain." He closed his phone.

"What the hell is going on?" Jason asked.

Chase looked up. "Hoke's Bluff police are at the plumber's. No one's there, but his house has been shot to Hell and back." Chase let out a frustrated breath. "They found over a kilo of cocaine. It appears like some kind of drug deal gone bad."

"Drugs? The plumber?" Jason said. "Ah, shit. Kathy— what about Kathy?" He shoved his hands into his pockets.

"She's not there." Chase frowned. "But Danny said there was blood. Lots of blood."

Jason looked back at the curtain. His chest ached thinking about Kathy, and panic slammed against his ribs when he realized that the people responsible for that blood were probably the same ones who had been with Sue. "So those men at Kathy's trailer were drug dealers? God *damn*," he muttered.

"We're not sure they're connected," Chase said—but neither of them believed in coincidences.

Jason made a fist and gripped it again. "What the hell were they looking for?"

"I don't know." Chase pocketed his phone. "The boys at Hoke's Bluff are going to want to talk to Sue as soon as she's able."

That piece of info had all sorts of bells and alarms going off in Jason's brain. His wife could possibly identify the people behind all the chaos and blood—people like drug dealers who didn't mind killing. People who wouldn't care his wife was pregnant.

He shook his head. "No!" He took two steps and then swung back around. "I don't want Sue involved in this until I know what the hell is going on."

"But she saw—"

Jason's mind raced. "I'll say *I* saw them. I'll find out everything Sue knows that might help this case and I'll give it to them. Sue's not getting involved."

"But Jason—" Chase started.

"Damn it, Chase, she's pregnant. Stop thinking like a cop and start thinking like a husband and father!"

The fight left his friend's expression. "Let me go find out what they know. Don't say anything until I call you." Chase turned to go.

Wait," Jason said, and leaned in. "What are we telling our wives about Kathy?"

Shit, Luke thought. The damn dog was covered in it. He and Kathy absolutely could not take the thing with them, and somehow he had to make her understand that. So far, she hadn't been totally unreasonable—oh, hell, who was he kidding? She'd pointed his own gun at him! The idea of just tossing her over his shoulder and dragging her out of the Goodwill trailer kicking and screaming began to appeal. He could do it, too. Yup, he had choices—and none of them involved taking the damn dog.

"Look at him," she cooed. The expression on her face, all soft and vulnerable, turned him inside out. It was how she looked at Tommy, and it always took Luke back to his own mom, the few memories he'd kept from his childhood.

Oh, hell no, he thought when he felt himself mentally taking a U-turn about the dog.

"We can't leave him!" Kathy cut a gaze toward Luke, wearing the same expression as when she'd pulled the gun on him.

Luke cursed under his breath. His gaze flew around the trailer, which was filled with other people's hand-me-downs. In the corner, someone had left a bottle of water. Reaching back into the bag he'd just dug through, he found the plastic bag of hotel soaps and shampoos that he'd seen earlier. "Bring the dog over there." He pointed to an empty spot in the trailer, jumped up, snatched a T-shirt from a pile of discarded clothes and went for the water.

Kathy moved where he'd told her. She knelt, head turned to the side, nose wrinkled as if the smell was getting to her, and held the dog. Luke poured the water over the puppy, which immediately started trying to drink. "Hold tight," he insisted.

"Poor thing's thirsty," she pointed out, and caught some water in her hand. The dog drank.

"Just hold him," Luke ordered. He poured all but the last inch of water onto the animal, recapped the bottle for her to give to the thirsty pup later, then squeezed a tube of hotel shampoo on the damn dog. He rubbed the soap vigorously into the squirming dog's fur, cursing the stink, unable to believe he was doing this.

The dog whimpered. "Not so hard," Kathy said, and then spoke softly to the mutt. "We'll have you smelling clean in no time."

The animal looked up at her with bug eyes. Damn thing was already in love with her. Not that Luke blamed the puppy; he was halfway there himself. Which explained why he was at this moment shampooing the damn thing and getting dog shit all under his fingernails.

"You're such a good doggie," she cooed.

Luke tuned out Kathy and listened for cars. If Lorenzo's men caught up with them, if saving this damn dog cost them their lives . . .

"Thank you." Kathy shot him the first real smile since everything went down. Her green eyes were soft with emotion, and Luke's chest swelled. "I knew you couldn't leave him."

I could have, Luke thought, but he didn't tell her that. His time working undercover had trained him to see life differently. Trained him to focus on his objective. Focus on staying alive. Not to let people in, not to care. Or maybe it was his ex-wife who'd taught him that. How could she have aborted their child? Hadn't losing his entire family in a matter of two years been enough?

But he was damn tired of being that person. There was a period in his life when that puppy would have mattered.

"Let's just get it done." Grabbing the dog by his feet, he wiped away most of the suds with a T-shirt, snatched up another garment, wrapped it around the puppy, picked the beast up and handed the bundle to Kathy. Then he handed her the water bottle. "Give it to him in the car."

Kathy pulled the wet animal to her chest. "It's gonna be fine now," she said.

God, Luke hoped everything would be fine. Deep down he knew what they were up against. It was him, a stubborn woman, and now a damn dog against men who killed for a living. The odds weren't in their favor.

Again he chewed on the fact that Calvin hadn't answered his call. If his link with Calvin was severed, he'd have to get with someone else. But who? The main reason the DA wanted him in protective custody and then WitSec was because they didn't know who they could trust. Having only been working on the task force two months before the undercover job became available, Luke couldn't say he trusted anyone.

Luke thought of all the friends he'd walked away from while trying to deal with the grief of his past, and it hit him that going undercover hadn't been his first attempt to hide from his problems. He'd started hiding long before that.

"I know you're hurting, but you can't just push everyone away!" His ex's voice vibrated through his head.

What the hell had she expected him to do? Invite everyone to his pity party? Men didn't do that. He didn't do that. All he'd needed was a little time. A little space to work through everything. The last thing he'd needed was for Sandy to give up on him and abort his baby without even giving him a choice. She'd been wrong. Damn wrong.

But that hadn't made him right, had it?

The thought took him to a place he'd never been on the issue, a place where one took some responsibility for past mistakes. He didn't want to go to that place. Not because he couldn't own up to his faults, but because he knew it didn't mean crap. That was the past. He needed to focus on the present.

He grabbed the box where Kathy had spotted some men's clothes and yanked out a light blue button-down oxford. Slipping his arms into it, he found it a little short, but this wasn't the big and tall shop. He snagged a jacket, draped it over his shoulder and glanced at Kathy, wondering whether they should try to find her something else to wear as well.

She had a silly grin on her face as she cooed at the snout of the semiclean puppy now wrapped in some old lady's pink worn-out robe. He found himself staring. The image showed all the reasons he liked her—the reasons he needed to make damn sure she got out of this mess alive. Tommy needed her. Hell, Luke needed her. He needed to find a phone and get Calvin on the line.

"Let's get out of here," he grunted.

"Wait." She ran back to the cage. "I think I saw a bag with a . . . Got it." She pulled out a leash and smiled again.

As Luke took a step to leave, he heard a car pull off the road and come to a gravel-crunching stop beside the trailer. That damn puppy might be the death of them yet.

Chapter Ten

Joey pulled up in front of a roach coach, a kitchen on wheels with big flowers and birds painted all over the front. Two Harleys were parked beside the truck, and two Harley drivers sat at a plastic table in foldout chairs eating off paper plates.

"They're not here," he said, and relief washed over him, but he didn't remove his hand from his gun tucked inside its shoulder holster.

"The van's not here," Donald corrected. His words almost sounded slurred. He had been dozing off and on during the drive. "Doesn't mean they aren't."

Joey looked back at the trailer, which had steam coming out over the open counter. He didn't think Hunter and the redhead would be hiding in there.

The phone call Donald received hadn't been about the blonde; it had been Lorenzo's contact, giving them the new location of Hunter's phone. On the rush over, Joey had envisioned the pictures of the mother and son hanging on the trailer wall, and he'd tried to prepare himself. If he had to kill Donald to protect that family, he'd do it. It wasn't as if anyone would miss the bastard. The world would be a better place.

Donald opened the car door. The smell of grilled onions and meat wafted inside the car. Joey's stomach rumbled. The three sausage and biscuits he'd eaten that morning had long since worn off.

Donald wavered when he turned to put his feet on the ground, and Joey wondered if the smell was turning the man's stomach. Donald had made him pull over a few miles back so he could throw up on the side of the road. Joey had watched the whole time, afraid his roadside request had simply been a ruse to kill him. But, no, Donald really puked.

"Maybe you should just let me check it out," Joey offered, more from hope of avoiding a showdown than worry about Donald. Hey, the man had threatened to kill him, so Joey was finished worrying about him.

"And let you fuck it up again?" Donald said, and pulled himself upright.

Joey stepped out of the car, ignoring the throbbing in his toe. He took in his surroundings, assessing all that might go wrong. Then again, maybe nothing would. Maybe Donald would see that Hunter and the girl weren't here and they could move on down the road. Joey always hoped for the best. Sadly, he was disappointed a lot.

The two motorcyclists were putting on their helmets, getting ready to take off.

"You two leaving?" Donald asked. He reached inside his jacket, and Joey reached for his own gun. He didn't want to shoot anyone. But if he had to, it would be Donald.

Luke heard the car door open and shut. Jumping in front of Kathy, he reached inside his partially buttoned shirt to pull the gun from the waist of his jeans. He stopped just as a uniformed police officer appeared around the corner of the open trailer.

The man nodded. "Hello."

From the corner of his eye, Luke saw Kathy's gaze shift to the officer. The thought running through her mind couldn't have been clearer if it had flashed in neon letters across her forehead: *We should tell him what happened at your place.* He shook his head and hoped like hell she listened. Being taken into custody would only make them a couple of sitting ducks waiting for Lorenzo's men. One of the other witnesses had been killed while at the police department trying to report a break-in. Another had been killed while in police custody. Until he spoke with Calvin to make sure who he could and couldn't trust, Luke wasn't trusting anyone.

Hoping to reassure Kathy, he pulled her against him and held her around the waist. "Trust me," he whispered. Then he said to the officer, "Just dropped off some old clothes. Cleaning out a few closets."

"Really?" The cop's gaze shot to Kathy, as if he'd read something in her mood. Luke felt her try to wiggle away. "I thought that was your van I glimpsed parked behind there."

"Uh . . ." Kathy muttered.

Kathy and the officer knew each other. Luke immediately started reassessing the situation.

"What the hell is that smell?" The officer took a step back.

From the cop's demeanor, Luke surmised that there wasn't a BOLO out on Kathy's van yet, or Kathy. The adrenaline tightening his muscles lessened a bit. Then he saw the cop studying the dog in Kathy's arms—or was he studying Kathy's cleavage?—and his muscles tightened again, but for different reasons.

"Someone actually left a puppy in a cage here!" Kathy answered, holding the trembling animal.

"You're kidding," the cop said. Again, he shot Luke a curious look. A look that lingered on his face. "You get into a fight?"

"Oh, I'm sorry," Kathy said. "This is . . . Stan Bradley. Stan, this is Cary Jenkins. Cary is a friend of Jason Dodd and Chase Kelly, my friends' husbands."

"Well, I'll be damned," the cop said, and looked back at Luke.

Damned about what? Luke wondered. Reaching up, he touched his black eye. "A couple asshole plumbers arguing about a job. Happened out there by Lacy Kelly's."

Kathy shot Luke another look, as if saying they should trust her cop friend. Luke ever so slightly shook his head no.

"I . . . I didn't know you were dating anyone." Officer Jenkins said, his gaze and smile now glued on Kathy.

Luke saw her start to open her mouth, and he interrupted, "Lucky me, huh?" He tucked her a bit closer to his side.

"Yeah, lucky you." The cop chuckled, but he didn't stop looking at Kathy. "So I guess the club has been officially disbanded?"

"What club?" Kathy verbalized the question running through Luke's head—but clearly the cop's question annoyed her. Funny, how annoying questions usually led to interesting information.

"You know what club," the officer said, not picking up on her tone.

But while Cary the Cop missed her tone, probably because of all the attention he was giving to her breasts, Luke was the third wheel in this conversation and knew it. He didn't like being third, especially when it involved Kathy Callahan and another man. Add the fact that the cop was still eyeing Kathy like a piece of birthday cake, and Luke found himself grinding his teeth.

Not that he was the only unhappy person present. Kathy was giving Officer Jenkins one of those feminine stares that usually had men covering the family jewels—and if the man would quit looking at her chest, he might see.

Finally the cop's gaze shot up, and the womanizing smile slipped from his face. "Er, I—"

"So Jason and Chase told the whole police force, huh?" Kathy's tone could chill a six-pack of beer. "How sweet. I'll make sure to give thanks for sharing that personal information the next time I see them."

The officer had the good manners to look embarrassed. "Well . . . they just . . . I mean, maybe they mentioned it in passing. It's not like they . . . really told me anything."

"What club?" Luke repeated, feeling sorry for the cop. Well, almost.

The officer shuffled his feet and redirected the conversation. "You're going to take the puppy? I'll bet Tommy will like that. How is he, by the way?"

"He's fine, thank you," Kathy said in friendlier tone.

So the cop had met Tommy? Luke remembered the day the freckle-faced kid had helped him work on the plumbing. Luke had never passed the chance to spend some time with the boy. And it wasn't just because of Kathy. Well, maybe it was in the beginning, but that had changed.

"Tell him I said hello," the cop suggested.

How close was this man to Kathy and her son? Good old-fashioned jealousy shot through Luke's veins. For some reason he hadn't even considered there might be other men.

Kathy looked at Luke and then back at Cary. "Can you excuse me for just a second?" she said to the cop. Then she leaned close to Luke's ear. "We can trust this guy. We really need to tell him about what happened at your place and—"

"No!" he said as firmly as he could without alarming the officer standing a few feet away. Feeling the man watching, Luke laughed, leaned in, and planted a kiss on her cheek—all to offset any negative vibes. It also might have been his way of saying hands-off. Leaning closer, Luke whispered, "You have to trust me."

"How about you trust *me* on this one?"

She pulled back and faced Officer Jenkins, and Luke's stomach muscles clenched. She was going to tell, and he had to decide what the hell he was going to do about it.

He sized up Officer Jenkins. They were approximately the same age, height, and weight. And they had the same taste in women, going by the cop's continual perusal of Kathy's breasts. Needless to say, he wouldn't be easy to take down. But damn it, Luke had to try.

Joey watched Donald just stand there, frozen, his hand inside his coat as if to grab his gun. But he didn't move. Was he getting sick again? About to puke?

The two bikers gave Donald an odd glance and then shifted their gaze to Joey, who nodded and tried to smile. With only Donald's back in his line of vision, Joey couldn't see Donald's expression, but the bikers didn't seem too worried. Damn it, he wished they would just take off, leaving two fewer people Joey would have to worry about.

One of the guy's bikes roared to life. Joey, hand on his gun, waited to see if Donald planned to let them ride off. He felt his heart thudding against his rib cage with the sound of the engine, but Donald didn't make any sudden moves. Joey's shoulders relaxed, and he let out a silent sigh. Someone inside the roach coach moved, and Joey heard a woman's voice, but the roaring sound of the bikes drowned out her words.

"We should go," Joey called.

Donald still didn't move, which Joey was finding really odd. The two bikers pulled away and onto the road, the sweet sound of their Harleys rising in the spring wind.

A feminine, heavily Spanish-accented voice came from the roach coach. "You want to eat?"

Joey looked over to see a woman in her early thirties with

her hair pulled back in a net. A few strands had slipped free and two, no three, black curls rested against her cheeks. Her brown eyes—large, almond-shaped eyes, slanted ever so slightly at the corners—gave her an exotic appearance.

Her forehead pinched in concern as she focused on Donald. "Your friend? He okay?" she asked, her English unsure.

Joey didn't have a freaking clue if Donald was okay, but he nodded. Then, staring at those beautiful eyes, he wanted more than ever to get away from the woman before Donald did anything stupid. "Yes, he's . . . fine." He moved between Donald and the truck. Keeping his hand inside his shirt, his fingers still wrapped around the Glock, he whispered, "Let's just get out of here, Donald."

The man didn't answer, and Joey noticed the strange look on his face, like Donald was sleepwalking. Joey took a step closer . . . and Donald dropped.

"Damn!" Joey swore, and tried to catch him. By the time he got to the man's side, however, Donald had landed face-first in the dirt. A puff of dust billowed all around his big frame.

"*Ah, Dios!*" the woman screeched. "You want me call 911?"

"No," Joey said. But even as he spoke, he saw the woman pick up her cell phone.

Chapter Eleven

Luke tightened his hand on Kathy's waist and said, "We should be going." He shot her another pleading glance before looking at the armed police officer standing a few feet away.

She shook her head. "Cary—"

The radio in the cop's cruiser blared. The officer held up his hand and spoke into the walkie-talkie pinned to his shirt, then said, "Sorry, Kathy, I have to go."

"But—" she exclaimed as the officer shot off. "Cary!" She started to jump down.

Luke caught her. "No!" He could hear the address being spilled out of the radio. It was *his*.

The sound of the cop car spitting gravel was a welcome relief. Luke didn't waste a second. "We've got to get out of here." He jumped down and reached back to help her.

Puppy clutched in one arm, Kathy accepted his help with her free hand. "I told you, he's friends with Chase and Jason. They like him. He's not a dirty cop."

"And I told you that doesn't matter." Luke put a palm on her back and rushed her forward. "If someone in the department is working with Lorenzo, word will get out and we'll be sitting ducks just waiting for them to finish us off. Which is all the more reason we need to find a new ride that doesn't have your name plastered all over it and isn't sporting bullet holes. If Jenkins was working for Lorenzo, we'd be dead right now. If he'd gotten a good look at your van, we'd be on our way to being dead!"

The puppy whined, and Kathy clutched the animal closer. "I just find it hard to believe that—"

"Get in!" he cut her off.

The moment she climbed into the van, Luke slammed her door and ran around the vehicle. Chances were that his name—and very likely Kathy's—would be played across the police radio at any moment, and Officer Jenkins would turn around.

"As I was saying . . ." she continued as he pulled himself up into the driver's seat. "I find it hard to believe that someone could hurt us if we're in police custody."

"Tell that to Beth Salzmann and Jim Leigh." He started the engine. It roared to life but stalled out.

"Who are Beth Salzmann and Jim whoever?" she snapped.

He turned the key again, holding his breath and praying that the van hadn't decided to quit on them. "Witnesses killed while either in police custody or at the police station."

Kathy stared at him. The puppy wiggled and started licking her neck.

The van engine roared to life. Luke sped back onto the road, driving as fast and as hard as he could.

"Please don't call them!" Joey begged. *"Por favor,"* he added, using the bit of Spanish he knew.

"Uh . . . he's fine," he continued babbling, giving a flinch and praying that Donald wouldn't roll over and do something stupid like shoot the woman for talking about calling 911. "Really, he's fine. Aren't you, Donald?"

He touched Donald's shoulder. The man didn't move. Not even to breathe.

"Christ!" Joey muttered, watching the man's back, hoping to see his shoulders rise as he took in air. They didn't. He rolled Donald over, and Joey's breath caught. The man's bug eyes were open, open wide. Joey had only seen eyes look that empty once—on Freddy's face. He pushed that thought away and touched Donald's neck, hoping to feel the flutter of a pulse; but as he expected, there was nothing.

"I call for help, *si?*" the Mexican woman asked, leaning forward to look down at them.

"No!"

Joey saw her move away from the counter and heard a door open and slam shut from the side of the truck. He brushed his hand over Donald's eyes to close them. "Are you sure? He need doctor, no?" she asked, hurrying toward him, cell phone in hand.

Joey yanked Donald's coat over his gun and holster. Then, using every bit of his strength, he heaved the big guy up on his shoulder. Donald's weight almost carried him over onto his butt. He readjusted, and the weight caused him to lean on his foot and his toe pinched in pain. He bit back a curse.

"He's fine. Just . . ." Joey met the woman's soft brown eyes and he almost let Donald fall. All words bounced right out of his head. Damn, she was pretty. Not *Playboy* pretty or glitzy pretty. He couldn't call her girl-next-door pretty, either, because he'd never lived next to anyone who looked like this. She looked old-Hollywood pretty, like the actresses in those old movies: clean, fresh . . . drop-dead gorgeous. It occurred to him that he probably shouldn't be thinking about women with a dead man on his shoulder, but Joey couldn't help it. He couldn't ever remember being punched in the gut by a woman's looks before.

"He's . . . he's just hitting the bottle a little hard. Too many *cervezas.*"

She took a step back, as if the idea of Donald being drunk disturbed her.

"Can you open the door?" He pointed to the car. *"La puerta?"*

She hurried to help. "Front or . . . *atrás?"*

"Back," he said, and motioned.

The woman opened the back door and stepped aside. Joey moved forward and dropped Donald in, yanking the man's coat closed again to cover his gun. Then, pushing Donald's big feet inside, hurrying before the woman caught on to the fact that Donald wasn't breathing, he slammed the door.

The door didn't shut. Joey tried again. He put some muscle into it this time. Again the door bounced back.

"Wait!" the woman screamed.

Joey didn't want to wait. Couldn't wait. Not and let her realize that Donald was dead.

He attempted to slam the door again. This time it bounced back so hard that it hit his shin and he flinched. The woman screamed. She pointed down. He followed her gaze to Donald's foot, which had slipped back out the door.

"Oh." Joey leaned down and pushed the man's foot inside the car. Now the door shut fine. "Thank you," he said, moving between the woman and the window.

"He going to have a hurt foot," she replied, her brow pinched.

"Nah, he . . . he's too ugly to feel anything." Joey smiled. "Besides . . . he deserves it for drinking too much."

He deserved it for killing Freddy. Deserved it for being a mean son of a bitch.

She made a face. "I not like men who drink too much. They get mean."

"I'm not much for drinking myself," Joey said. When his mom hadn't been high, she'd been drunk. He'd pretty much decided never to become addicted to anything.

The Mexican woman leaned over to peer in the car. "He not hurt himself when he fall down?"

"Him? No." Joey moved to limit her view. "You can't hurt him. Too big."

She chuckled. "You big, too."

Joey loved what her laughter did to her eyes. "I know—which is how I know he'll be okay. We don't feel pain, we big men." He took a step, and his big toe ached like a mother.

She shrugged. "I feel bad. He fall down while here."

"Oh, it's not your fault. Believe me." *The idiot should have worn a seat belt.*

"Maybe I fix coffee, and you take for him when he wake up? *Si?* It help mood sometime. Maybe he not be so mean when he wake up."

Coffee wouldn't have stopped Donald from being mean, Joey thought. For just a second, he wondered what type of person he was that he didn't care that Donald was dead. Then he remembered Donald volunteering to kill him.

The woman's words about mean drunks suddenly replayed in his head. "Someone you know drank too much?" he asked.

She flinched, as if the question was too personal. Then she nodded. "I leave him in Mexico. My life better without him."

"Good," Joey said, and looked back at the car. He should probably head out and find somewhere to dump the body. Strangely, getting rid of Donald wasn't going to bother him near as much as getting rid of Freddy.

Jesus, he needed to figure out what to do next. Should he call Lorenzo or just drop the body in some Dumpster and get the hell away as fast as he could? Maybe it was time to call it quits on this job. Hell, if he went back to Lorenzo now, he'd probably end up like Donald: dead in somebody's backseat. More likely the trunk. That's where they'd put Freddy.

"I not charge you for the coffee," the woman said.

There was a softness to her voice that went straight to Joey's chest and then lower. Amazingly, it had been a while since anything lower had been awakened by a kind voice and a pretty face. Staring at her, he wondered how the man she'd left in Mexico had been mean to her. Had he hurt her or just yelled at her the way some men did? Studying her closer, he noted a scar at the corner of her eye.

Joey had known a few women, but most of their relationships hadn't lasted long. They hadn't ended because Joey treated them badly, however; it was more because the girls wanted someone who could offer them nice things. Someone who drove a fancy car and took them out to fancy dinners. Until he'd gotten a job with Lorenzo, he hadn't much money to work with.

Joey stared at his car and then the woman. She was a little thing, not much over five feet, round and curvy. Curvy in all the right spots. Unlike American women, who ate like birds, afraid they'd gain a pound.

"Si? You take coffee?" she asked.

His six-feet-five-inches felt even taller standing next to her, and he met her soft eyes again. Hell, what was his hurry? It wasn't as if Donald was going to get pissy. The man was dead. And, as Joey had thought earlier, the world was probably a better place for it.

Realizing the woman was waiting on him to answer, he looked at her. "*Si,*" he told her. "Coffee would be nice."

"You speak a little Spanish," she said.

"Just a little," he replied.

"That is okay." She smiled. "I speak only a little English."

"You do pretty good," he said. He smiled, then realized he hadn't smiled in earnest in a long, long time. "You know . . . I'd like a cup of that coffee for *me*, if you don't mind. And maybe a bite to eat."

"Good," she said.

She went around the side and entered her truck, moved to the counter and filled a pot with water. Joey leaned against the counter as the smell of fresh coffee filled the air. He could have moved and sat at the nearby table, but he liked watching her.

As he shifted his weight to his other foot, trying not to put any pressure on his bad toe, a car pulled up behind him. It was a black and white state trooper vehicle, and it pulled up right beside his car with the dead Donald inside. The trooper got out. Joey's heart beat double-time.

Joey waited for the cop to look in the back. Would the trooper blame him for killing Donald? He supposed the woman would corroborate that Donald had just keeled over, but would that get him out of hot water? Hell no, not when the cops learned he worked for Lorenzo. They'd probably assume he was just as bad.

The officer walked past the car, right past Donald's dead body, and nodded at Joey. Leaning against the counter, he smiled at the Hispanic woman. "Hi, Lola. How about a glass of tea?"

"Sure, Trooper Foster," she said, and smiled. But Joey couldn't help noticing that her smile seemed forced.

"With lemon, right?" she asked, as if working hard to pronounce the words.

"You remembered," he said. "That's nice of you. Real nice."

Joey saw the way the cop's eyes traveled down Lola's body and how she looked away as if embarrassed or offended. Sure, Joey had noticed her body, too, but he hoped he'd done it in a less crass way.

Looking nervous, she filled a glass and then passed the officer his tea. He reached over and put his hand on her upper arm, left it there. "Thanks, babe." He brushed his thumb under her shirt sleeve. Her lips turned up at the corners, but the smile never moved to her eyes.

"I think my coffee is done," Joey remarked, hoping Lola would take it as an excuse to move away from the asshole. She did, and he could swear he saw her shoulders relax as the man's hand fell away. Then, without dropping a dollar on the counter, the officer walked off. It took everything Joey had not to watch him leave, to make sure he didn't spot Donald.

"Hey," the trooper called.

Joey felt his gut tighten. He turned around, expecting to see the trooper looking into the car, expecting him to have his gun drawn. Instead, he stood by his cruiser.

"You haven't seen a florist truck passing by here, have you? A white truck with big pink letters?"

So the cops were looking for Hunter and the redhead, too.

"No," Lola said. "But I watch birds, not the road."

"Can't say I've seen it," Joey added.

The trooper nodded, got into his car and left.

Lola looked at Joey. "I really, really don't like that man."

Joey looked at her sweet face, which was twisted with something that looked like fear. "Then that settles it," he replied. "I don't care for him, either."

*   *   *

"How are you going to do it?" Kathy asked, kneeling to fix the leash around the puppy as she watched Luke button his shirt. He'd pulled off to the side of the highway. Up the road at a makeshift car lot were about a dozen or so parked cars with FOR SALE signs in the windows.

She felt him studying her and glanced up. His gaze was on the scooped neckline of her tank top. She rose and adjusted it to cover the tops of her breasts. "You act as if you've never seen a pair," she snapped.

He raised his guilty gaze and grinned. "It's been a while." When she frowned, he brushed a hand over his mouth as if to hide his grin, then asked, "How am I going to do what?"

"How are you going to steal a car?" She gave the leash a little tug when the puppy tried to go out in the street. "What am I supposed to do?" She thought again about the ramifications of their actions. "Honestly, I don't want this to come back and bite me in the butt."

He stared at her. "You need to calm down. Act normal. We're just a married couple wanting to try out a new car."

"Gosh, less than an hour ago you told Cary we're dating, and now we're married."

He grinned. "I'll slow down on the honeymoon."

"Like that will happen," she said, but instantly remembered sitting in his lap at his house. Feeling her cheeks grow warm, she knelt again and focused on checking to make sure the puppy's collar wasn't too tight.

"Seriously, Kathy, you need to chill."

When she stood, she felt her stomach knot—if not from nerves, then from hunger. It was almost four in the afternoon and, other than coffee and a piece of toast, she hadn't eaten all day. "I can't chill. I'm about to become a car thief."

"You're not. I'm the one doing this."

He slipped on the navy suit jacket he'd stolen from Goodwill. Her gaze moved up and down his frame. In spite of being a little wrinkled, the coat actually went well over the blue oxford shirt. And the combo looked good paired with his jeans. Casual bad boy.

"I'm an accomplice." An accomplice who already has a record.

He ran a hand though his dark hair, as if to make sure it looked okay. Not that it needed it. His hair, even mussed, looked good. Not that she intended to keep noticing such things.

"I told you, as soon as I get in touch with Calvin, all this will go away."

"And you'll go away too, right?"

His gaze met hers, and they stood there for a second just staring at each other. Then, "Probably." He patted his pockets and pulled out a tie.

An empty feeling stirred in Kathy's chest. Considering what had happened these past few hours, the idea of him being out of her life should make her happy. All her attraction to him should have evaporated when she found out he was a cop. Why didn't it?

He stared at the tie for a second, as if debating wearing it or as if he didn't know how to put it on. Kathy moved forward, dropped the dog's leash in his hand and took the paisley tie and slid it around his neck. Measuring one side a few inches longer than the other, she looped one end around the other then tucked it inside the loop. It was only when she had the perfect knot and had given his chest the old one-two pat that she realized what she'd done. She also realized how close she now stood to him, how good it felt to be close. Lord have mercy on her, she'd missed having her body in close proximity to a man. And not just any man.

Her next intake of breath carried Luke's scent: fresh cut grass with that hint of mint. It took everything she had not to bury her nose in his shoulder and lean on him. It had been a hard day. If she ever needed to lean on someone, it was now.

"Sorry," she said. "Old habits."

He had his hands on her waist, just the way Tom used to do when she did his tie every morning. She'd pack his lunch, tie his tie, kiss him and send him off to work. And for what? So he could fall in love with a dumpy woman almost twice her age. Could someone please explain that? Kathy's chest grew heavy as she looked at the way Luke studied her. He wanted her. Desired her. That desire had fed her self-confidence for years, and before all of today's craziness she'd been about to give in.

Her stomach pinched with fear—fear that had nothing to do with men shooting at her or stealing a car. This was deeper, more personal. What if her ex was right that she just didn't have what it took to please a man? That she sucked in bed. And not the good kind of suck.

She took a step back. Luke continued to look at her. "It's back," he said.

"What's back?"

He shook his head. "That look you always get when I get close. Back at my place, I thought . . ."

"Thought what?" she asked, not certain why she wanted to know. But she did.

"We should go." He handed her the leash. The brief touch of his hand sent a jolt of emotion racing up her arm.

"What did you think?" she asked again.

He paused, took a breath and then said, "That you finally realized how good we'd be together. That I just might be the kind of guy you'd like hanging around."

"Oh." Okay, she'd had to ask, hadn't she? Now how did she respond? Clueless, she took charge of the dog and started walking. The puppy didn't move.

"And we *would* have been good," Luke added in a frustrated voice.

She gave the leash a tug, planning to ignore the remark. "Come on, Goodwill." The dog started shaking his head and whining.

"Why don't you carry it?" Luke asked, and looked back at the road as if watching for cars.

Kathy picked up the dog, gave it a scratch behind the ears and started walking.

"You named it Goodwill?" Luke moved in beside her.

"I figure Tommy will want to rename it, but for now Goodwill will do."

"He'll love it," Luke said. "Boys need a dog."

Her mind shot back to how long Tommy had been asking for a canine companion. "He's had lots of pets. Gerbils and the turtle. I haven't deprived him."

"I didn't say you have. It's just gerbils and turtles can't chase balls," Luke pointed out, and as his gaze met hers, it was as if he could read her insecurities. "Look, I didn't mean that you . . . Hell, you're the best mom I know. Tommy's lucky."

"I'm lucky," Kathy replied.

After she took a couple of steps, she glanced back at the White Elephant parked on the side of the road. "I hope you're right about me getting my van back."

"Don't worry."

He kept saying that, but it hadn't stopped *him* from worrying. She recalled seeing his brow pinch whenever he fell quiet, and she'd wager it wasn't from having positive thoughts. The gun he tucked in the back of his jeans pretty much made that a safe bet, too.

Chapter Twelve

For the first few minutes they walked in silence. Then he asked, "Your husband . . . he wore a tie?"

"Yeah." She answered without looking at him, and she could almost feel his hands on her waist.

"What did he do for a living?"

She swallowed, recalling he'd asked about Tom one day when he was over changing out her bathroom faucet. She hadn't wanted to talk about her past to him then, and she still didn't. "Can we change the subject?"

They made it couple of more feet. "He was a cop, wasn't he?"

She looked over at Luke. "No. Why would you think that?"

"Because you don't . . ." He paused. "What was he?"

The puppy whined and plopped his wet nose on her chest. "An accountant."

His gaze was on the dog or her breasts, but he looked up. "I suppose you don't like that I was an accountant, too? For the bad guys."

"It's on my list."

"Oh, so I made the list." A hint of tease played in his voice. "Wow. I've wanted to make a list of yours for a while."

She didn't reply, mostly because she wasn't sure if she had it in her right now to joke.

Luke sighed. "So who was the cop?"

She looked over at him. "I told you, his name was Cary Jenkins."

"No, who was the cop that caused you to dislike the

whole lot of us? Or was that him? Did you date him at one time?"

"No." She increased her pace. "I just got too many speeding tickets."

"You don't lie worth a damn," he said, catching up.

"Guess you could teach me how, huh? It's sort of your area of expertise. Do they teach that in cop school?"

He didn't have a comeback. They walked another minute in silence.

"Your father a cop?" he finally asked.

Don't tell anyone about your daddy, okay? We don't want the kids at the new school to tease you. She would bet her mom had told her that a dozen times. She never squealed, but somehow the kids always found out. How could they not? In Alabama her dad was famous. It wasn't until she was sixteen and she and her mom moved to Texas that her daddy's sins stopped being tossed in her face. It wasn't until she was nineteen, after her trip back to Alabama and her own adventure with the law, that she went to the library and discovered just how big his sins had been.

"What did *your* father do?" she asked, turning the tables on Luke.

He glanced over at her. "He was a plumber."

"Ahh, so that's how you know how to unstop a toilet, huh?"

"Pretty much."

His shoulder brushed up against hers. "So . . . he's a cop, isn't he?"

"Who?" she stalled. If she couldn't lie, maybe she could skirt the truth.

"Your dad."

Okay, so he wasn't gonna let her skirt. She shook her head. "He isn't anything. He's dead."

"Sorry." He looked behind them as he heard a car, but it

was nothing. After a few minutes he asked, "What did Officer Jenkins mean about a club?"

She was so relieved that he'd dropped the topic of her dad that she decided to tell him. "The Divorced, Desperate and Delicious club."

He smiled. "Delicious, huh?"

"Sue named it."

"The blonde?"

"Yeah."

"And what kind of club is it?" he asked.

"It isn't really a club. We just get together once a week."

"And drink Jack Daniel's." A smile pulled at his mouth.

She remembered him dropping by once during a meeting. "Sometimes we drink wine."

"What else?"

"Margaritas."

"No, what else do you guys do in this club?"

"We talk." She sped up again. "Just talk." But no sooner had she answered than she realized her mistake. Logically his next question would be . . .

"About what?"

She rolled her eyes at him. "About what dogs men are."

"And I know how much you love dogs." His gaze shifted to the puppy, who busied himself poking his nose in her cleavage.

Luke seemed to move a little closer. She could feel the energy that whispered through her every time he was physically near. But the closeness she felt now . . . it was different. And she'd never been a fan of different. Give her the ol' status quo every time. Was it boring? Heck, yeah. But boring was also safe.

"So . . . you talk about men at this club, huh?"

"Some," she admitted.

"Ever talk about me?"

"Never," she lied.

He laughed. "What did you say?"

"Please! Why would I talk about you?"

They were almost to the parked cars, and Kathy felt her stomach knot again. Glancing up, she wondered if he'd started this conversation just to keep her mind off what they were about to attempt. "Seriously, what do I have to do here?"

He draped an arm around her shoulders. "Just pretend you're my wife."

"That should be easy," she joked.

"Really?" His fingers toyed with her hair where it lay on her shoulder, and she could feel his hard body moving against hers.

"Yeah, I hate you almost as much as my ex." It was a whopper of a lie, but she decided that in these circumstances she shouldn't be held accountable.

A warm finger moved across her ear. "We'll have fun making up later."

"Keep dreaming," she said.

Nonetheless, things were different between them. He touched her freely now. Before, they had teased but didn't touch. He probably felt justified in touching her now, since she'd practically climbed in his lap and dry-humped him in his kitchen. Yet strangely enough, she sensed the difference ran deeper. It didn't just involve touching. It was as if somehow the last few hours had changed something emotional between them. She was not a fan.

"Oh, I'll keep dreaming about it," he replied, and stopped beside a red Chevy truck.

Kathy set the puppy down, and it started sniffing around for a good spot. The dog wasn't the only one who needed relief, either; her own bladder pinched.

"Tell me." Luke leaned in and bounced his shoulder against hers. "Do you ever dream about me?" His breath tickled her cheek.

"No!" The image of them naked in bed together—Matthew McConaughey feeling rejected and leaving the room—flashed in her head. She tucked her hair behind her ear and watched the puppy so he wouldn't see her lying eyes. "Why would I dream about you?"

He laughed, and that sexy masculine sound had her insides melting. And this melting wasn't different; the attraction had always been there. She could deal with that—or she'd thought she could when she'd decided to sleep with him. But things had changed, right? She shouldn't still be melting, because now she wasn't going to sleep with him.

"So what are these dreams about?"

"I don't dream about you," she repeated. She continued to look down.

He laughed harder. "What are we doing in these dreams?" He tilted her head back with a soft touch. "I've had a few dreams about you, too."

Meeting his eyes, she put her hand on his chest, over his paisley tie that she'd mistakenly tied for him earlier. "You . . . you might want to step back."

He ran a finger down her cheek. "Because you're finding it hard not to kiss me right now? Because, honestly, I'm finding it hard not—"

"Nope, that wouldn't be the reason." She looked back down and couldn't stop herself from smiling. "It's because Goodwill is peeing all over your shoe. And if I don't find a bathroom soon, I might join him."

"You want one more?" Lola asked.

"No, three soft tacos is my limit."

A smile started in her eyes and spilled onto her lips. "That one is number four." Reaching over, she gave him a refill. She had already filled a large to-go cup with coffee for him to take for Donald. Little did she know that the man wouldn't be savoring it. Joey cut a glance back to the car, not sure what he expected to see. Donald was dead. He'd recognized that look.

"You worry about your friend," Lola said. "You good man."

Not really, he knew. What Lola would think of him if she knew the truth—that he was a good-for-nothing bouncer/bodyguard who people paid to be a bully? Every time she smiled at him, he felt as if someone reached in and squeezed his heart. "I've eaten four tacos? No wonder I'm full."

He'd pulled a stool up to the counter, and they'd spent the last half-hour talking. She did most, while Joey ate, but that was fine with him. He liked listening to her. Once or twice she'd reverted back to her native language, but between his Spanish and her English they'd communicated just fine. Joey learned the roach coach belonged to her brother-in-law. That her sister was watching Lola's four-year-old daughter and Lola's young nephew.

Lola had eagerly shown him pictures of the child, saying, "She's a good girl. And smart. I make her speak English." The dark-eyed child looked a lot like her mama. When Joey asked about the girl's father, Lola said he was the man she'd left in Mexico—the man who liked to drink too much.

Lola didn't tell him, but Joey guessed she was here illegally. That would explain why she'd been so nervous with the state trooper. That, and because the man had undressed her with his eyes. Which suggested to Joey that the officer might be trying to pressure Lola into giving him some off-the-menu service.

"That trooper," Joey said. "Is he causing you trouble?"

The smile in her eyes faded. "He's not a good man. But I not let him be too much trouble."

Joey recalled the man's size, and he knew if that jerk decided to force himself on Lola she probably wouldn't be able to stop him. A few memories of hearing his mom manhandled played in his mind. His fist tightened around his fork.

"Maybe you could see if your brother-in-law will come with you to work here? Just in case," he suggested.

Lola shook her head. "He work in concrete, too."

"Oh." Joey wanted to add something else about her not being out here alone, but didn't think it was his right. So he just smiled and tried to hide his concern. "You make a darn good taco."

"Thank you," she said, as if she wasn't accustomed to compliments. "But this not *really* good food. When I cook at home . . ." She continued to talk about cooking big meals and about her family in Mexico.

Picking up his coffee cup, he noticed a magazine on the counter behind Lola—a bird magazine. The same one he had in his briefcase in the car. And he recalled what she'd said earlier. So when she stopped talking he asked, "You like birds?" He pointed to the magazine.

"*Si*. I . . . watch for them. It gives me something to do when I do not have customers. I usually bring birdseed. They come to eat and entertain me. But I run out of food and not go to store yet. You like birds, too?"

She looked surprised, and Joey remembered how most people thought an interest in birds made a man queer. Not wanting her to think that, he shook his head. "Not really."

His embarrassment was interrupted by the ringing of Donald's phone, which Joey just barely heard again. Someone had been calling every four or five minutes, probably the same person who'd called and given Donald the address to this place. It was probably Lorenzo's contact here. Or maybe it was even Lorenzo himself. But, damn it, Joey still didn't know what he was going to do. He had to figure that out soon.

He glanced back at the car. "I guess I'd better be going." He pulled out his wallet.

"No. I give you the food," she said. "Because . . ." She

hesitated, as if shy. "Because your friend fall down, I not charge you."

"Please. His falling down wasn't your fault." Joey pushed a fifty at her.

"No." She pushed it back. "I . . . enjoy talking to you, Mr. . . ." She pressed a hand over her lips. "Ahh, I don't even know your name. How rude of me, I do not even ask your name."

"Joey Hinkle." Joey held out his hand. "And you haven't been rude." She reached out, and when her small warm palm pressed against his a jolt of emotion shot up his arm. Not bad emotion but nice. So nice that he didn't want to let go of her hand.

"It has been very nice to meet you, Senor Hinkle." Those gorgeous eyes twinkled with a smile, and slowly she pulled her hand away, giving a shy expression that reminded him of his slightly more innocent youth. It made his heart beat faster.

"Call me Joey. Please."

"Joey," she repeated. She had a bit of trouble pronouncing the J, but the way she said it sounded so . . . nice.

"You come back, *si?*" she asked.

He almost told her he didn't live nearby. That he probably wouldn't be back. But something stopped him. Maybe it was because he didn't want to disappoint her.

The thought almost made him laugh. Why would his not returning disappoint her? He was nobody to her. "I . . . Maybe."

He stared at her, and that's when it hit him that she must really like him to not let him pay for his food; from all appearances, she didn't make a lot of money. It had been a long time since Joey felt as if anyone cared about him. People noticed him because he was big, but they rarely showed signs of caring about him one way or the other. It wasn't always their fault; he'd been accused by a lot of people of not being very social.

His own phone rang. *Shit.* They couldn't reach Donald, and now they were calling him. What the hell would he tell them?

"Your phone, yes?" said Lola.

"Yes." He nodded and pulled it out of his pocket.

The look on Luke's face when he saw the puppy's hiked-up leg brought a chuckle to Kathy's lips.

"Damn!" Luke jumped back, and a healthy stream struck the exact spot where his shoe had been. Kathy laughed so hard that she found herself leaning against him. Leaning against him felt awesome, too. "You enjoyed that," he accused, but his accusation sounded playful.

"Maybe," she admitted. The swelling in his eye had gone down, but he still had a bit of a shiner. She reached up and touched the bruise. "Does it hurt?"

"No."

He continued to stare at her. The closeness of his body to hers caused a rush of tingles to play chase in some private places. Kathy went to step back, but he wrapped an arm around her and tugged her close—so close that her breasts, still tingling, melted against his chest and her heart skipped a few beats. Her nipples tightened. He leaned in, and his five-o'clock shadow brushed against her cheek. The temptation to press her mouth to his played like soft music in her mind. The memory of how he'd tasted this morning had her gravitating closer.

Their noses brushed. "Did you know your eyes change color when you laugh?" Luke murmured. His breath brushed her mouth. "The green and gold specks meld and mesh, and it's like looking into a kaleidoscope. I can't help but wonder if they change colors when you . . . do other things."

"What things?" she asked, knowing full well what he meant.

"Probably the things we were doing in your dreams."

When she didn't deny it, his lips touched hers. She closed her eyes, and his tongue slipped inside her mouth.

Oh, sure, there was a little voice inside her that said she should stop him. Instead, she reached up and cupped her hand behind his head, threaded her fingers through his soft, dark hair and met his tongue with her own.

"Howdy!" a friendly voice called. "Can I help you love-birds?"

Kathy broke the kiss, but Luke's hand snaked around her waist and he held her against him. "Just keep on doing what you're doing," he whispered.

What she was doing? "I wasn't . . ." She hadn't been doing anything but responding to him. And hadn't she told herself she wasn't going to respond to him anymore? Holy crap, what was wrong with her? She was about to steal a car, and instead of thinking about that, she was making out with her partner in crime. "Let me go," she muttered.

He studied her, then dropped his hand and swung around to meet the salesman. "Hello," he said, and shook the middle-aged guy's hand. "Name's David Bradford. My wife, Kate, and I are just looking for a second ride."

"I'm Harry Johnson." The salesman dropped his hand into the pocket of his navy trousers. "I saw the way you were eyeing the red Chevy truck."

He gave Kathy a friendly nod. *Friendly.* Guilt bloomed in her chest. This beer-bellied older man was being nice, and she was about to become his worst nightmare. She remembered Luke had his gun. Surely he wouldn't use it, would he? Oh, gawd! She was about to become accessory to grand theft auto. Just because he had a badge, it didn't give him a license to steal.

"Did you have to teach him a lesson?" the salesman asked in a teasing voice, pointing to Luke's eye.

Kathy attempted a smile, guilt zipping around her insides like a trapped bird. "No, he . . ."

"I had to teach a few *other* guys some manners," Luke explained. He looked back at the Chevy. "I'd love a truck, but I promised to let her pick it out, and I think she's got her eye on that Dodge Charger." He reached out and took Kathy's hand and pulled her close. "She's got good taste, don't you think?"

The man grinned. "I'd say both of you do. You're a lucky fella to get such a pretty girl to marry you."

"Well, it wasn't easy. Took me over four years before she'd give me the time of day. And I even worked for her old man."

They walked over to the Dodge Charger. Kathy's first reaction to their made-up past was amusement, a thought that, considering Luke's current role, her father might indeed have hired him. He would have respected a car thief. Then the lies and the easy way they slipped from Luke's lips ran like rough sandpaper over her scruples—especially when she remembered he'd lied to her much the same way. She wondered if anything he'd told her during the last two and a half years was the truth. She recalled the few personal tidbits he'd shared: His sister and her kids had been killed in a car wreck. He'd lost his mom at an early age.

Had he lied to her about everything? She hadn't even known his real name until recently. And how did she know Luke Hunter was his real name? She didn't.

And yet, she believed him. She *wanted* to believe him. Even knowing he was a law-enforcement officer hadn't changed her core feelings. Here she stood, trusting Luke. Even knowing he'd lied to her, even knowing he was a cop. She had damn good reasons to never trust another cop. Sure, she accepted her friends' husbands and their friends, but she kept her distance. And while she agreed that her father wouldn't have won any daddy awards, his wrongs didn't make the police right. She knew, because she'd seen what happened.

She glanced at the puppy nipping at her shoe laces, then up at Luke through her lashes. She remembered seeing him with Tommy over the past few years, the gentle way he'd won over her shy son. Right or wrong, she trusted Luke Hunter. She trusted Luke on a gut level. But what if her gut was wrong?

Did she trust him with her life? Maybe. Probably. Obviously she trusted him enough to go along with this plan of stealing a car.

She swung around at the sound of police sirens. Luke squeezed her hand as if to tell her to relax, but when those sirens seemed to stop down the street—right down the street, where her van was—relaxing didn't seem possible. And just to make things worse, she remembered what he'd said earlier about those witnesses being killed while in police protection.

She gave his hand a return squeeze. He didn't react, just motioned to the Dodge Charger. She gave his hand a not so slight tug. He ran his thumb across her palm, slowly, as if to calm her.

"How does this baby ride?" he asked Harry.

The salesman stood with hands on each side of a protruding belly that would have put both Kathy's and Sue's pregnant ones to shame. "Smooth," he said, his focus on selling the car and not the police.

"Do you mind if we take it for a test drive?"

"Let me grab the keys." He waddled to the RV parked to the side of the lot, which was obviously his makeshift office. "Can I grab you two a cold bottle of water?"

"That would be nice," Luke called back, and then leaned in and whispered in Kathy's ear. "Just stay calm. You're doing great."

"I think the police stopped at my van," she said, her throat so tight it hurt to speak.

"I know," he said. "Breathe. You're doing great."

She looked at him. "Great? I'm so scared that my heart is chasing butterflies around my chest. I'm about to become a car thief and I gotta pee. Trust me, I'm not doing great."

Chapter Thirteen

Joey saw it was Pablo, and he let the call go to voice mail. He might pay for it later, but he didn't care.

"You not take the call?" Lola asked.

"Nah, it's not important," he replied.

"Maybe it's your wife." Lola's gaze went to Joey's left hand.

He wiggled his fingers. "Don't have one." Knowing she was interested enough to wonder if he was available brought a lightness to his chest. He wasn't fooling himself, though; nothing could ever come of it. But it still felt good. It made him feel younger and not so weighed down, not so muddled in the rut he'd created for himself.

His phone rang again. He should have known they wouldn't stop calling. "I should take it, so they'll leave me alone." He slid off the stool and stepped away from the counter. "Hello?"

"Where the hell are you?" Pablo snapped. "We've been trying to get Donald. He's not picking up."

Joey glanced at the car. "We're out where the last call was traced."

"Well, the phone's on the move again—but how the hell would you guys know since you aren't picking up?"

On the move? One of the motorcycle guys probably had found it.

"Put Donald on," Pablo growled.

Joey reached up and scratched his chin. "Donald's sort of . . . out of it right now."

"Out of it? Put him on the fucking phone!"

"I don't think he can talk."

"What?" Pablo snapped. "Lorenzo's contact wants him. Is he asleep again?"

Joey tried to think what to say. "Asleep?"

"He fell asleep twice on the ride over to the rental car. Wake his ass up."

"He's not sleeping."

"Then what the hell is he doing? Tell me he isn't with some broad? I swear, he eats Viagra like candy."

"It's not a woman," Joey said.

"Then fucking get him on the phone."

There was only one thing these men respected, and Joey wasn't above using it. He looked over at Lola to make sure she couldn't hear. "He . . . he's taking a shit."

"Oh. Well, why the hell didn't you say so?" Pablo paused. "How long is he going to be?"

"Probably a while. I think his breakfast didn't sit well."

"Ah, fuck it. As soon as Donald's ass is out of the crapper, get over to Highway 101 and Oakwood Drive—or leave his ass there and you get over there. Cops found the florist van. We've got to find Hunter and the girl before the police. Corky and I are halfway across the town and stuck behind some huge accident. I heard they're bringing in a helicopter. We could be locked up here for hours. We've only got one man on the inside, and if Hunter and the chick are brought in, it will be a lot harder to take them down."

Finding Hunter and taking him down isn't my job anymore, Joey thought. *I quit. Not that Lorenzo knows it yet.* But he would when Joey didn't return to New York.

Then Joey remembered the redhead and her son. Could he just walk away, knowing Lorenzo's men would probably catch up and take them out? Joey looked back at Lola, who smiled at him. She smiled at him as if he was a decent guy.

A decent guy wouldn't walk away and let an innocent mother get killed. Maybe if someone had been there to protect his own mother, she might have turned over a new leaf. Maybe Joey and his brother wouldn't have gotten separated and put in foster care. Maybe his brother wouldn't be doing ten to twelve years in a Jersey prison for dealing.

"Give the contact my number," Joey said. "I'll finish this."

"Thought you didn't want to get your hands dirty," Pablo sneered.

"Maybe getting my hands dirty isn't the worst thing."

Pablo laughed. "Lorenzo figured you'd turn around."

"Lorenzo was right." Joey *had* turned around, just not in the way Lorenzo expected. He wasn't cut out for this line of work—but he wasn't cut out to let the others do it, either.

Hanging up, he moved to the roach coach and looked at Lola. "I have to leave. It's been really nice talking to you."

She picked up his fifty, which still lay on counter. She held it out. "You take this."

"No." He took a step back. "I don't like owing people."

"And I no like it when someone not take my gift. I give you lunch. It was my gift."

She stepped away from the counter and came out the door. As she made her way toward him, he appreciated the way her breasts moved inside her red blouse. But not wanting her to think of him as she had the trooper, he forced his eyes up.

"Please. You take this." Rising on her tiptoes, she tucked the bill in his pressed shirt pocket.

He clasped his right palm over her hand and held it against his chest. Her feminine, lotion-soft skin had his heart drumming against his ribs. Was she that soft everywhere? Softer?

His gaze lowered to her blouse. He'd bet her full, round breasts were soft. It had been too damn long since he'd touched or been touched by a woman. Eight months, he figured. And that had been a girl he'd met in a bar when celebrating his new job—a girl he'd walked away from the next morning and never seen again. Yes, he was horny. But that didn't explain the emotional tickle he felt now and had felt earlier when he shook the woman's hand. It wasn't all sexual.

Realizing he still stared at her breasts, he jerked his eyes upward. Their eyes met, held. The tickle grew stronger. He reached up and brushed her cheek with his thumb, watching her closely to make sure his touch wasn't unwelcome.

"You are too pretty to be out here alone," he said.

She blushed. "Maybe you come back and we talk more. After you take care of your friend." She motioned to the car.

His friend? Damn, but he wanted to stay right here. He wished he didn't have to think about the redhead who might need him. Or about finding a place to dump Donald's body.

He moved his finger to the corner of her eye. His chest ached when he traced the half-inch scar there. "That man in Mexico—did he do this?"

She blinked and nodded, but said, "That's not important."

"It is to me," he said, and wished he could teach the guy a lesson. "Don't let anyone treat you bad. You don't deserve that." He remembered his mom and the nights he'd listened to what went on between her and her johns. More times than not, it wasn't just the normal bump and grind, and the bruises always told the story. Not for the first time, he wished he'd been big enough to teach those johns a lesson. And when he recalled a picture of Lola's little girl, he said, "Your daughter doesn't deserve to have to see it, either."

"She *not* see it," Lola said, confused. But then she smiled. "Don't let anyone treat you bad, either."

"I'll try not to," he replied.

He wanted to lean down and kiss her, but decided she

might think that was too forward. He supposed it was. So he nodded another good-bye and, feeling a little awkward, headed toward his car and Donald's body. As he drove away, she waved. He watched in the rearview mirror, knowing he'd probably never see her again; but crazy as it seemed, he knew he wouldn't forget her.

He hadn't gotten a mile down the road when a cop car sped up behind him, lights flashing and siren screaming. Glancing at the lifeless body in back, he knew he'd been lucky to convince the pretty Hispanic woman Donald was drunk. He doubted he'd be so lucky with a trooper.

Luke opened the back door of the Charger and waved Kathy in. He put his hand on her back as she lowered herself into the seat, hoping his touch would ease the anxiety in her expression. She quickly got settled, puppy and her purse in her lap, but then she looked up, her hazel eyes round with emotion. He needed her to hold it together just a little longer.

"She can ride shotgun," Harry suggested, smiling.

She motioned for him to shut the door. "This is fine."

"I'm ready to give this baby a ride," Luke said.

He hurried around to get into the driver's side. Harry the salesman maneuvered his rotund body into the front passenger seat and passed Luke and Kathy bottles of water.

"Thank you," Kathy said.

From the rearview mirror, Luke saw her draw the puppy to her chest as if a lifeline, and for a second he found himself jealous of the damn beast. Kathy glanced up, and he could see the fear in her hazel eyes. He'd give anything if she hadn't been pulled into this. But she had, and right now getting her out alive was more important than her emotional state—or her need for a bathroom.

He started the car engine and pulled out into the street, heading away from the van and the cops. One quick glance in the side mirror revealed they hadn't left a minute too soon—a group of cops stood by their cruisers, talking, obviously devising a search plan. And he hadn't made it a block before another police car came roaring past, sirens blaring. Luke held his breath until the trooper passed.

Harry twisted in his seat and glanced back. "Christ! Looks like a dozen cop cars are right up the street! I'll bet it's about what happened over in Piper earlier. I was listening to the police radio about it when you two came up."

"What happened?" Kathy asked.

Harry looked at her, then Luke. "Some men went into a house and shot it to hell and back."

"Anybody killed?" Kathy squeaked.

"They haven't said yet. But they did say some innocent gal got pulled in and kidnapped. They'll probably be finding her body off the side of the road somewhere."

Kathy's gasp filled the car. Luke tapped the gas a little harder.

Harry looked back at Kathy. "Sorry for my bluntness. I just . . . I just hate it. Senseless crimes tick me off. Cops think it's a drug deal gone bad. Poor gal."

"Drug deal?" Kathy echoed, her voice twice as squeaky.

Drugs? Luke thought. So, that was the way Lorenzo's men had decided to play it.

"Yup. They found cocaine at the house."

Luke could feel Kathy's gaze boring into the back of his head. Was she doubting him? He wanted to look back and offer her a bit of assurance, but damn it, he didn't have time. Lorenzo's men had to be close by, ready to finish what they started earlier. And like he'd told Kathy, he didn't trust anyone—not even someone with a badge. Lorenzo had too many lawmen in his pocket.

"Oh my!" Kathy said, and he heard her take a deep breath.

Luke glanced at the salesman. "Do you mind if I take this baby on some back roads? You know, just to see what it can really do."

"Have at it," Harry said. Then he turned back to Kathy. "What kind of pup is that?"

Kathy didn't answer, and Luke figured the game was almost up. If she lost it, Harry would be on to them. Luke really wanted a few more miles between them and Lorenzo's men before that happened.

"Part pug, I think," Kathy answered, her voice barely audible.

"He's so ugly it makes him lovable."

The puppy whined—or was that Kathy?

"You okay, missy?" Harry asked.

From the rearview mirror, Luke saw her nod and attempt a smile. *Hang in there, sweetheart.* Then he said, "You're right, she drives like a dream," hoping to draw Harry's attention.

"I knew you were gonna love her." Turning, the salesman ran his hand across the dashboard. "She's a bargain, too. Everything's in mint condition, except the radio. I was going to order one . . ."

Luke took a right turn off the main road. He'd looked at putting in a septic tank for a customer on some land about ten miles away. The land was about ten miles away from everyone—which would be the perfect place to get rid of Harry Johnson.

Joey looked in the rearview mirror at the cop speeding up behind him. Much to his surprise, the thing that bothered him most about being caught with a dead guy in his car and the likely subsequent accusations was that Lola would probably hear. Then he remembered the redhead and her boy. If he got hauled to jail, that poor mother was probably going to be killed. The boy would grow up without her. Joey recalled how much he'd missed his own mom, and she'd been a piece of crap. The woman hadn't even cared if they took a bath! He couldn't fathom how much a boy would miss the kind of mom who made sure he had toys by the bathtub.

He felt for his gun and wondered if he could get away without hurting the cop. While he wasn't really a religious man, he considered sending up a prayer—not so much for himself, but wasn't helping the kid a worthy cause? He could sure use a little help.

The flashing light caught his attention again, and letting go of a sigh he moved his hand from the gun. He couldn't shoot a cop. Nope, he might be able to kill a bad guy, but not a cop. He pulled off to a side street, expecting the police car with its flashing lights and siren to follow. Expecting that in a few minutes he'd be handcuffed and sitting in the back of the police cruiser. But the craziest thing happened: the cop didn't turn. Joey pulled over to the side of the road and sat in his car, studying the rearview mirror and listening as the police siren grew weaker.

Joey didn't shift his gaze. Had the cop simply missed the turn? Would he swing around and come blaring back after him? Obviously not, he decided after a moment.

"Well, shit," he said, and the tightness in his chest faded. He released a deep laugh.

He turned and eyed Donald. "Looks like it might be my lucky day. Not so much yours, though." The bluish tint to the man's skin had gotten worse.

Scanning the side of the road, Joey considered what he needed to do next. He glanced again in the backseat. "What do you think? This place okay for your final resting spot?"

He'd just put his hand on the door latch when he heard another engine. A truck turned down the road, and Joey faced forward and started his car, but before he pulled back on the road, the truck took another left and vanished. But it still made him reconsider his plan to dump the body. He should probably wait until night.

He spotted Donald's cap in the front seat. The man had bought it at a service station that morning. Joey picked it up and laughed as he read the words printed across the top: SHIT

HAPPENS AND THEN YOU DIE. "I guess you saw it coming," he muttered.

He looked at Donald, considered putting him in the trunk. But the memory of Freddy's body gave him pause.

That's when he remembered Bernie. From the movie. He'd loved that movie. A smile curled Joey's lips. He might be stuck hauling Donald's dead ass around, but perhaps he could make him look . . . a little less dead.

He put the car in park, got out and limped to open the back door. Damn, if his toe still didn't hurt. He grabbed Donald by the shoulders and sat the man upright. "You getting a little stiff, are you?" he asked. Then, setting the cap on Donald's coarse, gray hair, he tilted the brim downward to hide the man's bluish tint. "You just nap away," he muttered, and couldn't help snickering. "I'll bet you saw that movie, too, didn't you?"

Reaching around Donald, Joey pulled the seat belt over the big man's barrel chest and secured it. While fixing his collar, Joey laughed again. "I know you hate to be belted in, but it really might have saved your ass." His smile faded. "Your sorry ass.

"Damn, you really shouldn't have offed Freddy," he continued. "I know the boss told you to, but . . . I saw you two the night before, laughing and sharing stories about some gal you both knew. You seemed to *like* Freddy. How could you just go and kill him like that?" Letting go of a deep breath, Joey straightened the other man's jacket, pulled the sunglasses from his pocket and fitted them on the nose.

"How did you do it?" Joey asked, as if the dead man might respond. "How did you live with it? Or did you die with it?" He shook his head. "Guess I might be finding out soon, huh? I might not kill a cop, but I will kill Pablo or Corky if I have to. Not for me, but for that kid."

Joey hesitated, shaking his head. "I'd have killed you, too, if you'd gone after that pregnant blonde. Does that make me as bad as you? Maybe," he muttered in answer to his own question. "But some people just don't deserve to die."

Joey got out and crawled back into the driver's seat. He shifted the rearview mirror so he could see Donald. With sunglasses on, the man looked . . . well, alive.

"You ready?" Joey asked. "Let's go rescue us a redhead. Maybe by the grace of God you'll get some brownie points for being present—in body, at least, if not in spirit."

He pulled out his phone and made sure it was on; Lorenzo's contact should be calling soon. After securing his own seat belt, Joey drove out onto the road and headed toward the location where the van was found.

Glancing in the rearview mirror, he watched Donald's head bounce slightly with the car's movement. It looked like the corpse was nodding to some unheard music, chilled out and agreeable.

"I have to say," Joey admitted, "I think I kind of like you better dead than alive."

Chapter Fourteen

"Cocaine? Did you say they found drugs at the man's house?" Kathy asked, feeling some of her wits return.

"Yep. It's ugly, ain't it?" Harry said. "Hard to believe things like this happen in our neck of the woods."

Kathy held the puppy so tightly that it wiggled to get free. When she loosened her hold, the poor creature leaned back and tried to lick her face, but she arched her neck away. Luke glanced at her in the rearview mirror as if trying to send her a message. And if she read that unspoken message right, it was: *Relax, I'll explain it later.*

He'd better explain. He'd better have a damn good explanation, too. Because she'd halfway agreed to be part of stealing a car, but she hadn't said squat about being part of a drug deal. And, hey . . . she was picky about the crimes she wanted to commit.

Again she wondered, what if she was wrong about him? But then the mental image of Luke—as Stan—ruffling her son's hair and helping him fix his bike's tire played across her mind, and she knew she wasn't wrong.

She inhaled, hoping fresh oxygen would reduce the panic building in her chest. The smell of puppy, shampoo, and yeah, just a hint of the stench they had left back in the Goodwill trailer filled her nose.

"So what do you think? Are we going to make a deal?" Harry asked Luke.

"Yes, I think we're going to be negotiating, but there's just one little problem."

This was it, Kathy realized, and her heart pumped crazily.

"What's that?" Harry asked.

Luke pulled over to the side of the road.

Oh, crap! This was definitely *it*, and with the tension forming in her belly, her need to pee grew more intense. She closed her eyes and concentrated on not wetting her pants, on keeping that fizzy feeling from taking over her mind.

"Why are we stopping?" the man asked.

Kathy took another gulp of oxygen, and her gasp echoed through the car. Her eyes popped open. She didn't want to see Harry's face when he learned what they were up to, but she couldn't seem to stop herself from looking.

"You got a cell phone, Harry?" Luke asked.

"Sure." Harry pulled a phone from his pocket. "Why . . . ?"

Luke reached over and took it. Harry's jowls, dangling

down on each side of his face, dangled just a bit lower with his frown.

"Here's the deal." Luke gazed back at Kathy for a brief second, as if he knew this was eating her alive. "How much are you asking for this car?"

"Eight thousand." Harry's voice had lost its previous enthusiasm. "You want to give me back my cell phone?"

"Why don't we make it an even ten and I keep the phone." Luke ran his palm over the steering wheel while holding Harry's cell phone in his other hand. "I could even go as high as twelve if you play your cards right."

"Eight is fine." Harry's eyes, almost as bug-eyed as the pug puppy's, grew a tad bigger. "You're shitting me, right?"

Luke shook his head. "Serious as a heart attack."

Luke's tone must have rung Harry's warning bells, because the old man's round face grew pale—with exception of his ears, which grew red. Kathy suddenly wished Luke hadn't used the word heart attack.

"Why don't we just head back to the lot?" Harry glanced back at her, and Kathy saw the question in his eyes. "Start the car," he insisted. "I need to get back."

"Can't do that, Harry," Luke said. "You see, here's how this is going to play out. I'm going to pay you twelve thousand for this car, which is probably double what it's really worth. But it's going to be a few weeks before I can get you the money."

"I don't think so," Harry said, and he turned around again and his bugged out eyes found Kathy's. "He's the one they're talking about on the radio, right? You're the gal who—"

"That's enough." Luke reached over and turned Harry's face to him. "I'm the one you need to pay attention to. And here's what I want you to do."

"I'm not doing crap. You're going to start this car right now and head back."

"Harry, Harry," Luke said. "You're not listening to me.

And you've got to listen. You want the extra four thousand dollars, don't you?"

Harry, beer gut and all, dove over the gearshift, his fist swinging. His belly slammed into the steering wheel, and he looked like an angry Pillsbury Doughboy with his jowls jiggling.

"Noooo," Kathy moaned. The puppy whimpered.

Luke managed to dodge the rotund man's attack and pushed him back in his seat—but Harry came back for more. "Get out and run!" the guy screamed at her.

Luke grabbed the car salesman's right fist and held it tight. "Don't make this hard."

Harry swung with his left.

Luke ducked, and the driver-side headrest took the blow. Kathy could tell that Luke was trying not to hurt the man, but when Harry's fist hit Luke in the gut, she heard him groan and knew he was losing patience.

"Stop!" Kathy wasn't sure which man she was talking to, but the one-word order seemed appropriate. Of course, neither guy listened to her. Harry shifted more of his weight off the seat and onto Luke's, and they continued to tussle. Then Harry jerked back, and in his hands he had Luke's gun.

"No!" Kathy screeched.

Luke didn't waste a second. His face all seriousness, he grabbed Harry's wrist and slammed it against the dashboard. The gun dropped, and Luke snatched it up.

Upon leaving the hospital, Jason Dodd drove Sue straight to Chase and Lacy's. He'd spoken to Chase several times in the last few hours, and they'd decided to give their wives the news together. Neither Chase nor Jason looked forward to it, but both knew their wives would raise holy hell if they learned they'd been kept in the dark.

"Come in," Lacy said, her gaze concerned as she opened the door. "Are you okay?" she asked, obviously having spoken with Sue previously. "I can't believe what happened. And I still can't get Kathy on the phone."

"I'm fine," Sue replied. "And yeah, it's Kathy I'm worried about." She cut her eyes to Jason, letting him know she didn't appreciate him being so secretive. Whenever she'd asked about what he knew—which had been about ten times at this point; Sue was anything but patient—the only thing he'd tell her was that Chase was looking into it and that they were headed here now to find out. And in part that was true. He hoped Chase was here with more information.

He and Sue walked in and stood in the entryway, and Lacy shut the door. Jason moved to the living room, expecting to see Chase. His friend wasn't there, and Jason knew he had about thirty seconds before both Sue and Lacy started demanding answers. And while he'd learned to deal with Sue's plain and simple outbursts of emotion, Lacy scared him. The woman had once threatened to grind his male parts into sausage.

Where was Chase? Jason pulled out his phone. He'd spoken with his friend twice since he'd left the hospital—once when Chase arrived at Stan Bradley's place and again when he'd shown up at the van—and found out that Cary Jenkins, a friend and Hoke's Bluff police officer, had actually seen Kathy and the plumber. While they didn't know what the hell was going on, the news that Kathy seemed well had provided a big sigh of relief, but there were still a hell of a lot of questions yet to be answered.

The blood found at the plumber's place was right now being tested. Since Cary's report, they didn't think it was Kathy's, but whose was it? Cary swore Kathy looked fine, and other than a black eye, even Bradley didn't appear hurt. Cary also said that Kathy had introduced Stan Bradley as her boyfriend. But was Kathy lying because she was frightened? Did Bradley have a gun on her?

Jason's gut clenched again at how close his wife had come

to the men who shot up the plumber's house. He didn't have a clue why one of those men had made Sue hide in the closet, but Jason was damn sure going to shake that man's hand when they found him—right before he slapped a pair handcuffs on him if he had anything to do with Kathy's disappearance.

Glancing back at the women still jabbering in the entryway, Jason dialed Chase's number and waited for him to answer. He'd better not have stood him up with both their wives.

According to the last call from Chase, Stan Bradley's neighbor and landlady had given a detailed description of all the men. This made Jason feel better about tweaking his report and leaving out the fact that Sue had been at Kathy's. Especially when one of the guys described sounded just like the man who'd forced Sue into the closet: big, midthirties, thick sandy brown hair and light green eyes.

"Hey." Chase's voice sounded with the opening of the front door. Relief washed over Jason, and he shut his phone and swung around.

"What are you doing home?" Lacy leaned into her husband. "I tried to call you just a minute ago but—"

Chase kissed his wife, then met Jason's gaze. "Let's sit down."

"Sit down? Why? What . . . ? Oh, God, it's Kathy, isn't it?" Lacy's tone shot from mildly concerned to grave. She gave her husband's hand a tug. "Talk to me, Chase!"

"Let's sit down first." Chase nudged his wife forward.

Jason saw Sue's eyes tear up as she pressed a hand over her mouth. He went to her and wrapped an arm around her waist and walked her to the sofa. "It's going to be okay," he whispered.

He prayed he was right.

Luke kept the gun pointing away from Harry, but his scowl was aimed right at the used-car salesman. "Sit back!" he commanded.

Kathy watched Harry slam back into his seat, his face now the same beet red color as his ears and his gaze focused on the gun.

"That's much better," Luke said.

Harry raised his hands in the air.

"Now," Luke continued, "you're going to get out of the car and take your sweet time walking back. For every hour it takes you before you call and report this car missing, I'm going to throw in another thousand."

Harry shook his head. His expression went cold, and he cut his gaze back to Kathy. She could see the concern in his light blue eyes, and that it was for her. "No," he growled. "You can't do this."

"I'm going to pay for the car," Luke insisted. "You have my word."

"Your word is shit!" Harry spat out.

"You won't say that when you get the money."

"I don't want your drug money."

"Harry. Harry." Luke talked the way one might to a misbehaving child. "Just get out of the car. I promise you, everything is going to turn out fine."

"So you can shoot me in the back when I get out?"

"I'm not going—"

"He's not going to shoot you," Kathy interrupted.

"Let her go with me," Harry said. "She hasn't done anything to you."

Kathy saw Luke glance in the rearview mirror. She knew he was getting inpatient.

"Luke," she said, "Maybe you should just be honest. Tell him about—"

"I said get out!" Luke spoke to Harry but glared at her.

She ignored his warning. "Harry, he's not going to hurt me. Really. I'm fine. Just do as he says."

Harry puffed out his chest, as if wanting to be her hero, and guilt burned in Kathy's empty stomach.

The used-car salesman pointed a chubby finger at Luke. "I'm not leaving unless you let her go, too. I won't leave her with the likes of you."

Luke glanced again at the side mirror. He turned around in his seat, faced her, and then winked. The little flutter of his eyelid seemed to imply something, but she didn't have the slightest clue what.

Unfortunately, she found out.

"Get out, or the girl gets it," Luke said, and while he didn't point the gun at her, he held it closer.

Her heart stopped pumping. The wink hadn't been nearly enough of a warning.

"Get out!" Luke ordered. "Or I'll take it out on her."

He didn't say he was going to shoot her, but she knew that was what Harry thought. The poor old man looked horrified. And frankly, so was she. Not for one second did she think Luke would shoot her. But poor Harry didn't know that. This was Luke's ploy to get Harry to leave? He really didn't think he could trust random citizens? While she understood his motive, she didn't like his action.

Neither did Harry. His face got redder, his eyes wider.

"Don't do this," she snapped at Luke. Then, to Harry: "Don't worry about me. He's not going to hurt me. He's not like that. Just get out."

Harry didn't look convinced. So Kathy reached over and thumped Luke on the ear. "See? He's not going to hurt me."

Harry's gaze shot from Luke to her as if confused. Luke looked mildly affronted.

"He's not a bad guy. He plays good with kids and everything." Kathy grabbed a lock of Luke's dark hair and gave it a tug, and Luke yelped. "Seriously. See? Don't worry about me." She pulled his hair again. "I'm fine. Would he let me do this if he was going to hurt me?" Then, to prove her point, she gave his ear another thump. A hard one.

Luke flinched and twisted in his seat, his frown deepening.

He caught her by the wrist, but the whole time his gaze never left the used car salesman. "She's *really* getting on my nerves, Harry. I suggest—"

"Don't . . . don't hurt her." Harry held up his hands. He reached for the door handle, opened it and backed out of the seat as if he was really worried that Luke would shoot him. Before he pulled his head out of the car, he looked at her. "I'm sorry."

"Wait!" Kathy said. "Here . . ." Pushing the puppy out of her lap, she snagged the water bottle he'd given her. "Take this with you. It's a long walk back."

He took it but kept staring.

Spotting Luke's bottle of water in the cup holder, Kathy leaned over the car seat, her bottom hoisted in the air, and she offered it to Harry as well. "Take his, too. Just in case."

Harry nodded, looked even more confused; then, armed with two bottles of water, he backed away from the car and swung the door closed.

Luke nudged her back into her seat and then took off. The tires squealed. The pug puppy climbed back into her lap, found his spot and curled up.

"You could have been nicer," she accused. She ran her hand over Goodwill and glanced back to see Harry's rotund figure growing smaller.

Luke's dark blue eyes met hers. "I tried being nice. Didn't work," he said, suddenly digging around in the seat. Then he held his hand up, Harry's cell phone in his grasp.

"You could have tried harder."

"He snagged my gun," Luke snapped. "I nearly got shot trying to be nice!" He glanced at the phone, then focused on Kathy again as he tugged off his tie. "You could have been nicer, too. You didn't have to thump me. That took me back to the time my mom caught me . . ." He trailed off, almost smiling, tossed the necktie in the empty front seat, then hit some buttons on the phone. His expression fell back to serious.

Kathy held her breath and waited, praying he got in touch with whoever it was he needed. At the same time, her mind shot to him as a boy and she wondered what he'd been caught doing. What kind of kid had he been? Had he been outgoing? Or quiet and shy like Tommy?

The thought made her miss her son, and the air gushed out of her lungs. She wondered if he'd tried to call her. Did Tommy miss her? Or was he having too much fun with his dad and new elderly stepmom? Kathy's heart suffered a little tug-of-war.

She blinked away the beginning of her watery weakness and saw Luke clench his jaw.

"Calvin, damn it!" Luke spat. "Answer your freaking phone! Call me—at this number."

"What do we do now?" she asked, when he tossed the phone on the empty seat beside him.

"We come up with a new plan," he growled, shrugging out of the suit coat.

"What?" she asked.

He didn't hesitate. "It's called staying alive."

Kathy closed her eyes and sighed. "Could 'staying alive' possibly include a bathroom stop? And how about an explanation of the drugs back at your place?"

Chapter Fifteen

Jason followed the others into Lacy's living room. The moment Sue and Lacy were both sitting, Chase started talking. "As far as we know, Kathy is okay, so both of you can calm down."

"Where is she?" Sue and Lacy chorused.

"We're not sure." Jason sat on the arm of the sofa beside his wife and ran his hand over her back. "We're pretty sure she's with Stan Bradley right now."

"She went over to his house," Lacy said. "But what does that have to do with what happened at Kathy's? Is she in danger?"

Jason met Chase's eyes, and his friend finally jumped in. "Kathy left with Bradley from his place."

"And that's bad because . . . ?" Lacy guessed, staring at her husband.

"We're not sure Kathy went willingly," Jason explained.

"*What?*" Lacy said. "Why would you wonder that?" Her blue eyes found her husband. "What the hell is going on?"

Chase sat on the recliner close to Lacy, and Jason could see concern for his wife in his friend's eyes. "Police were called to Bradley's. Someone shot up the house. A neighbor saw Bradley with Kathy, and it appeared as if he forced her into her van."

"Oh, God!" Sue's eyes filled with tears.

Jason took her hand. If she needed to cry on him, that was okay. He'd given at least a dozen shirts to the crying-wife cause, and he'd give a hundred dozen if it made her feel better. Today, when he'd thought about losing her, he'd realized all over again how precious she was and how damn lucky he was that she loved him.

Sue wiped her nose with the back of her hand. "What if she's hurt? What if—"

"Don't what-if this," Jason told her. "We know she was okay not too long ago." As a writer, Sue's imagination always took off in leaps and bounds. Unfortunately, some of those leaps were in the wrong direction. "Right now we need to focus on finding Kathy. And staying calm. Both of you are in the baby-making business. Calm is important. Remember what the doctor said?"

"Exactly." Chase placed his hands on his knees and leaned forward. "Can either of you tell us exactly what the relationship was between the plumber and Kathy?"

Lacy and Sue met each other's gazes.

"She liked him," Sue said.

"A lot," added Lacy.

"Were they dating?" Chase asked.

"No." Lacy ran a hand over her belly. "Not yet. But she was thinking about, um, dating him. Why?"

Chase's gaze shot to Jason. "Cary Jenkins ran into her and Bradley at a Goodwill drop-off down Highway 101."

"When?" Lacy asked.

"This afternoon."

Sue leaned forward. "But if they thought the plumber forced her to go with him, why didn't Cary bring her back with him?"

Chase answered, "Because that was before he knew any of this. The good news is, he said she appeared to be fine. But he also said that it was implied during the conversation that Kathy and Bradley were dating."

Sue and Lacy shot each other a confused look. "They aren't as far as we know," Lacy admitted, and Sue nodded in agreement. "Although . . ."

"How well do you think Kathy knows Bradley?" Jason asked.

"She hasn't slept with him, if that's what you're asking," Lacy answered.

"She would have told us if she had," Sue added. "At least she hadn't slept with him when she left this morning," Sue admitted.

"That's not what I mean," Jason said, shaking his head. He didn't like to consider how much his wife and her friends shared. "I mean, what kind of guy is he?"

Lacy twisted a strand of hair around her finger. "She's known him as long as I have. As far as we know, he's a decent guy. She says he's always paying attention to Tommy." She pointed to her husband. "*You've* met Stan Bradley. Actually, both of you met him." She looked back at Jason. "Remember the day of the inside-out housecoat? When everyone showed up while Chase was hiding in my bedroom? And everyone suspected I was . . . having sex because of the housecoat mishap."

"You were having sex." Chase chuckled.

"I remember that day," Jason said, and grinned.

"I don't get it," Sue spoke up. "Why are you thinking he's a bad guy? And if he took Kathy, then who do you think shot up his place?"

Chase let go of a sigh. "They found cocaine, lots of it, at his house. It looks as if Bradley might have been dealing drugs."

"Bradley, the plumber, dealing drugs?" Lacy shook her head. "No. I don't see it."

"Me either," Sue said. "Just a couple of weeks ago, Kathy told us that she found the plumber helping Tommy change a tire on his bike. He was always really nice to both of them."

Jason met Chase's gaze, and the two men shook their heads.

Chase refocused on his wife. "Being nice doesn't mean he's not a criminal. If I remember correctly, I told you that I didn't care for him."

Lacy rolled her eyes. "You said he was too friendly to me. You didn't say you thought he was into drugs."

"He *was* too friendly to you," Chase growled.

"If he was fat and ugly you wouldn't have minded," Lacy tossed in. "But because he's good-looking—"

"Not true," Chase said. "And, personally, I don't think he was all that good-looking."

"Yes, he is," Sue laughed. "He's hot."

Jason frowned. "Guy's never working on *our* plumbing."

Chase stared at his wife. "It has nothing to do with how he looks. It bothered me that he seemed standoffish. And he knew I was a cop—which, if he was selling drugs, keeping his distance from me would make sense."

Lacy shook her head. "None of this makes sense! If he was into drugs, then who at Kathy's place made Sue go into the closet? And who would have shot up Bradley's place to start with?"

"Probably someone he's getting his drugs from," Chase answered. "Maybe this Bradley character owes someone else money. Kathy was driving the van, and it had her address on it. Maybe when Kathy and Bradley took off, the people looking for Bradley went looking for them at her place."

Sue made a face. "If they wanted money from Stan, why would they leave all of the drugs behind? For that matter, why would they go to Kathy's? Oh, jeepers! You two aren't insinuating that Kathy is in on any of this, are you? Because I can tell you right now that—"

"I'm not saying that," Jason interrupted—and he wasn't, but not everyone on the police force shared his and Chase's view. He knew Hoke's Bluff police, including Danny and Cary, were already looking into Kathy's life, as well as Stan Bradley's, with a fine-tooth comb.

Lacy rubbed her belly. "I don't think Bradley is a bad person. My grandmother liked him. She hired him to clean the septic tank."

"No offense," Chase said, popping up from his chair and slipping closer to his wife. "But your grandmother is almost ninety. Her character judgment isn't what it used to be. Look at the number of men she's married and divorced."

Lacy frowned. "Well, she's crazy about you. Should I be worried?"

"Probably . . . but it's too late." He brushed her curly hair from her cheek and gave a crooked grin. When she didn't return his smile, he leaned in and kissed her. Then he tapped her cheek with his finger. "Don't start worrying, Lacy. You've got my kid to think about. I'll do all the worrying, okay?"

"You've got to do more than worry. You've got to get Kathy out of this." Lacy leaned into her husband and let out a soft sob.

Chase's arms went around her. "It's going to be okay," he said.

Sue squeezed Jason's hand. "I want Kathy back home safe and sound and badmouthing men again."

He leaned down and kissed her head. "We're going to do everything in our power to make that happen."

Joey's phone rang, and when he reached over to get the cell on the seat he accidentally swerved. He grabbed the wheel a little too quickly and the car jerked back. In the rearview mirror, he saw Donald's body stiffly bounce back and forth. A smile tickled Joey's lips, and he remembered the movie again. Poor Bernie.

Glancing at the caller ID, he didn't recognize the number. Probably Lorenzo's contact. "Hello?" Joey said into the phone.

"Where's Donald?" the voice asked.

The speaker sounded vaguely familiar, but Joey couldn't place him. Looking over his shoulder he answered, "He's resting."

"Is he with you?"

"No." *Not in spirit, anyway.* "But I'm here and ready to do what I have to."

"Lorenzo's not going to be happy," the man complained.

"I can't do anything about that," Joey replied.

Silence followed, and then the contact spoke again. "There's a mom-and-pop café about a mile off Cypress and north on Newton. Where are you at?"

"A few miles off FM 101. Pablo said I needed to go back—"

"Meet me at the café in about thirty minutes."

"You got a location?" Joey asked, fearing the worst.

"Not yet, but we should have one by then."

"Really?" Joey asked.

"Really," the contact answered.

"How are we going to manage that?" Joey said, figuring if he was really setting out to protect the redhead, he needed information.

"How about you just show up?"

"That was my second plan," Joey grunted. "How am I going to recognize you?"

"I'll be the only one there who can legally carry a gun."

But you won't be the only person ready to use one.

Joey hung up and eyed Donald in the rearview mirror. "Is being an asshole a requirement to work for Lorenzo, or does the boss just get lucky?" he muttered to himself. He scratched his jaw. "Of course, since I worked for him, too, I guess I shouldn't be talking. But you know what? It's never too late to change."

Donald's dark glasses and the way his head was angled gave the impression that he actually listened.

"What?" Joey asked. "You don't think I can change?" Letting out a deep breath, he stared at the road. "Guess we'll just have to see."

He pulled over, shut the car off and got a map out of the glove box to find Cypress and Newton. After spreading the map out on the seat beside him, he looked back at Donald, all buckled up, looking cool in his shades and his Shit happens hat. Joey glanced at his watch. "You know what this means, don't you? I gotta drop your ass off someplace."

He spotted a couple of buzzards off to the right making dinner out of some roadkill. He thought about Donald's body being ravaged by the vultures. When he turned around to stare at Donald, he could swear the man looked right at him behind those glasses.

"I don't have time to bury your ass right now," he told the dead man. Guilt zipped through him as he spotted another buzzard land. "Fine. I tell you what: I'll *come back* and bury your ass, okay? But not right now."

Donald's stillness seemed to question Joey's honesty.

"I promise," Joey said.

He turned and faced forward. A block ahead, he spotted a place to do his dirty work. He thought again about Donald's hat: SHIT HAPPENS AND THEN YOU DIE. A laugh—a soul-deep belly laugh—fell right out of him, and he started the car.

"Perfect."

"I'm serious. The sooner the better," Kathy said about ten minutes after they left poor Harry on the side of some dirt road. Luke had told her that Lorenzo's men left the drugs as a way of explaining what went down. Call her crazy, but she believed him. Maybe because she'd seen it happen on all the police shows—or maybe it was because she really trusted him.

She'd climbed into the front seat, puppy in tow, tossed his tie and coat into the back, and plopped the puppy back in her lap. "You've got to find a McDonald's or a service station. I'm this close"—she held her fingers a smidgen apart—"to peeing all over the twelve-thousand-dollar car you just bought."

Luke glanced over at her. "I think the best I can offer you is a tree."

"A tree? I've never been good at the squatting position."

He grinned. "So which position do you prefer?"

She rolled her eyes. "Is it always about sex with you men?"

He cocked his head as if thinking. "Pretty much." A grin tickled his lips, and he reached up and loosened a couple of shirt buttons. "Isn't it that way with women?"

"No." Then the answer irritated her conscience. When she'd called last week to ask him over, she hadn't been asking for a serious relationship or marriage. She'd just wanted companionship. Okay . . . so she'd wanted sex. Tom had cured her of wanting anything long term. And so . . .

Luke looked back at the road. "I'll be damned. This might be your lucky day."

"What?" She glanced up, thinking he'd spotted a McDonald's or a service station. All she saw was a construction sign, without the construction men. And then she saw it: an orange and tan porta-potty.

She frowned. "Do you have any idea how badly those smell inside?"

He pulled the car over. "Well, it's like this. You got a tree." He pointed to a pine tree off to the right. "Or you got a porta-potty. And you've got about two minutes."

She grabbed the door handle. "It won't take two minutes. I can't hold my breath that long."

"What?" he asked, as she started looking around the floorboards.

"I'll need . . . Well, a job's never done until the paperwork is finished."

He shook his head. "Your two minutes are ticking." He reached over her lap and opened the door for her. "You're going to have to drip dry."

She shuddered. "Men are disgusting." She crawled out of the car, then looked back and suggested, "Why don't you walk Goodwill? He probably needs to go, too."

He frowned but reached into the backseat for the leash, and as she got to the porta-potty he was stepping from the car with the puppy in his arms. She saw him give the dog a scratch behind the ears. A flutter filled her chest. Then, taking a deep breath meant to last through the entire emptying of her bladder, she opened the door.

She actually had one foot inside before she realized the porta-potty was occupied. Letting out a yelp, she found herself staring at a man wearing shades, his pants pulled down around his ankles, a magazine in his lap, and a hat that read *Shit happens and then you die.*

She yelped again, "I'm so sorry—*so* sorry!" and slammed the door.

Jason and Chase left their wives in the living room to commiserate as they walked outside to the patio.

"What do you think?" Jason asked. "Where do we—?"

"I don't think he's that good-looking," Chase said.

Jason stared. "I wasn't talking about Bradley's appearance. I meant—"

"But do you think he's good-looking?" Chase asked, holding out his palms.

Jason sighed. "I don't know. I personally don't go around checking out other men. And I don't exactly like it when my wife does either," he added, frowning, remembering Sue calling the guy "hot."

"Well, I guess he's not bad-looking for a plumber," Chase mused.

"Right," Jason said, hoping to get back to business. "Now, back to my real question. Where do we start looking into Bradley?"

Chase pointed to the lot next door. "Right in front of you." A truck with a construction sign on its door panel was parked in front. Two men were walking around as if surveying the property. Chase explained, "We should talk to the contractor and see if he can enlighten us about what went down earlier—and what he knows about the plumber."

Jason nodded, falling into step beside Chase. Then he chuckled. "If you ask if he thinks Bradley is good-looking, I'm out of here."

Chase gave a brief smile.

"So you think this Bradley character kidnapped Kathy?" Jason asked.

"I don't know," Chase replied. "But something doesn't add up. Cary said she looked fine. Said she was even acting friendly with the guy."

"Then we both know it was an act," Jason replied. "Come on, Kathy friendly with a man?"

Chase chuckled.

"Seriously," Jason continued. "No offense or anything, but I always got the impression that men weren't her thing."

Chase looked at him. "Just because she didn't swoon over the Almighty Jason Dodd, you think she's a lesbian?"

"No. Not a lesbian. She just . . . doesn't like men."

Chase shrugged. "I just always figured she resented us for taking her best friends away. Also, if you remember correctly, neither of our wives was too keen on the opposite sex when we met them. I think Kathy's ex did a number on her, too."

"Maybe," Jason agreed, then let out a deep breath.

Chase stopped and turned. "You know the Hoke's Bluff PD is going to be asking questions as soon as they go over to Kathy's. You going to lie to Danny and Cary?"

Jason paused, knowing what his friend wasn't saying. "Do you have any reason why Sue being involved would help?"

"Right now I don't. But there's a lot we don't know."

"If it were Lacy, what would you do?" Jason asked.

Chase ran a hand over his face. "Probably the same thing you're doing."

"Thanks," Jason replied. "You know, I talked to Danny before I left the hospital. Hoke's Bluff PD is looking hard at Kathy for being involved in all this."

"Now, that I *don't* believe," Chase said. "She may not like men, but I don't think I've ever met a woman who cared more about her son. Drugs? No way. I can't see her doing anything illegal."

"Me either," Jason agreed. "That's why I'm thinking we

might be looking at the whole thing ass backwards. Maybe Bradley's not—"

"You think he's innocent?" Chase asked. "They found cocaine at his place."

Jason gave his friend a hard look. "Considering I'm talking to a guy who had a corrupt cop plant drugs under his bed a little more than a year ago, yeah, I think it might be a possibility."

"Damn. You got a point. And I really hate that." He stood there for a second, thinking. "But who would go out of their way to set up a *plumber?*"

They started moving again. "I don't know," Jason said. "You're the guy who always figures out the puzzles. I just point them out."

"True," Chase agreed. "But I think we'd both better get to work on this one, because if something happens to Kathy . . ."

"I know," Jason said. "It will break our wives' hearts."

"Yup," Chase said. "And you know what our jobs are?"

"To keep anything from breaking their hearts. Because they're our right arms."

Chase nodded. "You know, for a former womanizing son of a gun, I've taught you well."

"As if you didn't do your own womanizing," Jason muttered.

Kathy crossed her arms over her chest and tightened her thighs to keep her bladder from releasing. She stared at porta-potty. She did a little side-to-side dance, then leaned toward the door. "Are you almost finished?"

"What is it?" Luke appeared behind her, sounding concerned.

She swung around, and he gave the leash a yank when Goodwill sniffed at his shoe. "It's occupied." She bit down on her lip and gave the tree another glance. Desperate times called for desperate measures.

Luke turned to the road and then back to her. "Someone's in there?" he asked.

She nodded and motioned to the tree. "I'll be right back."

She had her pants down and was positioned in full squat by the pine, her jeans and panties as far away from spray danger as she could get them when she heard Luke call her name. She ignored him to enjoy the bliss of unloading her full bladder. It was better than sex, she thought. Well, better than sex with her ex, she amended. Remembering her fantasies about Luke, she reminded herself that maybe she just hadn't had good sex.

Then she heard someone behind her. "I said let's go!"

Startled, she nearly fell back and landed in the puddle she'd been making. Managing to catch herself, she twisted her head around to glare at Luke. However, stopping on demand wasn't easy. Fully aware that her bare bottom was exposed, she screeched, "Get out of here!"

"Now. Get up!" He had his gun in one hand and Goodwill in the other.

"Turn around," Kathy growled, both furious and embarrassed.

He muttered something and turned around, looking ready to unload his gun on someone.

Though she probably could have squeezed out another gallon, she jerked herself upright and hauled her panties and jeans up, too. "Have you ever heard of—"

He grabbed her by the elbow and started moving.

"Privacy?" she finished as he dragged her to the car. She started to give him a piece of her mind, but then she noted the seriousness of his expression. Remembering being chased and shot at, her gaze shifted around and she expected to see another car.

"What is it?" she asked when she didn't see any obvious danger.

He opened the car door and shoved her and Goodwill

inside. In seconds, he'd settled into the driver's seat. The tires spat gravel as he threw the car into gear and they spun out onto the road.

"You had better have a damn good reason for that," she growled.

He shifted the car into second gear. "I do."

"Would you like to share?" she seethed. "Because I could have done with a little more drip-dry time. And I don't think I used up my two minutes."

"Remember the guy you saw in the porta-potty?" Luke looked in the rearview mirror.

"Yeah."

"He worked for Lorenzo."

"Who's Lorenzo?"

"The guy I'm supposed to testify against."

"Oh." Kathy's heart started to pound. She turned to see if anyone was following them. "I don't think he's behind us."

"It's not him I'm worried about," Luke said.

"Then who *are* you worried about?"

He made a sharp turn onto another road but remained quiet.

"Answer me!"

He shot her a quick look. "The man in the porta-potty wasn't breathing."

"Nobody breathes in those things. They stink," she reminded him.

He shook his head and chuckled grimly. "No. He wasn't holding his breath. The guy in the porta-potty was dead."

Kathy's heart skipped a couple of beats. She bit her lip and stared at Luke. "Was he the guy I hit over the head with the toilet tank lid? Do you think I—"

"No. Different guy. I actually had the pleasure of meeting this guy when I was undercover. He was one of Lorenzo's top men."

Kathy closed her eyes, leaned her head back and tried

not to think about today being the absolute—the hands-down absolute, no questions asked—worst day of her life. Of course, she reminded herself, her bad day probably didn't compare to that of the guy in the porta-potty.

Chapter Sixteen

Joey pulled up at the café, checked the parking lot for any-thing suspicious. It hadn't occurred to him until a few min-utes ago that Lorenzo's contact probably already had info about the blonde. And if he knew about the blonde, he might suspect Joey of being up to no good.

Not that it was "no good" Joey was up to. Some would say his plan was "for the good." If Joey was successful, some kid would get to grow up with his mom. Maybe it wasn't a grand thing, his gesture, but to that boy it would be a big deal.

Reaching under his jacket, he checked his gun, then looked left to right as he got out of his car. Nothing. No-body. No cop car either. Since the guy said he'd be the only one legally carrying, Joey had suspected he was a lawman. Pulling his jacket closed, he hit the clicker to lock his car and walked inside the café.

The dark atmosphere smelled like grilled burgers. He shouldn't be hungry after the four soft tacos he'd eaten at Lola's, but Joey never passed up the opportunity to enjoy a meal—especially when it could be his last.

He blinked a few times, pushing his eyes to adjust. Look-ing from back to front, he counted only three of the booths occupied. The first held a couple of painters with splattered clothes. In the second sat two elderly women. The third was a man, alone. He wore a cowboy hat. Okay, it wasn't a cow-boy hat but a state trooper hat. Here was a man legally able to carry.

Joey took another step, and the trooper turned. Joey stopped so fast his expensive dress shoes squeaked on the floor. Trooper Foster? The man Lola hadn't wanted to smile at. The man whose touch had made the pretty Latina cringe. Lola's judgment was right on target. Not that anything explained her warm regard for Joey.

Foster's gaze met his. Joey saw recognition in the man's expression. Well, damn. This would be interesting. Or not.

Taking another step, Joey stayed ready to reach for his gun.

As Luke drove, his mind wandered back to that morning. To the tender way she'd cared for his wounds. Then his memory stuck to the teasing way she'd given him permission to kiss her.

"So if I kissed you right now, you wouldn't go Texan on me and freak out?"

"Haven't I told you? I'm originally from Alabama."

It was a piece of information about Kathy Callahan he hadn't known.

"You're not going to start freaking out on me again, are you, Bama?" Luke asked her, noticing her eyes were squeezed shut so tight that her brow creased. For the last ten minutes she hadn't said a word. Maybe he shouldn't have told her about the body in the porta-potty, but being honest had seemed his best option.

She rolled her head toward him and opened her eyes. She looked scared—and so damn vulnerable he ached to touch her. To offer her promises of not only keeping her safe but of a future with him. But those were promises she wouldn't want.

"Bama?" she repeated.

"You're from Alabama, right?"

She nodded. "How did you know?"

"You told me."

"When?"

He grinned. "Right before you kissed me back at my place."

"Oh." She blinked, and her brow pinched in thought.

He processed her reaction and joked, "Why? Is where you're from a secret?" But, damn, if he didn't want to uncover every one of her secrets.

She sat up straighter, and he read a surprising hint of defensiveness in her expression. "No. It was just a long time ago."

Obviously not long enough, if the look in her eyes was any indication.

She continued to stare. "However, for the record . . . I think you kissed me."

He didn't doubt the change of conversation was a cover-up, but if that helped, he'd play along. "Are we keeping a record? Like, a score? Who kisses whom?"

"No. But you're also the one who kissed me in the parking lot. I haven't kissed you . . ." She trailed off, blushing.

"Yet?" he asked.

"I didn't say that."

"It seemed to be implied. You didn't end your sentence."

She rolled her eyes. "I did end it."

"So we *are* keeping score?"

"No. But if we were, I'd win," she snapped.

"What fun would that be? Kissing me would be better."

"I don't know. I really like winning," she countered. Then she smiled, but it quickly faded, and she went back to being quiet, closed her eyes.

He reached out and brushed a hand over her shoulder. "Really. You okay?"

"If you're asking whether you need to start an argument with me again so I'll stop hearing and seeing things that aren't happening, the answer is no. But to answer the question if I'm okay . . . That's debatable. It's been a sucky—really, really sucky—day."

"I know. And I'm sorry," he said. He meant it. "I promise that I'm doing everything in my power to make sure it ends okay."

She fell back into her seat and looked at him. "It isn't all your fault."

"No? So which parts do you blame me for?" he asked, hoping that the question would help ease some of her frustration.

"I definitely blame you for throwing away my phone." Her mouth hinted at a smile, but then it faded and she nipped at her bottom lip. She shook her head and asked, "What do you think he died of? Do you think the smell could have killed him?"

Even though he knew she was half-serious, he couldn't help laughing. "I don't think so."

"Maybe a heart attack?"

"Could be, but . . . I doubt that, too."

"Why?" she asked.

"Because, considering what he's in town to do and the kind of people he hangs out with, him dying of natural causes just doesn't seem likely."

"So you think someone killed him." Concern darkened her eyes.

"That would be my first guess."

"Was he shot?"

"I didn't see a bullet wound."

"Was he bleeding, or did he have stab wounds?"

"I didn't see those either."

"Then how do you know he was dead? Did you even check?" she groused.

"He had his pants down."

She made the cutest expression, meaning *huh.* "And . . . what does that mean?"

He bit back a chuckle. "It means I'm a guy. And when a guy stumbles across another guy with his pants down, we don't do a lot of checking."

Kathy smiled, but the humor didn't linger. "You're positive he was dead?"

Luke sighed. "Afraid so. Not breathing, the bluish green complexion and the slight bloating around his face—that all pretty much nailed it down for me."

She crossed her arms over her chest and shivered. "Ugh. Do you think someone killed him while he was *in* the porta-potty?"

"Well, the only other option would be someone put him there after they killed him, and that wouldn't make sense." Luke shrugged.

"But he was reading a magazine. I think it was on birding."

"A birding magazine? That doesn't make sense either. I never figured him to be queer."

Kathy laughed. "You know what else doesn't make sense?"

"What?"

"That he wore sunglasses. It's dark in there. He wouldn't be able to read with sunglasses on."

"That's true," Luke realized. And for the life of him, he didn't know what any of it meant. Still, getting the hell away from one of Lorenzo's men, even a dead one, had seemed the right thing to do.

Half-crazed feminine laughter suddenly filled the car. "Oh, my gawd! Did you read his hat?"

"No." He studied her, concerned.

"It said: 'Shit happens and then you die'!"

Okay, she wasn't losing it. He belted out his own laughter, and then he had to wonder if maybe someone hadn't put that body in the porta-potty. But why? Then again, he shouldn't be spending too much energy worrying about who killed Lorenzo's man. Instead, he needed to figure out a plan to make sure he and Kathy stayed alive.

They drove a few more miles. "Where are we going now?" she asked, and gave Goodwill a loving pat. The dog, his head resting peacefully in her lap, opened his buggy eyes and glanced up at her.

Puppy love. For just a minute Luke remembered trying to talk his ex-wife into getting a dog. Sandy had been dead set against it. Unlike Kathy, she hadn't had time to nurture anything. Hadn't wanted to. Not even his child. The last thought sent a whole chestful of emotions rumbling through him, so he pushed it back.

"Do you even know where we're going?" Kathy asked.

"There's a place we can hide out for a while."

"Do you think Harry Johnson will be reporting the car stolen soon? Shouldn't we leave town?"

"That's what they think we'll do. And yes, someone could have easily picked up Harry, so there's a good chance he's already reported the car. We take it out on the freeway, we'll either be picked up by a trooper or spotted by Lorenzo's men. Lying low is safer. When we get in touch with Calvin, we'll meet him somewhere local." *If we get in touch with him.* He reminded himself it hadn't been that long.

Kathy reached for the dash. "Do you think they're talking about us on the radio?"

"It doesn't work," Luke said. "But I tried, too."

She leaned back and sighed, frustrated. He could relate wholeheartedly.

"Where is this place we're going to?" she asked.

"It's about six miles off Cypress Springs. I don't know about you, but I'm starving. Not too far from here there's a café-slash-convenience store. Figure we could grab something to eat—and maybe something to hold us over in the morning if I don't hear back from Calvin by then." He reached back into his jeans for his wallet and handed it to her. "See how much cash I got."

"I got credit cards, so we should be fine."

"We can't use those," he pointed out.

"Because they would trace them?"

"Right."

"I swear, I feel as if I'm living a *Law & Order* episode."

He shot her a sympathetic smile. "You should count all your cash, too."

She took his wallet, carefully set the sleepy puppy on the floor, unlocked her seat belt and then reached for her purse in back. While she was stretched across her seat, Luke shamelessly ogled her shapely backside.

Settling back, Kathy struggled to get her purse strap from Goodwill, who'd decided it was playtime. The puppy sank his teeth into the leather strap and yanked his head back and forth, mischievously growling. She finally managed to get the purse free.

"Do you really think this . . . this Calvin is going to call you back?"

"I'm sure he will," Luke replied and tried to remain positive.

Actually, the fact that Calvin hadn't already called was giving him a bad feeling. A *really* bad feeling. Like how deep was Lorenzo's penetration of the US justice system? Could he have found a way to infiltrate the US Marshals and Wit-Sec? It wasn't probable . . . but neither was it impossible.

He didn't want to jump to conclusions, though. Honestly, it had been only about six hours since he'd tried to reach Calvin. He figured he'd give his contact until morning, and between now and then he would come up with plan B.

While WitSec had preached against ever trying to contact anyone else, he knew a few names from the Bureau—names of people who four years ago might have considered him their friend. They were people who could check in with the US Marshals to see why Calvin was MIA . . . people whom he'd pushed out of his life while trying to deal with his grief.

"What if he doesn't?" Kathy asked.

"We'll handle it," he replied, pushing his past away and

concentrating on her. And damn, if she wasn't nice to concentrate on. Even frazzled, devoid of any makeup, she looked
great. A few light freckles spattered her nose. Without lipstick, her lips were a soft rose color.

And yet, while everything about her physical package,
from her hair to her toenails—which he'd noticed she kept
painted pink—had him enthralled, that wasn't what in-
trigued him most. It was who she was: the emotionally genu-
ine, dog-loving, kid-loving spirit.

He'd seen her cry once, when she found her son's turtle
dead in its fishbowl. Then she'd run out to the pet store and
bought another one the same size to spare her son the grief.
He'd seen her laugh herself silly when the pipe he was working on under her sink broke and water sprayed the hell out of
him—she hadn't given a damn about her carpet getting wet,
the way most women would have. He'd seen her push a
Tonka truck through the mud, getting down and dirty all
because her son asked her to play with him. She was so damn
unpretentious, so good-hearted—but still maintained a certain feminine sass.

Unexpectedly, a different image of her filled his mind:
pants down, squatting precariously behind that tree, furious
at him for interrupting her. Unable to stop himself, he
laughed uproariously.

"What?" Kathy asked.

He looked at her. "I'm never been so glad that I can pee
standing up."

Her mouth dropped open, and she slapped his arm. "I
knew sooner or later you would bring that up. You're not
gentleman enough to just forget it."

He continued to laugh and she continued to frown, but
he saw an amused twinkle in her eyes. Which was what he
loved about her most of all. They could tease each other,
laugh with and at each other. And damn, he liked who he
was around her. It reminded him of who he'd been before . . .

before all the bad stuff happened. The bad stuff summarized by the dead man's hat.

"Thank you," he said.

"For what?" Kathy asked.

"Everything," he said—and then felt silly. He pointed to his wallet. "Let's see how much money we have."

She opened his wallet, thumbed through, set the cash in her lap, then rechecked the billfold. "You have twenty-one dollars and . . ." She peered inside another compartment. Her gaze shot up, and her hazel eyes darkened.

"What . . . ?" he asked. Then he remembered.

"And two condoms," she continued.

He bit back a smile and took a chance that she was still in a teasing mood. "We could always buy more if you don't think that's enough."

Joey cautiously approached Foster, never forgetting exactly where his gun was, or where the other people in the café sat.

"Where is Donald?" the trooper asked.

When the man motioned for him to sit, Joey obliged. They had barely done more than nod at each other before the waitress, a woman in her midthirties with a pretty face, came to the table. Joey ordered coffee and a hamburger. No french fries. Normally, he'd have ordered the fries, but he remembered standing in front of Lola and wishing he hadn't been so lax about watching his waistline.

When the waitress walked away, Joey said, "The last time I saw Donald, he was sitting on the john, reading a birding magazine."

"Birding?" Foster chuckled. "I didn't know he was queer."

"Doesn't mean he's queer," Joey snapped.

"Right," said Foster. "Where was Donald when you were at the Latin Nookie's place."

"Latin Nookie?" Joey was more certain than ever that he disliked this asshole.

"Tell me you wouldn't want to tap that."

Joey breathed through his nose to try to get a handle on his composure; losing it right now wouldn't be good. Clenching his fists under the table, he spoke slowly. "I'd already left Donald at that point. Pablo said the redhead with Hunter had a cell phone, and the GPS led us to . . . that restaurant."

"Yeah, but it went back on the move." Foster pulled a phone from his front pocket. "Two Harley drivers picked it up off the road." He eyed Joey over the rim of his coffee cup. "Where did you leave Donald?"

"Some cheap motel off Highway 6." Joey hoped like hell that there was a cheap motel off Highway 6.

Foster nodded. "You know, Lorenzo is pretty unhappy with him. He was in charge of making Hunter disappear. I don't think Donald's long for this earth, if you know what I mean."

"I think you're right," Joey agreed.

"If you'd . . . take care of it, I'd bet Lorenzo would be ever so grateful."

The waitress headed back to drop off Joey's coffee. He picked up the cream pitcher and added some to his cup. "Normally, I'm not into taking care of those problems," he said, once the waitress was out of earshot.

"Lorenzo said as much," Foster admitted. "But he was hoping—"

Joey continued, "This time, I'll make an exception."

"I'll pass that along," Foster said. "I'm sure Lorenzo'll want to speak to you."

The idea of having to speak to his boss squirted acid into Joey's gut. "Where's Pablo and Corky?" he asked.

"Lorenzo has them stationed outside the local cop shop. He's worried Hunter will try to go there, or that someone will catch him and bring him in. He'd like the guy taken care of before the judicial system gets its hands on him."

"I thought he'd be halfway to Mexico by now," Joey mused.

"Which is probably why he isn't." Foster picked up his cup. "He knows it's what everyone expects, and so he's doing the opposite."

"Smart man," Joey said.

"Not smart enough to stay alive. We got to make sure of that."

"And how do we go about finding him?" Joey asked. "For that matter, how can you be sure he's still here?" The more information Joey had, the better.

"Lorenzo's sure. Hunter's attempting to reach someone. Someone your boss has already reached. All we—" The waitress headed over with Joey's burger, and Foster shut up. After the woman dropped off the plate, Joey picked up the conversation. "You said we'd have a fix on him by now. Do we have it?"

Foster looked at his watch. "We should have an exact location in a couple of hours. Best to take care of these things at night anyway. Don't you think? Besides, I figure that will give you just about enough time."

Kathy looked out the car window at the small café, while Luke checked the parking lot.

He'd left off his coat and tie. The blue oxford shirt looked good on him. It made his eyes looked bluer. Or maybe it was just the bruise under his eye.

He'd unbuttoned the top two buttons of his shirt. "I was just teasing about the condoms."

He'd already told her that once. She hadn't answered, because that would let him off the hook. And she hadn't let him off the hook because . . . well, for several reasons. The first was that she wondered whether he was really teasing. It appeared as if they may actually be staying the night together. And if they spent the night together . . . Her heart started to race. If they spent the night together, having sex was a real possibility.

Not that she wanted to have sex with him. Well, okay, so she'd wanted it that morning when she'd shown up at his place, frozen butter beans in tow. She'd admit that. Damn it, she'd also be honest with herself and admit that she probably still wanted it. But if Kathy had learned anything in this trek called life, it was that you didn't get everything you wanted—and sometimes when you did get it, you wished you hadn't. Just how unwise would it be to get sexually involved with this man, knowing what she knew about him? She needed to consider what she *didn't* know.

Which led her straight back to the condoms. The fact that he carried them in his wallet meant . . . it meant he was seeing someone. That he was having sex with someone. And the most logical suspect was still Claire, the landlady. Kathy didn't care that Luke insisted the woman was too old. Life had taught her different. Hell, for all Kathy knew, maybe all this pointed to a psychological defect on her part. Maybe for some unknown reason she found herself only attracted to men who ultimately wanted older women.

He touched her shoulder. "Why don't you go on inside, order us a couple of hamburgers to go. Then pick up some muffins or stuff to eat tomorrow morning. I'll walk Goodwill and take care of my own bathroom problems." Without removing his fingers from her shoulder, he glanced around, then reached down to grab the leash at her feet. "It's probably best if we're not seen together in public. If anything seems suspicious, just get out. Get out fast."

She nodded, desperately trying not to think about the tingle his touch was causing in her shoulder—a tingle that stemmed from the possibility of having sex with him tonight.

Which she wasn't going to do. Right?

When the answer didn't immediately echo back, she

pushed the question aside for another. "What do you like on your burger?"

"Don't make any special orders. The objective is to get the food and get out as soon as possible. You got that?"

She nodded.

His hand moved up to her chin, and his thumb traced her bottom lip. "Look around before you walk all the way inside. Lorenzo hires men by the pound. He likes them big, and he likes them to dress nice. If there are any big bozos in suits, get the hell out of there. You understand?"

She nodded again.

His hand shifted to the side of her neck, electrifying nerve ending upon nerve ending. "Have you forgiven me yet? For the condom remark."

"Not yet," she lied. She got out of the car and took off for the café.

Joey sat across from Foster and wanted to ask more questions about who Hunter was reaching out to, but if he appeared too curious he might make the trooper suspicious. Then Joey recalled what Foster had said.

"Time for what?" he asked.

"Time to eat your burger and take care of Donald. And make sure you dump the body so it won't be found anytime soon."

How could a person talk about eating and killing in the same sentence? Joey wondered.

The waitress moved in and smiled. "Is everything okay?"

Joey nodded. "Just fine."

"You know what? Bring me one of those, too, sweetcakes." Foster's gaze was on the waitress's breasts.

She frowned. "I'll get you a burger, as long as you don't call me sweetcakes again."

Foster frowned. "Just get me a freaking hamburger, or I swear I'll talk to Mr. James about firing your fat ass."

"This fat ass, as well as the rest of me—and not just my breasts you've been gaping at like a horny fifteen-year-old—is Mr. James's daughter's fat ass. So good luck with that." She swung around, not looking too worried about his threat or her slightly large backside.

Joey wanted to laugh, but something warned him any reaction might encourage Foster to become a bigger problem. Once again, he thought about Lola being out on the road alone with the likes of men such as this corrupt trooper dropping by.

Foster's phone rang, and he pulled it off his belt. "Yeah, I'm with him now. He said he'd do it." He paused. "Really. No problem. I'll be waiting. Yes."

A bell jingled, and Joey's gaze left Foster. The bright sunlight from outside spilled in as a woman walked through the café's front door. Recognition hit like a kick in the balls. Goddamn. If it wasn't the redhead. His gut went rock hard. His gaze shot to the trooper, who was still deep in conversation. Would Foster know what the woman looked like? Hell yeah, he would. God Almighty, this was going to get ugly.

Reaching into his suit, he drew his gun. Keeping it under the table, he pointed it at the trooper.

Chapter Seventeen

Luke watched Kathy walk inside the café. He searched the parking lot with his eyes again, checking one more time. Goodwill put his paws on the side of the car door, looked out and whined.

"You miss her already, don't you? Me too."

He picked up the puppy and attached the leash. The puppy looked up at him and then back out the window at the café, and whined as if he wanted out, to run after Kathy. Luke fought the same need, but he told himself she was fine.

"Separation anxiety," he muttered.

The puppy barked again.

"Only a few hours with her, and you don't want to let her out of your sight." He sighed. "I know—she's something, isn't she?" he asked the dog. "She got to me just about that fast, too. But you're lucky: she's easier on dogs than men."

Luke got out of the car and put the puppy down. "Nope," he said, when the dog started sniffing at his shoe. He gave the leash a tug. "I figure we both probably need to go, but my shoes aren't going to be involved this time. I work hard at not pissing on them, and I'd appreciate it if you'd do the same."

The puppy looked up at him with those soulful eyes and barked.

"Okay," Luke laughed. "Here's the deal. You make her happy. I like seeing her happy. So I'm tolerating you. But no pissing on my shoes."

The puppy hunched down on his paws and growled.

"Okay, you're cute. I'll give you that." Luke knelt and gave the dog a good scrubbing behind the ears, then stared at the café again. "You're one lucky son of a bitch. You see, you're going to get to go home with her. Me? Well . . . I'm not sure she's so willing." He smiled at the dog. "You'll like the kid. I do."

A Ford Taurus passed the café and slowed. Luke made sure it didn't pull in, made sure it didn't hold any of Lorenzo's men. When the car continued past, he relaxed. He stood and walked the dog to the edge of the lot where a tree would hide all the business being done.

"How about we make a pact," he told the dog. "My job is to get Miss Callahan back to her son safe and sound. No matter what the cost. If there's trouble, I'm getting between it and her. This means your job is to stay out of trouble's way. Because I'm not going to worry about your canine ass if trouble arrives—you got that?" He watched the dog raise its leg. "Oh, and you keep making her smile, too. I really like seeing that."

Goodwill barked, and Luke nodded. "Glad you see things my way."

* * *

Kathy had stood in the tiny, closed-off entryway of the café for a minute, collecting her courage to move inside. The moment the café door swished closed, darkness surrounded her. She blinked, giving her eyes time to adjust. Her pulse throbbed in her neck as she stood in the entrance, waiting and inhaling the smell of fat-laden food, like burgers, french fries, and were those onion rings?

Her stomach rumbled, partly from hunger but mostly from fear that someone might turn around, point a finger at her and accuse her of stealing a car. Then the memory of gunshots echoed in her head.

A couple more blinks had the darkness fading. Kathy cut her gaze around. Two men wearing white paint-splattered overalls sat in one booth. Two women, grandmotherly types, occupied another.

Blinking faster, she focused on a dark corner. Her heart dropped into her empty stomach when she spotted a man, his back to her, wearing a trooper hat and uniform. She took a step back, and then her focus flipped across the booth and saw another man . . . a big man wearing a suit.

The breath caught in her throat, and Luke's words shot through her mind: *If there are any big bozos in suits, get the hell out of there—and do it fast.*

She went to take another step back, but her feet felt nailed to the floor. Trying not to scream, trying not to call attention to herself, she realized that the suited big man was staring at her. Right at her. Oh, Lordie.

He shook his head ever so slightly, and his gaze flickered to the left. To her left. Left? Where the door was.

A scream climbed up her throat. She swallowed it. Mentally un-nailing her feet, she swung around and shot out of the café at a dead run. She ran toward the car but Luke wasn't there.

"What is it?" He appeared at her side, puppy in one hand, as he zipped his jeans with the other, as if he'd been "watering a plant," as her son referred to it. "What happened?" he asked.

"We . . . They . . . Shit!" Tears formed in her eyes. She couldn't talk.

He clearly saw something was wrong. He grabbed her elbow and rushed her to the car. In seconds he had her in the passenger seat, Goodwill deposited in her lap, and he was darting around the car.

"What happened?" he asked again, sliding behind the wheel and slamming the door.

"A trooper and a . . . a big guy in a suit."

Luke cursed. Starting the car, he swung around and looked back at the café. "Did they see you?"

She nodded.

He revved the engine. "Do you think they recognized you?"

She nodded again.

He flew out of the parking lot, tires squealing. Kathy's throat stung with emotion, so she allowed a few tears to flow. Hey, she deserved a good cry at this point. Then again, she didn't care if she deserved it or not; she was taking one.

"Buckle up!" Luke kept staring into the rearview mirror, his hands moving from the gearshift to the wheel so fast that she got dizzy.

"I want this to end. I want it to end now!" She ignored Goodwill, his paws on her chest, licking away her tears as fast as she could cry them.

"Are you sure they recognized you?" Luke's gaze kept darting from the rearview mirror to the road.

"Pretty sure." She hiccupped and set the dog on the floorboard.

Luke stopped looking in the rearview mirror to glance at her, concern flashing in his blue eyes. "I'm so damn sorry. I should have gone in myself. I didn't think—"

She shook her head. "They would have come after you for sure."

"Maybe, but—"

"No buts!" She dropped her face in her hands and tried to control her terror.

"Are you okay?" he asked.

She stared at him. "No. I'm not okay. It's not your fault," she added with a sniffle, "but I'm not cut out for this. I'm not ballsy enough. I used my quota of ballsy when I whacked that guy on the head. That's all the ballsiness I've got."

He changed gears, pushing the car to go faster. "As hard as it is to think of you with balls, I have to tell you that you've done better today than some guys I know who are quite proud of their own pair. You're doing great. Just keep telling yourself that." He turned the car onto another road without slowing. The back wheels skidded, and the back of the Charger swerved. "They don't seem to be following us. Are you sure they recognized you?"

"Yes," she answered. "The big guy in the suit nodded at me." She bit on her lip and tried to remember exactly what happened. "He shook his head 'no,' as if telling me not to come in. Then he . . . he looked at the door as if telling me to leave."

"Umm," Luke said.

Didn't he believe her? "What are you saying?" she asked.

"I just . . ." He frowned. "I'm not saying you're wrong. But I don't think Lorenzo's man would tell you to leave."

"Maybe it was because the trooper was there?" she suggested.

He scratched his five-o'clock shadow and divided his focus among the rearview mirror, her and the road. "If the trooper was with Lorenzo's man, odds are he's working for Lorenzo, too. Lorenzo's goal and his men's goal is to k . . . catch us. " Luke shook his head after stumbling over the word and continued. "If it was Lorenzo's man, letting you walk out of that café would not have accomplished his goal."

While she didn't like thinking she'd been wrong or enjoy him telling her she was wrong, she could see Luke's point. Could she have misread what happened? Maybe? Possibly? Oh, hell. Only a few hours ago she'd been hearing gunshots that weren't there. Seeing flashbacks of the big guy on Luke's bathroom floor. Perhaps it wasn't so farfetched that she'd thought the man in the booth made a few head gestures he hadn't.

Her empty stomach grumbled as she remembered the hearty aroma of the diner. "I guess I should have ordered the burgers, huh?"

"Oh, hell no. With that trooper there? Getting out was the right thing to do, no doubt about it." He reached over and slipped his hand in hers. "You did good." He squeezed tight. "I'm going to get you out of this, okay? I promise."

She glanced at their linked hands. His palm felt warm against hers. It was comforting, a little like a hug.

A tiny voice inside her said she needed to pull away, to keep her distance emotionally. Call her weak, but she didn't. Her hand remained snug in his, safe and protected. She needed the human contact, the warmth.

Not that she'd let it become a habit, or that she'd let it lead to anything else. As in something else that would require the use of the two condoms in his wallet. Nope. She was absolutely not going to let this lead to condom usage.

Sure, she'd thought about it, thought about it a lot, but she wasn't going there.

His thumb brushed over the back of her hand. Just a thumb, just a hand, but it all felt like so much more. Probably because she *wanted* more. Desperately. Was that insane?

She yanked her hand away so fast he glanced at her. "Cramp," she lied, and shook her hand.

Foster closed his phone and stared directly into Joey's eyes. Joey had stopped listening to the conversation, and now he wondered if his lack of attention had been a mistake. Had Foster gotten wind of the pregnant blonde Joey had told to hide in the closet?

"What?" Foster asked, just before the same question slipped from Joey's lips.

Joey shrugged.

"You were smiling," Foster accused.

"Oh." Hell yeah, he'd been smiling. The redhead had gotten the message and left the diner. "Since when is smiling a crime?"

"It makes you look like an idiot," Foster said.

Damn, Joey really didn't like this guy. He almost said as much; but then, Foster seemed the kind of jerk who'd take pleasure in knowing it, so Joey kept his dislike to himself. For now at least.

But later? Later, if Foster proved to be a threat to the redhead, that might be a different story. Foster would know exactly what Joey thought about him.

He picked up his burger, took a hearty bite, chewed and swallowed. "I'd say smiling makes me look happy." And he was. He was practically blissful. Hell, luck—or was it the Higher Power—had decided to shine on him.

Or, more than likely, fate had decided to shine on the redhead. Joey wasn't sure his ass was worth any shining. Not that his self-worth or lack of it mattered right now. He was just thrilled he'd done something right. While he knew his job was far from over, getting that mother out of the cafe without Foster seeing her was practically a miracle. And yeah, that made him want to smile.

Strangely enough, he'd been feeling happy since he'd laid eyes on Lola. But thinking about Lola and looking at Foster put an end to his good feelings.

The waitress dropped off Foster's hamburger. The man practically growled at her, but she seemed immune to his sour attitude.

"Thank you," Joey said, when Foster didn't. He might not be big on talking, but common courtesies he managed. The waitress smiled at him and left as quickly as she'd dropped off the plate.

"That was Lorenzo on the phone," Foster remarked. "Boss said for you to take care of Donald, but . . ." He paused. "He wants a finger. For proof."

Disgust hit Joey, and he dropped his burger. He'd give Lorenzo the finger, all right, just not one Lorenzo wanted. "Guess I'd better get going then."

"I guess you should," Foster agreed, smiling as if he enjoyed Joey's revulsion. "I'll call you as soon as I have something. Get Donald out of the way—and make sure he doesn't pop up anytime soon, if you know what I mean. We don't need people looking into that right now."

"Prunes, sauerkraut, deviled ham, Fiber One cereal, pickled beets and pork-'n'-beans." Kathy looked over her shoulder. Luke appeared to be checking the windows to see if they were locked, while Kathy had started to search for anything to fill the gaping holes in their bellies. She gazed again at the open pantry. "Who on God's green earth eats this stuff?"

Luke looked back and frowned. "She has digestive problems."

"Well, no wonder she has digestive problems if she . . ."

Until that moment, Kathy hadn't bothered asking who the tiny lakeside cabin belonged to. Or how Luke knew the key would be under the flowerpot on the side of the house.

"Whose place is this?" she asked. *Don't let him say his landlady Claire. Please, don't let him say—*

"Claire's."

Kathy rolled her eyes and grabbed the cans of deviled ham and pork-'n'-beans out of the pantry and set them, none too gently, on a counter. Then, unable to help herself, she turned and let him have it with both barrels. "She has the key to your place. You know where her little love cabin is and where the hidden key is. You know all about her sensitive digestive system, and you still want me to believe that you two are just friends? Do you think I'm an idiot?"

Luke held up his right index finger as if to make a point. "Believe me, if I had a choice not to hear about her digestive problems, I'd take it. I swear that's half of what she ever talks about."

"And what is the other half? Whispered sweet nothings?"

He pretended to shiver in repulsion. "You know, you obviously have a problem."

"*I* have a problem?" she shot back. "You're sleeping with a woman who has to eat prunes and yet manages to down pork-'n'-beans!"

His laugh filled the one-room cabin. And while she fought it, his reaction made her want to smile. She bit her lip. Then she wondered if her husband's new wife ate prunes. God, she hoped so. And she hoped they gave her gas. She hoped right now the woman was pooting her way across Paris. It would serve both the woman and Tom right. Although she felt sorry for her son.

"See, that's what I mean." Luke opened a cabinet door above the fridge and pulled out a toolbox, and Kathy watched his arm muscles flex. Yup, that shirt fit him well enough that it didn't hide his physique.

"What do you mean, that's what you mean?" she asked.

He set the toolbox on the small wooden two-person kitchen table and looked at her. "The fact that you don't believe me when I tell you that I'm not involved with Claire." He pulled out a pair of pliers, went to the kitchen window and twisted something on the lock. "Why don't you believe me?"

She arched a brow at him. "Because the proof is in the pudding. Or should I say 'the prunes'?" She reached back and pulled out the appropriate bag.

He smiled—the kind of smile that only appeared at the corners of his eyes. "Okay, correct me if I'm wrong, but you believe I'm with the FBI. You believe that I'm with WitSec."

"WitSec?"

He sighed. "The Witness Protection Program. You believe that, right?"

"Yeah." She looked for an electric can opener, and when one wasn't out, she started opening drawers. On her second try she found an old-fashioned, hand-crank kind.

"So why do you insist on believing that I'm lying when I tell you I'm not sleeping with a woman twice my age? To me it seems *that* scenario is easier to believe than the others."

She pulled out the can opener. She knew exactly why she refused to believe him: Because she'd found it so hard to believe when Tom had taken her out to eat on what she'd thought would be a romantic evening, only to tell her he was in love with his secretary. His much older, dumpy secretary. Something that went against every movie or book ever made. How did that happen?

"Why is that?" he repeated, pulling her out of her reverie.

"Because it's about sex. Men always lie about sex," she rationalized. And there was some truth to her statement.

"We do?" Luke asked.

"Yup. You do." She fought to get the can opener started in the can.

Luke's shoulder brushed hers as he pulled the device from

her hands. He opened the beans. Then he handed over the can and dropped the opener back on the counter and asked, "Who says men always lie about sex?"

"*Cosmo, Redbook,* and *Complete Woman.*" She looked around. "They all pretty much agree." She looked around again. "I don't suppose we have any bread, huh?"

"No. But I think I saw some crackers in the fridge."

"Crackers in the fridge?" she asked.

He held up his hands. "I didn't put them there."

She opened the refrigerator, grabbed the Saltines, dropped them on the table and then dumped the beans into a bowl.

As she looked around for a microwave, he cleared his throat to get her attention. "And you believe everything you read in those magazines?"

"Not everything. I didn't believe the article about how a woman could actually orgasm from sneezing. Not that sneezing doesn't feel good, but . . ." She looked up and found him staring at her, smiling.

"But you believe everything written about men involving sex."

"Pretty much," she admitted, and made a full circle, searching. "There's no microwave?"

He shrugged. "Claire doesn't believe in them. She's convinced that it's radio waves causing her irritable bowel syndrome." He snagged a pack of crackers, opened it, popped one in his mouth and groaned with pleasure. "Nothing like a good cracker. Almost as good as a sneeze." He grinned.

She studied him while she snatched a cracker of her own and savored it. Could he be telling the truth about Claire? She knelt and opened a few more cabinets until she found a pot suitable to heat the beans. While she was down there, Goodwill came bouncing over.

"I'm going to feed you too, buddy," she promised.

Standing, she pointed the pot at Luke. "So if you're not involved with Claire, how did you know about this place?"

She poured the bowl of beans into the pot and turned on the stove. The gas outlet gave a few puffs and clicks, and then the flame burst to life. She turned down the heat. Beans weren't her favorite, but with rations so low, burning them would be a felony. Right up there with stealing a car. She inwardly flinched and pushed those thoughts, along with the others, to the back of her mind.

Luke leaned against the side of the fridge, munched on crackers and studied her as if mentally chewing on something also. She hoped like hell the puzzle he was trying to solve wasn't her. Not that he would succeed—she hadn't really figured herself out yet. Probably because that would mean she'd have to sift through the crap that life had tossed in her lap, starting with her father and then her ex. Why spend time sifting through crap when she'd gotten so good at ignoring it?

"And how did you know where to find the key?" she added, opening the can of deviled ham. Crumbling some crackers on another plate, she added half the meat and set it down for Goodwill.

When she rose, Luke was staring at her chest. She gave her green tank top a good upward yank, and he frowned. Then he seemed to process her question. "Claire had me come out and fix the leaky toilet. I'm a plumber, remember?" He continued to stare, but not at her chest. He stared at her eyes, as if trying to read her.

That scrutiny annoyed her. She didn't want him figuring her out. If she could ignore all her own crap, so should the rest of the world. "And here I thought you were a cop," she muttered.

"A federal agent," he corrected, and crossed his arms over his chest. "And it's not the same thing," he cut her off.

She couldn't help it; she shot him a coy look. "What? Are your guns bigger than theirs?"

He smiled in response. "You know what I think?"

"That you need a bigger gun."

Happy with her retort, she turned and found the silver-ware drawer, retrieved a spoon to stir the pot. The slightly sweet smell of brown-sugar-seasoned beans followed steam up to her nose, and her stomach grumbled.

"I think you're scared. And I think you use humor to hide it." He moved next to her. "I also think the reason you don't believe me has something to do with some guy cheating on you, maybe with an older woman—and there was probably a cop involved." He pushed a strand of hair from her cheek and studied her.

He wasn't one hundred percent right, but he was pretty darn close to all her dirty laundry. Too close to her crap.

Almost as if he read the *No Trespassing* sign being nailed up in her mind, he leaned down and inhaled the steam rising from the beans. "I also think"—he looked up and met her gaze—"that I must be starving. Because when pork-'n'-beans starts smelling like ambrosia, something ain't right."

She dipped her spoon into the beans for a taste—not so much from hunger, but to have something to do with her hands. But the moment the food touched her tongue, her hunger returned. "They *are* ambrosia." A little sauce dripped onto her chin and she wiped it away with her finger.

"Really?"

He caught her hand and brought it to his mouth. His lips closed around her finger, and a warm wetness sur-rounded the digit. She felt his tongue slide against the un-derside of her knuckle. Then, slowly, he pulled her moist finger free.

God help her, if she didn't think about sticking her finger straight back into the pot and offering for him to lick some more. Of all the food and sex talks at the Divorced, Desper-ate and Delicious club, pork-'n'-beans had never been con-sidered. Wait until she told Lacy and Sue!

His soft gaze locked on her eyes again, but this time she

didn't think he was too close. To the contrary, she wanted him closer.

"Yup, ambrosia." He leaned in, so close his breath brushed her cheek. So close that the pork-'n'-beans lost all appeal, despite her hunger. All she wanted, all she could smell, was him. Fresh grass and mint.

"You know," he said, "I could probably stand here all day and just stare at you."

Her heart hiccupped. "You could?"

"I could if my stomach wasn't chewing on my backbone."

She looked down to get away from his smiling eyes, needing a second to sort through the feelings that were chasing logic right out of her. Feelings that said she wanted him to kiss her. That said, the hell with being logical about getting involved with him. Feelings that said: For God's sake you almost died today, shouldn't you learn to enjoy the moment? Go for it, take the most of right now. Use that pot of beans to the fullest.

Ah, but before she surrendered to those feelings, she needed to think. And to think hard.

She dropped her gaze and saw Goodwill. Then she smiled and let out a deep breath. "There might be another reason, too."

"A reason for what?" He ran a hand up her arm, goose bumps chasing after it.

She looked up. "For you not to stand here."

His mouth drew nearer. "Why's that?"

"Because Goodwill is about pee on your shoe again."

"Damn!" He jumped back right in time. "What is it with this dog and my shoes?"

"Maybe your feet stink," Kathy said, and laughed so hard she bumped into the counter.

"My feet don't stink! Well, they didn't before he pissed on them." He looked down at the dog, then at her. "You'd better make sure he doesn't go on the carpet. Claire will have a fit."

Kathy glanced around. "That carpet looks like it's thirty years old."

"Yeah, but she's at least seventy, so to her it's practically brand-new."

Luke grabbed some paper towels and cleaned up Goodwill's oops, then washed his hands.

Kathy didn't stop smiling as she found two plates and set them on the table. Then she emptied the rest of the deviled ham into a bowl, added some mayonnaise and gave it a good stir. "For our crackers," she told him. "We can pretend it's caviar."

"Yum," he replied.

"Yum?" She looked up, still stirring. "You like caviar?"

His gaze was on her chest again. "Do I like what?" He looked up.

If it was any other man, she would have called him on it. She didn't, though. Vaguely, she remembered not calling him on it when she'd first arrived at his house. Of course, at the time she'd been planning on sleeping with him. She'd dressed to impress, to elicit exactly this reaction.

It had seemed like such a good plan, then. Exactly what were her plans now?

Chapter Eighteen

Joey used the small flashlight on his keychain to see in the dark. He covered his nose and eyed the corpse still positioned on the throne just like it had been left, Donald still completely engrossed in the birding magazine. "Told you I'd come back. Bet you didn't believe me, did you?"

Even with his hand over his nose, the smell crawled up Joey's sinuses. "Is that you or . . . ?" He looked around the porta-potty. "It's the crapper, right? Yeah, I'd say so." He grabbed the magazine from Donald's lap and slipped it inside the waistband of his pants. "Get any good birding tips?"

Pocketing his flashlight, he reached down and used everything he had to lift Donald and yank up the guy's pants. The man's legs remained bent, which made getting him out of the enclosed plastic shithouse a little like getting a square peg out of a round hole. Finally, after several bangs and clatters, nearly knocking over the entire construction and hitting his toe at least twice, he managed to get Donald out.

If that wasn't hard enough, fitting a stiff, bent-legged man in the car proved even more trying. "Damn, you're just dead weight," Joey muttered. Then he laughed at his unintentional pun.

Thankfully, the potty position was almost the same as the backseat position, and once he had Donald in the car, getting him set up was a piece of cake. Nevertheless, Donald's hands were still open as if he waiting for someone to pass him a plate of food.

Joey picked up the man's hat, which had fallen to the ground, and set it on Donald's head. Then, just to make a point, he reached around the dead man and buckled him in again.

Job done, he leaned against the car to catch his breath. "I found you a final resting place. It's just a few miles up the road. It's got some nice trees, and there's a little creek close by. It's probably better than you deserve. Better than Freddy got. I picked up a shovel at Wal-Mart, and we should have you a few feet under in a couple of hours." Joey wiped some sweat from his brow and looked at Donald's hands, which were still outstretched. "You can keep all your fingers, too. Lorenzo can just go to hell as far as I'm concerned."

Looking up at the dark sky, he took his weight off his bad toe. Then, wanting to tell someone but having limited options, he said conversationally, "Oh, you'll never guess what happened. The redhead walked into the café where I met that Foster idiot. I don't like him any more than I liked you. Maybe even less." He smiled. "I actually managed to get her out of there before he saw her. I did a good thing, Donald! Damn, if that doesn't feel good."

Joey felt the smile slip away. "Of course, Foster swears we'll have their location sometime tonight. And if that's the case, she's not out of the woods yet." He pulled the birding magazine from the waistband of his pants and tossed it onto the backseat. "But you know, my mama used to say it wasn't over until you quit fighting. Not that she was amazingly wise, but she had her moments." In the distance, Joey heard an owl. "Point is, I'm not through fighting. And yeah, I know you'd say I won't win. I'll admit there's a good chance I'll end up like you—dead and waiting for someone to bury my ass."

Leaning his head back, Joey stared upward. "You know, in New York you would never see this many stars. I kind of like Texas. Met some nice people here." His mind went to Lola, her sweet smile, the way her eyes lit up. *Maybe you come back and talk to me,* she'd said, and damn, if she hadn't seemed to mean it. "Hell, if I live through this mess, maybe I will go back." He looked at Donald. "But what are the chances of me really living through this, huh?"

Closing his eyes a minute, he wondered about dying. Then he thought about his life. Not that his life offered a lot to think about. When he opened his eyes, he glared at Donald. "How sad is it that I'm standing here talking to a dead man? Hell, I've probably talked more to you these past few hours than I've talked to anyone in the past six months. Pretty damn sad, isn't it?"

He shut the car's back door, crawled behind the steering wheel and drove off to bury the man who was ostensibly his best friend.

Luke watched Kathy make swirly shapes in the sauce on her plate. "Hand me the rest of those beans if you're not going to eat them."

"I was going to give the rest to the puppy," she replied.

He swallowed a bite of cracker. "Do you know what beans will do a dog's digestive tract?"

A smile brightened her eyes. "The same thing it does to Claire's?"

He laughed. "Seriously, you're not feeding that dog beans if he's staying in this one-room cabin with us." He motioned for her to pass him the bowl.

She handed it over and grinned. "Maybe I shouldn't let you have more either."

"I think my digestive system can handle it." He emptied the last of the beans onto his plate and added, "Besides, I found another can of deviled ham. It was pushed in the back of the pantry. You can feed that to the dog.

For the last half hour they'd sat in Claire's tiny cabin, feasted on crackers spread with deviled ham and whatever Kathy added to it, a side dish of canned pork-'n'-beans, and washed the cuisine down with tap water. By all rights, it should have been a piss-poor dinner, but Luke couldn't remember ever enjoying a meal more. Hunger made one appreciate food, but he didn't fool himself; it wasn't the hunger. His pleasure came from the company—along with the fact that Kathy had seemed to shed the negative effects of the day.

The puppy nipping at their feet brought on a discussion of Kathy's son and how he'd been begging for a dog. The menu selection led the conversation to the kind of sandwiches their moms used to pack in their school lunches.

"Yeah, I've had deviled ham before, but mostly at friend's houses," he answered Kathy's question. Not that the subject matter was important. They could have discussed the different shades of black for all he cared. Watching the way she'd close her lips around her fork and daintily pull it from her mouth, the way her eyes crinkled at the corners when she laughed, he couldn't deny it—Kathy Callahan was under his skin, heating his blood, and he liked having her there.

Occasionally, their knees would brush against each other under the table, and the accidental touch had a tickle of lust swelling things down south. Of course, as much as he liked that tickle, he never completely let down his guard. His gun rested on the counter within arm's reach. He'd already checked to make sure the windows were locked, and from where he sat now, the kitchen window offered him a view of the dirt road leading to the house. He'd been out here several weekends and knew a car's headlights could be seen half a mile away. And the closest neighbor was more than a mile away.

"You've seriously never eaten a banana and mayonnaise sandwich?" she asked, and used a paper towel as if it were a fine cloth napkin.

"Bananas belong in pudding and muffins, not in a sandwich, and definitely not with mayonnaise. It must be an Alabama thing."

"It's a *Southern* thing," she corrected, and he remembered getting the feeling there was something about being from Alabama that bothered her.

"Where in Alabama did you grow up?"

He saw that disturbed flicker in her eyes again. "Mostly in the northeast."

The vagueness in her answer spoke volumes. He knew all about vagueness. It meant: don't go there. Normally, he respected boundaries. Hell, he'd been respecting her boundaries and barriers for almost three years. Somehow, today changed all that. His desire to tear down all her barricades was overwhelming.

Not now, a voice of wisdom warned.

Later?

Hell, he wanted a later with her, a later without barriers and boundaries. And, preferably, without clothes.

"How about fried bologna sandwiches?" she asked.

He stared into her hazel eyes, at the freckles across her nose, and he made a promise to himself: if they got out of this, he'd make "later" happen.

"I've heard of fried bologna. But no, I usually had tuna fish or peanut butter and jelly. With my mandatory box of raisins. My mom never forgot the raisins."

She smiled, but the expression was brief. "You . . . you told me once your mom passed away when you were young. Is that true, or were you lying about that, like you lied about your name?"

His knee brushed hers, and neither of them moved away. "She died when I was eight."

Kathy bit her lip. "And about your sister and your niece and nephew. The accident. Is that true, too?"

"Unfortunately." The memory stung, but amazingly, time had eased the grief.

Her knee bumped his again. "That must have been hard. I'm sorry," she said, and he watched her fold and unfold her paper towel. "So everything you told me before was true except your name?" She looked up, waiting, as if so much rode on his answer.

"Pretty much," he said.

While he didn't want to think about it, he knew his own vagueness had returned. He hazily remembered her asking once if he'd been married. He'd held up his left hand and said he'd never worn a wedding ring. And he hadn't. Sandy hadn't been much for traditions. Instead of rings, they'd bought each other expensive watches.

Maybe his unwillingness then to talk about his marriage, the abortion and the divorce, while open about the other losses in his life, was because it would have brought on more questions. Or maybe it didn't have anything to do with her, but about him. Maybe it was because he hadn't allowed himself to accept his own part in that marriage's failure. Sandy had aborted his child—and for that he would never forgive her—but the death of his marriage? How much had his grief over his sister and her kids played a part? Maybe more than he wanted to admit.

"What about Claire?" Kathy looked up at him through dark lashes while she rolled her napkin.

Luke shook off thoughts of the past. "Damn! There is absolutely nothing going on between Claire and me!"

"So who is she?"

"Who is who?" he asked. "Claire's my landlady. Like I told you."

"No," Kathy said. "Who are you involved with?"

"I'm not involved with—"

"Fine, don't tell me." She wadded her paper towel in her hands, jumped up and started to walk away.

"Wait!" He reached out, snagged her arm and pulled her back. She almost stepped on the puppy, lost her footing and landed in his lap with a thump. Not that he minded.

Her hands shot to his shoulders and she started to get up. He caught her around her waist. His intent wasn't to stop her if she really wanted to go, just to let her know he liked having her there. Their eyes met, and her attempt to rise faltered. She let herself settle back. Her breath caught, ever so slightly. He knew her mind had taken her back to the same place his had: his kitchen that morning.

Her backside was a sweet weight on his lap. His body reacted, and he was certain she could feel it.

He brushed her hair from her cheek and met her eyes. "I'm not involved with anyone. I swear to you." He said the words as an absolute, leaving no room for vagueness.

She pursed her lips. "You had condoms for a reason."

He bit back a smile. "Okay, that much is true."

"But you're still not going to admit it?"

He didn't answer for a moment. Then, seeing the look in her eyes, he caught her before she attempted to jump up. "Okay, I'll tell you. There was someone."

"So you lied to me earlier!" She tried to get up.

"Let me explain. Give me that much." Especially when he wanted so much more.

"Do I have to be in your lap for you to explain?" she asked.

"No, but I really like you here."

She relaxed again, and the feel of her bottom was heaven.

"Okay, explain," she said.

Her scooped top had slipped down an inch, and he found it hard to concentrate. "I wasn't involved, but I was hoping to get involved."

"What happened?" She sounded disbelieving.

"I don't know. She was hard to read. She'd invite me over to do odd jobs . . . some of them I knew weren't even real jobs."

He saw her eyes widen.

"She'd flirt with me something awful," he continued. "Tease me. Tempt me. I can't even begin to tell you how many cold showers she put me through."

"Not true!" She studied him beneath her lashes. "I read somewhere that men don't really take cold showers. They just . . ." She blushed.

He laughed, and damn how he enjoyed the color in her cheeks. Brushing her hair over her shoulder, because he didn't want his view blocked of her cleavage, he admitted, "Okay, you're right . . . we don't take that many cold showers." He had to stop himself from laughing again. "But what happened when I got home isn't the point. The point is, I'd get to her place and she'd be dressed in some cute short-shorts and some top just low enough"—he traced the scooped neckline of her shirt, careful not to touch too much, to overstep—"to drive a man wild. Sort of like this one."

"Maybe she wasn't dressing up for you. Maybe that's what she'd been wearing all day," Kathy suggested.

"Oh, she was doing it for me. Or at least to get to me. I knew that. She knows it, too."

His hands wanted to roam, to cup her breasts and hold her close, but his gut said it was too soon. To ward off temptation, he ran a finger over her lips—which brought on a different kind of temptation. The two kisses he'd managed to steal today had been amazing.

"You seem pretty sure of yourself," she said.

"I am. You see, I could smell the soap she used—it smelled like peaches. And when I'd go into her bathroom, I could tell she'd just showered. For me. Especially for me." He leaned in just a bit and could almost smell the hint of peaches on her skin now. Damn, he liked peaches.

She cut her eyes down at him. "A woman has to shower sometime." One eyebrow arched upward, giving her expression a touch of scorn, but there was just enough tease in her voice to let him know she was enjoying this.

That was all the encouragement he needed. "But then, whenever I'd try to get a little close, you know, just lean in a bit, she'd pull back. I'd ask her out to dinner, and she'd turn me down. But she never stopped smiling at me. Or dressing up or showering." He studied her mouth. "And she'd do this thing with her teeth and her bottom lip, gently tugging on it. I think she knew it drove me wild."

Kathy stopped doing precisely that. "I *know* she didn't do that on purpose. That's just a bad habit."

He grinned. "Needless to say, I kept hoping . . . hoping that the next time I leaned in . . ." He inched his mouth closer to hers. "That she wouldn't"—his lips brushed hers ever so slightly—"pull away."

Chapter Nineteen

Luke kept the kiss light and slow, hoping Kathy would deepen it. When she didn't, he did. He ran his tongue over her bottom lip. He was just about to go in for the kill when she slipped her finger between their mouths.

"There were *two* boxes of condoms," she said, sounding as breathless as he felt.

He grinned. "High hopes."

She tilted her head to the side, her eyes narrowed.

"Okay, I bought the first pack on the way over to her place one evening, hoping. I put them in my toolbox." He let his hand move up her back. The moment his fingers found the bra clasp, the temptation to release it was overwhelming. "When they didn't . . . come in handy, I tossed them in my bathroom cabinet. The next weekend she called, saying she thought the pipe was leaking again. I was out. Instead of going home, I bought another pack, hoping. But she turned me down again."

Kathy pointed at him. "What about when she called and asked you come over that last time?"

He caught her finger in his fist and considered putting it in his mouth. She'd seemed to respond to that earlier. Without thinking, he answered, "I'd heard from Calvin, and I was waiting for his call to say when they were going to meet me. I didn't think it would be right to start something and then . . ."

"Disappear?" She slipped her finger from his hand.

He nodded, disappointed, wanting so badly to get back to kissing her. He wanted to raise his hips and let her feel even more what having her on his lap was doing to him. He wanted to forget that his gun, less than a foot away, was there for a reason. A part of him kept insisting that no one knew they were here. There wasn't anything stopping them from having tonight.

"But if she'd stopped pushing you away earlier, before she called you, would you have told her that you were leaving . . . or would you have just left?"

"I'd have explained the best I could that I had to go somewhere but would be back. I wouldn't have just walked away."

"Why not?"

"Because I think we might actually have a shot at this."

She blinked, suddenly seeming skittish. "A shot at what?"

He sighed, cut his gaze to the window and then ran a hand over her shoulder. "This." He waved a hand between them.

"Sex?" she asked. He couldn't quite make out her tone.

"No."

The puppy was sniffing around his shoe again, and he gave it a nudge.

"No?" she repeated.

"Well, yes, sex. But more than that. A lot more."

"More?" She moved to rise.

He didn't try to stop her this time, mostly because of the seriousness in her eyes. Leaning forward, resting his palms on his knees and causally giving his jean legs a tug, hoping to give himself some relief, he continued to study her. "Yeah, more. Does that bother you?"

She shook her head. "No. I'm . . . confused."

"About what?" He watched her pick up Goodwill. "What are you confused about?"

"The 'more' part." She stared at him.

"What about the more part?"

She took that bottom lip between her teeth again and then released it. "I'm pretty sure all I want is sex."

Her words sifted through his head. He probably shouldn't have, but he couldn't help it: He fell back in his chair and laughed—really hard, too.

"What's so funny?" she asked.

That made him laugh harder.

What was so funny? *She* was! It had taken him two years and nine months to get a kiss from this woman, and now she stood there and announced that all she wanted was sex? Kathy Callahan was a mother, lover of puppies and turtles, as well as a woman who got excited at arranging flowers for weddings. Yeah, she was sensual as hell and impossibly tempting, but she was hardly the type who went to a man purely for sex.

He opened his mouth to say something, clueless to what that would be, when a cell phone rang. Not his phone, but the used car salesman's. He'd considered dumping it, in case it was reported missing and was now being tracked by the cops, but then he'd discarded the idea. Chances were that the cops wouldn't get around to doing that until tomorrow. As long as he kept the call under forty-five seconds, they wouldn't be able to track the calls to any tower. And while the caller might have been someone trying to reach Harry Johnson, it also could have been Calvin responding to the message he'd left.

He jumped up, grabbed the phone beside the gun and checked the caller ID. Glancing over his shoulder at Kathy, he smiled. "It's him."

Jason watched Sue and Lacy pick up the dishes from the patio and take them inside. It was almost dark. Chase had insisted they stay over and he'd grill hamburgers, and they'd eaten outside.

While he and Chase had tried to keep the dinner conversation light, their wives were both too worried about Kathy to eat or talk much. Still, Jason figured being here with company had probably helped.

The talk with the two contractors had proved baffling. The head contractor had a serious respect for Stan Bradley and had flat-out refused to believe he could be mixed up with drugs. "I know trouble when I see it, and believe me, that boy ain't trouble. Now the guys he taught a lesson to today, they're a rowdy bunch . . . but I wouldn't think they were into the drug scene either."

Chase and Jason had gotten the names of the guys Stan fought with and had given them to Danny to check out. Danny promised to call or swing by when he had something.

Chase picked up his beer and took a sip. "You know what doesn't make sense?" he asked.

"What?" Jason replied.

"What Cary said about Kathy and the plumber being at the Goodwill place. Why would they be there? And, if Kathy was afraid of Bradley, wouldn't she have said something? I know Cary, worked with him when he was with Houston PD. He's a good cop. I'd think he'd have picked up on it if Kathy was really afraid."

"Maybe she wasn't. Maybe Bradley convinced her he's the good guy." Jason shook his head. "We should check out the Goodwill trailer." His cell rang at that moment, and he looked at the caller ID. "It's Danny."

He flipped open the phone. "Hey, you got news?"

"'Fraid so," Danny said.

Jason's gut clenched. "Is Kathy okay?"

"As far as I know."

"Something turn up with the guys Bradley fought with?"

"Don't think so, I tracked them down at Molly's Pub. All of them went there to nurse their egos. The bartender vouched for them. That plumber must know how to fight. All four had the crap beat out of them."

"So what is it you got?" Jason asked, not caring if his impatience rang out. Getting info out of Danny was like milking a bull.

"We got some info back on Kathy and . . . let's just say I was a tad surprised."

"Surprised at what?"

"For starters, she has a record."

"Kathy Callahan has a criminal record? You're shitting me." Jason saw Chase's surprise, too.

"What kind of record?" his friend asked. Jason held up a finger.

"I shit you not," Danny continued. "Which is why I'm calling you. I was going to just drop by, but I didn't know if . . . if you wanted Sue and Lacy to hear. Why don't you and Chase meet me at the What-a-Burger by Chase's house?"

"How bad is it?" Jason asked.

"Bad enough," Danny answered. "And Cary just called me and said he stumbled across something weird about this Bradley guy. I'll try to get him to meet us if he can."

"It's about damn time," Luke answered Calvin's call. "Where the hell have you been?"

"I had a family emergency. Wife was in an accident."

"Is she going to be okay?" Luke asked, remembering a picture of Calvin's family on his desk.

"Yes, but let's get to your problem. Are you sure Lorenzo is behind this?"

"They had guns, were big guys in suits. They shot first and didn't bother to ask questions later. So, hell yeah, I know he's behind this."

"Okay. Where are you now?"

"Right outside Hoke's Bluff."

"You didn't leave the area?"

"I was in a van, very recognizable. And a woman got caught up in it with me. Figured hunkering down might be best."

"A woman? Is she still with you?" Calvin sounded nervous.

"Yes."

"Lose her," Calvin said.

"Too late."

"WitSec doesn't—"

"Have you forgotten who you're talking to?" Luke snapped. "I know the fucking rules. But Lorenzo's men know who she is. If I could have lost her, I would have. But she's with me now, and she's staying put until this is over."

Calvin sighed. "You dumped the van?" he said, as if forcing himself to continue.

"Yes. But the local authorities will be looking for the new vehicle shortly."

"Are you out of imminent danger now?"

Luke recalled that no one had followed them from the café. "For the time being, it appears that way."

"Where are you hiding out?" Calvin asked.

"A second home of one of my plumbing clients."

"Right outside Hoke's Bluff?"

"Yes." Luke didn't offer more info, because that's not how it was done. He knew that, and so did Calvin. Glancing at the clock, he remembered he should probably cut the call short, just in case.

"I'll need to set up a meet. It might be morning before I can get someone there. Is that soon enough?"

Luke looked at Kathy, who stood by the sink and was hanging on his every word. He thought about spending the night with her, but as much as that idea appealed, the sooner he had reinforcements, the less chance there was of her being hurt. "Sooner would be nice."

His contact was silent a moment. "Sooner might not be possible. Do you think they know where you are?"

"No."

"Then you should be safe."

He remembered again that no one had followed them. Chances were, Lorenzo and his goons thought he'd left town. "Okay," he agreed.

"I'll have them there as soon as possible," Calvin promised. "But it's probably going to be in the morning. I'll call you back as soon as I have a location."

"Then I'll just have to accept that," Luke agreed.

He met Kathy's gaze, and part of him was thrilled. They would have tonight. He was going to make it count. No doubt, when the US Marshals showed up he'd have to leave, but he sure as hell could give Kathy something to look forward to when he returned.

"Call me back with a place and time," he said wanting to disconnect.

"Might be a couple of hours," Calvin pointed out.

"Fine," Luke said. He hung up.

"They want you to lose me?" she asked as he set the phone back on the counter.

"No. He's going to call back with a place and time to meet some people."

"What people?" she asked. Uncertainty rang in her voice.

"US Marshals, probably."

"And what will they do with me?"

"They'll make sure you're safe until Lorenzo is in jail, and then you can go on your way."

"And you?"

"I'll be taken into protective custody until after the trial."

"And then what?"

"And then that's mostly up to me." But for the first time, he'd never been clearer about what he wanted—or who.

He leaned against the counter and studied her, remembering, *I'm pretty sure all I want is sex.* A smile pulled at his lips. "You know, I'd like to get back to something you mentioned earlier."

She shook her head. "We should forget about that. Your guys are coming to rescue us and—"

"No, actually, it's going to take them a while, and I'd really like to get back to it." He started moving toward her. "Because I have to tell you, I'm hurt. Crushed." He put his hand over his heart.

She backed against the counter as if nervous, but he didn't relent. He kept coming. When he stood right in front of her, he leaned in and put a hand on each side of the counter, trapping her. "So, when you called for me last week—and again when you came over this morning, dressed in that top—you were just planning on using me? For sex?"

She had her lip between her teeth again, but when she noticed him looking at her mouth, she released it. "It's not like . . . I didn't mean . . ."

"Is that all I am to you? A—what did you call Claire—a bang toy?" He enjoyed the blush on her cheeks.

"No! What I meant was, I didn't . . . I don't want . . ."

"A relationship?"

"Right," she said.

"So all you wanted was my body?" He waved a hand up and down his frame, and he had to work hard not to laugh.

Her mouth dropped open. Her eyes took on a suspicious glint, and she squared her shoulders. "I thought men liked that."

"Liked what? Oh, you mean a woman who just wants sex?" He leaned in closer. "Very hot sex with no emotional ties? Very, *very* hot sex . . . ?"

She tilted her head to look him in the eyes, as if she was onto his game. He loved the game, too. But he needed a new approach, because he still had a point to make, and he sure as hell planned on making it.

"You don't like that?" she asked.

"Oh, yeah. I love it."

He moved his hand around her waist and pulled her to him. Lowering his head, he kissed her—slow at first, but the moment he felt her relax, felt her lips melt against his, felt her soft body lean against him, he went in for real, and it was for the kill. He didn't hold anything back. He used his lips, his tongue, his hands and his body to make sure she got all the pleasure possible. This was probably his last shot at this.

He positioned his leg between hers, pressing his thigh between hers, raising it ever so slightly until he found the spot he wanted: the soft juncture between her legs. He knew he'd gauged right, because she ever so lightly moved against him. The rhythm was slow. And that was fine. For now. He wasn't finished making his point.

The kiss lasted longer than he intended; he almost forgot what he was doing. Then he pulled back.

He had to catch her when he let her go—which was exactly his plan. To catch her. But first he had to let her fall. She had to accept the truth. And the truth was she didn't want just a roll in the hay. He knew her. Maybe he even knew her better than she knew herself, but there was no way a woman like Kathy Callahan was in it for only the sex.

Sure, she wanted sex. So did he. It was going to be damn good sex, too.

They had played this game for two years and nine months. They'd teased, tempted and toyed with each other's affections. And he didn't mean toyed in a bad way. They'd had fun. But you didn't brush up against someone's life as long as they had without leaving an imprint. If he'd been honest with himself earlier, he would have admitted that, even if today never happened, if he'd left without saying good-bye, he'd have come back. He wouldn't have been able to walk away forever. Not without really trying to break down her walls.

And now, when she'd finally thrown open her doors . . .

He ran his thumb over her moist lips. "Men love pure sex," he admitted. Honestly, he had in his younger days. "But let's get the rules out of the way first."

"Rules?" Her voice was breathy, and her nipples pebbled against her tank top. Oh yeah, he had her right where he wanted her.

"Unfortunately, there are more rules in a purely sexual relationship than in a serious one."

"What kind of rules?" she asked.

"For example: can we bring in other people?"

Her brow crinkled in that cute way it always did when she was puzzled. "Other people?" she repeated.

"Yeah. You know, threesomes."

Her mouth dropped open. She tilted her head to one side, ever so slightly. "You're joking, right?"

"No." Inside he was howling with laughter, but he managed to paste a serious look on his face. "I'm just trying to figure out the boundaries. When a relationship is just sex, the sky is the limit on spicing things up, but we need to know the boundaries."

"No. Not happening," she snapped.

"What's not happening?" he asked, barely holding it together.

"Us. You. Me."

"Why, you chicken?" God, this was fun.

"Chicken," she repeated. "Yeah. I'm a chicken and you're a rooster and guess who's not going to be making eggs!"

"I can't believe you didn't find out what the crime was," Chase complained as they jumped into Jason's Mustang to go meet Danny.

"You know how he is." Jason backed out of the driveway.

"He can talk for fifteen minutes without getting to the point. Sort of reminds me of someone else I know." He shot Chase an accusatory glance.

"Yeah, Sue is like that, isn't she?" his friend replied, clueless.

Jason inwardly chuckled, but then his thoughts shot back to Kathy and his wife. Kathy was like a sister to Sue, and while Jason had never bonded with the woman, he'd respected her relationship to Sue. He had to. When Sue loved someone, they were family.

"It has to be, like, unpaid tickets or something," Chase said. "Kathy's not a hardened criminal."

"You'd think. But that's not how Danny made it sound."

Jason pulled up next to the fast-food restaurant at the same time as Cary's black Chevy truck. Jason parked beside a Hoke's Bluff police car, which meant Danny had invited Turner.

Danny stood in the parking lot, talking to a couple of women. "Look at him," Chase said, motioning. "Ink's not even dry on his divorce papers and he's already trolling for a replacement."

"I don't think it's a replacement he wants," Jason said. "Haven't you heard?"

"Heard what?"

"Cary, Danny and Turner have borrowed the idea from our wives. They started their own club."

Chase's laugh filled the car. "Please! They're going to take vows of celibacy?"

Jason laughed and opened his car door. "Well, they've got different rules and a different name. They call themselves the Balls-with-no-Chain Gang. Danny said the plan was to always get lucky and get out before you got yourself really screwed or weighed down by a relationship."

Chase reached for the door handle. "What you wanna bet that one of them will be married within a year?"

Jason laughed. "All it takes is the right woman."

He got out of the car. As he made his way to the building, he gave Danny's two women a look-see. Pretty packages, but he wasn't tempted to unwrap either. As Chase would put it, it wasn't worth risking the arm.

Danny waved bye to the ladies and followed Chase, Cary and Jason inside. Turner, in uniform, sat in a booth in the back. He waved at them.

Danny started to go to the counter, but Chase grabbed his arm. "Talk first, eat later." They walked over and sat down in the booth, and Chase didn't waste a second. "What do you have?"

Danny leaned back in the bench, as if enjoying the limelight. "Well, it's like this. I was looking around—"

"Just tell us what you know about Kathy!" Chase said.

"Terroristic threat. She threatened the life of a fellow officer."

Jason sat, dumbfounded. Chase too.

"Our Kathy?" Cary asked, obviously surprised as well.

"Yeah." Danny looked at Cary. "I got the info right before I left. She was arrested in Alabama about nine years ago."

"No shit?" Chase said.

"Did she do time?" Turner asked. "I can't see her being the type to do time."

"No. The officer supposedly went to the DA and had the charges dropped. But this is where it gets even better. According to the desk sergeant I spoke with, Kathy really should have gone down for it, because according to the assaulted cop, she was threatening all kinds of shit. And the desk sergeant informed me that Kathy 'came by her renegade spirit naturally.'"

"Meaning?" Chase and Jason said at the same time.

"Do you remember ever hearing about the Godsend Gang—they're, like, famous in Alabama."

Chase shook his head, but Jason spoke up. "Wasn't that the gang of men who killed six police officers and a bunch of civilians while robbing banks? I read something about it in a book of famous Southern crimes."

"Yeah. Well, Kathy's old man was part of that gang."

"Fuck," Jason said, and right then he remembered the most disturbing part of the story. "Please tell me she wasn't the kid who actually witnessed her dad getting blown to bits?"

Danny pointed a finger at him in acknowledgment. "That would be her."

Jason's chest filled with empathy. He knew all about childhood traumas. Suddenly Kathy's standoffishness made perfect sense. "Damn! I read it was, like, seven officers shooting at him. The guy took like thirty bullets, and the girl witnessed the whole thing." He ran a hand over his face. "No wonder she doesn't like cops."

"Oh, I also checked," Danny said. "She's registered for a nine-millimeter."

"That doesn't mean she's involved in this," Jason said, defending her.

"No, but it sure as hell sheds some new light on her," Turner said, crossing his arms over his chest.

"I'm with Jason," Chase said. "Kathy loves that boy of hers more than life. She wouldn't risk getting involved with drugs or anything like that."

"Her daddy did," Danny pointed out.

"Yeah, but we're not our parents!" Jason snapped. He damn sure was planning on being a better parent than his own mom.

"Come *on*, guys," Chase said. "All three of you have met her. If she'd given any one of you the time of day, you'd have been all over her."

"Maybe," Cary admitted. "But explain to me what was going on back at the Goodwill station. Because I'm telling you, she wasn't afraid of Stan Bradley. She either doesn't know he's into drugs—which would be hard to explain, considering his place was shot to Hell and back while she was there—or there's something else we're not seeing. And after what I discovered . . . well, it could be something else."

"What have you got?" Chase asked.

"According to the records, Stan Bradley lived and worked in Grandsville, Texas, before he moved here. My uncle is a contractor who lives there with his wife. His wife's family owns and runs a little lumber-slash-hardware kind of store. I called my uncle to just see if he had an opinion of the guy. And guess who's never heard of him."

"What are you saying?" Chase asked.

"I'm saying the man either lied about where he's been living, or Stan Bradley is an alias. Hell, maybe Bradley is somehow connected to Kathy's past."

Turner pushed up from the booth. "You guys can shoot the shit all day, but I've got to eat before I'm back on duty." He walked to the counter. Just as he got there, the radio attached to his belt went off, and they watched him speak into his walkie-talkie. He turned and walked back to meet them. "Bradley stole a Dodge Charger."

"Was Kathy with him?" Chase asked.

"I'm going to find out now."

"*We're* going to find out now," Jason promised.

Chapter Twenty

"Hey, if threesomes aren't your thing, I'm fine with it." Luke fought to keep a straight face. "Like I said, I'm just trying to establish the rules."

"Not happening," Kathy replied, looking appalled. She took a step away from him.

"I didn't say I had to have them. Threesomes are nice—the third person always being a girl, mind you—but I can live without them."

He watched her move across the room and scoop up Goodwill. It was a one-room cabin. Other than the bathroom, she couldn't run and hide. He took advantage and asked, "What about others outside the relationship?"

She swung around and stared at him. "Outside?"

"Yeah. Can we see other people, or do you want an exclusive?" He brushed a hand over his mouth to hide his grin. "Wait. If you were so concerned about the condoms, I suppose you want this to be a strictly sexual but committed relationship, right?"

Her hazel eyes darkened, telling him he'd hit his target.

"When are those guys showing up?" she asked, trying to drop the subject.

But there was no dropping it now. He moved close and slowly brushed his hand down her arm. "Do we go out in public? Can I take you out to dinner? Or do we pretend we don't know each other?"

"Why would we . . . ?" She watched his hand move up and down her arm as Goodwill readjusted himself to lick her neck. "Why would we pretend we don't know each other?" Unable to dodge the puppy's kisses, she put the dog down.

"Because"—he pressed his cheek to hers—"if someone sees us having dinner, they may assume that we actually care about each other instead of just being each other's bang toys."

She placed a hand on his chest. "You're making fun of me, aren't you?"

"Now why would I do that?" He took a step forward.

She took a step back. "That's what I'm trying to figure out."

"Could it be because I'm past the point of just wanting to get your panties off? That what I want from you is more than just to get you naked and make you my play toy?" He took another step forward.

She inched back, but she butted against the wall. He moved in for another kiss.

She resisted him for a half second, then gave in. Her tongue met his; her body inched off the wall and pressed into him. This was hotter, wetter and more intense than any of the kisses before. Anything else he'd wanted to say, any point he'd wanted to make was insignificant compared to what he wanted now.

He wanted her. Every inch of her. No barriers, no boundaries. No rules.

No clothes.

Oh, and he wanted the "more" she was so damn afraid of offering, too.

Slipping his hand around her waist and under her tank top, he unhooked her bra for the second time that day. Her breasts, already against his chest, gave a little when released. Amazing, how that slight release sent anticipation into his gut—and lower.

He slid his hand around her rib cage to hold a prize he'd freed. But his palm barely brushed against the round curve of her right breast before she pulled back.

"Luke?"

He lowered his hand just a bit and leaned his forehead against hers. "If that puppy is pissing on my—"

"No." She laughed, and it came out sultry and sexy. "But I would like a shower before . . ."

The thought of her naked under a soft stream of steamy water shot right to his crotch. "Sounds good." He pulled his hand from under her shirt and looked at her. Her lips were wet, her eyes dark with passion. "Damn, you look hot." He went back for another kiss, but she put a hand on his chest.

"A shower first." Her voice was breathy; her words brushed wet against his lips.

He nodded. "Okay, you get the water started. It takes a few minutes for it to heat up. I'll be right in."

She shook her head. "No, I didn't mean . . ."

He put a finger over her lips, knowing what she was about to say but determined to change her mind. "I promise you'll enjoy it more with me in there with you."

"But . . ."

"Shh." He leaned in. She watched him but didn't say a word.

"Think about it," he said. He ran his hand up under her shirt again.

"You." He kissed the edge of her lips. "Me." He moved his attention to her neck, running his tongue over the base of her throat. "Naked." He gently nipped the soft skin with his teeth. "Hot water." He passed his palm over her breast. The bra still clung to her, but he found her nipple and gently rolled the nub between his fingers. "Steam." He moved his hand down, over her jeans, past her zipper, and fit his palm to her soft mound, applying only the slightest pressure where he knew she needed it most. "My hands, all soaped up, moving over your wet skin. . . ." Her hips jutted out ever so slightly, and he knew he had her.

"Go," he said, and pulled back. "Get the water going."

She opened her eyes, blinked, stared at him but didn't argue this time. When she took that first step to the bathroom, a sense of power swelled in his chest. After all this time, she finally couldn't tell him no. The realization was one hell of an aphrodisiac—one he fully planned on taking advantage of to the fullest. For her pleasure, of course.

The bathroom door clicked shut. Luke cut his eyes around the room. He tossed the sofa cushions to the side, and pulled the folded-up mattress out. From his visits up here, he knew it was a piss-poor bed to sleep on, but he suspected they wouldn't be sleeping much.

He grabbed his condoms from his wallet and set them

next to the back of the lamp on the side table, reachable from the bed. Only two. He'd have to make them last. Then, having second thoughts, he picked up one of the foil packages and tucked it in his pocket. They might not make it to the bed.

He took off his shoes and socks, but when Goodwill, resting by the bathroom door, raised his head, he picked them up and set them on a chair. Giving the room one more check, he went for his gun, deciding to take it into the bathroom with him. Until Calvin called back, his goal was to make the most of his time with Kathy—but like the condoms, his gun would always be within arm's reach.

Joey pulled off to the side of the road and waited. The country lane felt too dark, too quiet. He rolled down his window, and in the distance he could hear the crickets. For some crazy reason, the sound made him feel lonely. Not that being alone was unusual for him.

Leaning forward, he looked through the windshield at the stars and wondered about Heaven and Hell. One of the foster homes he'd been in had insisted he attend church. Most of the kids living there had hated services, but for some reason Joey hadn't minded. Of course, he pretended he did, because not to wouldn't have been cool.

A few of the sermons whispered through Joey's mind, and he wondered if Donald had ended up in some fiery spot, paying for his bad deeds. Joey tried to think about the people he'd known in his life who'd died and *wouldn't* have gone to Hell. A couple of the foster moms who'd got stuck with him had been decent folks. Who knew if they had passed away yet? He hadn't kept up with any of them. Or they him.

His mind created an image of his mom—a druggie and prostitute, but at times he could swear he'd seen some goodness in her. What was the chance she'd managed to sneak into Heaven instead?

He gripped the wheel, and the blisters stung on his hands from digging Donald's grave. But at least his hands were clean. He'd stopped at a service station bathroom earlier and washed them and his face. His suit was probably covered in dust and dirt.

Lorenzo would have a fit if he saw him like this, but Joey couldn't help that. One couldn't dig a three-foot-deep hole and come out looking fresh from church. That's what Lorenzo always said: he wanted his men to look as if they'd just walked out of a Sunday service. Not that Joey really cared what Lorenzo wanted anymore.

Stretching out his fingers, Joey stared at his hands. It would have been easier just to have dumped Donald's body. Joey hadn't done that. Not because of what Foster had said about making sure the body didn't turn up, but because he'd told Donald he'd bury him. True, Donald had already been dead when Joey gave the promise, but Joey didn't make a lot of promises, and he always tried to keep those he did. Nevertheless, he didn't intend to promise that again. Burying someone was too much damn work!

He flexed the aching muscles in his arms. Digging had also aggravated his toe. The temptation hit to reach down and take off his shoe, but he figured it would hurt like hell to put it back on. So he didn't.

Foster had called and said to meet him out here. It was about a mile from where Luke Hunter lived. Joey had arrived before Foster. Only empty darkness waited. Of course, Joey wasn't sure what type of car the trooper drove when he wasn't in his state-mandated car. He probably should have asked.

Joey had also spoken to Corky and Pablo. They'd been told to lie low, and if Foster needed them, he'd call them. Obviously, Lorenzo felt Foster and Joey could handle the job—which was a good thing, too. The fewer people Joey had to deal with, the better. It was yet to be seen if he could save the redhead without offing anyone. His gut told him the possibility wasn't likely.

He closed his eyes and envisioned the redhead and her freckle-faced boy. He still didn't understand why Foster hadn't heard about the blonde. Surely the cops had figured out the two incidents were connected. Then again, he supposed he shouldn't question his good luck.

Glancing heavenward, he considered again if someone up there really did want him protecting the redhead. If he had to kill someone to save her, would that be an unforgiveable sin—the kind of sin that, if there was a Hell, would earn Joey a place next to Donald?

He recalled thinking it had been a miracle he'd gotten the redhead out of the café without Foster seeing her. Maybe by some act of God, he wouldn't have to kill anyone tonight. Maybe.

A car pulled up in front of him and parked. Joey sat, unmoving, watching as Foster got out. Only when he saw the man take his first step did it occur to Joey that maybe the trooper had brought him out here to kill him.

His breath hitched at the thought. Foster drew closer. The serenade of night noises stopped. All Joey could hear was the crunch of Foster's footsteps on the road.

When the trooper didn't pull his weapon, Joey fought back the panic and stepped out of the car.

"You take care of Donald?" Foster asked in such a casual manner that he could have been asking if Joey had eaten dinner. Did death and killing people not disturb these people at all?

"Done," Joey said, hoping he sounded equally casual.

Foster stared at him for a minute, trying to read him. "We're going to take my car," he finally said. "I heard you can't drive worth a damn."

"Where are we going?" Joey asked, ignoring his throbbing toe as he followed the other man back to his car.

"To do the job."

"You know where he is?" Joey walked around Foster's dark Honda, moved the passenger seat back about five inches, then got in.

Foster crawled behind the wheel. "There's a couple of possibilities. We'll check them both out."

"You really think he's still around town?"

"We know he is."

"How?"

"Because your boss is good. When money doesn't talk, he goes for the Achilles heel. Even if that heel is someone's wife. I respect that about him: ruthlessness."

A heaviness filled Joey's chest. What kind of person respected another for that? The same kind who took advantage of women. Joey remembered how the asshole had looked at and spoken about Lola.

Joey buckled his seat belt and tried not to think about some poor guy out there, worrying that his wife lived or died at the hands of Lorenzo's men. Right now, all he needed to think about was saving the redhead. And if by saving her he saved some pretty Mexican woman some grief as well? So be it. Because if he had to kill Foster, he would.

"We know he's out past Highway 101 at a place he did plumbing work. Lucky for us, Hunter kept great records." Foster picked up a black notebook from the dash.

"You went to his place?" Joey asked.

"Didn't have to. He kept it in his truck."

"Lucky us," Joey said.

"We got two addresses. With any luck, we'll take care of them both and get back in time to see *The Tonight Show*." He slapped the book against his thigh. "And I will be fifty thousand buckaroos richer."

"Money isn't all it's cracked up to be," Joey muttered, but he kept his eyes focused ahead. Focused on doing the right thing.

* * *

Kathy stood in the bathroom. Her heart raced to the beat of arousal, a beautiful yet dangerous song she hadn't heard in a long, long time. She glanced at the closed door and then the mirror. Her eyes reflected fear and exultation. Was she really going to do this?

Yes. She wanted to. She *needed* to.

How long had it been since she'd felt this alive, this truly turned on? Duh, never! And hadn't today—facing death— taught her to live for the moment? Why shouldn't she do this?

Because you suck at it, a voice of warning echoed. Her ex's words, jumping out of the past. *Can you say 'cold fish'?*

The two other guys she'd slept with before Tom hadn't complained. But what did horny teen boys know? They sure hadn't known anything about pleasing a woman.

She remembered the third guy she'd dated before Tom. She hadn't slept with him, but they'd come close. And sure, he'd complained about what happened, but she didn't see it as her fault. If he'd been wearing underwear like a normal person, it wouldn't have even happened!

She closed her eyes for a second and questioned again the wisdom of going through with this. What if it didn't go well? What if she couldn't make Luke happy? What if, after all this anticipation, she discovered she couldn't relax enough to get to the happy place? Tom had been the only one who'd ever brought her to orgasm, electrical devices not included—which probably explained why she'd married him. And probably why his insults hurt so much. What if sex with Luke wasn't everything she'd imagined? Would that prove that she was biologically deficient? Would it prove everything Tom had said and left unsaid?

Admittedly, she hadn't known anything about sex when they were together. Her mom sure as hell wasn't the type to explain things. Practically a loner from moving around so much, all due to her Daddy's reputation, she hadn't had any friends who shared their experiences. So she'd depended on Tom to teach her the fine art of bedroom games. But after a few months of marriage, he'd been so busy getting his rocks off, he'd stopped instructing—and his unspoken wishes had been easy to follow: just lie there. In less than a year, she was pregnant. He'd stopped trying to make her happy at all—and to be fair, she hadn't lost any sleep about making him happy, either. Well, not until late in the marriage when she'd started to sense something was wrong. But then her efforts to seduce her own husband had failed miserably.

But she knew more now. Hadn't all those Friday night sex talks with Sue and Lacy been her way of educating herself? She knew every man's hot spot and secret fantasy that *Cosmo* and *Redbook* had reported on for the last four years. Maybe she hadn't made sex suck, but it had been her past partners and their situations. She had to give this a shot, didn't she?

Yes! She was going to do this.

She reached into the small walk-in shower and turned on the hot water. But just as she started to take off her clothes, that inner voice, the one that seemed to yank on her emotions, spoke up again. *He's a cop.*

Not a cop. A federal agent, she argued with herself.

Same thing.

"Oh, Lordie," she muttered, and leaned against the bathroom counter.

She thought about Lacy and Sue and how happy they were with their husbands. Jason and Chase weren't bad men. And if her friends weren't lying—and she didn't think they were—their husbands were also gods in the bedroom. Wasn't it about time she stopped making the majority pay for the sins of the few? Luke Hunter had nothing to do with what happened to her dad.

Besides, it wasn't as if she was going to marry the guy. Chances were, tonight was all they would have. What was wrong with her taking tonight?

Nothing, she decided. Not a damn thing.

She stood up straight, took a deep breath and started to pull her bra from under her shirt. Then she heard Luke on the other side of the door. A light tapping sounded over the rush of the shower, bringing all her insecurities back to the forefront. She could ask him not to come in. Everything inside her said he'd respect her wishes.

She needed to figure out exactly what those wishes were.

Foster drove. Joey kept trying to find a place for his legs.

"Did you get the finger?" the trooper asked.

"I thought I'm supposed to give it to Lorenzo."

"Just checking."

"I don't like to be checked on."

Joey's lungs felt as if they couldn't get enough oxygen, and his palms itched like a son of bitch. Nothing but nerves.

He finally found a position where his knees didn't hit the dashboard. Funny, how people assumed because he was big that he wasn't afraid of things. He'd learned early on that a person's size didn't say anything about what was inside. His mother hadn't been as big as a minute, and he could remember her standing up to men twice her size. One of those times, when he'd been only seven, it had been on his account. One of their neighbors, a druggie much like his mom, had stolen Joey's basketball.

You weren't scared of him? Joey had asked.

Of course I was. The trick is to never let them see it.

Eventually, Joey had learned to hide his feelings. Maybe a little too much at times.

"Here." Foster handed him a gun. "You'll need this."

Joey stared at the gun with what looked like a homemade silencer attached. "I got my own," he replied.

"Yeah, but tonight we're using throwdowns. Belonged to a couple of drug dealers."

Joey took the gun, and it felt different in his hand. Maybe it was the balance, because of the silencer, or maybe it was because he knew he'd likely use it to kill the man who'd handed it to him. The memory of Freddy flashed in his mind, but he forced that back and instead thought of the little redheaded boy and his mom. Of the basket of toys he'd seen beside their bathtub. That boy deserved to have his mother.

Joey closed his eyes a minute, and when he opened them he saw a road sign and recognized where he was. About a mile up the road was the spot Lola parked her restaurant truck. His mind created an image of her sweet face. Then he remembered what Foster had called her earlier: *Latin Nookie.* Glancing over, Joey couldn't help wondering if Lola's life wouldn't be a better without the guy in it.

"Grab some gloves from the glove box," Foster said. "Then wipe the gun down."

Joey took a pair of plastic gloves. His hands were almost too large to fit.

"The first place is just up the road," Foster said. "We'll have to park and walk in. It rained last night and we don't want to leave tire tracks."

Joey's heart thudded against his sternum. His hands sweated and itched inside the rubber gloves, but he just kept telling himself that he was doing the right thing. That was all he had to hold on to.

Chapter Twenty-one

Kathy bit her lip and tried to decide what she wanted to do. Big mistake. Luke didn't wait for her to tell him to enter; he just walked in. Clicking at his heels was the puppy.

With Luke inside the small bathroom, it suddenly felt smaller. His dark blue eyes met hers, and he winked. His shiner had faded—or maybe it was the low lighting. Only one bulb over the small mirror spewed out any wattage.

He didn't talk. Instead, he studied her. Slowly he moved to the sink and set his gun and Harry's phone on the counter. Then, turning around, he put a hand on each side of her face and kissed her.

It wasn't the hot kind of kiss she'd expected. Instead, it was soft. Gentle. Sweet. Tender.

Then it got hot.

His tongue moved over her bottom lip before it delved inside her mouth. His hips brushed hers—just ever so lightly—and that brought back the achy feeling between her thighs, the hunger that she'd felt when he'd kissed her earlier.

His right hand moved under her tank top, along her back. Skimming, barely touching the skin that covered her rib cage, he slipped his fingers under her bra to cup her left breast. Her nipples, already tight, tightened some more.

"Do we really need all these clothes?" he whispered against her lips. And just like that, he caught the hem of her shirt and slipped it up.

Kathy raised her arms. The bra and shirt were whisked off, and they landed on the bathroom floor.

She had never been a shrieking, modest type. Sex meant getting naked. But it had been a long time since she'd bared her breasts for a man. Kathy found herself wanting to cover up, but then she looked at Luke—looked at him looking at her. He appeared to like what he saw. Feminine power helped her to fight the urge to cover herself.

Luke gently swirled his finger around her right nipple. "You're even more beautiful than I imagined," he murmured.

Kathy found herself nibbling at her lip.

He brushed his hand sideways, onto her left breast, and then with his index finger he traced a line down her abdomen, past her navel to the snap of her jeans. Pushing up on the tips of her toes, she pressed her lips to his. As soon as her lips brushed against him, he pulled back.

"For the record, you kissed me this time."

She recalled telling him earlier that she hadn't been the one who'd kissed him. This turnabout seemed fair play. She smiled. "Okay, you got me on that one."

"Oooh, I like a girl who knows when to concede," he replied.

He had her jeans loose in a trice, tucked one hand inside the back, slipped his palm down between her jeans and panties and cupped her left cheek. Then, with only a light pressure, he bought her against his body, where she felt the impressive bulge behind his zipper.

Breath held, she pushed herself closer to him. His fingers wiggled against her butt and every nerve ending in her body focused on where his hand would go next.

"You think that water's hot yet?" he asked. With his free hand, he stuck his arm behind the shower curtain. The hand inside her jeans moved around her hip to rest low on her abdomen, and his fingers toyed with the elastic band of her panties.

"Maybe . . ." Anticipation laced her tone, and she didn't try to hide it.

His fingers finally slipped inside the front of her panties. The sweet ache doubled between her thighs. Moisture collected deep in her center as she waited for his touch to slide lower.

Instead, he pulled his hand out of her jeans and knelt in front of her. As if taking his time, enjoying it, he untied the shoelaces of her sneakers.

She couldn't remember the last time anyone removed her shoes. She definitely couldn't remember the last time anyone removed her shoes while gazing up at her naked breasts. Probably because it had never happened.

He smiled at her and raised her foot to pull off her Reebok. "You know," he said, "you look good from all angles." After removing her sock, he looked down at her foot and ran a slow finger over the top of her painted toenails. "I knew they would be painted pink."

Chills ran up her foot and found the place between her legs.

"Even your feet are sexy," Luke said.

Kathy's gaze made its way down his pant legs to his bare feet. He must have taken off his shoes in the living room.

He started on her second Reebok, and when that was unlaced and removed, he stayed where he was, kneeling in front of her. Cupping his hands on the sides of her ankles, he ran his hands up the sides of her thighs, over her jeans. Then, hooking his thumbs in her belt loops, he whispered, "I want you naked."

Slowly, deliberately, he pulled her jeans and panties downward. She watched as the pale blue panties descended, exposing the clearly defined triangle of dark red hair at the V of her legs, and she saw his chest expand and his eyes widen. The look on his face—that one expression—was worth the torture she'd put herself though while waxing three nights ago. The tightening of desire low in her belly had her clenching her legs tighter together.

He pushed the jeans and panties the rest of the way down her thighs, past her calves. When they puddled around her feet, she stepped out of them. And then she stood there, with him kneeling in front of her, totally, completely naked. Nothing had ever felt so right.

Touching the inside of her ankle, he moved his hand up. His palm slid along her inner calf, past her knee and slowly inched between her thighs. But right before he arrived at her center, he slipped his fingers out from between her legs.

She frowned and shifted her gaze to his eyes. He was watching her, a sly smile on his lips. He knew exactly what she'd been wanting and had purposely held back.

Standing, he reached for the buttons of his shirt. He released one, then leaned in and kissed the edge of her lips. He pulled back and released another button. She watched his fingers move from one to another. Finally his shirt hung completely open. He slid it off his shoulders and let it fall to the floor. But instead of going to work on his jeans, as she expected, he closed the distance between them. Her hard nipples brushed his chest, and her breasts ached to be touched.

Kissing her on the cheek, he wrapped one arm around her waist and extended his other hand into the shower, testing the water temperature again. "You okay?" he whispered in her ear as he pulled it out.

That's when it hit her: She was standing there, not participating, just like she had with Tom.

"I'm sorry," she muttered.

His brow creased. "About what?"

"I . . ." She tried to remember some of the tips of what men liked, but for the life of her, not one piece of advice rose into her brain.

"I . . ." She met his gaze again. A swarm of butterflies started doing the tango in her stomach, and she looked away. "I'm really not very good at this."

"Good at what?" He turned her chin and forced her to look at him.

She felt her cheeks flush. "Sex." She forced herself say it, hoping it would stop at least some of her insecurities from eating her alive. "My ex . . . He said that I—"

"No." Luke pressed a finger to her lips. He gazed at her with a look that was part frustration and part compassion. "Stop."

"Stop what?" she asked, his finger still against her lips.

"That is wrong on *so* many levels," he said. He waved a hand around the room. "Do you see your ex in here?" When the puppy barked, he added, "Not you, Goodwill."

Kathy cut her gaze from the dog back to Luke. "No, he's not here."

"Good, because I sure as hell haven't invited him. And I'd prefer you didn't either." He touched his index finger to her temple. "Not even up here. This is you and me. No one else."

His smile touched something inside her, and she felt a surge of self-confidence. "Thought you liked threesomes," she teased.

He smiled. "We can discuss that later."

She sighed. "Can we start over?"

"Start over? No!" His gaze whispered down her naked body. "Let me make that clear. *Hell*, no." He reached around her waist and pulled her against him. "It's taken me over two and a half years to get you naked. There's no damn way I'm starting over."

Kathy laughed. "Then maybe you should get naked with me."

"Now that"—his hand whispered up her side to pass over her breasts—"sounds like a better idea."

He started to reach for his jeans, but she caught his hand. "Let me." She reached down to undo them.

Joey walked through the dark woods, letting Foster lead the way. Crickets and night birds sang in the distance. A soft wind stirred the trees, and the scent of pine filled the air. Their footsteps were nothing more than a soft padding accompanied by an occasional crack of a twig.

Another person might consider the surroundings peaceful, but the gun in his hand, the one Foster had handed him, sucked the peacefulness right out of it for Joey. The fact that he might at any minute be taking a life and possibly losing his own shot all inner peace right to hell.

The question was when Joey should do it. Foster had said there were two possible locations. What if this one wasn't right? What if Foster's information was wrong? He'd kill Foster if he had to, but what if he didn't have to? What if Hunter and the girl just disappeared? Call him a coward, but Joey really hoped that was how things turned out.

Then he remembered the look on Lola's face when the jerk had touched her, and he wasn't so sure.

After a few minutes, they came upon a small house. All the lights were out. The surrounding woods were silent.

"I don't think this is it," Foster said, keeping his voice low.

Joey listened to the nothingness, gripped the gun in his hands and hoped like hell the corrupt trooper was right.

"A man never tells a woman no when she wants to take his clothes off."

Luke dropped his arms to his sides to let Kathy do the honors. He watched her hands move to his fly and felt the tips of her fingers slip inside the front of his jeans to release the button. His body reacted as she brushed past sensitive skin.

She worked to release the button, and he let himself enjoy the view of her breasts jiggling ever so slightly with her movements. Her nipples were a peach color, several shades darker than that lovely spray of freckles across her nose, and her right nipple brushed against his chest as she moved. He ached to draw it into his mouth and taste it.

His gaze whispered down her breasts to her tiny waist. Then to her hips, which were flared, rounded and gave her body the perfect hourglass appearance. The red curls covering her sex drew his attention, and he felt himself grow frantic with need. His fingers itched to slip inside her folds and see if she was already wet for him. God knew he was already hard for her . . . and getting harder.

He realized she still struggled with the button. "Do you want me to do it?" he asked, trying not to sound impatient.

She looked up from his zipper. "Are you in a hurry, or is it that you don't trust me?"

"No." He grinned and sighed. "Take your time. The view is kind of nice."

Did the woman have a clue how beautiful she was? He didn't think she did. Her words replayed in his head: "My ex said . . ." And while he hadn't let her finish her thought, he assumed the memory wasn't a good one. He suspected that the vulnerable look in her eyes, the insecurity, had all come from what that asshole had said.

Her ex deserved to be tortured for any pain he might have caused her. At the same time, Luke delighted in the fact that he himself would be the one to turn her around. He planned on showing Kathy Callahan just how beautiful she was and returning some of the self-confidence she so rightly deserved.

She finally got the button free, as if a little clumsy from a case of nerves, and she tucked one hand inside his pants as she used the other to slowly undo the zipper. The back of her hand brushed against his dick, and a low hiss passed Luke's lips before he could catch it. His pelvis pressed against her hand.

Kathy looked up at him. "Wouldn't want this zipper to catch on anything."

"Ouch." He grinned.

She smiled back at him, and now that the zipper was

down, she placed both palms on his chest. "Of course, the last time wasn't my fault. I didn't know he wasn't wearing underwear!"

A laugh spilled from Luke's lips, and he pulled her against him. "Okay, I'm going to want to hear that story. *Just not now.*"

"Why, do you have other plans?" she asked, teasing. It was the tone he now knew she used to hide nervousness. But she slid her hands down and gave his jeans a little push.

His cock, freed of his boxers, brushed against her abdomen. That light touch brought another moan to his lips. But with his jeans pushed only to his thighs, she seemed to hesitate at finishing the job. She kept her gaze on his face, almost as if embarrassed to see what she'd uncovered.

"What's wrong? Scared to check me out?" he asked, hoping the joke would erase her tension.

"Not scared. I just like surprises." She pushed his jeans all the way down. They bunched around his ankles. Then she knelt in front of him.

He saw her gaze widen when she saw his surprise. And damn, if he wasn't a bit astonished himself! It had been a long time since he'd risen so proudly to the occasion—which meant the real Kathy did more for his libido than the fantasy Kathy he'd been making love to in his mind.

Seeing her, naked, kneeling, her mouth inches from his cock . . . it all took his libido and arousal up a notch. But in spite of the sweet fantasy flashing through his head, an escapade where she wantonly pleased him, he wanted tonight to be about pleasing her.

Telling himself they could explore his other fantasy later, he pulled her upright. "Ready for that shower?" he asked.

She nodded.

He slipped a hand around her waist, moved the shower curtain back and led her into the cascading water.

Chapter Twenty-two

Jason stood under the one streetlight in the makeshift car lot and took in every word Harry Johnson said.

"Hell, yeah—he had a gun and threatened to shoot me. And then he kind of threatened to kill the girl," the used car salesman was saying, leaning against a black pickup truck with a FOR SALE sign.

Kind of threatened? Jason waited for Turner to ask for clarification.

"What kind of gun was it?" the other cop asked instead.

Jason fought the desire to push Turner out of the way and ask his own questions. It wasn't that the guy was doing it wrong, but Jason had a separate agenda, which wasn't so much about catching Bradley as finding Kathy. Hell, he'd promised Sue to do just that.

Chase, standing beside him, muttered something under his breath. Jason's guess was that his friend was champing at the bit as well. But this wasn't their case. It wasn't even their jurisdiction; so they both had to wait until Turner finished questioning the man to move in.

The moment Turner closed his pad, Chase spoke up. "You said Bradley 'kind of' threatened to shoot Miss Callahan. What did you mean by that?"

The salesman passed a hand over his belly and pulled himself away from the truck. "He said she was annoying him. And that he'd take his frustration out on her if I didn't get out of the car. But . . ."

"But what?" Jason snapped.

"But then *she* told me that he wouldn't hurt her. And she thumped him on the side of the head and started yanking his hair."

"She did what?" Turner reopened his pad, clearly surprised.

Johnson looked back at him. "Yeah, it was strange. She just kept saying, 'He won't hurt me, see?' And then she'd give him another thump on his ear. I've had my ears thumped—it hurts!"

Jason and Chase looked at each other. "What did Bradley do?" Jason asked.

"Nothing, but he looked like he was getting pissed. I didn't want to chance it. I got out of the car. But Lord have mercy, I sure do hope that gal is okay."

Turner asked a few more questions, then thanked Johnson and explained how to fill out a stolen-car report. Then he, Chase and Jason all started to walk away. Turner headed for his car.

Chase growled to Jason, "None of this fucking makes sense."

"I know," Jason replied.

"Oh!" Johnson called out, and Jason and Chase turned. "There is one other thing . . ."

The spray of water hit her directly in the face, so Luke adjusted the showerhead. When he looked back at her, he was again struck by how damn beautiful she was.

"You look good wet," he said. He reached for the bar of soap and moved it over her breasts. She stood there, and he could tell from her expression that the pleasure wasn't all his.

After teasing her nipples with gentle caresses, he turned her around. He leaned down and whispered in her ear, "Do you have any idea how many times I thought about having you like this? Of us, naked in a shower?"

"How many?" she asked, her voice low.

"Every time I was in your bathroom with you. I could always smell that peach soap you use. I'd get hard just walking in there." As he moved the soap over her back, he got his first real look at her naked behind. It didn't disappoint. "Then there was the time I came over and you were prancing around in those cutoff jeans. Do you have any idea how hard it was to crawl under your sink after that?"

Moving his hands up from her waist, he followed her sides to her underarms. Once she was soapy and slick there, his hands again found their way to her breasts. She let out a soft moan and fell against him.

Her backside brushed his cock, and a bolt of pleasure surged through him. Unable to resist, he shifted his hand down to the little triangle of hair at the juncture of her thighs. Her skin was wet, but a wetter, slicker moisture met his fingers in the folds of her sex. Her head dropped back against his chest, and then her eyes closed and her mouth fell slightly open.

"You like that?" he whispered in her ear, watching streams of water roll down her breasts and bead on her nipples.

"Mmm," she said, and started rocking against his fingers.

The gentle back and forth brought her soapy backside sliding against him, and the pleasure almost took his breath away. Having gone without the real thing for so long, he knew he could come from this. But not wanting to appear like a randy virgin, he held himself in check.

Kissing her neck, mesmerized by the sight of his fingers disappearing into that patch of red hair, he shifted his hand down and found her tight opening. He slipped a finger inside, moving it in and out with the easy rhythm she herself set. Then, sliding his thumb up the crease of her sex, he found the little nub that drove most women crazy.

He heard her gasp, and the rhythm of her movements increased. In. Out. All the while, his thumb moved in tiny circles over her hot spot. She began to make soft noises, light purring sounds that were sexy as hell. His balls tightened and his dick throbbed.

He pleasured her the best way he could: slow, easy. He was eager to learn all the right moves—the moves she liked best. He took in her every reaction. With the side of his chin pressed against her temple, he watched. Watched the way her hips rocked back and forth, watched her nipples grow tighter, watched the way she curled her pink-painted toes. A sense of power mingled with the deep primal lust that grew inside him. She was almost to heaven, and he loved knowing he was the one sending her.

He felt her shudder against him, felt the feminine muscles in her sex spasm around his finger. Her knees gave way, and thankfully he caught her before she fell. He pulled her against him. His throbbing cock snug between their bodies, he leaned down to kiss her face.

She jerked her eyes open, tried to push away, but when her foot slipped in the bottom of the shower, he caught her a second time. "Slow down," he whispered, giving a half-laugh. "You're going to cause us both to fall on our asses."

The house looked like some weekend fishing retreat, and Joey could smell a lake not too far off.

"You want to take the front?" Foster asked. "I'll go around back."

Joey had been about to turn around and head back to the car. "Thought you said you didn't think they were here."

"I don't. But we can't leave until we're sure." The trooper kept his voice low.

"Fine." Joey started toward the front of the house, hoping beyond hope that the place was empty. If Hunter were here, he would probably shoot first and ask questions later. It was what Foster was betting on, too—which was the reason Foster wanted Joey to go in first. It was the same reason Donald wanted Joey to take the front door at the redhead's place.

Both thought he was expendable. But now Donald was the dead one, and Foster didn't seem far behind.

But how far? After debating his options, Joey realized if he killed Foster too soon, Lorenzo might contact Pablo and Corky to finish the job on the redhead and Hunter and himself. His best bet was to go along with the plan until . . . until he couldn't go along anymore. If by some miracle Joey was able to save the redhead and Hunter without taking out the trooper, then he would have to decide whether the jerk was a real threat to Lola. A threat that required elimination with prejudice.

And if he was? The image of soft brown eyes flashed in Joey's head. If Foster was really a threat to Lola, Joey would make sure Foster never had another chance to hurt her.

The trooper disappeared into a dark patch of trees as he walked around the back of the house. Joey moved closer to the porch and listened. Nothing. The muscles in his gut relaxed a little.

But, moving to the window, he peered inside. And in the corner he saw the tiniest bit of light flickering under a door. Christ Almighty! Maybe Luke Hunter and the redhead were here. Which meant Joey had to take Foster out.

His gloved hands began to sweat again, and he wished like hell he'd thought this through. Should he burst inside, risk getting shot by Hunter and take on Foster from the inside, or should he follow the trooper around back and try to take him on there? The visual of Freddy crumpled up in the trunk of his car filled Joey's head again. Fear of winding up like that, of having a bullet put in his head, made the next step harder to make.

Joey's stomach roiled, but he fought that nausea and moved closer to the front door. His footsteps on the wood porch sounded loud. He flinched. Taking in a pound of oxygen, he tried the doorknob. Locked.

The sliding glass doors off to the left caught his attention.

Joey moved off the porch and heard an owl hoot in the distance. Backing against the wall, he peered inside. Air seemed to be trapped in his lungs as his gaze shifted around the room. But it was empty. No one was there. Yet in the far corner, a closet door stood ajar and a sliver of light spilled out onto the floor.

The silence once again penetrated Joey's senses. His gut told him this wasn't right; Hunter and the girl weren't there. He hoped that was true.

He reached for the sliding glass door, and it opened—did everyone in Texas leave their doors unlocked? He walked into the room. A musty, unused smell flavored the air. He gazed around at the poor condition of the room's furnishings and realized the owners probably didn't lock the doors because there wasn't anything of value left here. It was like his boyhood home.

He moved through the house, suddenly confident no one was there and then went to find Foster. With any luck the other address would be just as empty and tonight he wouldn't have to kill or be killed.

Luke stared at Kathy's beautiful back. The shower spray hit her shoulders and sent a cascade of water running down it, and right before he reached out, she turned around. Her cheeks were bright red. The flush spread all the way down to the tops of her breasts.

"I'm sorry," she said before she even met his gaze.

He studied her, baffled. "For what?"

"For just standing here while you . . . did all the work."

He still didn't get it. "What were you supposed to be doing?"

She bit her lip and shook her head. "Maybe reciprocate."

He grinned. "You were kind of busy enjoying yourself."

"Yeah, selfish of me, wasn't it?" She halfway smiled.

He laughed, then pulled her close. "I certainly wouldn't

mind some reciprocation, but just so we're clear: Watching you come just now was friggin' fabulous. It's everything I wanted. You don't have a damn thing to apologize about."

She raised her head and rested her chin on his chest. "Really?" Her eyes were huge.

"Really."

"In that case, thank you. That was . . . amazing." She rose on her toes, pressed her hands to his wet chest and kissed him.

"That's the second kiss initiated by you," he pointed out, whispering against her lips.

He was considering stepping out of the shower and grabbing the condom in his jeans. But shower sex, great as it was, generally happened fast; and with only two condoms, he wanted to make the most of each. So he ran his hand down her back and deepened the kiss, thinking—

A sudden sharp pain ended the kiss.

"Damn!" he muttered against her lips, yanking his toe from the jaws of what he hoped was a puppy and not a baby gator that had made its way up the drain. When had the stupid beast slipped into the shower stall?

"What?" Kathy asked.

Luke looked down. "First he pisses on my foot and now he tries to eat it. How the hell is this dog named Goodwill?"

The animal barked and attacked his ankle again.

"Out!" Luke roared, and he literally had to shake the dog loose. There was no blood; the dog had only been giving him love bites. But Goodwill also didn't get the hint; he shook his head, crouched down playfully on his front paws, barked, then went after Luke's other foot. Luke adjusted the water spray, but Goodwill started biting at the water, as if this too was a game.

Kathy laughed. "He must have heard your threesome speech." She pressed a hand against Luke's chest and eyed

the dog, which was standing unrepentantly in the spray of water. "He's so cute! Tommy is going to love him!"

While Kathy stared at Goodwill, Luke stared at her. Damn, she looked good naked and wet, even cooing over a dog who'd just tried to remove his big toe. His body ached for release, and he passed a finger over her lips. "Yeah? You're not the one he's pissing or chewing on."

Kneeling, she gave the puppy a nudge out of the shower. "Now go be good," she told the dog. Then she stood.

Her gaze met and held Luke's. She stepped closer and placed her palms on his shoulders. The spray of water hitting his back was warm, but not as warm as her touch. Slowly, sensuously, her hands slid down his chest. Down they continued, all the way to his dick. And the moment one of her soft, wet palms wrapped around him, he almost came.

He grabbed her hand and turned off the water. "Okay. Shower's over."

"Over? Why?" she asked. Her face was serious.

"Because . . . the rooster is about to crow, and it's not done with the chicken yet."

Kathy grinned, wrapped her arms around his waist and rested her chin on his chest. When he looked into her eyes, he saw a glint of self-confidence that hadn't been there earlier, and her grin widened. "But the chicken already chirped."

"Ahh, but the chicken can chirp twice without needing a time-out." Laughter suddenly spilt from his lips. "Are we really standing here naked talking about chickens and roosters?"

"You started it," she chuckled.

"No, you did earlier." Running his hands over her smooth back, he realized that being with her was better than he'd ever imagined; through her, he'd found that part of himself he'd lost. His chest swelled with a sense of belonging, of

rightness. He *loved* her. There wasn't any other logical explanation. Why couldn't they have gotten together earlier?

"Okay, maybe I did mention it. But about this . . . time-out. I'm a patient chicken," she said, and slid her thigh between his legs. Her hand slowly inched down his belly. "I could suffer through a time-out."

"No suffering allowed." There had been a time when the thought of love or long-term commitment would have emotionally sent him scrambling for cover, but not now. Now he wanted to love her so completely that he'd mark her as his forever. Without a doubt, he wanted the "more" she was so disinclined to give.

A niggling thought surfaced, that he needed to tell Kathy about his first marriage, but he sent it packing. He didn't want to spend their time rummaging through his past. Tonight was about pleasure.

Her hand started moving downward again. "I could reciprocate. . . ."

He caught her fingers in his and walked himself and Kathy out of the shower, leaving the warm shower mist behind. His skin tingled from the cool air, but it wasn't near enough to dampen his lust. "I'll take a rain check. I've got *other* plans." Then he pulled a white towel from the stack neatly folded on the shelves and draped it around her shoulders.

"What kind of plans?" she teased, holding on to the ends of the towel.

"Good plans," he countered. "Naughty plans. I'll show you."

But as he took one step out of the bathroom, the ringing of his cell phone put his naughty plans on hold. And with all his blood down south, he swung around, snatched up the phone and hit the Talk button before he realized what he'd done. Or rather what he hadn't done. He hadn't checked the Caller ID.

Shutting his eyes in frustration, he answered with a brusque, "Hello?" He prayed it was Calvin.

"Bradley?"

Fuck. His gut knotted. It wasn't Calvin, and even worse, the caller wasn't someone wanting to speak to Harry Johnson.

"Listen to me," the caller said. "My name's Jason Dodd. I'm a cop, and I'm friends with Kathy Callahan. I think we met once. I don't know what you're into, but whatever it is, I'm sure I can help. But first I want to talk to Kathy. I need to know she's okay."

Luke pulled the phone from his ear and hit the End Call button before Dodd could trace it back to any particular cell tower and thereby get their approximate location.

Kathy moved behind him. "Who was it?"

He felt her press against his naked back, felt the nubby cotton material against his legs and knew she'd wrapped herself in the towel. He'd finally gotten her naked, and now she was covering herself up. But then her hand moved around his waist to rest low on his abdomen. That sweet yet erotic touch had things heating up again.

Who was it? The question vibrated through his head. "Wrong number."

A heaviness filled his chest, as if the air he breathed had turned to water. The weighty feeling felt vaguely familiar: guilt. And not just any guilt, but guilt for lying.

It had been a long time since lying had felt morally wrong. Lying meant survival, at least in his situation. Lying was required. How was this any different?

Did he not feel warranted in his decision of not involving the local authorities? Hell, yes. It didn't matter that the local authorities were Kathy's friends. And because he knew she'd disagree, not telling her the truth was just one way of not complicating things—things like her getting upset about him hanging up, things like her insisting he let her call Dodd back. Things like her getting angry and not letting him toss her down on that not-so-good mattress and make love to her ten different ways.

Shit. He raked a hand over his face. Was that the reason he'd lied to her: because telling her the truth might prevent him from getting laid? No wonder he felt guilty.

He turned, letting his gaze roam over her towel-draped body, eager to remove that covering. Desire still burned in her eyes.

Reaching out, he ran the back of his hand over her cheek, and she bit her lip again. The expression was part sex-kitten, part shy virgin. "Wanna tell me about those naughty plans?" she whispered.

Oh, hell yes, he did. He wanted that and so much more.

Slipping her hand into his, she led him out of the bathroom and didn't stop until they came to the sofa bed. Then, looking right at him, she unknotted her towel. It fluttered to the floor.

It took everything Luke had not to forget right and wrong. Not to push her back on that mattress and devour every inch of that body he'd wanted for so friggin' long. She put one fingertip on his chest. Then, slowly, she snaked it lower.

He caught her hand right before she caught his cock. "Wait." Damn, he couldn't do this. He stared at the phone.

"Wait—for what?"

He drew in air and released it in a huff. "That wasn't true."

"What wasn't true?" Her hazel eyes, huge with desire, blinked.

"It wasn't a wrong number."

Chapter Twenty-three

Joey and Foster got back to the car. Joey's toe throbbed, but he ignored it.

Foster got behind the wheel. He pulled off his gloves, grabbed his phone, hit a few numbers and listened. "Shit," he said, and dropped the phone in his lap.

"What?" Inside the car, Joey removed his own gloves and hoped for the best. Maybe Hunter and the girl were already miles away.

"That was a message from the trooper on duty. They say Hunter stole a blue, older-model Dodge Charger about two blocks from where he ditched the van. I'll bet my right nut that I passed that bastard on the way there this afternoon."

"The man's good," Joey said, and he realized he actually admired Hunter. The guy was a hell of a lot more of a role model than Lorenzo, whom his scummy companion seemed to idolize.

Foster must have picked up on the vibe, because he frowned. "He's a walking dead man—at least you'd better hope it ends up that way. If not, Lorenzo will be giving orders for some other guy to do to you what you did to Donald."

"Shit happens and then you die," Joey said, hoping that was only true for Donald. And Lorenzo would have to find him first.

"What?" Foster asked.

"Nothing. Just something on a hat Donald bought this morning."

"Speaking of Donald," Foster remarked. "Did you bury his ass good?"

"Good and buried," Joey replied. He cupped his hands and felt the blisters making the skin tight. *It's more than he deserved and, if it comes to that, more than I'm going to do for you.*

"It wasn't a wrong number?" Kathy repeated, confused, her mind more on getting Luke in bed than the phone call. Her body still throbbed with the pleasure he'd given her. She, Kathy Callahan, had come just from a guy's fingers. That had *so* not happened before. Tom had always had to—

Stop! Luke was right: She had to axe Tom. Thoughts of her ex didn't belong here tonight. And maybe it was time for her to stop thinking about him altogether. *Don't think about Tom. Don't think about Tom.* She needed to think about . . .

Luke. Her heart swelled as the vision of him playing ball with her son suddenly flashed through her head. Then she remembered the time she'd found Tommy's turtle dead, and Luke had stayed at the house to cover while she went to the pet store for a replacement.

She hadn't known his name was Luke then, of course. There was still so much about this man she didn't know—but also much she did know. And what she knew, she admired.

Except for the fact that after tonight he would be leaving. Her throat suddenly felt tight.

"It wasn't a wrong number," he said again.

Oh, yeah, she was supposed to be thinking about the wrong number thingamajig. There had to be a good reason he wanted to talk about that.

"So who called?" she asked.

"It was your friend's husband—Dodd, I think he said his last name was."

"Jason?" Okay, his reasons for discussing this suddenly started to become clear.

Feeling as if nakedness wasn't conducive to the conversation, Kathy picked up the towel at her feet. But when she did, Goodwill decided he wanted it, too. It took several careful yanks, while naked, to get the puppy to give up. Finally, the towel again around her, she looked at Luke.

"How did Jason know to call—?"

"I'm sure Mr. Johnson has reported the car stolen, and he told them that I took his phone."

She tried to recall what Luke had said when he'd answered the phone, but her mind was in post-orgasm mode and she hadn't taken in much of the conversation. "What did Jason say?"

"He said he wanted to help, but that he wanted to talk to you first."

"And you said?" Then she remembered. "You didn't say anything, did you?"

"No. I hung up. He could have traced us."

"Yeah," she agreed, her mind still finding it hard to focus. Luke was standing there without a stitch of clothing. "Couldn't I just have told him I was okay?"

"Maybe, but I didn't want to chance it. This is almost over. Calvin will send in some people. We'll get out of this in one piece. We just have to play it cool and by the book."

She stared at him, her mind starting to process. "So why did you tell me that it was a wrong number?"

He let out a gulp of air. "Because I knew we'd be having this conversation, and I didn't want to have this conversation."

"So you lied?"

"No," he insisted. "Okay, I did. But then I told the truth."

"Why?" she asked.

"I already told you!" There was a hint of frustration to his voice. "I knew we'd end up talking about this and—"

"No, I meant why did you tell me the truth?"

He closed his eyes. When he opened them, he reached

out and brushed a strand of wet hair from her cheek. "Because as soon as I lied to you, it felt wrong."

"Lying is always wrong," she pointed out, confused, her emotions running all over the place. It had to be the orgasm—normally she did a much better job of focusing.

"True." He moved a step nearer. "But this felt really wrong. And I don't want anything wrong between us. Actually, I'd prefer nothing between us." He glanced down at the towel.

She didn't say anything, because she wasn't sure what to say.

He moved closer, his natural scent filling her next breath, and moving his hand under her chin he tilted her head back so she would look at him. "You know what I want?"

"What?" she asked, but she was pretty sure she knew, because she was almost back to wanting it, too. The fact that he'd lied and then corrected it meant something. She wasn't sure what, but right now it didn't feel all bad.

"I want to forget about this conversation. I want to spend the next few hours being with you. Not thinking about calls or trials or any of the ugliness we've dealt with today, or any of the crap I've dealt with during the last four years of my undercover work and relocation. I just want to be with you. You think that's possible?"

Reaching up, she ran her fingers through his hair, which was still damp and curled up at the ends. "I think it might be possible."

He smiled and dropped his forehead against hers. "In that case, would it be wrong of me to say that, although you look lovely in that towel, I happen to know that you look even better without it?"

"It wouldn't be wrong," she said. "But it would be rude." She gave him an amused grin.

"Being rude I can handle."

He pulled the towel free and tossed it to Goodwill. The puppy raced to the terrycloth, latched his teeth into the soft material and shook it back and forth as if it were a chew toy. The next thing Kathy knew, she and Luke were on the sofa bed, facing each other, his mouth on hers. His solid body was pressed against hers. The light spray of hair across his chest teased her nipples. His hands caressed the sides of her breasts, and then moved over her back, following the arch of her spine. His palms cupped her bottom and ever so lightly rocked her pelvis against his.

She felt him, hot and hard against her thigh. Each time he brought her against him, his sex would slip between her legs, lighting a want, a need, a desire to take him inside her body. She felt herself grow moist again between her legs, and her need to be touched was almost painful.

"What do you like?" he whispered, kissing her again.

"This," she managed to say. "I like this." Then, remembering not to just lie there, she brought her hands up and brushed them over his chest. "What do *you* like?"

"Let me show you."

He rolled her onto her back and started his descent: her neck, her breasts and . . . lower. Slow. Easy. Wet. His lips and his tongue made an erotic, mind-spinning trail of butterfly kisses down her abdomen. He got between her thighs and placed a moist kiss on the tender skin inside each leg. Then he brushed his lips over her center, back and forth, never too fast, never too slow. When his tongue touched her there, moved against her, just like that, the world started spinning. It shattered into a starburst of pleasure. The next thing she knew, Luke held her in his arms, kissing her as she floated down to earth.

When he pulled back, he wore the cockiest of smiles. "Now aren't you totally, completely pissed at yourself right now?"

"For what?" she managed to ask. Had she done something wrong?

"For wasting all this time. We could have been doing this for the last two and a half years!"

She grinned. "Yeah, that was pretty dumb, wasn't it?"

He bundled her closer, and his chest moved with laughter. "Do you have any idea how much I love being with you?"

Love? The word caused the slightest wiggle of fear, but she pushed it back. Forcing herself to laugh, she said, "Don't you think it's time I reciprocate?"

"You must have read my mind." He reached over and dropped a foil package in her hand. "Mind helping a fellow out?"

"Not at all," she replied.

Feeling a little brazen, she pushed him down on the mattress, got up on her knees and straddled his upper thighs. His sex proudly saluted the ceiling. She couldn't help staring as she opened the foil package—or tried to open it. With her distraction, it took a while.

Luke didn't complain. He folded his arms behind his head, which accented his muscular arms and torso, and stared at her in all her nakedness. Not that this bothered her. She kind of liked staring at him, too. Oddly, she couldn't remember enjoying Tom being naked. Sex had been an undercover exercise.

At last, she slipped the condom from its package. She'd just placed the cool rubber on the tip of him when she recalled one of the discussions she'd had with Lacy and Sue—about the most sensitive points on a man's penis. Oh yeah, she remembered. Sue and Lacy had laughed themselves silly when she had brought out a curved banana for demonstration. She had to admit, this was much more exciting.

Pulling the condom away from his sex, she slowly ran her finger up the back of his shaft, tracing a blue vein. After twirling her finger around the head, she followed its cleft. Then she repeated the process, slower. She heard Luke moan, felt the moisture collect on the tip. Softly, she rolled the condom down his erection and used her other hand to caress his balls.

She didn't expect him to flip her over so quickly, but she wasn't complaining, especially when he settled on top of her. His weight felt right. Perfect, actually. Everything felt perfect as he entered her, stretched her, filled her.

There were no awkward moves, no tenuous adaptation to a rhythm they both understood. They moved together as if in a dance they'd practiced together forever: slow at first, then faster. He brushed the hair from her face and gazed into her eyes. Kathy Callahan had never felt so complete, so whole, or so beautiful.

Jason and Chase caught up with Turner right before he pulled off in order to tell him about the stolen cell phone. Turner didn't appear happy that Jason had collected the information, nor that he'd already made the first call.

"Give me the number," Turner said, frowning, standing outside his cruiser.

Jason handed over the paper where he'd jotted down the number that Johnson gave him. "I suggest you give him an hour. If we call him back right now, we'll piss him off. If we piss him off, he's more likely to hurt Kathy."

Turner shook his head. "Do you really think she's being held hostage? True, I know she . . . she doesn't seem the type to be in on the drugs. However, considering what Cary saw, what Johnson said about her yanking the guy's ear and saying he wouldn't hurt her, and what we discovered about her past, it's not looking too good."

Jason looked up at the dark sky and remembered what he'd read about Kathy witnessing her father's death. He factored in all he knew about her. She loved her son. She was about as loyal a friend as anyone could be to both Lacy and Sue. The fact that she was standoffish with him and Chase—well, it now made complete sense. And her being in on anything illegal, that didn't compute.

Grabbing his keys from his pocket, he looked back at

Turner. "If she's helping this guy, it's because she has a reason. A *good* reason. She's not into anything illegal."

"Maybe, but if she's helping him, that's illegal. And I don't like it any more than you two do, but I'm just calling it like I see it. Kathy Callahan is in a heap of trouble."

Chase and Jason watched Turner get in his car and drive away. Then Chase looked at Jason. "He's not the only one who's going to see things like that. We've got to get to the bottom of this, or Kathy could really be up shit creek."

"Why don't we go talk to Bradley's landlady? Maybe she'll give us something that might help." Jason rocked on his heels, trying to think.

Chase started to their car. "That's not a bad idea. Sure can't hurt."

Joey leaned back in his seat, ignoring Foster's rambling monologue about his ex-wives, and looked up through the window at the stars. In less than five minutes they would be at the second location, and God only knew what would happen then. Even Foster seemed on edge, or at least that might explain his constant jabbering.

While Joey's gaze watched the sky, a bright diamondlike streak shot across the blackness and faded into the horizon. It had moved too fast for an airplane. It had to have been a . . . Damn, he'd never seen a shooting star before. Thrilled, he almost turned around to tell Foster but caught himself. Men like Foster didn't give a damn about any shooting star.

"She caught me with the woman in the parking lot of the grocery store," Foster was saying. "And I told her, 'When you learn to suck dick that good, I'll stop seeing her.' So that's when I divorced wife number three." The trooper chuckled. "What about you? Got a woman waiting on you?"

"No." Joey looked back at the sky, vaguely remembering the singsong rhyme about making a wish on a shooting star. Wasn't it supposed to be good luck?

"You aren't much of a talker, are you?"

"No."

He remembered the conversations he'd had with Donald after the man died and wondered if they counted. Then he remembered talking with Lola. She'd been easy to talk to. He'd loved the way her accent lent a playfulness to her tone. *Yoey*—that was how his name had sounded, rolling off her tongue. A smile tickled his lips, and he thought again about going to see her.

Maybe tomorrow. If he had a tomorrow.

His focus remained on the sky until something crashed against the windshield.

Foster slammed on his brakes. "Shit!" The trooper jumped, and he must have hit the wipers, because a swishing sound immediately followed the crash, and then a thud, and then the wipers' motor started grinding.

Joey looked at the driver's side of the windshield. A bat lay trapped there, its wing pinned under the wiper. From all appearances, the animal was dead.

Dead? Joey's mind shot immediately to the bird that had slammed against the car less than an hour before Donald collapsed, and his heart skipped a beat. The dark sky seemed to grow darker, and he hoped the star had been meant to bring good luck. He also hoped like hell the luck was meant for him and not the dead bat trapped against the windshield.

Luke rolled onto his side, not wanting to drop his 200 pounds on top of Kathy. The moment he landed, he wrapped his arms around her and pulled her against him. He felt her breathing against his chest. Those quick wispy gasps matched his own.

He'd been lucky she'd been fast, or God help him, he would have gotten to the top of mountain without her. It had been too damn long since he'd been with a woman. It had—

The thought had no sooner flashed in his head than he

recognized the lie. His abstinence wasn't what had made him climb so fast and high. Abstinence wasn't what made the journey so damn special. It was her. All her. Kathy Callahan.

"I . . . didn't know," she said, and rested her hand against his chest.

"Didn't know what?" he managed to ask.

"That sex was . . . could be like that."

"That wasn't sex." He brushed his lips against her cheek.

"What was it?" she asked, and he couldn't believe he heard insecurity in her voice. Didn't she know she'd blown him away? He didn't have a clue what that asshole of an ex had said to her to make her feel this way, but the guy had to have been dumber than a pet rock dropped on its head.

"That," he said, "was heaven on earth." He cupped her chin in his hand so she'd look him in the eyes and know he meant business. "That was two and a half years plus of prep work, two and a half years plus of teasing, flirting, of two people who are meant to . . ." He almost said *love each other*, but her previous speech echoed in his head. "To be together. You were everything I thought you'd be and more."

She smiled her half-shy, half-playful smile. "So you really imagined how it would be?"

"Oh, hell yeah. During those cold showers that weren't really cold showers, you were there—or here." He touched his head. "Doing all sorts of naughty things."

"You're bad." She pressed a palm to his chest.

"I'm bad? *You* fantasized about *me*." He pulled her hips against his, loving how she fit against him. "Admit it."

The shy portion of her smile grew stronger. "Okay, maybe a little."

He saw the lie in her eyes and almost laughed. "And . . . ?"

"And what?"

"And did I live up to your expectations?"

She blinked, staring at him seriously. "Almost," she admitted—and then she started giggling. "I'm joking!"

"You think that's funny?" He rolled on top of her, snatched both her hands in one of his and held them above her head. When he stared down at her, he noticed her cheeks and chest were red. "You're chafed." He passed a hand over his face stubble. "Sorry."

She sighed. "Don't be. It was perfect. You were perfect." Wiggling her hand free, she brushed a palm over his jaw. "Thank you."

"No. Thank you."

The feel of her soft touch, the feel of her body beneath his, it all had things stirring again. Luke looked into her eyes, saw the way the gold and green flecks seemed to meld together and he said, "I was right."

She looked surprised. "Right about what?"

Right about what? That she was so damn perfect for him. That sex with her would ruin him for any other woman. He'd been right about so many things, but he wasn't allowed to say them.

"Your eyes change colors when you have sex," he said instead. Then he leaned in and kissed her.

Chapter Twenty-four

Joey, gloves on and gun in hand, trailed behind Foster. His gut felt like one tight knot. He kept thinking about that shooting star and hoped like hell luck had him in its sights. *Don't let them be here. Don't let them be here.* He repeated the words over and over in his head like a prayer. And, hey . . . maybe he was praying.

In spite of the fact that they were supposed to sneak up on

the cabin, Foster never stopped his nervous, low-toned yapping. Joey tried to tune him out, tired of hearing about the man's sexual conquests.

"What you want to bet I'll have her on her knees in front of me, unzipping my pants, within two days?"

Joey didn't care who Foster had in front of him. Damn! His foot came down hard on a rock and jarred his broken toe.

"You see, I know the magic word for all those Latinas."

His attention was wrenched from his throbbing toe, and his gut knotted even tighter. Was Foster talking about Lola? Joey imagined that sweet face with those exotic eyes. God help the man if he was talking about Lola.

"The magic word is Immigration. All I gotta do is say it real slow, point out that I know her brother-in-law is working as an illegal at that concrete company, and I'll have that roach coach babe between my legs anytime I want. Hell, I might have had her today if you hadn't parked your ass there."

Suddenly, Foster backed up—right into the end of Joey's gun. The temptation to pull the trigger was strong.

"Well, shit," Foster said in low voice. "We got those mother fuckers! Look, there's the blue Dodge Charger. And you thought Luke Hunter was good. Not as good as I am."

Before he nerved up to pull the trigger, Joey realized Foster had his phone out and was making a call.

Luke felt himself growing hard again, felt Kathy's sweet body moving against his. But the thought that he only had one more condom made him rein in his desires. He ended the kiss and brushed her hair from her eyes.

"Sex makes me hungry," he said. "Was there anything else in the cabinet?"

She chuckled. "You can have the prunes."

"Funny."

"Yeah, I thought it was."

The most adorable smile lit her expression, and his chest swelled. Leaving, even for the trial, was going to be hell. Not that he had an option. But he'd be back, and he hoped like hell she understood that.

"Actually, I think I saw some pineapple, and I don't think we ate all the crackers," she continued. The dog, which had been sleeping in the corner of the room, suddenly jumped up and barked. "I think Goodwill's hungry, too."

Luke shook his head. "Why? He ate half my foot just a bit ago." When Kathy laughed, he suggested, "Why don't you grab the food? I'm going to make a pit stop." He motioned to the bathroom. With some food in his belly, maybe he could figure out how to broach the subject of the future. Their future. It had taken him this long to win her over. No way in hell was he giving her up.

He rolled off the bed. At the same time, the phone rang. His gaze met hers, and he knew what she was thinking.

She sat up, pulling the sheet up with her. "Can't I just say that I'm okay? Doesn't it take a minute or two before they can trace a call?"

Luke picked up the phone from the side table and looked at the number. Relief whispered through him. "It's not him. Different number."

"Is it Calvin?"

"No. It's probably a call for Harry Johnson. So I'm not answering it."

Kathy nodded. From the look in her eyes, he could tell she didn't agree with his decision but didn't plan on arguing. For the latter, he was grateful.

The cell quit ringing. Luke leaned down and kissed her again, then headed for the bathroom, the cell phone snug in his palm. It wasn't that he didn't trust her, but considering that he knew she disagreed with his tactics . . . well, there wasn't a damn good reason to take a chance.

* * *

"We got them," Foster said into the phone. "Told you I was good."

Joey's heart raced with indecision as he listened to the dirty trooper talk to someone he assumed was Lorenzo. Imagining what Foster would do to Lola gave him courage but just not quite enough. Finger on the trigger, he wondered whether Donald had hesitated when he'd offed Freddy. Had it been hard at all?

"Nah, we don't need them," Foster continued. "I say, let Joey and me take care of this. We'll get the job done, and you make my deposit in the morning."

Joey looked back at the cabin and saw a shadow move across the front window. He thought of the redhead and looked back at his gun. He had to do this. He *had* to. Not just for Lola and the redhead but for her kid.

Kathy frowned as Luke walked away with the cell phone. Seriously, what harm would it do to call Lacy and in less than ten seconds let her friend know she was okay? From what Harry Johnson had said, her friends thought Luke kidnapped her. Lacy and Sue didn't need to be worrying, not in their conditions.

Kathy looked around the cabin for a radio or television. It appeared Claire thought those might be bad for her digestive system, because neither was present. Kathy supposed a weekend escape didn't require keeping in touch with the outside world.

She thought again about calling Lacy, about insisting Luke loan her the phone. Ahh, but arguing with the man who had just sent her to heaven didn't seem right. So she kept her mouth shut and watched him move into the bathroom.

Damn, if he didn't look good. His backside was round and tight. His thighs were solid, and no skinny knees for Luke Hunter. His legs were muscled, thick and finely dusted with hair. She'd read once in a magazine that a lot of men were waxing. She was glad Luke hadn't taken that route. No, she wouldn't want a man covered in fur, but a little hair . . . well, it seemed masculine. She remembered how sensitive her nipples had felt brushing against the soft hair on his chest. Yup, a little hair was fine.

A smile tugged at her lips, and she realized the light, airy feeling in her chest was all because of him. He made her . . . happy. Not that she hadn't been happy. She had her son to make her smile, to remind her of what life was really about. She had Lacy and Sue, her anchors, helping her stay sane whenever life seemed too crazy. She had her florist business. It felt good to make a living doing something she enjoyed. But Luke made her . . . well, he made her feel something more. As if she'd been missing out on something, a part of her that had been neglected. A part of her that had been dormant, a part that he'd brought back to life.

Who knew sex was so important?

His words vibrated though her head and heart. *That wasn't sex.* It certainly wasn't—not like any sex she'd ever had.

Pulling the sheet up to her chest, she fought back the fear that this was "more." That it involved things like promises and commitments. She had no problem offering those things, but she'd known the sting too often of having them broken; of having her love, her trust and her heart tossed back in her face—first from her father, then from a shitload of cops and then her husband. Did she really want to go there again?

Closing her eyes, she recalled several conversations she'd had with Sue and Lacy. She hadn't blamed them for falling in love, for relying on men to make their lives complete, but she'd sworn she would never want or need that security, herself. And yet . . .

Goodwill's bark brought her out of her thoughts. She looked at the puppy, who was dancing by the door.

"You gotta go?" she asked, feeling relieved to have something to pull her out of her reverie. God help her, but she didn't want to start regretting what had happened, and she didn't want to start thinking about the consequences. Couldn't she just enjoy the moment? Luke was going to leave tomorrow. She'd have plenty of time to reassess, to beat herself up for any mistakes then.

Standing up, she found her towel on the floor and wrapped it around her. Then she grabbed the leash that she'd left on the counter. After attaching it to Goodwill's collar, she opened the door to the dark, silent night.

Goodwill started barking—hard, serious barks—and yanked on the leash. It surprised her.

"What's wrong boy? You smell a raccoon or something?" Holding tight to the leash, Kathy gave a quick glance around the property. There wasn't another house for a mile, so no one would see her in a towel. She stepped out into the night.

The spring air held a tiny thread of coolness. As her feet met the damp ground, her gaze moved up to the dark sky. The stars seemed extra bright. Goodwill continued to bark and tried to run toward the woods. "No!" she ordered, and moved to another patch of grass, hoping he'd do his business before she lost her covering.

Foster had no sooner hung up when Joey saw the cabin's front door open. His breath caught when he recognized the redhead. With a couple of bushes and about fifty yards between them, she didn't have a clue of her danger. But the puppy on the leash, dragging her closer, seemed to have them in his sights.

"A little closer will make it easier." Foster let out a low groan, and the puppy started yapping louder. "Damn shame we can't get us a piece of that before we do the job."

The realization of what Foster meant made Joey wince in disgust, and he knew without a doubt the man deserved to die. While he didn't like being the one to do it, he also knew it had to be done. Maybe whatever Higher Power there was had put Joey here just for this reason—to do what had to be done. Maybe.

Foster released the safety on his gun. Sweat dripped from Joey's brow, and his hands felt sweaty beneath his gloves.

"She's even hotter than that Mexican piece of ass I'm going to get me some of later," the trooper muttered.

"You're making this easy," Joey whispered. He pointed the gun with its homemade silencer at the back of his companion's head.

"Making what easy?" Foster asked.

Joey pulled the trigger.

Chapter Twenty-five

Joey felt a splatter of what he assumed was blood on his arms and face. The *whoosh* from the gun, the gasp of Foster catching his last breath and then the thud of the man falling onto the soft ground, it all seemed drowned out by unrelenting barking. Bile rose in Joey's throat. Immediately, he realized he'd been wrong—not wrong to do it, but wrong about it being easy. Falling to his knees, refusing to look at the corpse of the man he'd just killed, he lost the contents of his stomach as silently as he could.

He, Joey Hinkle, had murdered a man. Did that make him damned to Hell, or had he done the job he'd been fated to do? Trying to control his gasping, he attempted to remind himself why he'd done it: the kid. He'd done it for the kid. Because that boy would have grown up without a mother like Joey and his brother had. Joey had also done it for Lola, because Foster would have forced her to have sex with him.

"Kathy?"

Joey heard a man call the name in panic. Hunter. Had the gunshot been loud enough for them to hear? Still on his hands and knees, Joey inched back farther into the woods. The ground felt cold even through his gloves, and dampness seeped through his suit pants.

"I'm here," the redhead answered above the dog's barking.

"What the hell are you doing outside? You scared the piss out of me!"

"Goodwill had to go."

Joey looked up and saw Luke Hunter rush over to the woman. His gaze shifted back and forth, checking out the area. While Joey couldn't be sure, it looked as if Hunter had a gun. Still feeling sick to his stomach, Joey crouched a little lower.

"What's got him all riled up?" Hunter asked, and Joey assumed he meant the dog. Relief fluttered through him.

"Probably a coon," the redhead answered.

"Has he done his business?" Hunter asked, impatient.

"Not yet."

"Well, he's had his chance." The man scooped up the dog. "Let's go inside."

"But . . ." She never finished what she had to say, as Hunter nudged her back toward the house.

Joey stayed where he was, on his knees, smelling the earth and the coppery scent of blood. His stomach still roiled.

Pushing his panic aside, he tried to think of what he needed to do now. He'd killed a man, killed him to save others. But unless he could stop Lorenzo from getting the redhead, his killing would be in vain. He couldn't let that happen.

Forcing himself to do what needed to be done, he moved to Foster's body and found the man's phone and keys. Then, grabbing Foster's feet, Joey pulled him deeper into the woods. He wouldn't bury him. Nope. If the buzzards picked Foster's bones, the man deserved it. Giving the body, face-down on the ground, one last look, Joey fought the need to puke again and started back to the car.

Remembering what Foster had said about the gun belong-ing to some drug gang, he tossed it out into the woods. When he reached the car, he had to adjust the seat before his 300-pound frame would fit. Sitting there, hands gripping the steering wheel, he focused on breathing and not think-ing. Then he saw it, out of the corner of his eye: another shooting star. It whisked across the sky like a message. Swal-lowing a lump, the ugliness of what he'd done didn't seem quite so ugly.

He grabbed Foster's phone from his coat pocket.

Lorenzo's voice echoed across the line when it connected: "Tell me the job is done."

"Sorry," Joey said. "Hunter shot Foster. He's dead."

Lorenzo let loose a long string of curse words that had Joey remembering his mother—a redhead like the woman he'd just saved. Someone needed to take a toilet brush to Lorenzo's mouth. Oh, hell, Lorenzo needed more than that.

"Here. Let me get that for you." Jason jumped up from the kitchen chair to help Claire Banks reach the glasses for the iced tea she'd offered him and Chase.

"Why, thank you. It's good to see at least *some* young men still have manners." The woman glanced at Chase, almost as if to suggest she found him lacking in the etiquette de-partment.

"We appreciate you talking to us this late," Jason said.

"No problem, I usually stay up to watch *The Tonight Show*."

When the woman turned back around, Chase shot Jason an annoyed expression, and Jason knew it went without saying he'd get his chops busted when they left. His friend was always ribbing him about his soft spot for the elderly. Not that he really had one.

He brought three glasses down. "Like we were saying, we would just like to go over everything you saw and see if there's anything you might be able to add about Stan Bradley."

The old woman handed Jason an ice pick. He stared at it.

"You'll need to chop the ice. It's in the freezer," she said, motioning to the fridge.

"Oh." He went to the freezer and pulled out a bag of ice. He looked down at the refrigerator and the ice dispenser in the door. "The ice machine is always the first to go, isn't it?"

"Go?" she asked, as she cut up a lemon.

"With refrigerators."

"Oh, it's not broken. I just don't use it. Makes the ice taste funny. And, if you ask me, it causes IBS."

"IBS?" Chase asked.

"Irritable Bowel Syndrome," the woman said. "Think about it. Probably five out of ten people have this problem now, and back before all this new modern technology started messing with our food, IBS didn't exist. Sure, we got gassy in the old days, but nothing a good walk around the block by yourself wouldn't cure."

Jason saw a look of suppressed laughter on Chase's face and had to swipe a hand over his own mouth. Then he turned around, dropped the bagged ice in the sink and started picking off chunks.

While he picked, he talked. "According to the reports, you said that you saw Stan Bradley kidnap Kathy Callahan."

"I didn't say he kidnapped her. Okay, sure, it sounds like he kidnapped her. I'll go so far to say it *looked* like he kidnapped her. But that boy is a good boy. He's never once turned me down when I asked a favor." She went to the fridge and took out a pitcher of tea. "And being the age I am,

I have a tendency to ask for a lot of favors. Of course, I cooked for the boy. Boy howdy, he sure did enjoy my meals."

"Exactly what did you see?" Chase asked.

"Why, one time I was out of my suppositories and he came through for me," Claire continued, ignoring Chase. Jason saw him make a face. "Can't see to drive at night, and that boy drove to five different pharmacies before he found them. My own son-in-law won't go pick up my supposito-ries—as if there's something ugly about them just because they go where the sun doesn't shine."

Jason heard Chase cough, which was really a laugh, and he bit the inside of his cheek to keep his composure. "He sounds like a nice guy."

"Which is why all this drug business is for the birds. Stan Bradley is a good man. If I were a few years younger I'd be smitten with him."

Jason dropped ice into their glasses. "So exactly what did you see this morning?"

"He was carrying her out of the house. Over his shoulder. He put her down. Well, he sort of dropped her down. Then I saw him pushing her into that big florist van. He ran around and got in the driver's side and drove off." She waved her hands back and forth. "That's when those no-good Yan-kees came out of the house and started shooting. Of course, I'd heard them shooting before."

Jason tried to imagine the scene. "So maybe the plumber was trying to get her away from the shooters."

"That's what I tried to tell those other police officers. But you know how most of you men are—stubborn dingbats."

"Do you know if Mr. Bradley had any friends or family?" Jason asked.

"Nope. Boy was a loner. Didn't even have a girlfriend. Don't know why either. He is what women your age would call a 'hottie.'"

"I don't think he's that good-looking," Chase muttered.

Jason turned and stared at him.

"What?" Chase said. "I don't."

Jason looked back at Claire Banks. "And that's when you called the police?"

"No, I'd already called the police."

"Why would you have already called the police?" Chase asked.

The woman put a finger to her temple. "You know, I think I forgot to tell this part to the other cops, too."

"What part?" Jason said.

"I called Stan when I saw those fellows pull up. He told me to lock my doors and to call the police."

Chase stood. "He told you to call the police? The plumber is the one who told you to call the police?"

"Yup. I'm telling you, he's a good boy. Any man who'll go after suppositories is a good one. Why . . . I *trust* the boy. Even gave him free rein to my lake cabin. Unlike some men, I knew he wouldn't be taking women up there, doing the dirty and using it like some cheap hotel. He's a good boy, that one. Loves my meatloaf like you wouldn't believe."

Jason looked at Chase, and a clear truth was rushing through his head: If Stan Bradley was into drug trafficking, he wouldn't have told her to call the police.

"Ten o'clock at the fruit stand."

Holding the cell phone to his ear, Luke repeated what Calvin said while he looked at Kathy. She was sitting at the tiny table in the corner of the room, wearing his shirt. When she'd asked if she could wear it, he'd told her no, that the towel gave him easier access. She'd rolled her eyes at him, sashayed that cute, towel-covered ass into the bathroom and donned it anyway. He couldn't complain.

They'd almost finished their after-sex snack when the phone had rung again. It was Calvin with the time and place.

"The stand is right off 101, a couple—"

"I know where the stand is," Luke answered. "We'll be there."

Kathy glanced down at her plate of pineapple and crackers. Was she thinking the same thing Luke was? Bringing an end to the mess would be heaven, but being separated from each other was going to be hell.

"About the girl," Calvin said. "If you could . . ."

"Could what?" Luke asked.

"Nothing."

Luke didn't like that. His gut twisted with an antsy feeling—the kind of feeling he'd banked on when working difficult cases. The kind of feeling that had helped keep him alive. Was he just getting paranoid, or was he picking up something in Calvin's tone?

"Who's going to meet us?" he asked.

A pause filled the line. Luke didn't like the pause either.

"Brad Chow and Kirk Paulson," Calvin finally said.

Luke recognized the names. He took a deep breath and tried to calm the inkling that something was wrong. He remembered Calvin telling him earlier that his wife had been in an accident. Was that why he seemed off the mark?

"How's your wife?" Luke asked.

"She's better." Calvin let out a breath. "Is everything still okay there? No problems?"

"It will be better tomorrow," Luke answered.

"But no troubles so far?"

The niggling feeling stirred in Luke's gut again. "Nothing I haven't handled—why?"

"Just checking," Calvin said. "Stay safe. Stay . . . alive."

Luke nodded and ended the call. Stay alive. He intended to do just that.

Chapter Twenty-six

He hung up and looked at Kathy while evaluating his paranoia.

"Everything okay?" she asked.

He wished like hell he knew. "We're set to meet tomorrow at ten." He looked out through the windows and reminded himself that no one had followed them. If they had, the shit would have already hit the fan. Setting his worry aside, he decided he wasn't going to let his doubts eat at him—but he'd be a fool to ignore them completely. And he was no fool.

He watched Kathy offer the puppy another cracker as she said, "He really needs some dog food."

"He'll get plenty tomorrow," Luke replied. The dog was lucky, because tomorrow he'd still be with Kathy. Luke knew without a doubt that they would whisk him to wherever the trial was being held. And since the trial might have to move, there was a chance of it being dragged out for weeks, maybe even months. That was a lot of time for Kathy to rebuild the barriers he'd just torn down.

His gaze swept over her. "You know, I was wrong," he said.

"Wrong about what?"

He grinned. "About you wearing my shirt."

She smiled that shy, seductive grin. "It's not really your shirt. You stole it."

"Yup. And after seeing it on you, they'll have to pry it out of my cold dead hands before I give it back. It's going into my keepsakes drawer."

That earned him another eye roll. "You have a keepsakes drawer filled with women's clothing—like underwear and such?"

"Why? Are you offering to add to my collection?"

"No!" Grinning, she raised one of her shoulders in a playful gesture that was so damn sexy he felt himself harden. "I couldn't offer you any panties. I'm not wearing any."

"I know." He ran a hand over his chest and grinned.

Nope, she didn't have a stitch on under that shirt. The shirttail hit midthigh, giving him plenty of leg to look at. Not that his gaze stayed on her legs, because every few minutes she'd shift those, and the shirttail would gape, offering him a peek at that perfectly waxed little triangle of red hair between her legs.

She shifted and uncrossed her legs, as if his gaze had lingered too long. Not that he considered it a problem. He simply glanced upward, where an equally nice view waited; the top two buttons of the shirt remained undone, and when she shifted just right, he got a glimpse of her breasts. His mind flashed an image of Kathy in the shower, the water trickling down those mounds of soft flesh and beading on her nipples. His mouth watered to taste them again. Obviously, the pineapple and crackers had recharged his energy, because he was hard again and getting harder. Uncomfortably hard.

Getting a glass of water, he readjusted himself. What he really wanted to do was remove his jeans, but he'd heard some women had rules about being naked before the guy. Something about a guy appearing too confident about her giving it up. Not that he was denying any such thing, because he felt damn confident she'd want to sleep with him again. Nevertheless, if following some dumb rule made her feel better about things, he'd be a by-the-book kind of guy.

He drank the water, put his glass in the sink, then he went and pulled Kathy upright before wrapping his arms around her waist. She didn't resist, but came to him in that soft, wanting way women do when they're willing. Then she rested her head on the spot between his shoulder and his chest. Her head fit perfectly, too—just the way he envisioned her fitting into his life, Tommy included.

He heard her sigh. It was the kind of sigh that usually meant a man could go ahead and take off his jeans. But before he got them both naked, they needed to talk.

"Did you get enough to eat?" she asked. She rested her chin on his chest and stared at him.

"It'll hold me over," he said, gazing into her eyes. "You?"

"I'm hoping I'll drop a pound."

"Don't you dare," he said. "You're perfect." He ran his hands down her sides to her waist, loving the soft curves that defined her shape.

"Ahh, the things men will say to get a woman in bed."

He laughed. And then, though he hadn't decided how to broach the subject of their future, the words just slipped out. "I think I'm in love with you, Kathy."

He knew he'd messed up by the slightest stiffening of her posture, and she blinked. "Don't say that."

"Why not?" he asked. It was too late to take the words back.

She swallowed and inched back. "Because . . . because it's kind of soon, don't you think?"

"You call two years and, what is it, nine months too soon?" He spotted the fear in her eyes. "Don't freak out." He tugged her closer to him. "I'm not asking you to take my name and have my baby." Although that idea appealed to him. "I'm just saying that . . . I want to give us a shot. That when the trial's over I'll be back, and I'd like it if I didn't have to chase off a dozen or so men attempting to take my place."

"Like there'll really be a lot of competition." She grinned. It appeared forced but was still a start. If humor put her at ease, he didn't mind.

"Are you kidding me?" He pointed to his eye. "Are you forgetting the reason I got this? Those men were all over you. And so was that cop Cory or whatever his name was. He—"

"Cary," she corrected.

"I don't care what his name is. The point is, I saw the way he eyeballed you. It's no secret that any one of those men would give their right eye and probably an extra limb to trade places with me right now. And since I'm going to be MIA for a while, I'd like a little assurance that you won't fill my shoes."

She softened against him. "I don't think your shoes are easy to fill."

He leaned down and kissed her. "You just keep thinking that."

She ended the kiss that he'd meant to lead somewhere. "The thing is, I . . . I don't . . . I'm not sure I can . . ."

Her words made no sense, but her expression spoke loud and clear. "We'll take it slow, Kathy. As slow as you want."

She nodded. "Slow is good."

He started to go back in for a kiss, but she slipped a hand between their mouths. "How long do you think you'll be gone?"

"I don't know. Could be a week or a month."

"That long?" she asked. Her brow creased, and he could tell she felt the same way he did.

"Yeah. It's going to be hell. I wish I could ask you to come with me, but I know the DA and the US Marshals wouldn't agree."

She made a face. "I couldn't go anyway. I have to work and . . . Damn!" She pulled back. "I haven't even thought about work. I'll bet I had eight deliveries to make this afternoon! I was supposed to deliver to a baby shower. And there was a convention at the Chambers. I was supposed to deliver fresh flowers for their vases. How could I have forgotten—?"

"Hey." He interrupted her by pressing his forehead against hers. "You sort of had a few other things to worry about."

"True, but still I should have remembered."

He shot her his best sexy smile. "What you wanna bet I can make you forget everything again?"

She looked up and grinned. "You really are a bad boy, aren't you, Mr. Hunter?"

"Sweetheart, I'll be anything you want—a bad boy, a rogue or even a pirate. You seem to fancy those in the naughty books you read."

She put a hand on his chest and gave him an accusing grin. "You've been checking out my books?"

"It's not like they were hidden. You kept a stack on the back of your toilet. I had to move them, and one just sort of fell open in my hands."

She shrugged. "Okay . . . but they aren't naughty. They're romance novels."

"Yeah, well, that's my kind of romance. Naughty."

He picked her up. She wrapped her legs around his waist, and when the moist spot between her legs met his naked abdomen, he groaned and started moving to the bed. Their talk had lasted too damn long. It was time to move to the good stuff.

Jason sat beside his wife, shooing the cats away as Sue read the pages in the true-crime book that told Kathy's childhood story. Both he and Chase had debated telling their wives everything they'd learned, but then, because they were both afraid of what their wives would do after discovering they hadn't been forthcoming, they'd decided to spill their guts.

This time, however, they'd done it separately. After he and Chase phoned to tell Cary what they'd learned about Stan telling Claire to call the police, Jason took Sue back to their place. When he'd told Sue what he'd read about Kathy and her father, she'd immediately insisted on seeing. He knew it was going to be hard for her to read, but when his wife's mind was made up, there was no changing it.

Jason heard Sue's breath catch, and knew she'd just gotten to the part about Kathy. She covered her mouth with her hand and tears filled her eyes, but she continued to read. He dropped his arm around her shoulders.

She turned and pressed her face into his shoulder and sobbed. "That's . . . terrible." After a good cry, his shirt was a mess and she pulled back. "I don't understand why Kathy never told us about this. Didn't she trust us?"

Jason cupped his wife's chin in his hand. "Sue, it doesn't have anything to do with how she felt about you guys. When bad things happen when you're young . . . it does something to you. It messes with your head. Sometimes you think that if you don't think or talk about it, it'll go away."

"But something like that doesn't go away," she pointed out.

"I know. But until a person wants to deal with it, it just feels safer not talking."

"You're talking about yourself, too—what happened with your mom leaving?"

He nodded. "And you, too. Remember how hard it was to tell me about your dad's death?"

She wiped her nose with the back of her hand. "I guess. But my God, this was . . ." She picked up the book. "I can't imagine a kid seeing her dad shot over thirty times. And the way they described her hugging him. That was"—more tears flowed—"so awful!"

"I know." Jason pulled his petite wife, pregnant belly and all, into his lap, and he put the book to the side. "But what's important is that she has you and Lacy now. And both of you excel at helping people you love get over things. Look what you did with Chase and me. You turned us into card-carrying, pussy-whipped husbands."

She hit him on the chest and smiled, but the smile didn't linger. "You really believe Kathy is okay?"

"I believe Stan Bradley was trying to protect her by getting her out of his house this morning. And I believe he's probably still trying to protect her. From what you've told me, this guy has been knocking on Kathy's door for a long time. A guy doesn't keep coming back unless he cares. And if he feels anything for Kathy like what Chase and I feel for you and Lacy, then he's going to do his best to keep her safe."

She nodded. "Please tell me that you don't think she has anything to do with the whole drug thing."

"I never thought she was involved with anything illegal," he pronounced.

She touched his chin. "Have I told you how much I love you lately?"

"It's been a whole twelve hours. I'm having withdrawals," he said, which caused her to kiss him. He pulled back, cupping her face in both palms. "I love you, woman. I was so scared today when you were at Kathy's. You are my world. Nothing better ever happen to you." His chest grew heavy with emotion, and he blinked the moisture from his eyes and dropped his hand to caress her belly. "You or this kid."

She wrapped her arms around his neck. "I think she's going to be a daddy's girl."

"She? Yesterday it was a boy."

"I know, but now I think it's going to be a girl. Is a girl okay?"

"A girl's fine. But I'm taking lessons from your grandpa on how to keep the boys away. I might even have to start a roach collection to make sure it works."

She grinned, thinking of her overprotective relative. "Wanna go to bed?"

"To sleep?" he asked, and waggled his eyebrows.

"Well, if you're good, I'll let you rub my back."

"Mmm. You know what happened the last time you let me rub your back?"

"I think I remember," she said. Then she got up, took him by the hand and led him into the bedroom.

Kathy shot straight up in bed. All she could see was blood. Lots of blood. Her own scream had woken her up.

"Hey!"

A pair of strong arms embraced her. She almost screamed again, until she remembered who those arms belonged to. It wasn't the cop trying to pull her away from her daddy, and it wasn't one of the cops who'd shot him and kept shooting. It was Luke. She trusted Luke.

"You have a bad dream?"

"Yeah," she said. "A dream. Just a dream."

She fell into him and blinked away the tears she hadn't realized she was crying. Why was she dreaming about this now? The dreams had stopped. They'd stopped a long time ago.

Then she remembered how seeing the blood and hearing the gunshots had taken her back. God, she hoped they weren't here to stay. She couldn't deal with that again.

"You want to tell me about it?" Luke asked.

She looked at him. "No. I don't want to . . . talk. I'm fine."

He leaned in close. "You gotta work on those lying skills."

She shook her head and then pulled the sheet up around her breasts. Her gaze moved to the window, and she saw a sliver of sun spilling in. "What time is it?" she asked.

He reached over and picked up the phone. "A little after five."

They had made love again last night, and it had been even better than the first time. She recalled waking up several times during the night, unaccustomed to sleeping with someone—and each time she stirred, she'd realized he was awake. "Did you even sleep?" she asked.

"I did fine."

"Your lying skills are waning, too."

He grinned.

"So you didn't sleep?" she asked.

His smiled widened. "Too busy peeking under the covers." He ducked his head under the sheets.

She yanked the sheet back and tucked it around her body. "Stop that!"

"Killjoy," he accused.

She looked around the cabin. "Where's Goodwill?"

"Sleeping." Luke pointed over to the kitchenette area, where the dog had fallen asleep on the rug. "He woke me three times to take him outside."

"You should have woken me. I'd have done it."

"We did okay. We had a long talk about him pissing on my shoe."

She smiled, and her chest filled with a warm wash of emotion as some of the sexier memories from last night filled her mind. But then she remembered that in a few hours they were going to meet with people who would separate them. And while he'd promised he would come back, which did take away a bit of the sting, that scared her. Was she ready to jump into a real relationship?

We'll take it slow, Kathy. As slow as you want it.

His words took a lap around her head and heart. She hoped he meant them, because there was no telling how slow she'd need him to go. It was downright amazing that she was willing to try.

"Where's that head taking you now?" he asked.

Realizing she'd been lost in thought, she looked up. "Uh, just thinking about you leaving."

"Why don't you think about me coming back?"

"Actually, I sort of was thinking about that, too."

The humor in his eyes faded. "Why do I get a feeling that you're not having all positive thoughts?"

"They're positive," she said. Then: "I'm just scared."

"Why?"

When she didn't answer, he ran a hand over her cheek. "What happened, Kathy? What happened that makes it so hard for you to trust?"

Chapter Twenty-seven

"Nothing happened." Kathy started readjusting the sheet, mentally stuffing her dirty laundry into a virtual closet.

"Bullshit." He caught her face in his palm and forced her to look at him. "Your ex did a real number on you, didn't he?"

"Maybe. Okay, yes, he did a number on me." She opened the door of the mental closet just a bit.

"What did he do?"

She hesitated, but he seemed so determined. "He left me," she admitted.

"How come I get a feeling there's more to it?"

She let go of a deep gulp of air and gave the door another nudge. "He left me for his secretary."

"And?"

"Does there need to be more?"

"There usually is." He continued to stare at her.

"She was older." Kathy tightened the sheet around herself. "A lot older."

His gaze never wavered, as if he was waiting for more. She reached for the mental door handle and prepared to fling it wide.

"You hear women complain about their husbands leaving them for younger, prettier models. And I'm not saying that wouldn't hurt. But let them walk in my shoes. This woman was old, she was fat, she didn't even have a big bank account . . . and yet he chose her over me." Kathy's throat grew tight, and for one second she wanted to pick up her laundry and toss it back in the closet.

"He was an idiot," Luke said. "A friggin' idiot."

Something about his tone chased away her need to hide. "He called me from work and asked me to meet him for dinner. Our anniversary was in a week. I thought . . . I thought he was going to take me out on a romantic date. I went and bought some new lingerie. I got a babysitter for the entire night. Then I sat there with a pair of thong panties crawling up my ass while he told me that he loved a woman who was almost as old as my mother!"

Kathy felt her stomach tremble. Oddly, it wasn't so much from pain—that part had mostly subsided over the years—but just because she'd never, ever told anyone about it. Never aired her dirty laundry to anyone.

She continued, "He said that I was a cold . . . fish in bed, and that I didn't know how to . . ." Realizing what she was about to say, she closed her eyes.

"Okay, he's even a bigger idiot than I thought." Luke pulled her against him and tugged some of the sheet over himself. Not that she hadn't already noticed his condition.

She swallowed, and for reasons she didn't even understand, she wanted to tell him the rest. "It wasn't all a lie."

"I beg to differ. Last night was—"

"That was different. I've . . . I've learned a few things since . . . since then."

He cocked his eyebrow up. "With who?"

"With Lacy and Sue."

His eyes widened.

Realizing what he thought, she giggled. "Not like that! None of us were having sex, so we talked about sex. Every Friday we would choose a topic, and we'd all research it and then share what we learned. Different positions. The most sensitive parts of a man's body. Oral sex, food and sex, sexual fantasies, anything to do with men and sex. Sometimes Lacy would insist on adding a discussion about history or something, but mostly we'd talk about sex."

Luke's mouth hung open, and he continued to stare. He blinked. "Food and sex?" he managed to eke out.

"Yeah, foods that go with sex: strawberries, chocolate, grapes. Oh, Sue's husband Jason brought home a moon pie. And Sue got *very* creative."

He started laughing, and Kathy couldn't help it; she joined him. When at last their laughter faded, he asked, "Exactly what did she do with the moon pie?"

Kathy giggled. "It's one of those things you can't explain."

"Oh, come on. I gotta know!"

"Nope." She reached up and pretended to lock her lips with a key.

"You can't do that! Come on!"

She shook her head and giggled. And then they were kissing. Touching. His hands were everywhere, giving pleasure upon pleasure.

Kathy felt his sex hard against her thigh. Pushing him onto his back, she crawled on top and with one swoop took him inside her.

"Here's another thing we talked about," she said in her best sultry voice. She concentrated on squeezing all her inner muscles surrounding him, remembering that she'd read this could bring a man to orgasm quicker than almost anything else.

He let out a deep moan. His hands found her waist and held her in place, and he pumped into her hard and then harder. She rode his movements, trying to concentrate, to keep her muscles squeezing, and all of a sudden the pleasure became too intense, and she was almost ready to explode when—

"Shit!" he growled. He picked her up and tossed her off him. Catching his breath, he rolled over and wrapped his arm around her. "Sorry. I . . . No condom." He pressed a hand over his face. "Are you on the pill?"

Kathy dropped an arm over her face. "No." What the hell had she been thinking? Okay, she hadn't been thinking. She'd just been feeling. Which was a prime example of why she couldn't just let her emotions rule.

"I'm sorry," he said, his voice still husky. He swallowed, hard. "I didn't mean to be so abrupt. But when I realized what we were doing, I was a fraction of a second from coming."

She shook her head, feeling embarrassed. "I was the one who started it."

"Hey." He picked up her arm and leaned his head down to peek at her. "That was fucking amazing. Promise me that when I come back, you'll do that again. Jeez, that's all I'll think about while I'm away."

His smile chased off all embarrassment. "You know," she said, "there's more than one way to skin a rabbit." And suddenly struck with a jolt of self-confidence, she trailed a finger down his chest until she found his sex, which was still rock hard, and wrapped her fist around him.

"Did you guys have a Friday night discussion about this, too?" he asked, his voice throaty.

She grinned. "We might have."

Joey had parked in the empty lot where Lola was yesterday and watched the sunrise. He hadn't slept. He couldn't. After he'd left the cabin, he'd driven to a service station and washed up. And washed up. He wasn't sure how long he stood in the bathroom, scrubbing his hands and face over and over. It was as if he could still feel the blood on him.

Not that he had any now. He'd changed, then gone back to where he'd buried Donald's body and burnt his blood-stained clothes.

While there, he'd talked to Donald again. He knew Donald couldn't hear him, but he'd talked anyway. He confessed about killing Foster, about how he'd hated it. How he couldn't understand how Donald had done such things. And the only time he'd felt better about what he'd done was when he thought about Lola—about saving her from Foster. Which was when he'd decided he had to see her. He had to see her one more time before he met Pablo and Corky, before he went with them back to the cabin and probably had to do to them what he'd done to Foster. That, or he'd die by their hands.

He didn't want to sound pessimistic, just realistic. Which was another reason he wanted to see Lola: He didn't have much to his name, but why let what he had go to the state of New York?

He actually considered going to the police and confessing everything, but then he realized that his confession wouldn't save the redhead or her kid. Lorenzo would still get Hunter and probably the mother, too. He looked at his watch. It wasn't quite six. He wondered what time Lola showed up. In less than an hour he was supposed to meet Pablo and Corky. All he wanted was to see her.

Almost as if he'd wished her there, the big truck pulled up. Lola looked too small to drive the vehicle. She turned her head and stared at his car.

He got out. Instead of dressing in the damn monkey suit Lorenzo insisted his employees wear, he had put on his jeans and a T-shirt. It felt good to be in his own clothes, too.

When Lola got out, she smiled. Damn if that smile didn't put everything into place. All guilt evaporated.

He met her halfway across the lot. Her smile widened. "I . . . not know if I ever see you again."

Don't ask him how he knew it would be okay, because he didn't have a freaking clue, but he leaned down and kissed her. When he realized she was kissing him back, another sense of rightness exploded in his chest.

He didn't let the kiss go too far, just enough to hint about his feelings. When he pulled back, he smiled. "I hope that was okay. I wanted to do it yesterday and . . . I didn't, and I was sorry that I hadn't. So . . ."

She grinned. "It's okay. I sorry you didn't do it yesterday, too."

He laughed. "I don't have much time, but I needed to see you."

"You have to go to work?"

"Sort of," he answered.

She looked down at his clothes. "You look different."

"Good different or bad different?"

"Good different," she said, and smiled. "You want some coffee?" She looked back at her truck. "I need to start cooking. Maybe you talk while I cook? Maybe you tell me about your job, that one day you dress in suit and the next day you don't."

His gut tightened. "Can I help you do anything?" he asked, and walked with her, wondering how he would explain his profession.

"You get the tables and chairs set up, *si?*"

Ten minutes later, she poured him a cup of coffee. He leaned against the counter, watched her scramble a big skillet of eggs.

"You eat?" she asked.

"No."

Her brow creased. "I not charge you."

Reaching over the counter, he touched her face. "I know. I'm just not hungry." He took a deep breath. "I need to ask a favor of you."

"A favor?"

"I want you to keep something for me. Just keep it until . . . Just a minute." He went back to his car and got his briefcase. Setting it on the counter, he tried to think of how to say this.

She looked down at the briefcase and frowned. "I not . . ." She shook her head. "I not do anything illegal. If this—"

"No. It's not illegal. I promise." He opened the briefcase, which contained his bank records, his checkbook and some personal items.

Her expression changed when she saw the three birding magazines. "You read about birds, too!"

"Yeah. But I'm not queer."

"Queer?" She didn't understand the word.

"I like girls," he said.

She laughed. "I not think you . . . you like boys." Her gaze cut back to the briefcase, and she pointed to a picture resting on top of the magazines. "Is this you? May I?" She asked permission to pick it up.

He nodded. "It's my mom and my brother . . . and me." He pointed himself out. It was the only picture he had of his mom. "I was probably eight. My brother was six."

"You cute boy."

"Nah, I was always too big."

"You not too big. You are just right size."

He grinned, then picked up his checkbook. He'd already made out the check. The only thing lacking was her name. "This is . . . my checkbook. I don't have a lot of money."

Her brow creased, and she looked in confusion at the written check. "That is a lot of money."

"Fifty thousand really isn't a lot," he said. "The thing is . . ." God, how could he explain this? "I have to do something in the next few days and I might not . . . I might not be able to use this money."

She stared at him. "What are you saying?"

"What I'm saying is, if I don't come back in a week, I want you to have this."

She shook her head. He saw something like fear in her eyes. "Why you think you not come back? What you do to make so much money? I do not understand. But I do not want this." She pushed the briefcase back and dropped the picture. "I not get mixed up in anything bad."

"I didn't do anything bad to get that money!" he told her. "I was a bodyguard. Yes, the man I worked for, he . . . *he* did bad things. And I took care of his mess one time, but I never got paid to *do* bad things."

She blinked and stared at him. "You not hurt anyone?"

He let go of a deep breath. He couldn't lie. She deserved the truth.

But would she understand?

"The only time I hurt anyone, it was to protect someone else."

She took a step back, almost as if she was afraid.

"Please . . ." He closed his eyes and sent up a prayer. "The man was going to hurt a woman. Two women. And I couldn't let him do that. So I did what I had to do to protect someone else. You have to believe me."

She met his gaze, hesitant at first, and then she moved closer. "I believe you. But I still do not want your money. I do not understand why you say you might not need it."

Joey couldn't ever remember anything being so hard to explain. "I have to do something, and if I don't come back . . ."

"Why you not come back?" Her expression was worried.

He ignored her question. "If I do come back, I would like . . . I would like to get to know you better. Actually, I'd like to get to know you a lot better."

She shook her head again. "I do not understand. Why you think you not come back? Do you . . . you think you die?"

He didn't answer, but neither did he deny it. And he didn't look away from her.

Her eyes were awash with emotion. He put his hand over hers. "I have to do this."

"What do you have to do, Joey? What are you saying?"

"I can't explain. I just want you to keep this." He moved

his briefcase closer to her. "And if I don't come back, I want you to use this money to help you and your daughter."

"No! I do not want this." She moved away. "I do not want you to do something that maybe get you killed. You keep your money. And you stay safe. If you want to know me better, then you not . . . you not go do this thing that maybe get you killed."

"I have to." He glanced at his watch. His time was up. "I have to go."

"No! You take this! I do not . . ."

He didn't listen to her. He did what he had to do and left. The image of her standing in the parking lot, his briefcase in her hands, would forever be etched in his mind. He just hoped that would be more than a few hours.

Chapter Twenty-eight

Jason was jolted awake by a thought—a thought that, at the exact moment of alertness, did a U-turn and left him with only a vague feeling that whatever the thought had been, it was important.

He rolled over and looked at the clock. Almost six. It was Saturday, and he didn't need to go to work. So he lay there, stared at the ceiling and tried to find the thought that had bounced right out of his head.

Sue stirred beside him, and he turned over and looked at her. It never failed, his first glimpse of her every morning sent the same message right to his heart: He was one lucky bastard to have her in his life. The sweet love they'd made last night was foremost in his mind. He felt himself grow hard and was tempted to wake her up for a repeat performance, but then, just like that, the thought that had bounced out of his head bounced right back in. He heard Claire Banks's words echo in his head: *"I even gave him free rein to use my cabin."*

He shot out of bed and ran into the living room to find his cell. Picking it up, he called Chase.

There were five rings before his friend picked up. "This better be damn good!"

"It is. It woke me up. Mrs. Banks said she gave Bradley free rein to use her cabin. Maybe—"

"Where's this cabin at?" Chase asked, understanding completely.

"I don't know, but it might be worth checking out."

"You call her."

Jason could hear Chase getting out of bed. The idea of waking the woman at six in the morning didn't hold much appeal. "Why don't *you* call her? You're senior."

"Because it's you she's sweet on. Call her and get an address."

Joey watched Corky and Pablo eat their fast-food breakfast sandwiches. How could they eat when they thought they were about to go kill someone, maybe two someones? They were no better than Donald or Trooper Foster. Even the few sips of coffee Joey had drunk at Lola's were now acid in his stomach.

Still, Joey would have loved to have left them out of this. But Lorenzo had made it clear that the three of them were to do this together. He'd even arranged the meet this morning. Taking a deep breath, Joey decided to put an end to all this. It was risky. They might turn on him, but at least he'd know he tried. Moving a paper napkin on the table, he said, "You know we don't have to do this, right?"

Corky added his seventh pack of sugar to his coffee. "Do what?"

"We can walk away. All of us walk away alive. Let Lorenzo take his chances in court. If he goes to jail, so be it."

Pablo laughed. "You think Lorenzo would let us walk away?"

Corky snickered. "Are you fucking nuts? We walk away, Lorenzo will find us and feed our balls to us one at a time."

Joey decided to try a different tack. It wasn't altogether the truth, but lying was much less a sin than killing. "Foster killed Donald. Lorenzo had him do it." He expected to see something in their eyes like grief. They'd worked with Donald for five years or more.

For one second, he thought he spotted something in Corky's eyes, but it faded quickly.

Pablo said, "Donald screwed up. He was in charge. This whole thing was supposed to go down like clockwork."

Joey stared, amazed by their indifference. But then he added, "Donald isn't the only one Lorenzo blames."

This got their attention. Both hit men stopped feeding their faces.

"What are you saying?" Corky asked.

"I'm saying Lorenzo blames all of us."

"Who told you this?" Corky asked.

"Foster. Right before Hunter killed him. He said that we had all disappointed Lorenzo and that he plans to teach us a lesson."

"Foster's dead?" Corky asked, his eyes wide with what looked like fear.

Joey was surprised Lorenzo hadn't filled them in; nevertheless he decided to play on it. "Hunter isn't just any ordinary guy. He was trained in special ops or something." Joey didn't even know whether special ops was real, but it sounded good. "He's not going to go down easy. We could all die. And if we don't, Lorenzo might just do us in anyway. Just like he did Freddy and Donald. We're nothing to him, just bozos with guns."

"No," Corky said. "We take Hunter down and Lorenzo will be happy."

"*If* we take him down," Joey allowed.

Pablo dropped his sandwich on the table. "I'd rather take my chances with Hunter than Lorenzo any day of the week. Because if we double-cross the boss, as long as he's alive he'll be after our asses. He doesn't let people screw him."

As long as he's alive. Pablo's words echoed in Joey's head as he leaned back in the booth. "Fine. I just thought I'd tell you what I know."

He saw Corky and Pablo look at each other. All he could think was that he'd tried. Tried to get them to turn back. Tried to save their sorry asses.

As they got up to leave, Joey wondered how he should do this—or, rather, when. With his heart already racing, he told himself to wait, wait until they got to the woods. He'd fall in behind them and then he'd do it.

But he didn't have the silencer anymore, so the shots might warn Hunter. The man might come out and investigate. That meant even if he managed to stop Corky and Pablo without getting killed, he would very likely end up shot by one of the people he was trying to protect.

It was just a chance he had to take.

Luke heard Kathy start the shower, but he didn't join her because he just kept feeling antsy. Was that because everything was coming to an end? Was it because he knew he'd be walking away from Kathy for who knew how long? Or was it more?

He hadn't slept all night. He'd kept going over and over his conversation with Calvin, searching for the reason something didn't feel right. But as hard as he tried, he couldn't put his finger on anything. It was just a hunch—but damn it, his hunches had been right before.

Suddenly, Goodwill came up to the bed and barked.

"What, you gotta piss again?" Luke asked. The animal wagged its tail and tried to jump on the mattress. Luke grunted an acknowledgment, got up, donned his jeans, got the dog on the leash, grabbed the gun and the phone, and headed outside.

He hadn't cleared the porch when the phone in his hand started vibrating. He'd put it on silent when the calls last night kept coming. He glanced at the number on the screen. What did the guy want now?

"What is it, Calvin?" he answered.

"Luke Hunter?"

Luke hesitated, fear building so fast he couldn't breathe. It wasn't Calvin's voice.

"Who's this?"

"Jacob Wells, US Marshal. Wherever you are, get out. There's been a breach in security. If you had a set place to meet, don't go there. Get out, and when you feel safe, call me at Calvin's number and I'll set a new meeting place."

"What do you mean?" Luke said. Goodwill was yapping again.

"I repeat: Wherever you are, leave. Lorenzo's men know where you are."

"Fuck!" Luke grabbed the dog, swung around to head back to the cabin—and that's when he heard the first shot.

Gun held ready, he looked around. He didn't see anyone. Another blast sounded, but too far away to be aimed at him. Nonetheless he ran back into the cabin, locked the door behind him, put the dog on the floor and pushed open the bathroom door. Kathy stood outside the shower, naked and dripping wet.

"Get dressed!" he yelled. "We've got company."

He saw the panic in her face, but he didn't have time to comfort her. She grabbed her green tank top and slung it on.

"Hurry!" He ran to the front window. He could swear he saw movement to his right, through the trees. But whoever was out there was staying in the woods.

Another bullet was fired. Luke stood there listening. The bullets weren't coming toward the cabin. What the hell was going on?

Silence echoed. Goodwill started barking again. Luke's gaze shot to the Dodge Charger parked in the drive. Could they make it to the car without getting shot?

A noise sounded toward the rear of the cabin. Luke swung around. A man passed by the back window. He wasn't dressed in a suit, but he sure as hell was big enough to fit Lorenzo's type. Luke took his first shot and shattered the glass.

"Luke!" Kathy screamed from the bathroom.

"Don't come out!" he yelled in reply. He'd seen the man drop, but he wasn't sure if he'd hit him.

Kathy appeared at the door, fully dressed.

"Don't come out!" Luke yelled again. "Shut that door and lock it."

Another shot sounded outside, in the distance. Luke's heart thudded. Then he heard a bullet hit the back wall of the cabin. Who was shooting at whom? He kept his gun aimed at the window—and that's when he heard the sound of a car pulling up out front. More of Lorenzo's men, he feared.

Car doors opened and then slammed. Luke's gut clenched. His thoughts were on Kathy, on keeping her safe. How many of Lorenzo's goons were there now? How many could he possibly fight off? How in the hell was he going to get Kathy out of this alive?

Another shot sounded from the back of the cabin. Seriously, who was shooting at whom? He went to the front door, counted to three, and then went out, gun held ready. His gaze flicked left then right, but he saw nothing. Nothing except the classic Mustang parked there. It was familiar. He'd seen it at Lacy Kelly's house. It belonged to Jason Dodd, the cop married to Kathy's friend.

His gut twisted. Were Kathy's friends working with Lorenzo?

"HPD! Hold it right there!" a familiar voice boomed behind him. "Put down the gun, Bradley."

Then Dodd came around the side of the cabin, his own gun drawn. "Do as he says. Put the gun down and then let's talk."

"About what?" Luke asked, his weapon still held tight. He figured the man behind him was Officer Kelly. But could he trust these people? How did they know he was here if they weren't with Lorenzo?

"Where's Kathy?" Dodd asked.

"You leave her out of this. I swear to God if you lay one finger on her, I'll—"

"Why would we hurt her?" Kelly asked.

Right then, something caught his eye. A big guy, this one wearing a suit, stepped out of the woods holding a pistol. Luke raised his gun and fired at the same moment he felt something slam into his shoulder. The man standing at the edge of the woods dropped. So did Luke. Officer Dodd spun toward the man, and a few more shots were fired.

The pain was crushing Luke's shoulder, but he forced himself to roll over, gun still tight in his grip. "Who sent you here?" he demanded, pointing his gun at Kathy's two supposed policeman friends.

Chapter Twenty-nine

"Are you with Lorenzo?" Luke ground out, the pain in his shoulder getting worse by the second.

"Put that gun down!" Officer Kelly had Luke covered as well. The tension in the air thickened, but Luke refused to drop his weapon until he knew they weren't a threat.

"Neither of us knows any Lorenzo," Dodd spoke up. "Your landlady told us she let you use this place. We took a chance you'd be here."

"Claire?" Luke tossed down his weapon.

"Noooo!" Kathy screamed, barreling out of the cabin, a toilet tank lid held in her hands. God help him but he loved that woman, whatever she thought she was doing. "You're shot!" she realized. Then, looking at her two friends, she flung the tank lid down and ran to Luke, dropped onto her knees. "You shot him!" Tears were running down her cheeks, she looked white and pasty. "Oh, God, no."

Luke tried to reach out to her, but it hurt like hell to move his arm. "I'm fine," he promised. "It's not bad. And they didn't shoot me. Someone else did."

Kathy continued to sob.

Luke sat up a bit and reached for her with his other hand. "Kathy?" he said. He touched her face. "Look at me. I'm talking to you. I'm going to be okay. You understand?"

She blinked, and he thought he'd finally got through to her. She nodded, but her tears seemed to flow even faster. Then she fell into him.

Her weight hit his shoulder and he let out a hiss. "I'm

fine," he whispered in her ear, "but my shoulder is hurting like hell. Can you not . . . lean on me quite so much?" Then he saw over Kathy's shoulder that her friend was reaching for his phone. "Please don't call this in."

"Why?" Officer Kelly asked.

Kathy drew back. "He was working undercover and—"

"You're a cop?" Officer Dodd asked, clearly surprised.

"No," Kathy said, and hiccupped. "He's a federal agent."

Officers Dodd and Kelly did a quick search around the property because Luke realized they'd lost track of the big guy he'd seen in back of the cabin, but the investigation turned up nothing. Then Luke made a call to Calvin's number. Jacob Wells answered, and he had men pulling up at Claire's cabin within thirty minutes. Luke, Kathy and her two friends spent the whole time on alert.

Right before Luke was taken away by US Marshals, Kathy leaned in and whispered, "I'll be waiting."

I love you, was on Luke's lips, but he held the words back.

Five hours later, and less than sixty minutes after he woke up from surgery, he wanted to kick himself. He should have told her his feelings. But he hadn't because he'd been afraid the words would scare her. Now he was scared about not having said them. About leaving her. About Kathy pulling away, closing him off again.

On the drive to the hospital he'd insisted that she be protected, in case any of Lorenzo's men were still around. The marshals had assured him she was safe, and he'd assured them that if anything happened to her, he'd give them a personal escort to Hell. His shoulder had been hurting like a son of a bitch, and he was already missing her, so he wasn't at his calmest.

He was still trying to clear the post-surgery cobwebs from his head when Jacob Wells walked in. "I hate to do this to you, Hunter, but they want you moved to a safe house and put under protective custody ASAP. Do you think you're up to traveling?"

Luke looked up. "Shoot me up with another dose of morphine and I'll go wherever you want. When's the trial?"

"It's set for next Wednesday."

It took a moment for Luke to recall what day it was. The last thirty-six hours had sort of messed up his internal calendar. Suddenly, he remembered a question he'd thought to ask right before they'd taken him into surgery: "The security leak. What happened?"

"They kidnapped Calvin Hodges's wife. They were forcing him to cooperate."

"How is he?"

Wells shook his head. "He didn't make it. Lorenzo's men shot him just before he managed to get away. But his wife is going to be okay."

"Damn," Luke said, truly aggrieved.

"The last thing he did was report in about you, admit what had happened."

"I'm sorry," Luke said.

"Yeah. I didn't know him personally, but I've heard from several who said he was a good man."

"He seemed like a decent guy," Luke agreed. "That's why I didn't want to believe . . . I mean, my gut kept telling me something was up, but . . ."

"Guts are always right." Wells handed over a bag with clothes in it.

Luke hoped like hell that the US Marshal was wrong—and not because of anything to do with Lorenzo, but because right now, despite what Kathy had told him, Luke had a gut feeling that he wasn't finished fighting with Kathy about them being together. His gut said that this time apart was only going to make things harder.

Shaking off those worries, because there wasn't a damn

thing he could do about them, he focused back on Wells. "Where's the trial going down?"

"In Dallas."

"Home sweet home," Luke said, remembering how after he'd signed the divorce papers he hadn't been able to leave town fast enough.

"Do you need me to get a nurse to help you get dressed?"

Luke glanced into the bag and saw the pants were sweats. "I think I can manage," he said. Then, as Wells started to walk away, he remembered to ask, "How did things shake down back at the cabin?"

The marshal turned around. "Oh. In addition to the guy at the edge of the woods, they found two other bodies. One was a state trooper."

"The other guy—a big fellow—he was one of Lorenzo's, right?"

"Yeah . . . although Kelly and Dodd said you told him the guy was wearing a gray T-shirt."

"He was."

"Well, the guy they found was in a suit and tie."

Luke's gut clenched. "So one of them got away?"

"Sounds like it. But we think he was wounded. There was blood at the back of the cabin, so you probably hit him. We got people checking the hospitals. Or maybe the guy went somewhere and died. We'll find his body sooner or later."

And if they didn't? "You've got Kathy Callahan in protective custody, right? Because I swear—"

"We've got her in protective custody," Wells reassured him. "Last time I talked to my guy, she was giving him hell."

Luke smiled, remembering her snagging his gun. "She's good at that. Make sure she knows I'm okay. She'll worry."

"So that's the way it is," Wells said, a cocky grin on his face. "We'll make sure she hears you're okay. The men who picked you up saw the way the girl acted, and they were talking."

"Well, tell them to stop," Luke growled. He didn't like the idea of anyone discussing Kathy.

Wells tucked his hands in his pockets. "The trooper they found dead—he'd been dead for at least twelve hours. We found the gun that we think killed him. We're running it through ballistics."

"That can't be right," Luke said. He thought back to what he was doing twelve hours before the body was found. Shoot, those men could have stormed the house and killed him and Kathy both, he'd been so preoccupied with making love to her. He started to beat himself up mentally, but as the memories of his time with Kathy replayed in his mind, he decided to let himself off. He'd made a mistake, but nothing had happened. And he wouldn't trade in their time together for the world.

"If they knew we were there, why wouldn't they have stormed the cabin?" he wondered aloud.

"We don't know. The coroner put the trooper's time of death between eight and ten last night. The other two bodies each had multiple bullet wounds . . . by different guns. It appears as if you had help, or someone was just trying to take out Lorenzo's men."

Luke shook his head, confused. "Who?"

Wells shrugged. "God only knows. Lorenzo doesn't make friends, but few people have the balls to go after him."

Luke tried to remember. "Right after you called, I heard shots and they didn't seem to be coming toward the cabin. But . . . this doesn't make sense." The information took a few laps around his head. "Did you find the dead guy in the porta-potty I told you about?"

"No," Wells said.

Luke shook his head. "Something is happening here that we don't understand."

"Yeah," Wells said. "We were hoping you might be able to

shed some light on things—after you'd had some time to think."

Luke met the Marshal's gaze. "I don't have a friggin' clue. It's like I had a guardian angel."

"One hell of a guardian angel," Wells agreed. "Let's hope he keeps it up until we get Lorenzo behind bars." The marshal shrugged and pointed to the bag of clothes. "Get dressed, and I'll be waiting right outside the door."

Twenty-four hours after leaving Claire's cabin, Kathy sat in the kitchen of a cheap apartment in Houston, held against her will in protective custody. She had thumbed through the same magazine at least a dozen times. A magazine about insects. Who in their right mind read magazines about insects?

She groaned and was almost to the point of telling Mr. I'm-in-Charge that *he* was the one going to need protective custody. A person could die of boredom here, so killing him would be self-defense. And, hey—she knew where the toilet tank lid was.

Hoping for anything to take her mind off Luke and off all the crappy memories the last few days had churned up, she started reading about the life of a housefly. When she got to the part about mating, she tossed the magazine aside and dropped her head on the table. He'd been shot, for Chrissakes! She just wanted to hear his voice and know he was okay. Sure, Mr. I'm-in-Charge had told her that Luke was fine, but she wanted to hear that from Luke himself. Why couldn't they understand that? But each time she asked, all she got from Mr. I'm-in-Charge was, "No can do. No can do."

"Hey," the U.S. Marshal said as he popped his head into the kitchen. "You've got company."

"Luke?" Kathy jumped up so fast that her chair crashed

backward, and she whizzed past the officer, but disappointment filled her as she saw who was standing in the living room. Her two pregnant best friends both opened up their arms for a hug. Kathy spotted Jason standing behind them and ran right past Lacy and Sue. "Have you heard anything?" she asked. "Can I please talk to him?"

"Well, I guess we know how we rate," Lacy muttered.

"Oh, that hurt," Sue said.

Jason looked from them to Kathy. "I heard he got through the surgery fine, and they've moved him to a safe house to await the trial. But they don't allow phone calls."

Kathy felt her throat tighten, but she swallowed that super-sized lump down. "Why not?"

Jason held up his hands. "I didn't make the rules."

Kathy faced Lacy and Sue, who from their downtrodden expressions, felt ignored. Since nothing was more pathetic than two dejected pregnant women, she walked over and embraced them. The group hug drew out. The women's arms held Kathy so tight that the stupid lump in her throat rose back up. This time, she couldn't stop the tears.

"Lord have mercy," Sue said, sniffling. "You scared the pee out of us."

"I'm sorry." Kathy wiped the tears from her face. "Let's go to the kitchen." They walked into the small, sparsely furnished room. The U.S. Marshal now sat at the table, flipping through the bug magazine.

Kathy stared at him and pointed to the door. "Out."

He rolled his eyes, stood and joined Jason in the other room.

"I guess you have him toeing the line," Lacy snickered.

Kathy sniffled and looked at her friends. "You gotta help me break out of here. I swear, I'm going bat-shit crazy."

"I don't think we can break you out, but we did sneak you something in."

Lacy pulled a small bottle of Jack Daniel's from her purse,

which Kathy took and hugged like a long lost friend. "God, I love you guys."

The trio sat down at the table. Sue found some glasses, filled two with water, for herself and Lacy, and poured a couple fingers of whiskey into the third. Kathy picked up the glass, ready to feel the burn and hoping it might relieve some of the ache in her heart, and she forced herself to take a little sip. Heat slid down her throat as the smell filled her nose.

"Goodwill sends his love," Sue mentioned.

"Oh, gosh! I forgot to ask about him. How is he?"

Sue smiled. "He's giving my cats hell. But he's so sweet. I think I've finally talked Jason into our getting a puppy."

"Thanks for keeping him," Kathy said. "I don't know why they wouldn't let me keep him with me here."

"You'd have to walk him," Lacy pointed out, "and they don't want you outside."

"I guess." Kathy picked up her glass again and took another small sip.

"Okay," Sue demanded, no sooner than Kathy set her glass down, "you've had the truth serum, now spill it."

"It was awful. Terrible." Kathy took another sip of Jack.

"It was?" Sue asked.

Lacy giggled. "I don't think she's talking about the sex."

Sue chuckled. "Well, duh—what does she think we came all the way over here to talk about?"

Kathy couldn't help but laugh. "How do you guys even know I *had* sex?"

"Please," Lacy said. "Both Jason and Chase said you were all over him. That there was only one bed in the cabin, and . . . well, Chase said it was really messy, as if someone had gone at it really good."

Sue jumped in. "And Jason said, even after the plumber was shot, he wouldn't put his gun down because he thought they might hurt you. According to my husband, a wounded man doesn't put his life on the line unless he's gotten lucky."

Sue and Lacy both laughed again, but to Kathy the thought of Luke shot and trying to protect her didn't seem funny. More tears threatened.

"Why won't they let me talk to him?" she muttered.

"Stupid rules," Sue complained.

Kathy picked up her glass and swirled its caramel-colored contents. "They *are* stupid."

"Okay, we all agree it's a stupid rule," Lacy said. "Now that we got that figured out, spill it."

"Yeah, we want to hear the good stuff," Sue said.

Kathy brought her glass to her lips again. "There was a dead guy in a porta-potty."

Sue's and Lacy's mouths fell open. Kathy knew this wasn't the story they wanted to hear, but for some reason she wasn't ready to bare her soul about the sex. Maybe after a few more drinks.

"How did he get in the porta-potty?" Sue asked.

"That's still a mystery." Kathy went to take a big gulp of whiskey, but only managed to get down a sip. "But the funny part was, he had the perfect hat."

Kathy told them the whole story. She went back to the beginning and explained being at Luke's when the gunfire started. Her friends' reactions changed quickly. But when she got to the part about the cabin, Kathy paused again, still not wanting to share.

"And . . . ?" Sue said.

"Okay." Kathy held up her hand and knew she wasn't going to get out of telling them at least part of what happened, though some details were too raw to share. Or too special. "I slept with him. I'm not really certain what it means. He says he's coming back but . . . you know how men say one thing and then do another." Her throat felt tight, and she swallowed really hard.

"If he said he'll be back, I bet he'll be back," Lacy said.

"Do you want him to come back?" Sue asked.

"Yes. And no. I mean, yes." She dropped her face into her hands. "I'm so confused. I want him to, but I don't know if I can do this."

"Do what?" Lacy asked.

"Do a serious relationship. I failed at it once."

"Duh!" Sue said. "Lacy and I failed, too, and look at us now."

Kathy stared into her drink. "Yeah, but . . . Tom left me for a woman twice my age."

"Seriously?" Lacy asked.

"Seriously," Kathy said.

For some reason, telling them was so much easier than she'd thought. Was it because she'd already bared her soul to Luke? She let go of a deep breath and added, "Tom said I was a cold fish in bed, and—"

"Did the plumber think you were a cold fish?" Lacy interrupted. "Because, let me tell you, my ex said pretty much the same thing. It took me a while to accept that he just didn't have what it took to turn me on. Still, I know how much that kind of self-doubt can eat at you."

Kathy looked down at her drink again. "At least your ex left you for a younger model."

"She wasn't that young," Lacy replied.

"Yes, she was," Kathy said. "I found the video on the Internet where he did her in the elevator."

"Oh gawd, wasn't that funny!" Sue chortled. "Did you see him fall when he first tried to take off his pants?"

"It wasn't funny," Lacy retorted—but then she laughed. "Oh, hell, did you see how she kept telling him 'go deeper,' but he couldn't because he's got a little bitty dick?"

They all chuckled, and then Sue broke in, "Hey, I made my ex want to be a woman, so I don't know what you two are bitching about."

They laughed some more. And it felt so good.

When Kathy finally stopped laughing, she pointed out, "But my husband's TOW was old and not even a cougar."

Sue and Lacy regarded each other, then Sue leaned in. "Did she have false teeth?"

Kathy stared at her. "Why?"

Sue chuckled. "You didn't see that movie? Older women take their teeth out and . . ." She stuck her finger in her mouth.

"Oh, that's gross," Lacy said.

Kathy leaned back in her chair, laughing some more. It felt calming just having them there, having a bit of normalcy back in her life. Now all she needed was her son home and everything would be fine.

What about Luke? The question bounced around her head.

Lacy noticed Kathy's worry, and reached over to pour her another shot of whiskey. "You're not drinking," she said.

Kathy looked at her glass and lifted it to her lips, then lowered it. "Maybe it's a wine night."

"You gotta drink *something*." Sue spared Lacy a quick glance before fixing back on Kathy. "Come on, let's toast."

Something about the look that passed between her friends hinted at secrets. "Why do I have to drink?" Kathy asked, and her mind raced. "Do you guys know something about Luke that you're not telling me? Is he okay? I swear to God, if you two know—"

"No," Sue said. "We just want you to spill the beans."

"I did spill the beans!"

"All the beans?" Sue asked.

"What other beans are there?"

Kathy's thoughts were on pork-'n'-beans. But one look into her friends' eyes and she knew what beans they were talking about. They knew. They knew about her father. A lump crawled back up her throat and she swallowed, not sure whether she was relieved or mortified.

"Hey." Jason walked into the kitchen. He clutched his phone in his hand. "You're not going to believe this."

"What?" all three women asked at the same time.

"There's not going to be a trial. They just found Richard Lorenzo dead. Somebody capped his ass and saved the taxpayers a whole heck of a lot of money."

Chapter Thirty

Luke stood in his hotel room and tossed the few clothes the US Marshals had provided him into a plastic bag. He was more than ready to be gone.

The moment he'd learned Lorenzo had been killed, he'd been ready to head back to Kathy, but the DA and US Marshals planned otherwise. There was tons of red tape yet to be untangled. Also, with Lorenzo dead, one of his ex-wives had come forth and offered to name names, primarily people her husband had had in his pocket. Supposedly she'd already gotten a book deal for a tell-all. The heads of some high-powered people were about to roll . . . but Luke was thankful his time was mostly done.

He'd called Kathy at least six times but only got her voice machine. He'd left messages. The last time he'd even left a number. She hadn't called back. It had forced him to break down and call Jason Dodd, who had told him that Kathy was taking some time off to see her mother. But knowing Kathy the way Luke did, he figured she wouldn't abandon her business long.

She was probably back, and she still hadn't called him. His gut told him she was trying to push him away. Sure, he'd expected it, but it still hurt. Not that he was going to let her succeed. No more phone calls. In person, he'd have some leverage. If she gave him fifteen minutes alone with her, she'd be naked and putty in his hands. At least, that was the way his fantasy went.

The memory of their time together was never far from his mind. It was difficult to focus on anything else, no matter what other details threatened to intrude.

The job is yours if you want it.

His old boss with the FBI had dropped by yesterday and offered him his old job back. Luke admitted it had been good to see John Patterson but he'd turned him down flat. The truth was, all he wanted was a certain redhead. And if she wasn't so inclined to get naked in fifteen minutes . . . ? It didn't matter. If it took another two and a half years, he would win her heart for keeps. He loved her, and he knew she felt the same way about him.

As Luke stuffed his last pair of jeans into the plastic bag, he recalled the conversation with his old boss about the whole Lorenzo case. The fact that they hadn't found Lorenzo's killer left a lot of questions. Questions Luke wasn't sure they'd ever answer. He felt pretty damn certain, though, the man who'd killed Lorenzo was probably somehow connected to whoever took out Lorenzo's men back at the cabin and the state trooper, who evidence was now showing was dirty.

Patterson had gone so far as to warn Luke that he might want to watch his back, since he might be a link to putting away the killer. Luke had chewed on that thought for a minute, thinking more about Kathy's safety than his own. But then he remembered that the trooper's autopsy put his time of death hours before the shootout at the cabin. If the trooper's killer wanted Luke or Kathy out of the way, he could have easily made a move then. And considering this person had taken out Lorenzo's men without ever taking a shot at Luke on that day, Luke just didn't feel the need to be paranoid. Chances were this person had a personal vendetta against Lorenzo and had enough balls to see it through. Not that Luke wouldn't be careful. Who knew how a killer's mind worked? That said, Luke pretty much owed the guy a freaking huge pat on the back.

A knock sounded at the door, and he hurried to answer, thinking it was US Marshal Wells with his walking papers. The thought that in less than six hours he might be with Kathy put a bounce in his step. But the moment he opened the door, he realized his mistake. The media had been hounding him, wanting an interview.

It wasn't a reporter, but someone he wanted to see even less: his ex-wife. Luke swore rather colorfully.

"Not exactly the warm welcome I was hoping for." She smiled and pushed her way inside. She still looked like she'd just walked off the page of a fashion magazine, was tall and blonde.

Luke didn't return the smile, even considered pushing her right back outside. But then he recalled some of the other things he'd been thinking about the past few days—at least when he wasn't thinking about Kathy. He'd been determined to figure out where everything went wrong with his first marriage so that he wouldn't make the same mistakes again. And yes, after being honest with himself, he realized he'd made a hell of a lot of mistakes. Sure, he'd been dealing with a shitload of grief. Add to that a job he didn't like, living in a fancy condo that his wife required for mixing and mingling with her high-profile friends he hated, and plainly put, he'd been miserable. Part of him had resented her for being happy when he wasn't. Which had led him to a more important conclusion: His marriage had been in trouble long before people started dying on him. He and Sandy had simply wanted different things in life.

"Can't you at least say hi?" she asked.

"Sorry, Sandy," he said. "I was expecting someone else."

She nodded, and her gaze moved over him. "I heard you were shot. How's the shoulder?"

"It's fine."

She smiled in earnest. "You look healthy. Still as good-looking as ever."

He just stared, confused.

She set her purse on the sofa. "That was your cue to tell me that I look good, too."

He shook his head. "I must be missing my cues today."

"Three and a half years and you're still in a bad mood, huh?"

He raked a hand over his face. "What do you want, Sandy? You want an apology? Okay, I'll admit it: I spent the last two years of our marriage in a bad mood." He held up his hand. "Granted, I had reasons. But they weren't your fault, were they?"

"No, they weren't," she said. "But for the record, if I had to do over again . . . I would be more understanding."

Her words shocked him, and he wasn't sure what to say.

She sighed. "We both made some mistakes, didn't we?"

He wondered if she was talking about aborting his child. He looked into her eyes and saw the answer. She regretted it. That didn't change the past, but knowing she regretted the abortion brought some consolation.

"Yes," he agreed. "We both made mistakes."

She looked around the room, as if nervous. "I'd hoped you would come to see me."

"Why?" Her reasons for being here still puzzled him. Was facing him and admitting her mistake that important to her? It sure as hell wouldn't have been to the old Sandy. But then again, he'd changed these last few years. Who was to say she hadn't also?

When she didn't answer, he continued. "Look, I don't understand what you want. To rehash things is futile. Plain and simple, we were wrong for each other."

"It wasn't all bad," she said.

He remembered that there was a time when he loved her. But what he felt for Kathy was so much more. He liked Kathy, respected Kathy. His relationship with Sandy had been based on lust. Sure, he'd grown to love her, but until this moment, when she'd admitted she'd made some mistakes, he hadn't found a lot to respect. Sandy, an only child of rich parents, had been accustomed to getting her way. Making her happy had made him happy—at least in the beginning.

"You're right. It wasn't all bad. But it's in the past."

She shook her head. "It's not in the past, yet. That's why I'm here."

"What do you mean?"

"The day you left, I lost it." She took a step toward him and then a step back. "I ripped up the divorce papers, Luke. I never filed them. Legally, we're still married."

Kathy sat in the middle of her living room floor with the television remote control in her hand. Every few seconds she'd hit play and rewatch the segment of the news that she'd TiVo'd hoping to get an update on the Lorenzo case. She'd gotten more than she expected.

When she'd gone to her mom's last week, she'd been running away—running away from talking about her father with Sue and Lacy, running away from what she felt for Luke. But the time she'd spent watching daytime soaps and painting her mom's bathroom had just proved something Kathy should have known: Running away never worked. The crap in her lap had to be dealt with.

She'd arrived home late last night, prepared to call the number Luke had left on her answering machine. Prepared to tell him she was willing to give everything a shot if they could just please, *please* take it slow. But then, first thing this morning, she'd been hit right in the gut with the realization that slow wasn't possible for her and Luke. Because she'd been hit by a serious bout of nausea. Oh, she'd wanted to deny it. For God's sake, he hadn't even come inside her. But as she'd discovered seven years ago, all the women in her family were prone to suffering from morning sickness extremely early in the pregnancy. A man's sperm just had to wink at one of their eggs, and the stomach went south. And once you'd dealt with morning sickness once, you knew that monster's face when he popped in to say howdy. Of course, trying to deny it now was even more impossible. Kathy stared at the fifteen early-results pregnancy tests littered around her.

Finding out she was pregnant had taken its toll—a big freaking toll, more toll that she had available in her emotional bank account. However, there might have been the chance she could have dealt with it. Maybe. But an hour after puking her guts out and using all fifteen sticks, yup, she'd prayed one of them would have given at least a little bit of hope, she'd taken the second blow. Funny, how one little sentence on the news could chew her up and spit her out.

She held out the remote and clicked it again, and the reporter once more spoke into the camera. "Federal Agent Luke Hunter, the primary agent responsible for bringing down Richard Lorenzo's operation, is still refusing to talk to us. However, we spoke to Special Agent Patterson and he informs us that Agent Hunter is making up for lost time with his wife."

Pause. Rewind. *Making up for lost time with his wife?*

Pause. Rewind. *Making up for lost time with his wife.*

Yup, Kathy Callahan was not just a TOW, she was a pregnant TOW. And it was her own fault! She'd been the one who'd climbed on top and ridden him like some horny cowgirl. Make that a horny TOW cowgirl.

Pause. Rewind. *Making up for lost time with his wife.*

Kathy heard someone at her door, but she was in no mood

for company. Goodwill, who'd been sleeping in her bed, came trotting out of the bedroom and barked. He stopped to smell her pregnancy tests, but in a firm voice she said, "Leave them alone." The words came out sounding like they'd been voiced by some evil demon. Poor Goodwill dropped to the floor and started whimpering.

"Sorry," Kathy said. Her own voice was hoarse from all the whimpering she'd done.

Pause. Rewind. *Making up for lost time with his wife.*

"Kathy?" Sue called.

The sound of a key turning in the lock had Kathy sweeping all fifteen positive test sticks under her sofa as the door swung open. Lacy and Sue came barreling in. And yes, they barreled; pregnant women barreled. In just a few months, she'd be barreling too.

Both Sue and Kathy stopped when they saw her on the floor, her eyes obviously swollen. Goodwill, thrilled to see Sue, ran around her feet yapping.

"What are you doing?" Sue asked. "Why didn't you answer the door?"

"Because I didn't want company."

Kathy stood up. Ordinarily, she would have felt terrible about being rude to her pregnant friends, but considering she'd joined their ranks . . . well, all bets were off.

Lacy and Sue looked at each other. "What's wrong?"

So they hadn't seen the news. "Wrong? Why does anything have to be wrong?" *I'm pregnant with a married man's child.* "I'm just in the mood to be alone. So if you two will be so kind as to skedaddle—"

"It's Friday," Sue said.

"Is it a law that people can't be alone on Friday?"

"We always meet on Friday," Sue pointed out.

That's when Kathy realized she was crying again. She wiped her eyes. "Okay, I forgot it's Friday. Now we've met. Now can you leave?"

"No," Lacy said. "We're not leaving until you tell us what's wrong."

"Did Luke call again?" Sue asked.

"No. But if he does, I'm killing him."

Kathy saw the looks on her friends' faces. Had the word "kill" put the fear of God in them? What did they think of her?

"What did he do?" Lacy asked.

Kathy had avoided all conversation about her father. After their meeting at the apartment in Houston, she'd realized they knew it, and she was pretty sure they knew she knew they knew. But during their few conversations while she was at her mom's, they hadn't mentioned anything, and neither had Kathy. Head in the sand was one of her favorite positions. The next time they had their favorite-position talk, she'd mention it.

"Why are you going to kill him?" Lacy asked.

"Maybe because it runs in my family. You know: like father, like daughter." Okay, for someone who preferred things not to come out in the open, she'd sure as hell opened up a Pandora's box.

"What?" Sue asked.

"Don't lie. I know you know about it. You know what he did. His gang killed people. Fourteen of them. But don't worry, he took at least two bullets for everyone who died!"

They didn't deny they knew the truth. But then Kathy saw the sympathy and pity in their faces—a look she hated almost as much as when people were afraid of her. Her tears started flowing harder.

"All I need is a gun," she sniffled. "And mine just so happens to be at my mom's. Do you think maybe one of you could loan me one of your husband's?" As another knock sounded at the door, she took a step back. "I just want to be alone. Please."

The knocked sounded again. Sue stepped to the door. She opened it, and just as quickly slammed it shut. Then, in a panic, she worked the lock.

"Who is it?" Kathy asked.

Sue turned around, and her wide eyes shot to Lacy. "No one," she squeaked.

There were no more knocks. But then Kathy heard him: "Kathy?" *Luke.*

Calmly, she reached over and picked up a lamp, looked at Sue, let out a deep breath and warned, "Move." Sue did. The lamp shattered against the front door, and the noise scared Goodwill so bad that he ran under the sofa. Kathy dropped to the floor and hugged her knees. "I just want to be by myself."

Goodwill wriggled out from under the sofa. Walking over to Sue, he dropped two positive pregnancy tests at her feet. Kathy saw her two friends glance down.

"Oh, shit," Lacy said.

Kathy buried her face between her knees and started sobbing.

Luke paced back and forth on the front porch of Kathy's trailer. He knew she was in there; all sorts of noises were coming forth. Hell, the blonde woman had even opened the door to him for about a second. But now, ten minutes later, his knocks were still going unanswered.

Suddenly, Jason Dodd's Mustang pulled up. Luke watched Dodd and Chase Kelly, get out of the car and walk up to the porch.

"Hey," Jason said.

Luke looked at them, then back at the front door. "Why do I get the feeling you're not just dropping by?"

"You figured that out, huh?" Chase gave him a rueful smile.

"What the hell is going on?" Luke demanded, keeping most of his fury in check, having felt the three of them had parted in good terms back at the cabin.

Jason shrugged. "Our wives called and said they didn't think they could hold Kathy back much longer."

"She's pretty much plotting your murder," Chase explained. "She wants to borrow one of our guns."

Luke considered the half-assed smile on the man's face, and it downright pissed him off. "And why is that?" he asked. But then a cold ache hit his heart and a colder fear: Could Kathy have heard about Sandy? The only thing worse than having to tell her he'd been married when he'd implied that he wasn't, would be her finding out on her own and thinking he'd been using her.

"We'll tell you all about it if you'll come with us."

Chase winked. But what the hell did that wink mean? What did these two know?

Jason turned his back to the trailer and leaned in close to Luke. "Look, our wives are probably watching right now. We gotta make this look good. But the truth is, we know what you're up against."

Luke shook his head. "I'm not going anywhere until I speak to Kathy."

Chase turned his back to the trailer and replied, "I know how you feel. But maybe right now isn't the time. Let her cool off."

"Cool off from what?" he asked, more frustrated than ever.

Jason stepped closer. "Let's go back to my place. It's just up the road a few miles. Let Lacy and Sue calm Kathy down."

"But I don't even know what's wrong!" Luke said. At least, he hoped he didn't.

"That's women for you," Chase said. "They like to keep us wondering. They want us to have to work at figuring out what they're mad about."

"But I haven't had a chance to make her mad. Don't get

me wrong, I've got crap to tell her and she'll have plenty of reasons to be pissed off, but—"

Jason leaned in close again. "Look, we know what's bothering her. Just come with us and we'll explain. Trust us on this. What have you got to lose?"

Chapter Thirty-one

Luke sat at Jason Dodd's table, holding a beer while he waited for the two bozos to explain. Sure, he'd expected Kathy to have her barriers up, but this? It didn't make sense. Could she have somehow learned about Sandy? How?

Jason sat down across from him. "Do you know about the club?"

"What club?" Luke asked.

"Our wives and Kathy started this club, and all of them swore they wouldn't have anything to do with men anymore."

"Oh, that club. Yeah, I know about that," Luke said, wondering if he should have left Kathy's trailer. Sooner or later she'd open the door. She had to, didn't she?

"They were all really hurt by their exes. And that's what makes it so hard for them," Chase explained. "According to what Lacy said, Kathy's ex ran off—"

"With his secretary," Luke interrupted. "Kathy told me about it. I don't think that has anything to do with this."

"Did she tell you about her father?" Jason asked.

Luke stopped rotating the beer in his hand. "No. He was a cop, wasn't he? I know she doesn't like cops."

"No, he wasn't a cop," Chase said. "But it does explain her dislike for cops."

"What happened?" Luke asked.

Jason stood and walked over to the coffee table. When he came back, he dropped a book in front of Luke. "Page fifty-five. But let me warn you, it's not easy to read."

"Remember, park your car about two houses up," Chase warned. "Because they might be looking for cars. They're smart like that."

It was the next morning, and Luke was leaving Jason Dodd's. After downing more beers, he and Chase had slept over—at Jason's insistence—as Sue and Lacy had spent the night at Kathy's. The wives had called the husbands late the evening before, though neither woman had explained what was going on. Lacy *had* informed Chase that if she ever had the misfortune to run into Luke Hunter, she'd be making sausage out of his man parts. Jason just laughed and assured Luke not to worry; she'd threatened to do the same to him and he still had all his parts. When the girls called that morning, saying they were taking Kathy out for brunch, Jason and Chase concocted their plan for Luke to go to Kathy's, pull a few wires in her car, let himself into her place, unplug her phones and be there when she came home.

"Yeah," Jason agreed. "Park far away. Sue writes mystery novels, so she has a suspicious mind. I swear, she's plotting a whole novel around that dead guy Kathy said you saw in the porta-potty."

"Oh," Chase said. "You'd better hide in her place until you know it's just her, because my wife has one bad-ass swing."

"Especially if she's got a fish," Jason said. "She hit him with a singing fish."

Luke wasn't in the mood to appreciate their humor, even though he'd admit he was grateful for their help. If things worked out between him and Kathy, Luke could see them all becoming friends.

Damn, what was he saying? Of course things would work out. They had to.

"And whatever happens, you did *not* get that key from us," Jason warned.

"I got it," Luke said as he started to walk away, Jason's phone rang.

"Yeah," Jason said and cut Luke a frown. "Yes, ma'am. I'll see to it. I agree, that's terrible." He rolled his eyes. When he hung up, his gaze shot back to Luke. "I swear, when this is all said and done, you're taking back the responsibility for Mrs. Banks. Between her IBS and shot-up cabin—and let's not even talk about her suppositories—she's driving me crazy! I already deal with my mom and Ms. Roberts, the cucumber lady, and I don't think I've got time to take care of another old lady."

They all laughed.

When Luke started out again, Chase gave Luke a thump on the back. "Go get the girl."

Luke took a deep breath. Reading about Kathy's father and what happened hurt worse than being shot. And he completely understood why Jason and Chase thought this could be behind Kathy's reluctance to see him, but he kept fighting a niggling doubt that they had gotten past the cop thing. If this was what had Kathy up in arms, it would be an easy fix; he wasn't sure he even wanted to get back into the law enforcement field. The hard part of his talk with Kathy would come when he had to tell her about Sandy.

Chase must have read his concern. "It's going to be okay."

"I don't know," Luke said. "I've made some mistakes—"

"Just walk in, look her right in the eyes and say you're sorry. They like that," Chase said.

"And say you were wrong," Jason suggested. "They really like hearing that. Unfortunately, they're mostly right about us being wrong. At least Sue is, anyway."

"And tell her you love her," Chase said. "You do love her, don't you?"

"Hell, yeah," Luke growled.

"Then practice saying this: 'I was wrong. I'm sorry. You were right,' and tag on an 'I love you,' and you should do just fine."

Jason reared back on his heels. "You don't have to tell us if you don't want to, but I'm curious—what is it that you have to tell Kathy that you think she's going to be pissed about?"

Luke almost snapped that it was none of their damn business, but then he remembered how helpful they were being. "I was married."

"You didn't tell her you'd been married?" Chase asked. "That's it? Hey, I did the same with Lacy. Lacy got over it."

"That's not the worst part," Luke confessed. "I just found out I was still married when we were together."

"Crap!" said Jason. "You're married?"

"No, now I'm divorced," Luke said. "Got the paperwork to prove it."

"But you were married when you were at the cabin?" Chase's expression was grave.

Luke nodded. "But I didn't know! I'd signed the papers before I went undercover. My ex just didn't file them."

"Oh." Jason shook his head.

"What do you think?" Luke asked Chase. "You think she's going be able to handle that?"

"Sure," the cop said. "You didn't know, so how can she hold you responsible? Go break a leg." He grabbed Luke's hand and pumped it up and down.

Luke walked out the door, but right before he shut it he heard Chase say, "Dead man walking."

"Yup," Jason agreed. "And a shame, too. I kind of liked him."

"Me, too," Chase said. "But I still say he's not that good-looking."

Sue pulled up in Kathy's driveway. "Do you want us to come in, stay awhile?" She turned and looked at her friend, who was sitting in the backseat.

"No, but thanks. I love you guys." Kathy reached forward to squeeze their hands. They squeezed hers back.

"You know we're here for you," Lacy said.

"I know," Kathy replied. "I'm sorry I was such a bitch. It's the hormones, you know."

"You weren't a bitch," Sue argued.

"What are you going to do?" Lacy asked, giving Kathy's hand another squeeze.

"I'm having this baby. I thought I made that clear."

"No, we know *that*," Lacy said. "I mean, about him."

Kathy pulled her hands free. "If I don't have to see him for a few months, maybe I can refrain from trying to kill him."

"Are you going to tell him?" Sue asked.

Kathy admitted the truth. "At first I decided I wouldn't, but then I realized he deserves to know. Even assholes deserve to know about their kids. Look at Tom. He's an asshole, but he loves Tommy."

"And he deserves to pay child support," Lacy said.

Kathy shook her head. "I won't ask for it."

"Why not?" Sue asked.

"It's my fault I got pregnant."

"Your fault?" Lacy repeated. "You must have missed that film in high school. You see, it's his little wigglies meeting up with your little eggs that got you pregnant. Meaning, it takes two to tango."

"Yeah, but he didn't want to dance without a condom, and I just kind of jumped on top and started dancing."

Sue let out a chuckle. "Now that creates a visual."

They all laughed. After one more group hug, Kathy walked to the porch and watched her two best friends in the whole world drive away. Somehow she knew that everything would be okay. How could she go wrong? She didn't need a husband. She had friends.

She let herself in and quickly locked the door. The last thing she wanted was to have to face Luke right now. In a month or so when—

"Hi, Kathy."

She swung around. Holy mother of pearls, the father of her child was sitting at her kitchen table.

"I didn't mean to scare you." Luke's chest swelled with emotion at just seeing her. He moved the puppy from his lap to the floor and stood up. He wanted so much to go to her and pull her into his arms, but he didn't move. "I didn't know if it would be better if you saw me first or I spoke first."

"What about neither?" She pointed to the door. "Leave, Luke. I . . . I can't deal with this right now."

"You see, that's my problem, Kathy. I'm not one hundred percent sure what it is you're dealing with."

"Leave, Luke." She pointed to the door again.

"Why?"

She didn't answer.

His insecurities started to build. What was it that Chase Kelly had told him to say? "I'm sorry. I was wrong. You were right."

"Wrong about what?" she asked, her eyes narrowing with anger.

Okay . . . that hadn't worked. "Is this about me being a cop?"

When she didn't answer, he was almost hopeful. "Kathy, I don't have to be a federal agent anymore. I kind of like being a plumber, and the money is a hell of a lot better."

She closed her eyes and pointed to the door. "I'm calling Jason and Chase again if you don't leave."

"Give me five minutes." He didn't think saying that her phones wouldn't work was a good thing right now.

"What for, Luke? What can you say that will make this right?"

"Make *what* right, Kathy?" Had she somehow gotten wind of Sandy?

She walked over to the coffee table and turned on the television. After hitting a few buttons, the screen came on, and he saw a news clip. And then he saw and heard: *"Making up for lost time with his wife."*

Kathy stared, and her eyes grew moist. "Can you tell me that it's not true? Can you tell me that the reporter got it wrong?"

He nodded. "I'm not married."

"So she just lied?"

He saw hope in her eyes. Never had he wanted to lie so damn bad in his life. Instead, he pulled out several folded papers. "Okay, here's the deal. I left Sandy three and a half years ago when I accepted a transfer to New York with the agency. Before I left, she asked for a divorce and I signed the papers and dropped them off so she could file them."

"And?" she prompted, the hope in her eyes growing stronger.

He hesitated. "She didn't file the papers. I swear I didn't know."

Kathy just stood there.

"I went undercover a month later, and as far as I knew, I was divorced. I hadn't even seen her since I signed those papers. Until yesterday morning."

Kathy folded her hands under her breasts. "You didn't even tell me you'd been married!" She started to walk away, then stopped. "Wait. I'd asked you point-blank, and you told me you never had! You lied to me! You deceived me! You deceived me about everything!"

The pain in her eyes hit him like a hot poker across the face. "What I told you was that I'd never worn a ring. And I didn't. We bought . . ." He let out a deep breath. "Fuck. You're right. I lied. What I did was the same as lying. But I was conditioned to lie, Kathy."

Her arms tightened. "Is that supposed to make it okay?"

"No! I was wrong, but that doesn't—"

"We made love! I—" Her voice caught. "I thought . . ." She covered her face with her hands. "You should have told me."

"Yes. I should have. But . . ."

She dropped her hands. "There are no buts, Luke."

He felt as if he was losing, but then something occurred to him. "Yes, there are buts! People sometimes don't admit things because the truth hurts too much."

"If they care about the other person, they do," she snapped.

He picked up the book he'd brought. "Is that why you didn't tell me about this? You don't care about me?"

Her face paled as she recognized the book. "Get out!"

"We're alike, Kathy." He dropped the book on her table. "I didn't tell you about my divorce because it hurt me to talk about it."

"You love her that much?" she asked, crying.

"No. We stopped loving each other years ago. It hurt be-cause she had an abortion without telling me. I got furious at her." He fought the panic building in his chest. "I'd lost my father. I'd lost my sister and her children, and I felt guilty because I was supposed to go with them on that trip. The guilt ate at me."

Kathy turned away.

He moved so she'd have to face him. "I blamed myself. Then, when I confronted Sandy about the abortion, she said it was my fault. She said she did it because I wasn't there for her. And while I'll never forgive her, I knew she was right. And that hurt. It hurt so badly that I buried it inside, just like you buried what happened to your dad all those years ago. . . ."

She said nothing.

He walked over and reached out to touch her, but she stepped back. "What do you want from me?" he asked.

She shook her head. "Leave."

He had nothing else. No words to offer. Nothing. So he did what she asked and walked away.

Chapter Thirty-two

Kathy went to the sofa. She dropped down and hugged herself. She wasn't sure how long she sat there feeling numb— thirty minutes, maybe more. Then she heard his words again: *"It hurt so badly that I buried it inside me, just like you buried what happened to your dad all those years ago.*

"We're alike."

She looked up and saw the book. She'd known it existed, but she'd never read it. Why go there? Why deal with crap when she didn't have to?

"We're alike.

"I didn't tell you about my divorce. I didn't tell you because it still hurt me to talk about it."

What the hell was she doing? What was she doing letting him walk away?

She fell to her knees and raked out the pregnancy sticks from under the sofa, then dropped them in her purse. Where had he gone? His car wasn't out front, so he must be walking.

If she hurried, maybe she could catch him. Oh God, if he got away, she didn't even know how to find him, where even to start to look.

She ran out the door and got as far as the steps.

"You going somewhere?"

Kathy swung around. Luke sat on her porch swing—just sat there, one arm outstretched on the back of the swing, as if waiting for someone to come and take the spot beside him.

Forcing herself to breathe, she took a few steps closer. "I thought you'd left."

"I thought I had, too. But this is as far I got, because I realized everything I want is still right here. An obstinate redhead with a heart of gold. A damn dog who pisses on my shoe. A boy with freckles and his mother's smile."

Kathy bit her lip. "So . . . what was your plan? Just going to sit out here forever?"

"I figured if you wouldn't let me inside, I'd live right here." He pointed to the side of the house. "I happen to know a water line runs right through there. I figured I could tap into it, put me up a shower."

She felt a few more tears run down her face, and she wiped them away. "You were going to shower on my front porch? The neighbors might complain."

"Oh, I was planning on putting up a couple walls." He pointed behind him. "And I envisioned running a few lines from your bathroom and puting a toilet over there. Then I could throw a few blankets and pillows on the swing to sleep. I could stay here . . . I don't know, maybe forever. Or until you came to your senses."

"You had all that planned?"

"It beats the hell out of the other option."

"What's that?"

"Leaving. I don't think I could do it."

She walked over and sat down beside him, in that spot

that seemed to be waiting for her. The moment her side touched his, an emotional pain rocked inside her. But it faded into a sense of rightness, of being where she should.

Slowly, she leaned against him. He dropped his arm down from the back of the swing and let it fall around her. Leaning in ever so slightly, he pressed his face into her hair and she heard him sigh, as if he'd been holding his breath. She closed her eyes and inhaled his scent, and they just sat there and rocked.

Back. Forth. There was something cathartic about the movement.

"He . . . my dad threw out his gun. When he stepped out of the truck, he didn't have his gun." She felt Luke's arm tighten around her as she began to explain. "I know that doesn't change what he did," she went on, "and I know that when he picked me up that day, it was because he knew the cops might come after him. He was wrong. I know that he was a bad person. But . . ." She pressed her face against his chest until she heard his heartbeat. "But I was crying, and he said he was sorry and told me it would be okay. He gave himself up for me. And"—her breath caught—"they shot him anyway. They shot him so many times."

She felt Luke draw in a deep breath. When she looked up, he had tears in his eyes.

"They were wrong," he said. "What they did was so damn wrong."

She nodded, wiped her face and leaned back against him. He set the swing in motion again and they just sat there, softly swaying. Having him beside her, things just felt right. Better than right, they felt perfect.

She swallowed. "I'm sorry. I shouldn't have been so stubborn in the house earlier."

"Then you wouldn't be you."

She heard the smile in his voice and gave him a little nudge with her elbow. "You were right. We're alike."

"Are you calling me stubborn?" His hand stirred in her hair.

"Yeah." She took a breath and found comfort in his scent—still mint and fresh-cut grass. "How's your shoulder?" she asked.

"Still throbs, but it's going to be okay."

Minutes passed. They didn't speak, but the silence brought peace.

Then his words came. "Maybe we could stop keeping secrets."

No more secrets? "Okay." She sat up. He looked at her as she picked up her purse and turned it upside down on his lap. Tumbling out came her wallet, her change purse, a couple of pens, a tampon, and then . . .

His brow crinkled, and he looked at her like she was crazy. "What . . . ?" His expression changed as he noticed all the pregnancy sticks. He picked up one that had fallen between his legs, and he looked at it. He breathed in. He breathed out. "Please tell me you were always planning on telling me about this."

"I was." She looked up at him. "I thought you were married, so I wasn't planning to ask for anything from you. But I was going to tell you."

His arm found its way around her again. "I'm not married. Yet." He pushed a strand of red hair from her damp cheek, leaned in close and kissed her cheek. "Will you marry me, Kathy Callahan?"

She ran her palm over his chest. "That depends."

"On what?" His right eyebrow arched.

"I don't want you living on my porch."

His eyes crinkled into a sexy grin. "And where would I live?"

"I think I could make room for you inside."

"Can I sleep with you?"

"It's a big bed," she answered.

"Do I get my own drawer?"

"I think I could spare one or two." Their smiles met. "Oh, and I'm keeping Goodwill—I don't care if he does pee on your shoe or bite your toes."

"I think I can handle that."

He started filling her purse back up; then he stood and held out his hand.

"Where are we going?" she asked, standing beside him.

"First, I'm hooking your phones back up."

"Back up?"

"I was afraid you'd call Chase and Jason again."

"Oh," she said.

"And then I should probably hook the wires back up in your car."

"My car?"

"I was afraid you might try to drive away."

"Oh."

"And then I'm calling Chase and Jason and telling them I'm not a dead man walking. Those jerks had no faith in me."

"They said that?" she asked.

"Yeah."

"So they gave you the key to my place?"

"I can't answer that one," he said.

She grinned. After a moment she asked, "And *then* what are we doing?"

"Then you're keeping your promise to me."

"What promise?"

He shot her his sexiest grin. "To do that thing again."

"What thing?"

He waggled his brows and held up the pregnancy stick he still carried. "The thing that caused all these test sticks to turn pink."

"Oh, that thing." She laughed and leaned against him, loving how it felt. Which is when she realized she hadn't said it yet: "I love you."

"That's good," he replied. "Because I'm kind of crazy about you, too."

Kathy walked him inside her living room and shut the door. Then she released the first three buttons on her blouse. "You know . . . I'm very disappointed with your priorities. I thought I'd come first on your to-do list."

Smiling, he moved in and tilted her head up for a kiss. It seemed Jason and Chase's advice would come in handy after all.

"I'm sorry," he said. "I was wrong. You are right." He cupped her face in his palms. "I love you."

Epilogue

"There they are," Kathy told Luke as she saw Lacy and Chase and then Sue and Jason pull up in their cars. They all met outside in the parking lot: six adults, three babies—all girls—and an eight-year-old boy.

Today was the celebration of the completion of Sue's novel—a book that shamelessly included a dead John Doe in a porta-potty and the mysterious assassination of a high-profile drug lord. It was called *The John's Secret*. Sue didn't deny that the book was inspired not only by events in the Richard Lorenzo case but also by several unanswered questions. One of which was: Who killed Lorenzo? The US Marshals didn't know . . . and from what Luke told her, they didn't care.

"Hey!" Kathy hugged Sue.

"I'm telling you guys, I love this place," Lacy said, walking up holding Chase's left hand. His other hand held the baby carrier with their daughter, the nine-month-old Marissa Kelly, who had blue eyes and a head full of dark curly hair just like her mama. "It opened last week and the food is fabulous. Best Mexican I've ever had."

"I'll be the judge of that," Luke said, moving in beside Kathy, holding the carrier of their own sleeping daughter, Kylie Hunter—who, at six weeks old, didn't yet have a hair on her head. His other hand rested on Tommy's shoulder. The boy still wore his soccer uniform.

"Hey," Luke said to Jason, and pointed to Tommy. "Did you see this boy score two goals?"

"I did," Jason said, and gave Kathy's son a thumbs-up. "It's because I practiced with him last week."

"Oh, bull crap! I'm the one who taught him that move—aren't I, Tommy?" Luke said.

Kathy poked him in the ribs. "Language."

"Sorry," he muttered.

"Who taught you how to play soccer?" Jason pushed Tommy.

"Uh, both of you?" the boy answered.

Sue moved next to Jason and started fixing their daughter's hair bow. The beautiful blonde girl rested her head on her daddy's shoulder, blissful and content.

Blissful and content, Kathy ruminated. Sometimes she couldn't believe how life had changed for them. They had come a long way, from swearing off men to becoming wives and new moms. And loving it, she admitted.

"Lacy, are the margaritas good?" Sue asked.

"The best," Lacy answered.

"Hey, Mom? What's the name mean?" Tommy asked, pointing to the sign.

"It means 'Shooting Star,'" Kathy told him as they piled into the restaurant. "And this is Lola," she introduced the pregnant hostess, who also happened to be the owner, and who led them to their table.

After everyone got seated, Kathy watched Luke set up the high chair to hold their baby carrier. In the corner of her vision, she saw someone step to the table with a tray of chips and salsa. Her stomach grumbled at the smell of food. "Man, it smells good in here."

"What would you like to dri . . . ?" The question of the big man setting the chips down in front of Kathy faltered as his gaze smacked right into hers. Not that it mattered, because Kathy wouldn't have been able to answer, anyway. She was too busy trying to understand why seeing his face made her want to bolt out of the restaurant.

She finally remembered, and her gaze shot to Sue, who sat frozen, eyes wide, mouth gaping—the same expression Kathy guessed was on her own face: sheer shock. This was the guy who'd put Sue in the closet, the same guy who'd sat in the diner with Lorenzo's dirty state trooper and who'd let Kathy walk out of the diner that day.

"What would you like to drink?" the barrel-chested man finished, and he looked down at his pad as if collecting his thoughts.

"I want a Coke. My sister won't be drinking anything," Tommy said. "She only drinks yucky milk that comes out of a can. I tasted it, and it tastes like crap. But Goodwill my dog likes it."

Kathy was still staring, and she barely noticed her son's language.

Thankfully, Luke was on top of it. "Hey." Luke nudged the boy with his elbow. "Crap's not a nice word."

"But you use it all the time," Tommy replied.

Several chuckles echoed from Jason and Chase, badly disguised as coughs.

"You even say the F word," Tommy continued.

Kathy managed to look away from the waiter, to Luke, who looked horrified.

"I do?" he said.

"Yeah, at the game this morning you called Jason a *fff-fool*," Tommy said innocently.

"Oh, I guess I did," Luke muttered, relieved. Then he looked over at Kathy. "And from the look on your mom's face right now, I'd say she's upset about that."

Kathy only managed to nod, trying to change her expression. Little did her husband know, her concerns didn't include his language right now, but rather the big guy wearing an apron.

The waiter looked up and smiled at Tommy. "So that's your sister, huh?" He gestured to the carrier.

"Yup." Tommy made the perfect big brother face: a mix of disgust and pride.

"You're a very lucky boy," the big man said, and his gentle tone and smile did something to ease the knot in Kathy's chest.

"I know." Tommy reached for a corn chip. "My mom tells me that all the time. I got a dog, a baby sister, a new dad who gets his shoes tinkled on by the dog." Tommy chuckled along with the men. Goodwill's continual fascination with Luke's shoes was a constant joke. "Plus I get to go to Paris every year with my real dad and stepmom. But it's not a lot of fun, because she spends most of the time in the bathroom." Tommy leaned closer to the waiter and whispered, "And she's old, too."

Kathy managed to clear her throat in warning.

Tommy looked at her. "Of course, my mama says I ain't supposed to say it."

All the men at the table laughed. Even the waiter. The sound of that laughter lightened Kathy's concern a little more.

"Well, your mom's right about you being lucky." The waiter's gaze returned to Kathy, his smile fading a notch.

Kathy remembered how he'd perhaps motioned for her to leave the diner that day. Had he saved her life? He had— probably twice, if the things she was now thinking were true. He'd likely shot several of Lorenzo's goons at the cabin. But why?

"Hey, don't hog the chips," Chase said, joking with Tommy, who'd devoured half the basket.

"Oh, I'm sorry," Lacy piped up. She'd been fiddling with her daughter's blanket. "I didn't introduce you guys. This is Joey, Lola's husband. And a soon-to-be father, too!"

A round of congratulations echoed up from the table.

"I guess you are a lucky man, too," Tommy said.

Kathy saw Joey look over at Lola, who was talking to a little dark-haired girl sitting at one of the booths coloring pages of a coloring book. "Very lucky," the big man replied and smiled when the little girl looked up and smiled at him.

Then Joey's gaze shifted to Sue, who held Nikki in her lap. "What would you like to drink, madam?"

Sue opened her mouth, but nothing came out—and that was a true rarity for Sue, who seldom shut up. "Uh," she finally eked out. "A margarita." But when the waiter walked away, she dropped Nikki in Lacy's lap and jumped up. "I gotta pee." Her gaze smacked into Kathy's and she darted toward the bathroom.

Tommy looked questioningly at Luke. "Why is pee an okay word, but crap isn't? You do them both in the bathroom."

Luke glanced at Kathy. "That's a good question, and I'm going to let your mother answer it."

"Sorry." Kathy stood. "But you're going to have to do the honors, because I've got to pee, too. I mean, I've got to use the restroom." She dropped her red cloth napkin on the table and followed Sue.

She heard Luke chuckle as they walked away.

In the bathroom, when the door had closed behind them, Sue and Kathy both turned and stared at each other. "It's him, isn't it?" Sue asked.

"I think so," Kathy said.

"Do you think he . . . he could have been the one to kill Lorenzo?" Sue asked.

Kathy shook her head. "I don't know. But if he is, he's still the guy who saved both of our lives. Not to mention my husband's."

"And Nikki's," Sue said. "He saved my daughter's life, too. So what do we do?"

Kathy let the options roll around her head for about two

seconds. "I say we go eat Mexican food. And we celebrate the fact that we're all okay."

"Right." Sue smiled. "And we won't say a word about this to anyone, because . . . because, honestly, the man probably just *looks* like the same guy, right?"

Kathy nodded. "Right. There's probably dozens of six-foot-five guys with bright green eyes."

"Right," Sue said.

They walked out, and Sue immediately joined the others, but Kathy stopped and stared at everyone she loved. Luke, their daughter in his arms as he fed her a bottle, looked up and winked. Her heart swelled with happiness, and she realized just how amazingly blessed she was to have each of these people in her life.

Suddenly, Kathy realized that the waiter stood beside her. His green eyes met hers. "Is . . . is everything okay?" There was a touch of uncertainty in his voice.

She looked back at the table. "It's perfect. Thank you. *Really* . . . thank you," she said.

"No," he replied. "Thank you."